Demon Eyes

To Joe and Grant,
and journeys left unwritten.

SCOTT TRACEY

Demon Eyes

flux
Woodbury, Minnesota

FIRST EDITION
First Printing, 2012

Book design by Steffani Sawyer
Cover design by Kevin R. Brown
Cover illustration: Steve McAfee
Cover images: Lighthouse © iStockphoto.com/Luca Marchesi
          Clouds: iStockphoto.com/TommL
          Eyes: iStockphoto.com/Ivan Bliznetsov

Flux, an imprint of Llewellyn Worldwide Ltd.

Library of Congress Cataloging-in-Publication Data
Tracey, Scott, 1979–
  Demon eyes/Scott Tracey.—1st ed.
      p. cm.
  Sequel to: Witch eyes
  Summary: When girls begin disappearing, Braden realizes anew that while he himself is not a demon, there are demons in the dead of night and as he continues to explore the history behind Belle Dam's darkest secrets, friendships and alliances are tested.
  ISBN 978-0-7387-2645-8
  [1. Witches—Fiction. 2. Demonology—Fiction. 3. Magic—Fiction. 4. Gays—Fiction.] I. Title.
  PZ7.T6815Wit 2012
  [Fic]—dc23
                                                    2012017410

                          Flux
                  Llewellyn Worldwide Ltd.
                    2143 Wooddale Drive
                  Woodbury, MN 55125-2989
                      www.fluxnow.com

Printed in the United States of America

O N E

"Power is a problem," a dead man said to me.

It had been two weeks of silence. Fourteen days of stomach-twisting rot and guilt. *You killed him. He's dead because of you.* The thoughts kept circling, like vultures that didn't mind waiting for dinner.

It didn't scare me that I was dreaming about Lucien Fallon. Even in death, he would have to have the last word. Some part of me had been waiting for this.

I was in one of the upstairs hallways where a gold-lacquered table rested against a gilded mirror. My fingers brushed against edged scrollwork, and I stared into the mirror. His reflection stared back.

Lucien looked just like he had … *after.* His hair was caked with darkness that hinted at crimson and smelled of copper. His suit, always impeccable, was rumpled and streaked with blood. No dry cleaner could have salvaged it, even if they could find the shallow grave he had been buried in.

The worst of it was the killing wound. Part of Lucien's

face was simply *gone*, the gunshot had torn through his skull like it was Play-Doh. It had looked worse the night he died. Now it looked strange and plastic, like a badly designed horror movie effect.

"It's a key," he continued, before clarifying, "Power." His mouth moved, but the rest of his face was mannequin-still. Maybe being dead was a kind of Botox. "It unlocks all the best doors. Hidden, crawling parts of your inhumanity."

"I'm not a demon," I said, the words tasting strange against my tongue.

"Humans make the best demons, Braden," Lucien responded, his one good eyebrow quirking upwards. "We may inspire, but you're the ones who act."

Feeling a trickle against my skin, I reached up to touch my mouth. In the mirror, Lucien's hand also rose. A single tear of blood dripped down from the devastation. Our hands touched skin in tandem.

I moved my hand and pressed my fingers against the glass. "You're dead." This was just a mirage. A hallucination. Artificial.

"And you killed me," he responded easily.

Something shifted inside the reflection, brushing against the corners of my perception. Phantom thoughts that tickled just out of sight. There was something I should have noticed, but the specifics eluded me.

The tone of the dream changed—a discordant trill that made my stomach sink. Fear and a muscle-freezing kind of panic stirred, but for the moment, I was still in control.

At first, I couldn't see it. Everything was fine. My eyes

searched his face, the ruined fabric of his eye, his hands. One moment it was invisible and then the next, it was all I could see. I didn't know how I could have missed it.

My fingers were splayed against the surface of glass. But Lucien, my mirror half, held his just shy. We were reflections out of sync.

"You're supposed to be dead," I whispered again.

The dissonance between us grew. Behind him, things shifted. Colors blurred, walls faded away, and the hallway went from night to day.

"I'll never tell," Lucien said, his good eye sparkling. "We are ever the same."

"I'm not like you," I retorted, feeling blood rush to my face. I realized that I wasn't wearing my glasses, but the freedom of the dream soothed me. It would be okay as long as we were here. Nothing bad could happen in a dream.

"You have never been more of me," he said, his lips peeling back into a smile.

The shifting colors behind him slowly gained shape again and a picture formed—a little girl in a blue dress with auburn hair trailing down her back. The more I watched, the larger she grew and the room came more and more into focus until it was like I was there with her.

The walls were covered in posters of smiling children and cupboards with plastic locks on their doors. The girl sat on a makeshift exam table, her legs dangling idly: once swinging clockwise, the other counterclockwise. A doctor's office, I realized. But the lights kept flickering and the shadows in their corners grew bold. A storm rumbled in the distance, thunder shaking the walls.

The girl's serious expression never wavered, even when a man sat in front of her with his back to me. He wore a suit the color of old iron, coarse and gray with a hint of rust.

"Hi," the girl said warily, not exactly shy but recognizing the importance of stranger danger. I liked her already.

The man leaned forward with his hands clasped in prayer. "Do you remember me?"

The girl shook her head.

"I came to see you once. Just a few weeks ago."

What was this? Part of my dream?

The girl was still dubious, but she wasn't scared. The man in the suit rested one hand on the side of the exam table, not touching her, but infecting her space. "Your dad used to work for me. At the big office building downtown?"

Finally something the girl knew. She nodded. "Dad's gone."

The man inclined his head. "You miss him."

She struggled with that, letting it turn over in her head before finally nodding.

"I bet he told you all kinds of stories, didn't he?"

"I liked the one about the witches best."

The man chuckled. "Of course you do." He leaned forward, his voice taking on a conspiratorial tone. "I'm going to tell you a little secret. Just between us, okay?"

That was something the girl could get behind. A secret? Her eyes lit up like the man had announced he was really Santa in disguise.

"He wouldn't have been a good father. Not anymore."
She frowned.

"Mom's been pretty angry since he left, hasn't she?"

"I'm not supposed to talk about that," she said, sounding very prim all of a sudden.

"It's okay," he said, holding up his hands in surrender. "All you have to do is remember. You're going to pack up all your toys and move to a new house. Not today, but soon. You'll have problems with school, but that's okay. We want you tough." His voice was soothing, like a lullaby or a campfire tale. "Your mom's problem," he said as he mimed taking a drink, and the little girl's eyes widened, "that's going to take longer. But she'll get it under control."

"Who are you?" the girl asked.

"Someone who wants you to remember," he said. There was nothing comforting and tranquil to his voice now. "Because someday I might make a mistake. Something bad will happen to me. And if it does, you're going to die."

The threat hangs between them, reflected in the girl's wide eyes. *Why was he doing this? What was the point of torturing a little girl? Scaring her half to death?*

"I'll make sure they find everyone you care about, everyone you've ever met, and they'll die, too. It's going to hurt, they're going to suffer, and it's going to be. All. Your. Fault."

It didn't make any sense: he was going to kill her, but only if he was already dead? How was that even possible?

Despite the horrible things he was saying, she didn't react. I expected tears, panic, or for her to beg—anything a terrified child would do. But the girl was stoic and still.

I stepped to the side, revealing what I'd already figured out. The man in the chair was Lucien, looking exactly as he had my first day in Belle Dam. But he had eyes only for the girl now. He reached out with his right hand, only the pinkie extended. His smile was reassuring but blatantly plastic. Then he whispered, "Pinkie swear."

The girl looked down. Hesitated. Unable to resist the childhood code, she hooked her pinkie around his and allowed him to squeeze tight.

Another Lucien stepped behind me, his voice like snakeskin against my ear. "What *are* you looking at, dear boy? What horrors do you see?"

The scene melted, and we were in the hallway again. Well, *I* was in the hallway. Lucien was still in the mirror.

"This isn't real," I protested. "This is my house. Not yours."

His mouth mimicked the shape of my words. Lucien laughed, and even the echo was off, growing louder instead of softer. "Forgotten already?" Lucien leaned forward, his nose pressing against the mirror like it was only a window between us. "This house has always been ours," he whispered. "There *is* no way out."

Without warning, Lucien's fist thrust forward. I tried to turn away, duck, or hide. But my body wouldn't cooperate, and the air was like tar. The mirror shattered. Glass struck my face, my hands, my arms. More glass than even a dozen mirrors could have held. In seconds, my body was riddled with painless wounds and my shirt was cut to ribbons. The fabric stuck to skin slickened by flowing blood.

But that wasn't enough for him. One hand grabbed my ear, braced against the side of my head. His other hand bobbed in front of me like he was savoring the moment.

And then he plunged his thumb into my eye socket.

The agony was instant. Pain that struck like a firebomb to the face, flaring through my veins. My whole body clenched, every inch of me shrieking. And his thumb, foreign and wrong, *was in my eye*.

I woke up screaming.

The bed was soaked, sheets weighted down and tangled around my skin. I tried to tug myself free, only to land on the floor, my right arm still caught in the sheets and hanging over my head.

"Braden?"

Jason's voice came from the other side of my door. My voice had choked into silence when I slammed into the hardwood floor. With my free hand, I felt my face, tracing over my closed eyes, assuring myself that they were still there.

"Just a dream," I said, exhaling.

Dream or not, Lucien was still dead. He might not have been human, but it didn't make me feel any better. He was dead because of me. I could still feel the click of the gun, the punch of recoil, the smell in the air afterward.

I gagged, the memory suddenly so pungent I couldn't help myself. The door handle jiggled, my heart seized, and I went cold. *He's here.* Then I remembered that the presence on the other side was Jason. He was very much alive.

A deep breath. Then another. "I'm okay," I called, trying

to keep my voice steady. It was hoarse and half gone. *How long was I screaming this time?* "Just a nightmare."

I could feel him waiting on the other side. Jason Thorpe. My father. Our relationship wasn't strong enough to even call a relationship. I lived in his house. Ate his food. Suffered his belated attempts at parenting.

Did he think I'd ask for help? I didn't need to be coddled. I didn't deserve it, either. I slowed my breathing and waited. He'd give up and walk away sooner or later. He always did. And once that happened, I could climb up onto the window seat and find something to read. I was done sleeping for the night.

two

"I don't need to see another doctor. And I definitely don't need to keep talking about what's wrong," I said later that day. I wore the neon green and black sunglasses this morning just because I knew how much Jason hated them. But he was running late, as usual.

"Is that what you think I'm doing here?" the doctor asked.

Here was one of the forty-seven offices in Dracula's castle. The Thorpe estate had a certain resemblance to a Transylvanian monstrosity, dark and somber with lots of arches. Jason's personal design aesthetic was office formal. Most rooms had at least one desk, if not two, and singular seating for wayward employees. *Maybe he has a different office for every day of the week?* It wouldn't surprise me—not that he was ever home for more than an hour.

The Thorpe house was in the southeast corner of Belle Dam, Washington, a city on the Olympic Peninsula. As far as I was aware, it was a city whose main exports were secrets and lies. Not that I was one to judge—I had more than my fair share of both.

"Aren't you supposed to be waiting on Jason?" I asked, glancing back toward the door. The doctor was behind Jason's desk, white haired and dressed like someone's grandfather. Shirt and tie, with a cardigan over top. He probably had a pocket full of sweets for when the session was over.

Jason had been threatening to make me talk to a shrink since the moment I crossed the threshold. If I couldn't talk to my friends, and I *wouldn't* talk to him, he figured that I'd better talk to someone. After waking him again last night, he must have decided that now was the time to get all my feelings out there.

"Mr. Thorpe? Well, we can wait if you would prefer."

I shrugged. "He's the one paying you to make a house call. He should get his money's worth."

Ever since I'd left the hospital following Lucien's death, it had been one specialist after another. My body had taken a beating. Between the physical therapists, who really just wanted to torture me with "workouts," and the nutritionists force-feeding me calories every hour, everyone thought they were helping. They weren't, and it was becoming too much.

Now Jason had brought in a therapist. *Fantastic.* He thought he could just *do* things like that. Like being my father gave him the right. Jason Thorpe, the man who'd had me shipped away to be raised in seclusion. Never making contact, and letting me think he didn't exist.

Now that I was here, it was a constant struggle of Jason saying "do this" and my refusal. He was used to employees, not teenagers. And that was just the beginning of our problems. "I don't want to talk about my feelings," I said suddenly, glaring across the desk.

The doctor looked surprised, but nodded. "You don't have to do anything you don't want to."

I snorted. Clearly, this man wasn't a local. Doing things you didn't want to was the Belle Dam way of life.

Jason swept into the room a moment later. That was another thing he was used to—making an entrance. He couldn't just walk in like a normal person or slip in under the radar. He had to be the most important person in the room. Always.

"You haven't started already?" he asked immediately, looking annoyed.

"Braden wanted to wait for you," the doctor said.

I wanted to—no, he was getting it all wrong! Making it sound like I wanted Jason here for support! "No," I jumped in immediately, "No, I didn't! That's not what I meant!"

The doctor inclined his head, as if suggesting *if you say so.*

"But I didn't!"

"Let's get on with it, then," Jason said, emphasizing his point with a flick of a wrist. He pulled out a tablet computer and stood somewhere just behind me, tapping out something clearly more important. Another fun Jason fact—he didn't believe in undivided attention. In his world, everything was divisible.

"Braden," the doctor said gently, "do you know why I'm here?"

You want me to talk about how I killed someone. Why I'm

having nightmares. Why I hate my father. "He thinks some-thing's wrong with me," I said, nodding to the side I thought Jason was on. "So he wants to make sure I'm not broken *and* crazy."

The tapping stopped. "What?" Jason sounded genuinely confused.

Even the doctor looked caught off guard. "I . . . no. Not exactly," he coughed.

"I get it," I snapped, talking over him. "I 'experienced a trauma' and that was before I almost died in the hospi-tal. Jason wanted a healthy, reasonably well-adjusted protégé, but he got stuck with me instead. And I'm not *dealing* well enough for him."

There was a moment of silence in the room, where no one took a breath. Then the doctor leaned forward in his chair. "I'm an ophthalmologist. Do you know what that means?" he asked, gently.

I opened my mouth for a quick retort and froze, the words dying on my tongue. *Not a therapist.* One part of my stomach unclenched but another locked up into ice. *Jason still thinks he can fix me? Enough money and the right doctor and I'll be cured.*

I fixed the *ophthalmologist* with another glare. "I'm sev-enteen and I've been seeing doctors all my life," I snapped. "I'm not an idiot."

"Get on with it, doctor," Jason said.

"Right, of course," the doctor said, looking flustered. "Your f—, err, Mr. Thorpe thought it might do you some good to see someone who specializes in rare eye conditions."

He kept talking, using a slew of technical terms. I tuned him out. At least I wouldn't have to talk about Lucien. About what happened. I didn't even have to be here, not really. They could talk about my eyes all day if that's what Jason wanted.

It was a curse that didn't have a name. At least not one I knew of. Growing up, we'd called them *witch eyes*. My eyes had to be constantly shielded: sunglasses, goggles, even keeping my eyes closed would do it. Otherwise, I saw the world as it truly was: an unfiltered collection of every action, word, emotion, and darkness that had ever left a stain.

It all came at once: a thousand images, scents, voices, and rages that clawed for every inch of my attention. I could see colors that the human eye couldn't, relive horrible breakups, moments of grief, and remnants of spells over twenty years old.

Even on a good day, it was like uncorking a dam and trying to catch all the water in a little bucket. The human mind wasn't meant to be deluged with information like a supercomputer. Not even mine.

I'd ended up in the hospital because I pushed too hard— using the witch eyes and my magic to save my life and stop a monster.

"I'd like to get him into the hospital and run some tests," the doctor said, looking over my shoulder.

"No more hospitals," Jason replied. "I sent you all the relevant files."

"But without actually examining him, I'm—"

Jason cut him off with a hand. "I explained it to you over

the phone," he said evenly. "Braden's ... problem is unique. The slightest exposure will ravage him."

The doctor nodded. "And you want him protected."

"I want him fixed."

Fixed. Because I wasn't any good to Jason broken.

The doctor took a moment to gather himself together. "You have a seizure condition," he finally said, looking over his notes, "somehow related to a light allergy. And your eyes have to stay covered or ..."

He trailed off and I finished the thought for him. " ... or I get nosebleeds, migraines. Sometimes pass out. The seizures were more rare."

"And you recently had an episode where you were exposed to a lot of natural light without protective covering?"

The battle in Lucien's office that night had pushed me further than I knew I could go. I'd never had to fight like that before. "Yes."

"Mmhmm," the doctor said. "The concern now is that any future exposure could do irreparable harm, like loss of vision entirely. Or that it could prove fatal."

"The doctors at the time believed that whatever triggered Braden's seizures will continue," Jason said. "I want to know if that's true. If their ... predictions were true."

The doctor looked at me. "You nearly died?"

I shrugged. "That's what they said. I don't remember it." Most of the hospital stay was blank.

He hmmed again, studying the files. "You have to understand that this ... condition ... doesn't conform to any pathology on record."

"I know that," Jason responded, "and I don't care. What I want is answers."

"You want me to predict the future," the doctor clarified. "And I can't do that anymore than you can."

Jason's lips tightened. I knew what he was thinking about. Or who. There had been a man in Belle Dam who could predict the future. He was dead—and the reason we were here.

"But it's possible," I asked. "If I take the sunglasses off, even for a few seconds, I could die?" My voice, faint and wavering, didn't sound like me.

The doctor didn't answer right away, and that was all I needed. I left the room.

three

"I have a bad feeling about this."

Jade didn't respond.

"Are you sure this is a good idea?" I pressed.

"Braden? Do you want to see him or not?" Jade rolled her eyes and pulled open a compact, checking her makeup.

After walking out of the doctor's visit, I spent the rest of the day avoiding Jason. I'd given up trying to call Trey—he never answered—and Riley hadn't picked up any of my calls since I was in the hospital. Along with Jade, she had been one of my first friends in Belle Dam. Emphasis on the *had been.*

When Jade texted, the siren call of sneaking out was too much to resist.

The plan was simple. Sneak out of the house and cut through the woods to the utility roads that sheared the back half of the Thorpe property. Jade would be waiting a quarter mile down the road.

After that it was a simple drive into town with me slouched down in the passenger seat, and into the over-twenty-one club in question—if we could manage to fly under the radar. Jade, in her thousand-dollar dress decked with diamonds, wasn't exactly the textbook definition of "stealthy." I doubted she knew the first thing about avoiding attention.

Now we were on the street and heading towards the club, which was located somewhere in a maze of warehouses.

"Jason's going to kill me if he finds out I'm gone," I muttered, glancing back at the way we came. The moon was glinting off the water in the harbor. Any other night, I might have stopped and stared for a while.

"Oh, he definitely will," Jade said heartlessly. "But you're here anyway. So enjoy the moment." Her voice dripped with dark joy. "It might be the last night of your life, after all."

"Not helping." I squinted back towards the town. "Are you sure we'll get in?"

Jade Lansing, the prom queen with a rebellious streak that matched the pink one in her hair. Her mother was Catherine Lansing, a powerful witch and no friend to the Thorpes. Jade had been one of the first people to welcome me to Belle Dam. And despite her mother's demands to cease and desist, our friendship seemed as strong as ever. For the moment, at least.

For generations, the Lansings and Thorpes have warred against each other, using the town as a giant chess game and the people as their pawns. We were the latest generation, dancing on strings they'd tied to us. Yet somehow we'd managed a friendship.

There were only four people in Belle Dam who knew that Jason was my father, and Jade was one of them. As long as I remained the outsider Jason had taken under his wing, I had a measure of safety. He'd explained it to me in detail. Everyone in town knew that Jason's wife and son were dead. There were graves. They all would assume he was trying to replace the child he'd already lost.

But if Catherine figured out the truth—that I was the son that Jason had lost—there was no telling how she'd react. Except that it would be terrible and I, most likely, would be dead. It was a dangerous secret. Jason had put a plan in motion seventeen years ago. That was a long time to pretend to grieve without a payoff, so Catherine would do anything to disrupt him. Even without knowing his endgame, she'd know this was huge.

Jade snapped her fingers, pulling my attention back to her. "Of course we'll get in. Have you seriously never been to a club before?" She glanced over her shoulder, arching her eyebrows.

"I'm only seventeen!"

She looked mystified, but just as quickly brushed it off. "You have so much to learn," she sighed, then looked me over. "New sunglasses?"

I felt the edge of the frame, trying to remember which ones I'd set out for tonight. "No," I finally decided. It was one of the many unremarkable pairs I owned, solid black and made of plastic.

"Jason bought you every pair of sunglasses Dior ever put out," Jade said, sounding annoyed. "And you haven't even tried them on."

"I like the ones I've already got," I replied, trying not to feel defensive. Jade didn't eat breakfast unless her silverware had a Chanel double-C logo, but I was used to buying things like sunglasses in a gas station.

She shrugged, bored already.

It was October, and the night was sharper and damper than I'd expected. For being in the Pacific Northwest, it didn't rain as much as I would have thought. When Jade told me to dress warm, I'd figured that meant a long-sleeved shirt. But here, dress warm meant *warm.* Like "you don't want to lose your extremities" warm.

I'd been in Belle Dam for over a month, and I still felt like I didn't understand anything. There were parts of town where I wasn't welcome because everyone knew that Jason had taken me in, and parts of town where Jade wouldn't dare show her face. There were rules everywhere, and people watching. Always watching.

That's what made tonight so dangerous, and part of why it was appealing.

As we closed in on the warehouse, the ground started to throb. A steady, pulsing beat reminded me of magic so much my fingers itched. The bass got louder with every step, and my skin hummed with it.

"And you're sure he's here?" I asked, raising my voice over the loud music. That was the point of our entire adventure. Jade had promised me.

I didn't need to see the mischievous look she had. I could hear it in her voice.

"Don't start getting nervous now."

"I'm not nervous!" I had passed that about an hour ago.

This new feeling was like combustible electric anticipation. Trey was here.

Trey was short for Gentry. Lansing. Jade's older brother. I liked him, and we'd kissed a few times, but he was as frustrating as he was distant. He liked me, too—at least I thought he did. But he had been raised in the feud and had chosen his side. It just wasn't mine.

He said things were different now and that we couldn't be together. I didn't want to believe him, and I just felt like if we could *talk*—just sit down in a room together and talk— that everything would start to make sense. Because it didn't right now. The more he ignored me, the stronger the compulsion to see him grew.

"C'mon!" Jade laughed, as a couple of guys walked outside, one going out of his way to prop the door for her like a gentleman. She gave him the eye, scrutinizing him the way only a girl can size up a potential guy. Given how quick her gaze flicked to the other one, I think Gentleman didn't have much of a shot.

I hesitated, my nerves getting the best of me. *Maybe this is a bad idea.*

"Stop being such a bore," Jade said as she sauntered back and snagged my sleeve, tugging me forward long enough for her to link her arm around mine. "It's going to be fun. And if he's not here ... then we'll just have a night out."

"Jason's going to know I snuck out. He always does." I couldn't figure out how he did it either.

"Is he going to ground you? Lock you in your room. You can just—" she waggled her fingers. Jade didn't like being bothered with tiresome things like curfews or parental supervision. She dragged me inside, allowing me only a second to glance up and see the name scrawled in neon above the door.

DOWNFALL

Oh yeah. Tonight couldn't *possibly* be a bad idea.

"Uhh, nice shades, guy," the nongentleman muttered just before the music surged and the rest of what he was saying was lost in a throbbing dance tempo.

Jade glided past the bouncer without even a pause, and he nodded his head respectfully in her direction. She laid her hand on his shoulder while she passed, murmuring something that sounded flirty. The bouncer's lips started to rise into a smile, and then his eyes slid over to me. The smile froze in place, no more than a half twitch of the lips. "Isn't he—" he began, but Jade cut him off.

"—with me. Thanks, Bobby." Jade turned and beckoned me with a finger, eyes dancing with deceit.

God, I was so screwed.

Bobby let me pass, but I could feel his stare as we stepped into the club. It was a Thursday night, and the place was busy but not packed. Groups were surrounding small tables that circled the bar in a complex pattern. The lighting was dim, making it harder to see than normal.

Jade moved next to me, sliding her arm around my waist. "So how about that guy by the door?" she shouted, jerking her head back the way we'd come.

I looked at her in confusion.

"He was totally flirting with you, hello? How did you not see that?"

He was? I glanced back towards the exit like I'd catch another look at him. "But he was old."

Jade leaned in closer, drawing the scent of her perfume in with her. It was spicy and exotic, not quite the usual stuff she wore. "He wasn't *that* old. Besides, I thought you liked older guys?"

I shook my head, my thoughts conflicting. "What was that with the bouncer? He acted like he knew me," I shouted, battling the music pulsing around us.

"He did." Jade brushed a lock of pink and blond hair out of her eyes. "Better get used to it. Paparazzi's watching."

Easier said than done. People thought I was either Jason's protégé or a hard-luck case he'd pulled in off the street. Either way, I wasn't anonymous anymore. People took notice when I walked into a room.

I hated it.

Jason said doors would open for me. Jade said that if I hoped to survive school, I needed to accept my position. The doctors said I needed to take it easy. Everyone had an opinion. But I didn't want people treating me differently just because of where I was living.

"Where is he?" I shouted into the crowd, scanning for any sign of my blond-haired crush. It was easier to focus on that, than on all the things spiraling out of control elsewhere.

"Let's get a drink. He'll still be here in a minute."

She walked away from me, and I swore under my breath. Navigating this place by myself was a bad idea. I tried, and failed, to avoid bumping into anything, hitting the side of a table my first time, and then a group of girls on my second. I wasn't interested in a drink, I just wanted to find Trey.

The closer I got to the bar, the better the lighting was, and I used that to my advantage. I stepped in between crowds of college students, navigating my way through circles of energetic conversations. The farther from the entrance, the more chaotic things got. People stumbled and flailed about, girls carried their heels and still weren't able to stand straight. Dancers moved in frenetic, seizurelike motions to the beat. A strobe light kept flashing, and all the added light at the corners of my eyes grated.

I was so out of place. I didn't belong here. And I couldn't shake the sense that someone was staring. Every time I turned, there were eyes on my back for sure, but no one really seemed to be looking my way.

"Where are you?" I whispered to myself as I grabbed the corner of my sunglasses. It would be so much easier to find him if I could just take them off and really *see*. But the doctor's warning was still fresh in my ears.

The crowd cleared in front of me, and there he was. Trey's lanky form was stretched out at one of the small circular tables against the wall. A bottle of something that wasn't root beer dangled between his fingers, his attention focused on the person across from him. I couldn't get a good look. The other half of the table was swaddled in shadows.

My heart thudded in my chest, which tightened with every breath. *He was here.*

One of the spotlights in the ceiling highlighted the wall

behind him, so I could soak up every detail. Trey wore a blue V-neck over a white T-shirt, and he'd cut his hair. At first, he was smiling, but he looked more annoyed than anything. His forehead knotted up, and he stabbed his finger down on the table, emphasizing whatever was being said.

He looked better than the last time I'd seen him. And then he looked up, and our eyes met.

I froze. Every muscle in my body chose that moment to mutiny. My skin split with sweat, and tangles of nerves felt like they'd burst out of my stomach.

He slid off the bar stool and started towards me, his companion forgotten. All I could do was stare, soak him up, commit every tiny detail to memory. But in the back of my head, guilt bled through. If only the last month hadn't happened. If I had stayed ignorant about who I was and why I was here. I wouldn't be a killer, and we wouldn't be in this mess.

"What are you doing here?" There was no warmth to his voice. *It's just too loud, that's all,* I told myself. His companion slunk into the crowd, head dropped down. I couldn't get a good look at him, but I assumed it was a guy. Another college guy, maybe.

I focused back on him, a smile on my lips. "I needed to see you."

Trey shook his head, dropping closer to me. I leaned forward to catch that hint of aftershave he wore.

"You can't be here. Go home, Braden."

All the knots in my stomach, already warring with the butterflies determined to take control, were drowned by gallons of ice water. I must not have heard him right. "What?"

Trey didn't repeat himself. His eyes narrowed, and he stared coldly down at me.

It was this stupid music. I couldn't hear anything at all. My irritation was so great that I reacted before I even realized what I was doing. I drew in magic as easily as drawing in a breath, and smoothed it into a spell.

I pictured every sound registering like one of those heartbeat monitors in the hospital. Hundreds of lines jerking up and down, each a different vibration. One by one, I smoothed them away, and the cacophony died into eerie silence.

It only took a couple of seconds, but still I took a step back and tried to catch my breath. I'd barely used any magic since the hospital, too scared of how closely it was linked to my visions. If the visions would kill me, wouldn't the magic? I waited it out, expecting something worse than a few light-headed moments, but it never came.

Magic was all about will and demand. I wanted things to happen, and then I made them. Every spell had a shape and a form, and the more I learned, the more I could do. But it was still instinctual to use my power instead of thinking it through. Most of the time, I caught myself. But being around Trey took me off my guard.

"What are you doing?" Trey's voice dropped to a more normal tone, as he swiveled to look around the room.

Everyone went around their business: laughing, joking, drinking. To everyone else, the status stayed quo. To us, the silence was a strange thing—a separate presence in the room. The walls seemed to bulge inward, dwarfing the place into something alien and claustrophobic. A club without noise yet filled with people really didn't feel the same.

"What's wrong?" I reached for him, but he pulled away.

"No." Just one little word, but it was thick with Lansing disdain.

"Trey, we need to talk."

For a second, there was a glimmer of the boy I knew behind the icicle chips in his eyes. "Do you even know where you are right now?" His arm twitched, like he was going to grab me and thought better of it.

"It's a club," I said, stating the obvious. "Jade told me you'd be here."

His mouth snapped shut, and his face tightened even more. "Jade?"

I nodded.

"She's here too?" It was a rhetorical question. His attention was off me the moment her name was said. Instead, he was searching the crowd, eyes flicking from group to group. I looked towards the bar, and saw one of the bartenders staring at us. He had his phone in hand, and his fingers were moving, but he barely looked at the screen.

"Trey," I said, nudging him. "The bar."

He looked up, but didn't glance towards the bar right away. He took his time, and when his eyes shifted past, it was almost casual. Then he started swearing.

"What's happening?"

"You're leaving," he snapped. "Now."

Was this some kind of joke? "I'm not going anywhere.

Not until you talk to me." I crossed my arms in front of me, and closed in on his personal space.

Trey grew more agitated by the second. He cut through the crowd, and I was forced to follow him. Wherever Jade was, I bet she was having a better time than I was.

And then, it all made sense. My jaw dropped. I caught up with him and grabbed his arm. "Are you on a *date*?"

Trey turned back, caught by surprise. He shook his head, but I swear he almost smiled. "You are *such* an idiot," he said.

"Oh my god, you are."

"Not now," he muttered. He kept looking over my head, continuing his search.

"Then what is it? Explain it to me." I got into his face, straining to close the height difference between us. "Why are you being such a dick?"

Now I wasn't the only one who looked like he wanted to punch something. "C'mon," he growled, grabbing my wrist and moving for the exit. "Where's my sister?"

Trey's fingers were cold against my wrist, but his grip was gentle. "I don't know! We split up at the door."

We found Jade by a group of Neanderthals in flannel. The center of attention, of course. She saw us first and was already grabbing her purse and making apologies before falling in behind us.

It wasn't good enough to get us outside. Trey didn't stop until we were two blocks down from the club. He turned to Jade, but didn't let go of my arm. "Go get your car and go home," he said over his shoulder. "I'll take Braden."

She didn't argue, which wasn't like Jade. She gave me an

inquisitive look and sauntered past, like leaving so soon was *her* idea.

Trey watched her go, and I watched him. "What's going on? What's wrong?"

He turned to look at me, except his eyes glossed past mine and focused on some point beyond my shoulder. Back toward the Club. "You have to stop this."

"Stop what?"

"You know what." His eyes flashed from ice to fire in an instant, and his grip on my wrist became a vise. "Shit." He pulled me forward only to change directions and swing me around. I almost lost my balance, but the next thing I knew Trey had a hand around the back of my head, we were facing each other, and he was guiding me back into darkness.

The building extended out around us on either side, and after a second I realized we were in some sort of entryway, pressed against a door.

Trey leaned against me, his mouth tucked against my ear. "Quiet," he whispered.

A second later, a pair of guys went running down the alley—the bartender and the bouncer. Trey's arms tightened around me, and I rested my cheek against the side of his shoulder, watching them. They ran right past the corner we were hidden in and kept going.

I turned back to him to see that Trey had forgotten the other men. He glared down at me, and my heart stuttered into my throat. "What were you thinking?" But his question lacked heat. The tension in his face kept wavering, like he was cycling through emotions too fast for any one to settle. "Why aren't you getting this?"

"Getting *what*?" I demanded.

He laid out the facts like it was just another presentation in one of his business classes. Cold. Analytic. "Jason let everyone believe his son died. He *wanted* everyone to know he died. There's a reason we don't trust the Thorpes. They'll lie, and they'll use you." Trey's eyes were hard, betrayed blue diamonds. "Exactly what you've done since you came here."

"I didn't do anything," I protested. "You know why I—"

"You've been lying since you got off the bus," Trey said, his voice short. "Out of everyone in Belle Dam, you've been circling Jade and me since the beginning." I opened my mouth to argue, but he didn't pause long enough for me to interrupt. "You have the kind of power that could change the game entirely. And Lucien tried to kill me for getting too close to you."

"That's not why he wanted you—"

"*It doesn't matter*," he insisted. "How are you not seeing this? Do you think showing up at a club and pouting in my direction will make me forget all of that? That because I feel this," he gestured between us, "*thing* that I'd turn my back on my family so easily? Come on, Braden. *Think.*"

"But I don't want to be your enemy," I whispered, my voice cracking halfway through.

The stern, angry expression on his face slipped, and his eyes trailed down to my mouth. His thumb trailed along my jaw, and he sighed. The fight seemed to leave his body, and he leaned forward.

"I never said I wanted to be yours," he admitted quietly. "But try seeing things from my side for once. You came to town and started asking questions. Digging up rotting skeletons and secrets. Witches don't come to Belle Dam, but you stroll in like you owned the town. And then I find out you've got the Widow's eyes?"

Grace Lansing. Trey's ancestor, and known at times as the Widow of Belle Dam. The only other person who I knew to have had the witch eyes.

"You didn't tell me who you were in the beginning, either," I pointed out, unwilling to let this go.

"That's fair," he admitted. "But I *told* you the truth. You never told me, I had to find out for myself. That night in the cemetery, and then again in Fallon's office."

The first night, he'd seen my uncovered eyes. There were stories about Grace, fairy tales or legends, and Trey had made the connection easily, as soon as he'd seen what I could do. And Lucien had been the one to reveal my parentage, doing so with relish.

Even as I was thinking furiously, trying to find a retort, the truth of what he was saying hit me.

Trey was right. Maybe not about how all Thorpes go to hell, but about me.

"Maybe I haven't told you the truth all the time," I said, waiting until alarm faded like a morning frost, "but you know *me.* They all want me to be some kind of weapon. That's not what I want."

"I know," Trey said, the hand behind my head gently rubbing my scalp. He looked uncertain, but still struggling.

"Trey, please."

"We shouldn't be doing this," he whispered, lips hovering just over mine. I tilted my head to the side, breath caught in my throat. I knew he was right, that it was dangerous for us to be like this, but in the moment I didn't care.

Just before our lips would have touched—before tension turned to kissing—Trey pulled back. He smirked, teeth exposed. "*'Are you on a date?'*" he mimicked, pitching his voice high.

"Shut up," I responded, my cheeks reddening.

"Yeah," he said, but he wasn't listening to me, his eyes still trained on my mouth. "Yeah, okay." His lips descended, and suddenly everything made sense. Trey tasted like bitter beer and a hint of chocolate. The first kiss was slow, like a reintroduction, but it still sparked a coil of fire that started raging through me. If this was what a wildfire was like, I could understand why the forest burned.

I had to grab the front of his shirt, claw my fingers around the fabric, just to ground myself. My mouth fit to his perfectly. *This was right. It was...* everything. Kissing Trey was perfect.

Someone groaned, but I don't know which one of us it was. Didn't care. I pressed tighter against him. At some point I shifted, or Trey shifted me, and instead of having my back against the wall, we fell against the corner, our flanks flush against the door. Trey carded his fingers through my hair, and I slid my hand under the fabric of his shirt.

When we pulled apart, I gasped for air. Real air, not the meager inhales I'd managed when we were kissing. "What was that tonight?" I managed to pant, while Trey continued to press his lips against my jaw.

"Shut up," he muttered again, his voice sounding a lot less stable.

I grinned stupidly, then laughed when his nose kept brushing against my cheek.

Everything was going well, and then it all changed. "I missed this," I said.

Trey pulled back, and as I watched his expression shift, the steaming bubble we were in collapsed. His open, happy expression faded, replaced by a cold mask. He pulled away, even though I was still tangled up in his limbs.

"You can't come here again," he said. "Not to Downfall. Promise me."

"What? Why?"

He shook me. "Promise." After a moment, he added a desperate "please."

"Why? What's wrong?" Now I was nervous.

"My mother owns the building." One of his hands slid down to mine, and he threaded our fingers together. "She's the reason I'm here tonight." My skin went cold, and Trey kept talking. "She's putting out feelers. Looking for someone."

That sinking feeling powered up a bit and became a whirlpool in my stomach. "What does that mean?"

He struggled, clearly trying to decide what to tell me. "Things are about to escalate. Again."

four

"How are you?" Trey asked, the first words we'd spoken since the alley.

He'd driven me home in his SUV just as promised. Before we'd even left, he rummaged in the back, emerging with a sweatshirt he wrapped around me. What should have been a sweet moment was almost clinical, and he wouldn't meet my eyes. The drive back was filled by a mix of the radio and a hissing static. Trey smacked the dash a few times, but the signal didn't get any better.

Jason's house was still a short walk through the woods. It wasn't like Trey could drop me off at the door.

I shrugged, hiding behind nonchalance. "I'm okay. For now." I stood in the access road while he sat in his car. His door was open, one leg dangled out, but he never unbuckled his seatbelt. It enforced a distance between us.

Trey looked exhausted. *How much of that is my fault?* I hesitated, wanting to say … I don't know, something. But what came out is something else entirely. A confession. "I dreamt about him last night. Lucien."

Trey sighed, like this was to be expected. "It was just a dream. Lucien's gone. You know that."

"I know, but it was so … real. The things he was saying to me."

"He's dead. We killed him."

"*I* killed him," I corrected. The act itself was complicated, but I'd been the one who pulled the trigger.

"He was a demon. A bad guy."

"But he didn't die like a demon," I said quietly. That was the part that bothered me. "He died like a person, bleeding and everything."

"Braden." My name trailed off on his lips and then he pulled me forward. To him. It was awkward, the one-armed hug with him in the SUV and me outside. I had to stand on my tiptoes and lean to one side. I closed my eyes. Nothing else mattered, because he was right here.

"You did the right thing," he said, lips against my ear.

Then why was I dreaming about Lucien? Why couldn't I let it go? The memory of his body on the ground lived in my head now, taking up squatter's rights in the back of my mind.

We stayed like that for a couple of minutes, until my body began to cramp. I pulled away and wiggled my toes.

"What do you think happened to him?" I asked.

Trey seemed surprised. "Lucien? Either he's back in Hell, or he went wherever things like him go when they die, I guess."

Was that it? All Lucien had wanted was a way to escape this town, to escape the prison he'd been trapped in. But if he was sent back the way he was, weakened and fragile, then wasn't it a fitting punishment? "Did I tell you? In my dream, he looked like he did that night. After."

"Braden," Trey sighed again, dropping his head back and staring at the roof, "you have to let this go. It's not like you killed someone. You killed a *thing*. You don't need to feel guilty about that."

"How do I know that Grace didn't make him human when she did ... whatever it was that she did?"

"He would have been over a hundred fifty years old, then," Trey said. "Still doesn't make him human."

Trey had very distinct lines between what was okay and what wasn't. And supernatural creatures were things, not people. *Does that include me? Would he feel guilty if he had to kill me someday?* The thought got me shivering, and I huddled down in his sweatshirt even more.

"What?" he asked. I shook my head.

It was somewhere between midnight and dawn, and I had school in the morning. I had to go, or I'd never get any sleep. I bit down on my lower lip. "When can I see you again?"

He struggled to answer, the first attempt pushed down and suppressed. His jaw stiffened, and his eyes grew hard. "Be serious."

"I am!"

Trey shook his head. "You have to move on. Think what Jason would do if he caught us together."

I knew the realities of the feud—at least I thought I did. "We can keep it a secret. Find ways to meet up." I knew it was desperate, but I'd try anything.

Trey snorted. "You should know by now. Everyone is

desperate to know everyone else's secrets. There's no such thing as privacy."

"I don't hear you coming up with any suggestions," I snapped.

He tried to sound severe, but ended up sounding beaten down instead. "That's because I didn't offer any." His mouth opened, like he wanted to say more, but he cut himself off with a shake of his head. The door slammed shut a moment later.

Trey drove off, and I was alone.

¤   ¤   ¤

Lucien was still stuck in my thoughts the next morning. I couldn't shake the nightmare, but I also couldn't shake Trey's suggestion that it was all based on my guilt. If that was all it was, well, I wouldn't be relieved. But I'd be at peace.

There was only one place I could think of to get help for my problem. But first, I had to get through Jason's morning routine. I climbed out of bed after my alarm went off for the third time—I set it to wake me up an hour earlier than I had to just so I could lie in bed and gradually work towards consciousness.

"Mister Braden, breakfast is served."

The iron-haired British woman vanished back into the hallway. Everyone that worked for Jason called me that. Mister Braden. I didn't know what to call any of them because they never stayed in the room long enough to find out their names. And Jason never bothered to introduce them. I had a sneaking suspicion he didn't know, either.

"Coming," I called, even though by now she was too far away to hear. Or care.

By the time I made it to the kitchen, Jason was already on his way out. I stepped to one side of the doorframe and held my breath. He looked down at me as he passed, slipping back into his suit coat. I waited, sure that there was *some* criticism on the way. He couldn't really let me leave the house and return to school without something, right?

But Jason didn't say anything. At all. I finally exhaled once he was gone and headed for the table. Mrs. Irons (which is what I decided to call the maid, in absence of a name) had set out enough breakfast for the entire swim team.

Jason cleared his throat from the hallway behind me. "Braden?"

I stiffened.

"Next time you sneak in, use the front door like a civilized person."

I slumped down into the chair, my stomach in knots, and forced myself not to look back at him. *He knew. Of course he knew. I told Jade!* I sat in silence in front of a mountain of bacon, eggs, and toast. I tried to eat, but everything tasted like ash.

Half an hour later, I left the house. I was supposed to show up for a meeting with a guidance counselor before returning to classes. I had the feeling that whatever this meeting was about, I wasn't going to enjoy it very much.

The drive into Belle Dam wasn't long, but the driver

didn't talk and the radio was off, leaving me to my thoughts. I had a plan for my morning, and it wasn't a meeting at school I was interested in. I waited until we were half a dozen blocks from the high school.

"I'll get out here," I called up to the front seat once we pulled up to a stop light. I hopped out of the car before the driver could react. He trailed me for a full block before the protest of car horns finally urged him to speed up and leave me behind.

Once the town car was out of sight, I switched directions. Gregory's 'Mix wasn't far. It was the only comic book/occult supply shop I'd ever heard of. The owner, Greg, was overbearing and annoying, but he knew more about the Lansings and the Thorpes than almost anyone in town.

If anyone had dug up information about Lucien, it would be him.

I kept my head down as I navigated the sidewalks, giving myself a wide berth around other people. There were whispers, and a few double takes. I couldn't even walk down the street without people noticing me now. This was ridiculous.

The front doors of Gregory's 'Mix were locked and the lights were off. But I'd learned that Greg lived in the back part of the building, in a second-floor rear office. I circled the block, then ducked into an alley so narrow I could almost touch both walls at the same time.

I climbed the black iron stairs. There was a tattered, blue duffle bag at the top. The door to Greg's apartment was open. Like "there's a serial killer inside who would happily go for seconds" open.

"Greg," I called cautiously, one hand still clutching the railing.

Inside the apartment, someone groaned in annoyance. Gregory appeared in the doorway a second later. He looked like he was on the wrong end of a love affair with his espresso machine.

"What are *you* doing here?"

I looked around at his apartment. There were piles of boxes everywhere, and the mess was impressive. "What's going on?"

"Nothing," he said, too quickly, stifling back a laugh. "Everything's great. Just real busy." He peeked out the door, scanning the stairs and alley. "Gotta go." He disappeared back into the apartment.

He gets weirder every time I see him. I didn't even think that was possible after the last few visits to the shop. Greg stuffed things haphazardly into a suitcase as I followed him inside. At first, I assumed it was clothes, toiletries, or something important. Then I took a closer look.

"Are those … toys?"

He glared at me for one a moment before going back to arranging them. "They're action figures, and they're in the original boxes." His tone suggested I was an idiot for not knowing better.

Okay, then. "Listen, I need some information."

If possible, Greg's motions sped up.

I walked into the apartment, and stood across the couch from him. "I need to know more about demons."

"And you're asking me?" Greg huffed, zipping up the

suitcase. "You're living with *the man*, now. Ask him for help. He's probably got three times the resources I do."

That was out of the question. "This doesn't have anything to do with Jason. I'm asking you."

"This is me being polite and telling you no."

"Just tell me what you know about Lucien. What kind of demon was—is he?" I hoped he didn't notice my slip. Gossip suggested that Lucien had taken a job in New York. Only a few people knew what had really happened. And that wasn't something I trusted Gregory with.

Greg looked at me funny. "Carmen kept asking that, too. She thought it was important."

It took a moment for the name to register. "Carmen? That witch who died?"

Ten years ago, two witches had come to Belle Dam and . . . applied for some sort of work visa. Jason took on one, and Catherine the other as proxies—who didn't violate the feud's truce. Everything had been fine until the witches came to blows. There was some sort of magical showdown that released so much power that it set everyone's teeth on edge. Neither one of their bodies had been recovered.

"Yeah," Greg responded. "She and Adele were fascinated by the connection between him and Grace. They bought into all those old stories about the Widow's treasure. I tried to tell her to forget it, but she wouldn't listen."

Grace had a treasure all right. It was a grave full of demon power. "Wait, Adele? Wasn't that Jason's witch?"

Greg nodded, but didn't say anything else.

"They were . . . working together?"

He lifted a shoulder. "I don't know if I'd say that, but their interests were definitely in sympathy."

We were getting off topic. "But do you know anything else about Lucien? About where he came from, what he was?"

"Like I said, you're better off asking Jason. Lucien Fallon worked for the Thorpes for a *long* time. And not all of them were as warm and trusting as Jason."

Jason? Warm and trusting? "I think you've been drinking the cough syrup again," I replied. "I can't ask Jason for help, anyways."

"Why? Because you killed his pet demon?" Greg asked, arching an eyebrow. "Don't look so surprised, I know a cover-up when I hear one."

I pressed my lips together, thoughts whirling through my head. *He knew. If he knew, Catherine knew. Other people were going to find out. Everyone was going to know what I did.*

"You still don't get how it works, do you?"

"How what works?"

He looked at me, and gestured to the suitcase, smiling sadly. "Do you know who's not a threat? The comic book guy you're embarassed to know. No one takes him seriously, with his toys, his conspiracy theories, and his comics. *Geek* was my armor. They look beyond his 'cute' little obsession with Belle Dam's dark side." The smile turns bitter, his eyes far away. "I always stayed under the radar. Until *you*."

We both heard the click-clack of footsteps on the stairs at the same time. Greg froze in place—so still it looked like he'd stopped breathing. A sound curled around the silence, high and soft, but it took four stairs before I recognized it. Humming. It was the sound of a little girl humming.

"*Yesterday, upon the stair,*" she sang.

Greg grabbed my arm, nearly yanking it out of the socket. "You have to get me out of here!"

"*I met a man who wasn't there.*"

The steady clang of the girl's shoes against the stairs was putting me on edge, too. "Who is she?"

"Please, just get me out of here," he begged. And then his eyes focused on the window, and he let out a squeak.

At first, I thought it was a trick of the light, and I almost pulled my sunglasses down to find out for sure. Starting at the bottom right corner, a pattern of frost grew like vines across the surface of the nearest windows, dimming the light inside the apartment. It spread like a virus from one window to the next until they were all covered over.

"Who is she?" I repeated, my voice more urgent.

"*He wasn't there again today.*" Both her voice, and the sound of her shoes was getting louder. It was definitely a child's voice—for a moment, I'd worried that Catherine was coming for a visit, and this was the last place I'd want to be, then.

"Please," Greg begged, sweaty and gross and in my face.

"*Oh, how I wish he'd go away.*"

She appeared in the doorway, her features washed out in the light. It was indeed a little girl, but it wasn't until she took two steps into the apartment that I saw the billowing pink princess costume and tiny plastic tiara tangled up in her hair.

I recognized her. After all, the girl had tried to kill me.

five

It was a standoff. Greg and I standing near the couch ten feet away, and the little girl in the doorway.

"I spy two very naughty boys," she said, breaking the silence. Then she giggled. There was something in her hands, but it wasn't until she was out of the light that I realized what it was.

It was a towel, and she was carefully, methodically, wiping away the dark substance coating her fingers. A dark *red* substance. It wasn't the haphazard scrubbing of a normal five-year-old. These were practiced and thorough strokes, like a surgeon scrubbing up before they cut someone open.

"What do you want?" I asked. Gregory scrambled behind me.

The little girl's voice hardened. "I told you you shouldn't have come here." Then she relaxed and flashed a big smile. "Then I introduced you to Mr. Bus."

"You're a demon," I said flatly. "Aren't you?"

"Guessing games!" She clapped her hands together and

laughed, exposing the gap between her two front teeth. "I love games. Hot or cold?"

"Don't make her angry," Greg whispered from behind me.

"Hot or cold? Who *are* you?"

"A friend, silly."

I shook my head. "You're not a friend of mine. Or his."

She giggled. "Warmer. Who said anything about you *boys*?" she asked, drawling the last word with the snips and snails kind of emphasis that only a girl can give. She dropped her towel onto the couch. Her hands were still a smear of red stains, though how she kept it off of her dress, I didn't know.

"Make her go away," Greg whispered.

"You're making lots of people angry," the girl said, dragging out her words into an almost sing-song.

"Are you a demon?"

One side of her mouth slowly rose. "You're getting colder."

"But you're here because of me?"

She eyed me, her lips resisting a smile. "You're a snowman! How come you're not shivering?" There was something in her eyes, a kind of savvy that didn't belong there. Like she knew something I didn't.

There was a clattering sound behind me. I turned to see Greg scuttling backwards.

The little girl's face lost any trace of humor. "You keep *talking*. Simon says no talking!"

I held up my hands and tried to placate her. "He's not. Just tell us why you're here. Did Jason send you?"

"You've got ice in your veins," she sang, and then she laughed again.

And you've got blood on your hands, I thought but didn't say. Like she'd heard me anyway, the girl smirked.

"Someone's not very happy with you either, mister."

"Who?" I demanded. "Catherine?"

She clapped her hands together rapidly and started bouncing up and down on her toes. "Cold as ice, cold as ice, the stupid head is cold as ice!" Her sing-song was really starting to irritate me.

"I'M SORRY!" Greg burst out, now fully shaking behind me. Both the girl and I stopped. "I-I-I didn't mean it. Whatever I did!"

The princess exhaled, scuffing one foot on the carpet.

"Leave him alone," I said, crossing my arms in front of me. I'd stop her if I had to. I didn't know *how*, but I would find a way.

"I'm not scared of you," she huffed while mimicking my pose. "You're just a stupid boy."

"And what are you supposed to be? Princess Barbie, psycho killer?"

She stuck her tongue out at me, which I definitely didn't see coming. In terms of threatening gestures, it wasn't exactly the first thing to come to mind.

Greg whimpered behind me. "I said I was sorry. I said I was sorry." He kept repeating the phrase, and I had a feeling if I turned to check on him, I'd find him rocking back and forth.

"I don't want you to be *sorry,*" the girl spat. "I want you to shut up." She turned to me. "And *you.* You just mess everything up, don't you? You big … stupid head!"

"What'd I mess up?" I said, challengingly. "I didn't die the first time?"

"You didn't die *any* of the times. Now there's blood on your hands, and you *broke the rules*."

"So?"

"You think your daddy's going to help you now? She's so angry at you."

I looked, involuntarily, at Greg. Did Catherine know about me? Jason wouldn't tell anyone. That left only the people I'd told.

The little girl narrowed her eyes. "You'd better watch it," she said, pointing at me with her stained finger. A second later, the windows were clear and sunlight came pouring in. I blinked a couple of times, even through my sunglasses.

"Where'd she go?" Greg whispered.

The little girl was gone.

¤   ¤   ¤

"I'm getting out of town," Greg had told me. "If you're smart, you'll do the same."

Leaving wasn't an option. At least not now. I still held out hope that I could pull something of a life together, despite the feud.

So I went back to school like everything was normal. People's eyes followed me wherever I went. No one said anything about the meeting I'd skipped, and I walked into third period just as the bell was ringing. Throughout the day, there were a few whispers, but the silences whenever I walked into a room were the worst.

There weren't any friendly faces in the halls. The school had closed ranks so far, no one willing to be the first to extend an olive branch.

I didn't run into Jade once, and I wondered if that was on purpose. She said things would be different when I came back, but it couldn't be that bad, right? And not only was Riley still not answering my calls, but she was nowhere to be found as well. The only two friends I'd made in school were both MIA.

Then there were the classes themselves—I'd already missed so much. It was a little overwhelming, but I tried not to let it show. The teachers had assembled a packet that was so thick it couldn't be stapled together. Every class, and a list of all the assignments, readings, tests, and projects that I'd missed during my all-expenses-paid vacation inside Belle Dam Memorial. It would take me approximately seven years to catch up.

But for the most part, I made it through half the day without any problems. It wasn't meant to last.

"Watch it," some kid in a letter jacket snarled, just as his hand connected with my shoulder. He shoved, hard, and I went flying towards the wall, nearly stumbling off my feet.

I regained my balance, pressing my fingers against the wall I'd almost run into. Letter Guy swerved; I recognized him. Carter something. One of Jade's friends from the football team. He wasn't a threat. I relaxed. "Carter, hey. What's going on?"

The fist that clocked me in the face made me reconsider my definition of "not a threat." I stumbled back, unsure how I was even still on my feet. With his other hand he shoved me, fingers digging into my shoulder and slammed me into the concrete wall.

What the hell? It took a few seconds for reality to settle, split between the sudden shakiness of everything and the more pressing *ow, my face!* The side of my sunglasses dug into my skin, scraping rough. But they stayed on, and I exhaled in relief.

"What are you staring at, faggot?" He got in my face, but around the edges of his reddening ears I could see a group hesitating. A mob that wasn't sure if it should settle into mob form just yet.

My mouth opened and closed as I tried to think of something to say. Besides a confused "Huh?" So this was the "gay bashing" part of the Belle Dam welcome wagon. In lieu of an actual fruit basket, because that would just be inappropriate.

"I asked you what you're staring at, bitch," Carter kept snarling, which really made him look like some sort of constipated Neanderthal. He punctuated the last word with another shove, this one to my chest.

Finally, I found my voice. "The hell's your problem, Carter?"

"You're my problem, freak."

Later, I'd realize this was the point where I signed my own death warrant. But my mouth opened anyway, and the first thing that slipped out was, "You shave your chest with that mouth?"

The next thing I knew, my head smacked against the wall, my jaw was on fire, and the buzzing in my ears sounded exactly like a bunch of kids from *Lord of the Flies*.

Best. Day. Ever.

Everything finally started coming together once I realized I was on the ground, and Carter was on top of me.

Wait. Focus, Braden.

The fist to my stomach knocked the breath out of me. My one fear was that he was going to knock my glasses off. I went to say something, and he hit me in the jaw again. My eyes blurred, filled with tears, and through the haze I saw him.

Lucien. He wore sunglasses just like my own; his hair was flat, and his suit wrinkled, but it was him. I knew it was him. It was like the crowd, Carter, all of it was gone. There were only the two of us. He stared at me impassively, and I watched as blood started trickling down from his ruined eye.

Even though he didn't say anything, I could read the expression on his face like words on a page. *You could stop this. Him. End it.*

Carter's fist brought me back to reality, such as it was. "Fight back, asshole," he snarled. "Thorpe's little bitch." His fist rose again, ready to keep punching me.

But he didn't.

"Get off of him, Carter." Jade was standing there in front of us, one hand on her hip.

Carter held off long enough for my eyes to finish watering.

"Stay out of this." The switch from badass jock to sullen boy was instant.

"If you think that's best," she said, chiding him with her best "I wouldn't if I were you" voice.

"J-Jade," I managed to spit out, along with a little bit of blood.

"You know what Thorpe will do to you if Braden runs home and tattles?" Jade asked, towering over us like some sort of Gucci-wearing Amazon.

Carter's fist clenched. And then all at once, the giant weight on my chest vanished. In my case, it was a linebacker. Or a point guard. I didn't have a clue what sport he played. Golf, maybe?

It took a minute or two to struggle to my feet. In the aftermath of Jade's arrival, the crowd had dispersed. The whole thing took about two minutes, but it was like no one noticed.

"Carter's not a thinker. I'm sure, in his head, this was a good idea," Jade said, her tone even. Her eyes, though, showed her regret. "I doubt anyone's dumb enough to report this to the office, but word will spread. You should get out of here." She'd stopped the fight and given me a reason to leave, all while playing her part.

I kept my eyes open as I headed for my locker. I was less concerned about the fight than I was about what I'd seen. *It wasn't him*, I tried to convince myself.

It couldn't be.

six

It was barely noon when I walked back into my bedroom. I'd gone four blocks before I decided to call someone at the house to pick me up. That meant Jason would hear about my leaving school early, but it still beat walking home.

My face was throbbing, for once because of something other than my eyes. I took a shower, which only reminded me that my face was going to be a mess of bruises later on. By the time I got back into my room, Mrs. Irons had dropped off an ice pack and vanished back into the house.

I didn't know what to do with myself. I *could* start working on the never-ending packet of homework I'd missed, but after leaving early that seemed like the wrong answer. For a few minutes I curled up on the bed, ice pack against my face.

My nerves were too jittery to sulk. *I have to get out of the house.* I did the only thing I could think of: sent a text to the one person still talking to me, and changed into sweats and running shoes.

I waited a few minutes and stretched with all the exercises the personal trainer had shown me. Then I headed out the back of the house and jogged down the east trail and into the woods.

The Thorpe property lines were murky. I'd asked Jason, but he gave me some runaround answer that didn't clear anything up. But from my understanding, the property covered most of the woods southeast of Belle Dam along the peninsula. The house was somewhere smack-dab in the middle, which meant it was a drive into town every day, but on the bright side, there were no neighbors.

The east path was my favorite because it was the fastest way through the woods to the cliffs. Just when the house vanished from sight, the path was dominated by a pair of fallen trees. Giant clods of dirt and root were exposed, the trees were nearly horizontal, and both were covered in moss. It was creepy and awesome at the same time.

Eventually, I emerged out by the cliffs and sat down on one of the rocks. I never actually approached the edge—the whole idea of there being that far of a fall unnerved me. But I liked looking at the water in the bay. The tide came in below, a quiet sound for a quiet day.

"Let me guess," a voice announced from behind me. "No one asked you to Homecoming? And now your life is over?" Drew appeared on the path I'd just come from, swallowed up in a red hoodie and track pants.

Drew Armstrong thrived on his status as the wild child rebel of Belle Dam and he *loved* getting under people's skin. Especially mine. It didn't help that he was also absolutely gorgeous—built like a football player, with dark hair buzzed close to the scalp. What did help was that he was an arrogant ass.

Somehow, since moving in with Jason, I'd become the closest thing Drew had to a friend. And vice versa. Maybe because I knew his secret. Drew was a Shifter—he could shift into animal form at the slightest provocation. But he also had to deal with heightened animal instincts—instincts that sometimes took control. Ever since one of those instincts nearly hurt Jade, Drew's been persona non grata in town.

"Just thinking," I protested, climbing up off the stone.

"From a distance maybe," he said. "But up close, it's definitely sulking. There's more of a pout going on. Dare I say it's adorable?" He reached out, finger nearly touching my lips while he smirked.

I jerked backwards and glared. "I'm not in the mood."

"You'd be surprised how often I hear that," he said. Drew didn't care what other people thought about him. It was one of the few good things about him. He leaned forward. "Ouch, I hope the other guy bought you dinner first. Rough first day, sweetie?"

"I got Thorpe-bashed."

Drew nodded knowingly. "Took them long enough. I hope you did more than curl up in the fetal position. Unless that was your master plan all along."

God, how I hated him sometimes. "I castrated him," I said, deadpan. Then something occurred to me, and I snorted.

"What?"

I shook my head. "Just … a jock without his balls. That's the kind of stupid joke you'd make."

He straightened and looked entirely too pleased with himself. "My influence over you gets stronger every day."

"Yeah, my life is on a real downward spiral."

"So what else is on your mind?" he continued. "You went to the tower to see your precious little Romeo, but alas, he wouldn't throw down his hair? And you had to flee, lest the evil witch catch you poaching her golden prince's virtue."

The best thing I could do was ignore him. But Drew grabbed onto one of the tree branches and hoisted himself up like a gymnast. A very needy gymnast desperate for attention. Ignoring him was hard.

I tried to resist, really I did. But he stared down at me, an enigmatic grin on his face. Finally, I couldn't take it anymore. "What'd you hear?"

He shrugged, then dropped back down to the ground effortlessly. "I hear things. I know people. They like to talk about romantic entanglements in dank, nasty alleys. Over-dramatic declarations of lust and avoidance. The usual."

"Does anyone else know?"

He shrugged.

I shoved him. The only reason he fell back, that he moved at all, was because I'd caught him off guard. I repeated the question, trying to resist the urge to start yelling.

"Relax, boy wonder," Drew snapped. His eyes flashed like he was seriously considering a reprisal, but he didn't. "No one that'll run back to tattle. But if you don't mind a little friendly advice—"

"I mind."

"—you should be a little more discriminating where you put your tongue."

I rolled my eyes. I don't know if the relationship between Trey and Drew could be called a rivalry, exactly. At first glance, Trey wanted Drew dead, and all Drew wanted was to antagonize Trey as much as possible. But neither one spared their opinions about the other.

"You're the recluse living in the woods. Who would take your advice, anyway?"

"I'm not the one that's too scared to fight for what he wants," Drew retorted, a sharpness to his words.

"You don't know what you're talking about," I said.

He snorted. "I don't? Just because you spend all your free time journaling about your feelings, or whatever it is you do, you're not the only one on Belle Dam's shit list."

No, I'm just the only seventeen-year-old who is both still breathing and has his own headstone. Which reminded me. "Any luck figuring out what they did with it?"

Drew shook his head. "Your dad covers his tracks well. Almost like he's a professional."

Jason refused to talk about Lucien, or what happened the night he died. Drew had been looking into it for me. I'd hoped that his Shifter senses would allow him to figure out what Jason had done with the body. Even before the last couple of days, I wanted to see for myself that Lucien was gone. I needed to.

At first, I'd thought that finding his grave would give me some closure. Or that it would, at the very least, help me come to terms with what I'd done.

I thought about telling Drew about my dream, but he'd probably say the same thing Trey did. *It's just your guilt talking,* and *dreams don't mean anything.* Instead, I told him about what happened at Gregory's apartment this morning.

"A little girl?" he asked dubiously, once I was done.

"Something that looked like a little girl."

"And she was there to what? Threaten you?"

"Not me. Greg. I think she wanted to scare him. Keep him from talking any more than he already had. He was packing when I left. Probably gone by now."

Drew looked surprised. "Well, shit. Not that he was the most trustworthy source, but he's been keeping his ear to the ground for a long time."

"Riley changed his passwords and downloaded most of what he knew about the town," I said after a moment. "So it's not exactly square one." I paused, trying to figure out the best way to approach the next topic. "Have you ... talked to her lately?"

He looked out at the water, pointedly ignoring me. He probably thought he was a lot more subtle than he was. "Of course." His voice betrayed nothing.

"She's avoiding me."

"Uh-huh."

"Do you know why?"

"Maybe she doesn't like liars?"

Not exactly the response I was looking for. "What?" Riley fancied herself a junior reporter—the student newspaper was her life, and she had a fascination for the strangeness in Belle Dam that rivaled Gregory's.

"What lie? Don't you mean 'which one'?" Drew smiled a little too wide.

"Look, I kept things from her, but it was for her own good."

"I'm sure she completely understands," he said with mock sympathy.

I rolled my eyes. "It's not like you've been completely honest with her either."

That kept him quiet for almost thirty seconds. A new record. "Are we running or what?" he finally said, jogging off down the same path he'd emerged from.

The doctors and therapists thought running in the woods was a terrible idea. Something about pushing myself too hard or putting myself at risk. All I know is that running with Drew was one of the few times lately where I felt like myself.

I couldn't keep up with him by any means, but running behind him wasn't without its perks.

After half a mile, I barely even felt the bruises.

SEVEN

Jason was already seated at the country-style table when I walked into the dining room the next morning. *People actually eat in dining rooms.* Another surprise about life with Jason. Most of the time, Uncle John and I ate in the kitchen, or the covered porch if the weather was nice and we were feeling particularly fancy.

"We shower before breakfast," Jason said quietly from behind his newspaper. Another surprise—Jason read the paper front to back every day. Then again, I think he actually owned the paper, so that was probably a factor.

"It's the weekend."

"Saturday's as important a day as any other, Braden." He turned the page. No surprise, he was reading the Business section.

"Fine, I'll shower after I'm done."

"After you're done," he corrected, "we have another session."

"Your sessions are a waste of time," I snapped, throwing myself down into my chair. Jason might have been my father biologically, but he didn't look at me the way a parent was supposed to. To him, I was a means to an end. A tool, or a weapon.

"Manners." Jason's voice was sharp from across the table.

My stomach soured at the plate of food in front of me. Today it was a fruit plate, a giant bowl of oatmeal, and yogurt. I made a token effort of stabbing into the oatmeal.

"I'm leaving this afternoon," Jason added, folding the paper and staring at me across the table. "I'll be back late tomorrow. You know the rules. Stop leaving the house without an escort."

This was the second trip this week. I should have been happy about almost two days without him telling me what to do, but the house was already empty enough as it was. "Do you always travel this much?"

His lips thinned. "My job keeps me busy, Braden."

That wasn't an answer. "You already left once this week. There weren't so many trips when I first got here."

"When you were fresh out of the *hospital*," he emphasized, "you were in an unfamiliar house, with a list of enemies longer than my arm." His tone grew dry. At least I knew that sarcasm was a genetic trait in this family. "I can't imagine *why* I would have stayed close."

I didn't have a witty comeback, so I continued playing with my food. After a few minutes I gave up, walked into the kitchen, and set the plate on the counter.

"Go shower and meet me downstairs," Jason called after me.

¤ ¤ ¤

"You need to learn some control, Braden." Jason scrubbed his hands over his face, the tension that had been there for weeks had been pushing out gray hairs faster than he could hide them.

"I have control," I replied, freshly showered like he'd ordered. There'd been something wrong with the hot water— no matter how high I turned the dial, it wouldn't go above lukewarm. And there was no point in showering if I couldn't scald myself.

"Yes, I can see that," Jason said blandly. "It's written all over your face."

I flushed, having forgotten the bruises for a few minutes.

We were in some sort of sub-basement, fully finished with deep oak walls and flooring. Jason called it his "working room."

In the center of the room was a small, rectangular coffee table on top of a square patch of carpet. I sat on one side of the table while Jason worked on the other. The carpet was a recent addition—the floors were freezing without it. Jason had made himself hoarse trying to get me to concentrate on something other than shivering.

In front of him was the journal that was the only constant to these sessions. Jason took notes on *everything:* time of day, phase of the moon, spell ingredients, intent, his time of the month. I'd learned quickly that he was just as meticulous about note keeping as John had been.

My heart sank a little, thinking about Uncle John. I hadn't spoken to him since I'd first come to Belle Dam. I'd needed information about the city and learned that as a condition of helping John escape with me, Lucien had bound my uncle against revealing any secrets about his past, or my birthplace. John had hung up on me the last time we spoke, and since then hadn't picked up.

I'd chosen to come to Belle Dam, a place he'd vowed never to return to. It sucked that my choice had separated us so completely.

"Some of this stuff is new," I said, looking down at the table. There was a golden carving as big as my fist, etched with symbols that looked like chicken scratch. A vial of murky liquid that was most likely gutter water. A ram's horn.

At first glance, the gems, herbs, and charms looked casually scattered around the table. But each was charged with its own particular magical energy, and each wove seamlessly into the next. Jason could put together, in minutes, a spell as strong as something it took my uncle days to replicate. After the first few experiments, I'd learned that there was a pattern to their placement.

It was all to find a way to contain, or control, my power. Jason had become obsessed with finding a way to use magic to control the witch eyes. He didn't like it when I referred to this project by its real name: a waste of time.

He looked up from his notebook, already scribbling away. "Are you ready?"

I nodded, leaning back a little, closed my eyes, and slid

the sunglasses off. Then it was a lot of waiting, as Jason began his spellcasting.

Pinpricks ran along my hands, like a dance of needles twirling across my skin. The magic intensified, making my hair stand on end and my body start to hum. The sensation crawled up past my wrists, into my arms, and up towards my face. Alternating waves of heat and cold washed over me as many different threads of power wove themselves together according to Jason's design.

I tried to count to one hundred, but my thoughts kept intruding. Trey. Lucien. Gregory. It was too quiet. Finally, I couldn't hold it in anymore. "Well?"

"Shut up," Jason muttered. The strain in his voice worried me. I'd seen him use magic to rewind time as casually as breathing. Bending natural forces around like wire hangers wasn't anything to sneeze at, so for Jason to be winded was slightly disturbing.

The magic kept building around me, but Jason was its focus. At a moment's notice, I could draw on a huge surge of power, but nothing like what Jason could do. He and Catherine had twenty years of experience on me, if not more. They both have control and finesse, where I had only strength. We could tap into the same amount of power, but Jason could direct it like a surgeon with a scalpel; and I had a chainsaw.

The spell rippled across my face, turning from streams of power into rivers, and then into raging torrents of energy that warped and bent and formed patterns that settled over my eyes like contact lenses.

Jason tried for calm, but I could still hear the strain in his voice. "Now."

I reached for my sunglasses and slid them back over my face. They were my safety net—if Jason's spell didn't work, the sunglasses would block out the visions of anything but the spell laid over my eyes.

"Open them."

I did, instinctively wincing.

The instinct was right.

Silver shadows retreated against the darkness burned contained fire and darkness crowed she will not defeat me all I have left of rose remorse bundled like ashes against heart rhythm have to save him but he won't stop he's iron and copper the rising son so fragile.

I saw the spell in its entirety, spinning across multiple levels of power so tightly constrained it was almost a thing of beauty. It only lasted for one perfect, solid moment before my eyes unraveled the magic, revealing its deepest secrets before me. As strong as it was, the power of my eyes was stronger, neatly slicing through the magic as it did every day.

The vision vanished, replaced by the tinted world I was used to. Jason's jaw tightened the moment the spell was broken.

"Damn it all," he snarled. His hand swept across the table, throwing a metal dish off to clatter near the wall.

"It's not you, it's me," I said tiredly, pulling my legs up in front of me and resting my forehead against my knees.

"External forces aren't—" Jason muttered. Suddenly, he went silent.

I looked up, and Jason had stopped in mid-sentence. Not just stopped. Froze. His eyes were glassy and his hand was poised in the air.

Everything had frozen, even the metal dish that had been wobbling against the ground. The supplies on the table looked flat, two dimensional. In a moment, it had become a postcard of a room, rather than the reality.

"The Thorpe men, together again."

I fell back, scrambling on the floor. That voice.

Lucien appeared from behind Jason, like his shadow given shape and come to life. He was crouched down on his haunches, a hand on Jason's shoulder to brace himself.

The lawyer's hair was shaggy now, cut in a fashion that might have looked good a hundred years ago. Even his suit had a rougher quality to it, like fashion somehow plucked out of time. Unlike in my dream, he wasn't wearing a bullet hole through the side of his face. It was undamaged, if even more irritating than I remembered.

"How exciting," he said, his eyes flashing. "How many traditions started in this very room? Passed down from father to son. Aren't you curious?"

"Are you real?" My hand hesitated as I reached for the sunglasses. I knew I could answer that question once and for all. The witch eyes would reveal the truth.

"If you think that's best," he said coolly. "Killing me almost killed you once."

"So you're dead?" Relief unclenched the knot in my stomach.

He lifted a shoulder. Shrugged. "Keeping you from slumbering sound gets me to sleep at night."

"What is this? How are you doing this?" I looked at Jason, and the annoyance frozen on his face.

Lucien chuckled. "We're a bit too far for questions so deep, don't you think?"

I closed my eyes. Counted to ten. This was just like the dream. All I had to do was wake myself up, or force myself to move back to reality. *He won't be there*, I told myself, before opening my eyes again.

Damn.

His smile brought out creases on either side of his eyes. "Have you asked him about the family legacy yet? Aren't you curious about the blood running through your veins?"

"How real are you?" I wondered instead. "Face-punchably real?"

"Sarcasm. How droll." Lucien's vulpine smile widened. "Jonathan was never a quick study, not like his brother. But every now and then, he would surprise your grandfather."

"Don't talk about my uncle."

"The best we can say for *him*," Lucien cocked his head towards Jason, "is that he always did his duty. Save once. There is the most fascinating tradition of patricide among the Thorpes, but Jason was blindly loyal. He would never have done what he needed to. Vincent, like his father August before him, grew tiresome. I have no patience for fanatics." Lucien dragged his finger across his throat slowly. His voice became a whispered secret. "Would you like to know your father's fortune, Braden?"

I swallowed.

He kept talking. "Would you like to know who kills him?"

I shook my head.

"Are you curious if it will be you?"

Snap.

"—working." Jason's voice picked up exactly where it left off, irritation and all. There was no sign of Lucien. No indication that it was anything more than a hallucination.

But it wasn't. I was sure of it.

Lucien was still alive.

eight

Jason wouldn't let me leave until he smeared my face with some nasty gray-green paste. As far as beauty secrets went, I'd pass next time. The paste smelled like bad guacamole and feet. But he promised it would take care of the bruising, so I didn't scrub it off immediately. I did, however, scrub it off after only a few minutes. I couldn't stand the smell.

I didn't say anything about the conversation with Lucien. *Lucien was alive.* He had to be. This was more than just guilt.

Jason's latest failed experiment put an end to his attempts at containing my witch eyes, at least for now. He said something about "more research" and "incorporating circles of protection" but that it would take him a few weeks to put together the necessary materials. That, and something about "going back to the source."

Drew had left four messages in the few hours I'd been awake. When I tried to call him back, it went straight to voicemail. I checked my text messages, and there was only one from him.

Go for a run. Now.

For once, I didn't argue. Ten minutes later, I was deep in the woods when Drew appeared in front of me.

"What's going on?" I asked, but almost as soon as he appeared he was in motion again.

"Something you need to see." His voice echoed against the trees.

With a sigh, I started after him. On a normal run, he paced himself. Today, I barely saw him. Every few minutes, I'd catch a glimpse of his scarlet hoodie before he disappeared again.

The overgrown path eventually opened up into a real path, complete with tree roots that threatened to trip me, sinkholes that appeared out of nowhere, and deceptively thick underbrush coverage. I was scratched and thwacked and passively assaulted by the forest at every turn.

I picked up speed as the path smoothed out and Drew got farther and farther away. "This better not be another stupid hide-and-seek game!"

"You'll want to see this," his voice echoed against fir and pine. I gritted my teeth and kept going. My lungs burned, and my legs ached, but I wouldn't stop until I caught up with him. I wouldn't give him the satisfaction of knowing I couldn't keep up.

I was so intent on catching him that I didn't realize the woods were getting thin and sparse. I flew out of the forest and onto a dirt path scrambling up towards the road before I managed to stop myself. Drew leaned against a pine tree, not even pretending to be winded. We must have run at least two miles, but he acted like it was a sprint.

We were south of town—*very* south of town.

"Took you long enough," he said. "You'll never outrun the bullies at school like that."

I somehow managed a smile while trying desperately to restart my heart. "That's why God invented magic."

"Been working great for you so far, hasn't it? Throw some sparkles and watch them panic?" He snorted.

"Don't be a dick."

He looked down at me and headed up to the road. "Come look at this."

Instead of walking right up the path, he moved to the side and walked through a mess of weeds. Each step was careful, like he was afraid of disturbing something. "You see it?" he asked, his voice hushed.

I looked around but didn't see anything. "It's dirt," I said, feigning shock. "That's it, we can plant those magic beans here! Eureka."

"Just look at the ground," he snapped, his annoyance growing. "You don't see that?"

I looked where he pointed, and didn't see anything. At first. I leaned closer. "It looks like … " I followed along, seeing tracks cross over to the concrete, and a sudden acrid smell.

Animal tracks, at least that was my initial thought. But where the tracks met concrete, they turned nightshade black. Charred into the stone itself.

"A hellhound," Drew announced.

"I stopped the hellhound," I said, turning around. "Remember?"

"You stopped *a* hellhound," he corrected. "There's always more, and this one's new." He hopped up onto the street, stepping out into the lane of traffic before whirling dramatically around. "So you want to tell me why your new sugar daddy's been outsourcing?"

"Jason didn't do this," I said, but I was already doubting myself. There were only two people I knew who were strong enough to randomly summon up hellhounds. Jason and Catherine.

I'd done it once, but only with some unwanted help. There had been a magical booby trap I accidentally triggered, which infected my spell like a virus and summoned a pack of hellhounds into the city.

"Get a better poker face," Drew said seriously. "And let me ask again. Why's Jason summoning hellhounds?"

I shook my head, trying to think it through. "They're too dangerous," I said. "No way he'd summon one. They're too hard to kill or control. Best bet is to find something bigger and badder to kill it for you."

"Yeah, yeah," he said. "You can kiss my ass later." Drew had killed the rest of the hellhounds I'd accidentally summoned. "The leader of that group was a real bitch, though. Let me chase her for hours and then sneaks up and goes for the jugular." He touched his neck. "I gotta admit, I was pissed you got her before I could."

I shrugged, and kept looking around. The tracks just … stopped. It was like the hellhound walked into the street only to turn around and vanish. "Where'd it go from here?"

"No clue," Drew said. "Bitch was gone by the time I realized something was going on."

I glanced over at him. "What do you mean?" It took a huge surge of energy to summon a hellhound. One of the benefits of being a Shifter was the ability to smell magic coming, like rain on the horizon. Drew would have known from the moment the warlock started casting their spell.

He glared at me. "By the time I caught on to its trail, it was long gone."

"But didn't you sense it when they summon..." I stopped, realizing what Drew was saying. "No one summoned this thing, did they?"

He lifted a shoulder. "Hell if I know. Unless they had them flown in special."

"So how'd you know there was a hound?"

"This ain't my first time at the rodeo, cowboy," he said. Drew pointed up the road, towards Belle Dam. "Girl got off the bus last night. Supposed to be visiting some friends. Only she never makes it."

I winced. "The hellhound killed her?"

He shook his head. "Not exactly. There were signs of a struggle. Then the thing dragged her into the woods." After a moment, he added, "She was still alive."

"Hellhounds don't take prisoners," I said, trying to be patient. "They kill, eat, and move on. They're not smart enough to take their food along in a people-bag."

His eyes narrowed. "I'm telling you, I followed both trails up to right here. She was still alive when they were here."

"So what, you're saying the hellhound really dragged her off for later?"

"Or someone got the hellhound to fetch her for them."

Hellhounds are violent, vicious creatures. They can't be controlled. That was one reason I thought that Jason would have been crazy to summon one. A warlock could control them for a little while—point them at a target and let them go—but their sole skill is murder. Not retrieval.

"Then it wasn't a hellhound," I said. "I don't know what it *was*, but none of those facts add up to hellhound."

"Smelled like a hellhound. Moved like a hellhound. Burned the ground like a hellhound. I'm guessing it's not a duck."

"Do you know anything about this girl?" I asked. "Was she a witch or something?"

Drew shook his head. "Totally vanilla. Just some girl."

I reached down and touched the ground near one of the prints. "This doesn't make any sense," I murmured.

He cleared his throat, and I looked up to find myself under his scrutiny. Drew had this way of staring, never blinking. Just waiting for you to back down and look away first. "Gentry never told you about us, did he?"

Things in my stomach started churning uncomfortably, and my vision blurred. Even though some part of me knew he was probably just baiting me, I couldn't stop picturing it. Thinking about it. Trey and … Drew? Like *that*?

"Don't go getting your panties in a bunch, little buddy," Drew said, sounding as affectionate as an older brother. "I'm not that kind of cowboy."

I licked my lips, sucking oxygen in through my teeth. My lungs burned. "What are you talking about?"

He shook his head. Just one more person in Belle Dam that hated answering questions. "Ask him about it sometimes. Unless you're scared it really was something more."

I huffed. "You're not even his type."

Drew smirked. "And you are?"

I shook off his words, even though a part of me wondered if there was some truth to them. It was hard to tell with Drew—his need to screw with people seemed to overwhelm any other facet of his personality.

"What's this have to do with anything?" I demanded. I wouldn't put it past Drew to try to mess with my head.

"Just that once upon a time, he was the one helping me track down wayward demon spawn. Maybe he knows something. No offense, junior, but boyfriend's easier on the eyes."

"Mine, too," I muttered. I took a breath. "Lucien's alive."

To his credit, Drew didn't look surprised. "When did that revelation appear?"

I shrugged. "About an hour ago? But I've been seeing him for days. He's haunting me."

"Thorpe's gotta be pissed. Billable hours from beyond the grave? That shit adds up." Drew sobered when I didn't laugh. "You think they're connected?"

"A hellhound shows up right around the time Lucien starts popping up for visits? There's no such thing as a coincidence in Belle Dam."

"I think that's on our postcards, actually." He crossed his

arms in front of him. "Can you, y'know, and figure out who she is?"

I closed my eyes and sighed. "Doesn't work like that." I realized I was shivering. I started running my hands up my arms, trying to create some friction, and thereby some warmth. "When did it get so cold?" I muttered.

Drew looked at me in surprise. "What are you talking about? It's gorgeous outside."

I glanced pointedly at his red hooded sweatshirt.

He looked down and shrugged. "Stop undressing me with your eyes, and I'll stop covering up." His tone dried. "I just feel so dirty."

"Maybe it's all the filth coming out of your mouth," I argued.

Drew stopped to consider that, and then ultimately shrugged. "You're insane. It's nice outside."

But it wasn't. And I couldn't figure out why he wasn't noticing. "Is there a storm coming in?" I asked, glancing east as if I could see the water through the forest.

"Braden?" Drew's voice was a warning. I looked over at him, to find his movements fluid but wrong. Like someone had pressed the Slow button on the remote.

My skin tingled. Ten thousand snowflakes landing on the surface, a spark of friction and feeling lasting only a microsecond before melting to water. Ocean spray. Water. Ice. I felt, vibrations in the air. Closing in. Getting near.

Visions.

My hands cupped around the sides of my sunglasses

instinctively to block as much light as they could—to keep me from slipping.

But the visions weren't sneaking around corners and edges and slipping under the sides. They were coming from straight ahead. Straight through the plastic that had always shielded me.

They slammed into me like a wayward train, throwing me back.

I was swallowed up in the frost.

¤ ¤ ¤

The girl stepped off the bus with a black and gold shoulder bag with scuffed leather straps and gold that had long since tarnished. Her mane of thick and curly black hair framed her face, giving her a sense of danger.

—Black lace fantasies zippers and lips twisting, burning, teasing hungry fingers, tips razor-sharp like poison and scorn—

An hour from town, and the bus had broken down in the middle of nowhere. At first, the few of them on the bus had thought it was a flat, and they'd be moving again in a matter of minutes. But whatever was wrong, it required a new bus to come and collect them, and continue the route.

Someone got off behind her. Followed her. She smirked. A casual toss of her hair and a glance over shoulder revealed the guy that had tried engaging in a conversation on their way out of Seattle. The one who kept calling attention to his wrist, and the still-flush skin of fresh ink. Boys in costumes, dressing up for pretty girls. Nothing ever changed.

"Not interested," she laughed, heading for the street. Billy's house was only a few blocks from the bus station. She'd never minded the walk before.

—clamor of garnet breeze warnings come up frigid changing coast everyone hides and things come to die never sober sickness like violet and sin charmed innocence tripped and flaunted summer girls in autumn grief—

"You sure you don't want a ride," the guy asked, his voice high.

All she did was laugh.

Two blocks later, night had swallowed the town. Her feet chafed in the heels—she hated them, but Bobby loved her in them. The city kept getting darker, even though the opposite should have occurred this far past midnight. The streetlights weren't lit up like normal. Not a single porch light blazed. The city slept on.

"Maybe I should have taken him up on that ride," she whispered. And then she heard the growl from behind her.

Just before the vision ended, I saw something else. Something that wasn't a vision at all. It was a memory.

Lucien's face, the moment of absolute surprise right before I pulled the trigger.

¤   ¤   ¤

I was on my hands and knees.

"You're lucky there wasn't any traffic," Drew announced

from somewhere behind me. I pulled myself up and away from him, steadied my feet and braced myself for the pain.

Except there wasn't any. Cold seeped along my bones like a soothing, frosty balm. Everywhere it spread, my body relaxed. I could feel it spilling over my skin. Sating some fire I didn't know was raging.

"You want to tell me what the hell that was?"

My wonder at not being immediately crippled with pain forgotten for the moment, I turned around. Avoided his eyes. "I saw ... her. The girl. But it won't help. It wasn't ... anything." In the vision, I'd been in her head, but I had also been outside and separate from her. Like someone had been following her, and I'd watched through his eyes.

"Then why'd you see it?" Drew asked, like it was the most obvious question in the world.

"I don't control what I see," I said, resting one hand on my stomach, which had started cramping sometime before I came out of the vision.

"Well, that's kind of pointless then, isn't it?"

I shook my head and walked away, back into the woods. "She didn't even see it coming," I muttered to myself.

"Do you think she's still alive?" Drew asked, coming to stand next to me.

My stomach roiled. I had to keep moving. "Do you?"

Drew followed me for about fifty feet, absolutely silent. Even as a person, he prowled through the woods like a hunter. "I'll let you know if I hear anything," he said. I glanced over my shoulder. Silver was spreading along his fingers, glossy and metallic energy that was something like magic, but still different somehow.

It spread across his body, swallowing up his features and then contorted down. A few seconds later, a wolf emerged from the quicksilver, looking at me for only an instant before darting down a different path.

I was alone.

The afternoon shower started a few seconds later. The trees blocked most—but not all—of the rain, but within a matter of minutes I was soaked.

"I hate Washington," I muttered.

NINE

Main Street was unusually quiet later that afternoon. The rain had let up, but the streets were still clear. Maybe everyone knew something I didn't.

After I left Drew, I tried to call Trey but his phone went straight to voicemail. Being the only other person who knew about the hellhounds, I told myself he needed to know they were back. Or *more* were back. However that worked.

While I listened to Trey's recorded message, I couldn't help but remember what Drew had implied. My stomach soured, but luckily, there was nothing in it.

I went into town because, even with Gregory gone, there was a collection of mystical texts on the shelves that could be useful. Only when I walked up, there was a giant blue tarp over the front of what had been Gregory's 'Mix only yesterday. Sawhorses were set up on the sidewalk, keeping pedestrians away from the building.

"What the hell?"

"Water damage. Funny how all the pipes just *burst* like that." Riley came up behind me, staring up at the building. She was thin and birdlike, auburn hair and Seventies fashion sense. Her arms were covered in a legion of chunky plastic bracelets that rattled when she moved. Riley was always in motion.

At least she *usually* was. Halloween had come a few weeks early, and Riley was a statue.

My heart dropped. Burst pipes meant that anything I might have found would be waterlogged and more likely useless—if I could even find anything at all.

"I've been calling," I said.

She didn't look at me. "I've been ignoring."

"Riley, what's going on?" The last time we'd really talked—before the hospital and the incident with Lucien—everything had been fine. Well, as close to fine as Belle Dam ever got. She knew Jason was my father and had a front-row seat when Drew and Gregory, and later Drew and Trey, had nearly come to blows.

But ever since the hospital, a switch had flipped. She only visited once; a short, one-sided conversation that ended the moment a nurse walked in. Riley made excuses about school and deadlines, and vanished. I still didn't know why.

"I hope you didn't need anything. He's gone," she said, voice wan. She looked like she hadn't been sleeping.

"I know."

"Of course you do," she nodded.

"What's going on with you?"

She barked out a laugh. "Do you even think about him?"

"About Gregory?"

"I saw him," Riley said slowly, her tone morose. *Not Gregory.* She wrapped her arms around herself, warding off a chill. "Jade called me that night; told me what happened. I went to his office. His body..."

I took a step forward. "He was a demon. I had to," I begged. Pleaded. *She has to understand. I don't even understand.*

"Was he?" she asked quietly. "Why? Because you say so?"

"Riley," I said again, extending my hand.

She looked at me then, and I wished she hadn't. I remembered the innocent, earnest Riley I'd met on the first day of school. The inquisitive, determined Riley I'd gotten to know later. But this was a new Riley, and the way she was looking at me made me want to squirm away in shame.

"Gregory tried to help you," she said, and looked pointedly towards the building.

I dropped my head, studying the cracks in the sidewalk. "I didn't mean for that to happen."

"Doesn't matter," Riley said. "Gregory helped you. He's gone. Lucien worked for you. Now he's gone. I...I can't be next." Her voice caught, and I looked up, but she was looking away from me, her face in shadows.

"Something's happening," I said, my voice low. "There's a girl...and Lucien, I don't think he's—"

"I don't want to know!"

"I thought we were friends!"

She turned around, her face a marble mask. "It's dangerous to be your friend, Braden. They all get hurt."

¤   ¤   ¤

The next day, I texted Jade, wanting to talk about what had happened at school.

"We really have to stop meeting like this," she announced, as she swept up red velvet stairs a few hours later. Meeting at the theater was Jade's idea. I'd picked the top row, and Jade sat herself one row below me.

"Can we shorthand the melodrama? It's been a bad couple of days," I said, hunching down in my seat.

"No one's going to see a movie on Sunday afternoon," she sniffed. She was suddenly concerned about being seen together. Sneaking into a club at midnight was okay, but being seen together in the daylight was not. I still didn't understand all the rules of Belle Dam, but this one most of all. At this point, I was basically just doing what she said.

"How's your face?" She acted like this was a spy movie, speaking over her shoulder and never looking at me directly. I wanted to kick the back of her chair.

Like Jason had promised, the goop he gave me stopped most of the swelling and bruising. The skin was still tender, but I wasn't black and blue. "Since your friend tried ripping my head off?"

She tsked. "Don't be like that. I told you, tensions are high now. People feel like they have something to prove."

"I'm not the school's new Thorpe piñata!"

"They don't see it that way."

I shook my head. "I can't believe you just stood there and didn't do anything."

"Didn't do anything?" Jade was annoyed. "In case you forgot, I was the one that *broke up* the fight. And I reminded

Carter why fighting you was a bad idea. Something *you* should have done right from the start."

"You could have just told him it was a mistake. That we're still friends."

"Look," she sighed. "I like you. I'm glad we're friends. But this isn't a game anymore. As far as everyone at school is concerned? We're exactly who they expect us to be. Either rivals, or enemies."

"You've got to be kidding me," I muttered under my breath.

"The Thorpes and Lansings don't mix. You already know this."

"I'm not a Thorpe!"

Jade smiled sadly. "You know that ship has sailed." She made a face. "Then it caught fire. And then it sank."

"Why is this a big joke to you?"

"It's not," she said, looking back at me for the first time. It was only so she could glare properly. "Don't you get how this works? There are people who'd be more than happy with tearing me down just to gain a little favor with Jason. And now you've come in like their new mascot."

"So?"

"So that's how wars begin. One side lobs a bomb. Then the other side retaliates. How far do you think some of these people will go? Tensions have been simmering for a long time. And with my mom taking off the kid gloves, it's open season again."

"We go to *high school*," I argued. "Not the front line."

"Now it's both," she fired back. "Those kids we go to school with? They've got stakes in the feud, too. They may not cast spells in the halls, Braden, but high school is already a war zone. Ours is about to go pro."

"We go to school with a bunch of teenagers," I protested. "Not soldiers."

"And they have parents who are even more invested in the feud than we are. You don't get it. People are *desperate* to keep my mother happy. Jason, too. Being on their good side means good things happen to you. You're safe. Protected."

"Yeah, but—"

"But, nothing. The best thing we can do is give them a show. If we're fighting, people will spend their time trying to get on *our* good side, instead of doing something crazy."

"And if we're not at each other's throats..."

"Then a lot of people will get hurt for no reason. So we have to keep them otherwise occupied." She pulled a folded-up piece of red paper out of her purse and handed it back to me. "Winter Formal's in a couple of months. You should think about running. It'll get your name out there."

I looked down at the paper, and tried to suppress the panic. The last time I'd had anything to do with a dance of any kind, it had been Homecoming, and I nearly started a riot. "I'll ... pass."

"You're going to have to get involved somehow," Jade said pensively. "Take Drew. He'd love another chance to make a scene."

There was something in her voice. A catch when she mentioned Drew. "I think he's still into you, actually. He's not the one I'd want to go to a dance with, anyway."

"Well, that's not going to happen," she said, sharper than

I expected. Her expression softened. "I just mean that, you know you guys can't. And Drew's the perfect substitute. He doesn't care what anyone thinks."

"I used to think you hated him," I said, my tone slow. "But that's not it at all."

She snorted. "I stopped feeling anything for Drew Armstrong a long time ago."

The lights dimmed some more and the previews started. We were the only two in the theater. "You guys used to go out…"

"And then he tried to kill me," Jade said, oh-so casual. It was just another fact of life: the sky was blue, fashion was life, Drew had tried to kill her. "Don't read into it. He's not my secret Romeo, and this isn't a star-crossed affair."

I looked away and watched the screen. Some actress I didn't know was emoting at some actor I didn't know. And then there was a tambourine falling down the stairs in slow motion. "If you say so."

"Drew knew what he was to me, Braden. We went out because it drove my mother absolutely crazy."

"So you didn't care that she and Trey ran him out of town?"

Now it was Jade's turn to look away. "Of *course* I care about that. I didn't want his life ruined. But…"

The movie started a few seconds later, and we were lulled by the quiet. "We can't keep doing this," Jade said finally.

"Doing what? Talking?" I grabbed the bag next to me.

Jade's eyebrows raised in surprise. "You bought popcorn?"

I shrugged. "I didn't know how long you were going to make me wait," I muttered.

"It's probably really old," she cautioned, but she got up and moved to the seat next to mine.

"Have you talked to Trey?"

She shook her head, grabbing only a single kernel of popcorn. "I think he's been staying in the city. My mother doesn't seem to care very much. She's barely home as it is."

"Maybe he's staying with your dad?" I remembered Trey telling me how their parents had separate homes. His father taught at the community college in town.

She shook her head. "Doubtful. My father lives in a tiny studio a block from his school. There's no room for Trey. Besides… they don't get along."

"Really?"

Jade nodded. "Trey says it's the gay thing, but I'm not so sure. They never talk. Dad never asks about him."

We didn't say anything for a long time, and if it hadn't been for our hands occasionally meeting in the popcorn bag, I wouldn't have realized she was still there.

I walked home, if only to gather my thoughts. The weekend had been a total bust. I was on the outskirts of town, still about a mile from home, when I stopped on the sidewalk. There was a prickling at the back of my neck. *I remember this from the last time.* I eased into the shadows casted by a line of trees and waited. If someone was following me, they'd show themselves sooner or later.

After five minutes, the feeling of being watched hadn't faded, and no one had appeared.

It came to me then, how pathetic things had gotten.

Whether it was my closest friend or some kind of stalker, the only way we could hang out was in the shadows.

TEN

That night, Jason came home.

At first, I didn't even realize what was going on. I was in the formal dining room and had the few books that I'd brought home spread across the table. There was so much to do that it was basically pointless. I could barely focus on one subject for more than a couple of pages before I had to switch to something else.

A flurry of activity swept past me: suitcases, servants, and Jason at the rear like a king at court. "You're studying," he said in that clipped way of his. "Excellent."

"I have to catch up." Never mind that it was Sunday night, and I was just starting to dig myself out of the hole.

I don't know what he thought I had been studying, but when he realized it was for school, he got annoyed—looked like he smelled something foul. "I told you the private tutor was a more logical choice."

"I'm going to a regular school," I said, my knuckles turning white around my pen. "I want to be with kids my own age."

"You're not *like* children your own age," Jason said, as if

I needed the reminder. "This obsession with the mundane is silly and wasteful."

A new record. Jason walked into the room and fifteen seconds later we were disagreeing about something. "*You* went to public school," I said, my voice rising in challenge. "You went to the same high school I'm going to."

"And it was a waste of time," he reiterated. "But my father felt—wrongly, I might add—that I should learn influence and leadership from my peers."

"*Over* your peers, you mean."

Jason didn't refute me.

I tried a different approach. *Pretend you're talking to John. Be calm, remember that you can convince him.* "I like being a part of something normal. Maybe you think of them as nothing more than serfs and vassals, but I don't."

Jason was quiet for so long I was suddenly worried that he'd had a stroke. But when I looked back up, expecting to see him standing at the edge of the room like he had been, he was gone. He'd walked out in the middle of our argument.

Typical.

An hour later, I'd given up on any actual homework and grabbed the Faulkner novel we were reading in English. I headed to the library, and curled up in one of the black leather Barcelona chairs.

"I don't care what kind of offer they're presenting," Jason said as he strode in through the library's open doors a few minutes later, cell phone propped against his ear. "The planning commission is going to turn it down, do you understand me?" He didn't even notice me.

He vaulted up the steps, and I sank lower into my chair. *What was going on?* "She's calling it a restoration. Those buildings were renovated ten years ago." Jason continued. "I don't know what she's up to yet. That's enough reason to reject the proposal. I don't have time to hold your hand on this. I'm still looking for—" Jason cut himself off suddenly. "Take care of this."

Catherine? I didn't understand a lot about how the feud worked nowadays, but I know it was more passive. Catherine tried to do something, and Jason blocked her. Jason showed interest in a project, and Catherine snatched it up. The way Jason had explained, the cease-fire between the Thorpes and the Lansings kept things stable in Belle Dam.

What was Catherine up to? Restoration, like a building?

"No, I know exactly why she bought it, and how she managed it. The boy—" Jason cut himself short. He was directly above me now, leaning down over the second floor railing. "That's not the issue, Tom. Tell the planning commission to do what I've said."

I heard the phone snap shut, but Jason didn't move.

"Catherine's trying to restore some old building?" I asked, as much to announce my presence as to find out the answer.

"It's nothing to concern yourself with." Still he didn't move.

Should I push? I couldn't see how Catherine's interest in construction had anything to do with me. Unless she wanted to drop me in a cement mixer.

"You've familiarized yourself with the library, I trust?"

I looked around. Oh, right, because it was so easy. *I know where you can shove your library.* I bit my tongue. "Nothing's in order. I can't find anything because it's all shelved at random. Aren't you supposed to have books on magic? Grimoires? History?"

I heard him sigh, which only annoyed me more. I leapt out of my chair and turned around. "I didn't ask for this," I snapped, staring straight above me. Jason still leaned over the railing, not looking down.

"Calm down," he said.

"No, I won't." Everything at school, all the changes with my friends, even what happened with Lucien: it was all because of Jason. "You barely say two words to me unless you're criticizing everything I say and do." I looked up at him. "You're not the only one disappointed about me being here."

He came down the stairs silently, eyes locked on me. I expected him to walk out of the room again, but he didn't. He came right up to me. "You're in my home. Watched over by my people. Protected from my enemies. I provide everything you've needed. Doctors, maids, drivers. Clothes. Money. Try showing some respect."

"Try earning it." I honestly didn't know what he expected from me, but I'd had enough this week. "You want me to start a war," I said, my voice hardening with every word. "Lucien demolished my life to get me here. The two of you let me start a life just so you could tear it out from under me. I almost died because you let a demon into your life."

"Everything I've done," Jason said, unwavering, "has been to keep you safe. To give you a fighting chance."

"I had a fighting chance in Montana." It bothered me, how much Jason looked like Uncle John. Growing up with John had been easy—I'd learned to read his moods, his expressions. Our life together wasn't perfect, but I knew he cared about me. But I could never get a read on Jason, and the only expression I'd learned was his disappointment.

Jason cleared his throat, and looked over my shoulder. "If you're done, I'll show you how to use the library."

There wasn't any point in studying now. "Fine," I said. "Show me."

He walked to one of the bookshelves, where a wooden panel divided one shelf from the next. Casually, he reached into it, his fingers sliding *through* the wood. *An illusion.* He pulled out a leather-bound book, and then a pen and ink-well.

"You dip the pen in the ink," he said. "You write the subject you're looking for in the book. And then the book will tell you where to find what you're looking for. Simple enough for anyone to manage."

He stepped away, leaving the opened book and the tools on the makeshift table.

"So it's some sort of eighteenth-century magical search engine?" I asked, studying it. My outburst had made him only more quiet. I turned, about to repeat the question, when I realized I was alone in the library again. That was getting *really* annoying. "Nice talking to you, too," I muttered, then started playing with the book. An hour later, I found it wasn't quite that easy to allay all my fears. It was exactly what I thought: a search engine. When I wrote the word "demon" the book flooded with books, authors, shelves, and rows. Ink spilled in from the side and filled pages faster than I could flip past them. Crossing the word out was the book's version of a Backspace key, the ink vanishing from the page.

It took me half an hour to figure out that each of the bookshelves had a number, and the book would track down whatever I was looking for and tell me the bookshelf, which shelf it was on, and then how many books from the left.

A search for "Lucien Fallon" turned up only one entry. A historical guide to Belle Dam. Paging through all two hundred pages, I found that the book only referenced a Lucien de Laurent and Tiberius Fallon, one an athlete who once visited the city, the other a lumberjack. But no Lucien Fallon. I stifled a yawn and put the book back on the shelf.

I continued searching for another half-hour, ending up with a stack of books to study in depth later. But my eyes were starting to glaze over, and I still had school in the morning.

I prayed to not dream.

eleven

The hallways on Monday morning were tense. Every group I walked by caught their breath, waiting until I passed before they exhaled. I wonder if it there was a Belle Dam myth about that—like the one that said you have to hold your breath while passing a cemetery or else a ghost will slip into your body. Except in this case, it was a Thorpe. Or Thorpe adjacent, which is what I technically was.

I tried to act like it didn't bother me. I *loved* being the school leper. *It's like every high school movie I've ever seen come to life. I'm living the dream!* But there were only so many times I could watch people avert their eyes or turn their backs to me before it started sucking.

An auburn-haired girl in an ankle-length skirt swished past me, the clack-clacking of her bracelets keeping time.

"Riley!" I called after her, but she turned the corner without looking back.

"Hey!" I shouted again, pushing my way through crowds of freshman. My English class was down by the freshman wing, where all the youngest kids congregated. The bell rang, and it was like the aftermath of the Red Sea parting. Everyone was sucked into a classroom, and the hallways cleared.

It looked like she'd been heading towards the Journalism room. She'd pointed it out a few times when I first started here, but writing for the paper wasn't something that interested me.

I threw the Journalism door open and saw . . . an entire class.

Crap.

Staring at me.

Double crap.

A couple people giggled.

Triple.

"Can we help you?" the teacher was a bespectacled young man with dark brown hair. He couldn't have been much past thirty. The enthusiasm for his job still was there.

"I need to talk to Riley." After a moment I added, "Please."

"And you are?" He wasn't annoyed. Far from it. The teacher was amused. Probably thinking this was some sort of young love thing.

"Braden Michaels." I winced, waiting for it.

There it was. The flash of recognition. The understanding in his eyes. "Oh." The teacher pulled his glasses off and wiped them on his vest. "Riley?"

From a distant corner of the room, a small but strident voice said, "I've got a story to proof before school's out."

"Riley?" His voice took on more of a warning tone.

I stood at the door, on display for the rest of the class. Some of them I recognized. Others stared at me with varying degrees of loathing and interest. After what felt like an hour of scrutiny, Riley got up from her chair. She brushed past me and into the hallway. I followed behind, letting the door close behind us.

"What?" She had her arms folded in front of her and was glaring at me.

"What do you mean, what?"

Riley huffed. Clack. "I've got a lot of work. Just leave me alone."

"I told you," I said doggedly, "I need your help. Please."

"And I told you that I can't help you," she responded.

"Someone kidnapped a girl over the weekend," I said, lowering my voice. "That trumps what's going on between you and me. Or at least I thought it did."

She raised her eyes. "What are you talking about?"

"There was a girl, our age maybe, and something took her after she got off the bus."

Her face clouded over, and I could almost *see* the gears in her head shifting. "There hasn't been anything in the papers," she said slowly. "How sure are you?"

"I saw it." I waggled my fingers, the international symbol for *mystical*. "Drew tracked her until she vanished."

"She vanished?"

"That's not the part I need help with," I said, and felt something on the back of my neck. *Someone's behind me.* The feeling took hold of me all at once, a presence just out of sight. I shifted around, slowly at first, but there wasn't anyone in the hall. The feeling vanished the second I moved.

"Braden?"

He's not here, I told myself, trying to cage the panic currently running like a current up my spine. *He hasn't come for me … yet.* "It's fine," I said, then immediately after added, "I'm fine, I mean. I need to know who the girl is. This isn't random. It's Belle Dam."

"Do you know where she was coming from?"

"No."

"Do you have anything else to go on?"

I shook my head.

"So … " Riley trailed off, her eyes focused—or rather unfocused—above my head as she lost herself in thought. "You want me to find a girl who could be anyone, who came from God knows where, and who could have been heading anywhere?"

"She was going to see someone named Billy. He lives near the bus station."

"That's not a lot to go on," Riley said, her voice uncertain.

I shook my head. "If we find out anything else, I'll have Drew give you a call," I said.

Riley seemed to understand a dismissal when she heard one. "You said something took her. You mean something like—"

"—something like Lucien, yeah. Maybe. Who knows? Maybe it's something worse?"

¤   ¤   ¤

I skipped study hall and went to the library instead. As long as we signed in at the door, no one seemed to care. I threw my bag down and was barely seated at one of the round tables when someone coughed next to me.

The first thing I noticed about him was that while the rest of us were attending a public school, he must have thought this was a prep school. His black Oxford shirt was set off by the bright-purple undershirt visible behind the top three open buttons, a slim silver and violet tie hung loose around his neck. All he was missing was the suit jacket and pocket square.

"Braden, right?"

Dark hair swooped around his face, bunched up with too much product. I blinked, realizing I was staring. I couldn't place him. "Sorry, yeah. You are?"

"I'm Ben. I've seen you in art a few times. You have it third period, right?"

He was looking at me in open curiosity and something like amusement. I wondered if the blind kid rumors were still going around school.

Had I noticed him there before? I looked again, but he wasn't any more familiar to me. I shook my head. "I mean, yeah, I do," I said, realizing my stupidity. "But sorry, I don't think I've ever seen you."

"Not surprised. You're always so busy." he said, smiling. His teeth were toothpaste-commercial white.

"Okay?" But it was more of a "Okay, why are you talking to me?"

He gestured to the chair next to me, as if asking permission to join and then sat down anyway before I could give it. He leaned forward, dropping his voice like we were suddenly sharing secrets. "I thought you could use a friendly face. I heard about what happened with Jock Boy the other day."

"Is that what you are? A friendly face?"

"It's been said once or twice," Ben said with a shrug.

"Thanks, but I'm doing alright on my own."

"Are you?" Ben played with the strap of his book bag. "I just—I know what it's like to be on the outside."

"Look, I appreciate it and everything, but things are kind of … complicated for me right now."

"Yeah, I heard you were antisocial," he said. A moment later his eyes widened. "I didn't mean it like that."

"No, that's kind of right," I said, laughing. Ben had the guts to say something about me to my face. I couldn't fault him for that.

"People talk, that's all," he said.

"So, how'd you end up on the outskirts? Did you tell Jade that vintage was last season or something?"

He smiled again, but this was a more subdued one. No teeth. "My family made a few mistakes. Sins of the father passed down and all that."

I wanted to sympathize with him—I *did*—but no one knew about the sins on my hands. "That sucks."

"We should hang out sometime," Ben said, cheering back up.

Hanging out. That wouldn't be so bad. "Sure, that sounds like fun. It's just that I'm kind of busy right now." I gestured down at the papers in front of me.

"No, right, totally. I get it." Ben started to get up.

I realized something, and laughed. He looked at me, curious. "You're the first person with a normal name that I've met here," I said. "Everyone else is an Astronomica or a Chevelle, y'know?"

He looked at me, weighing me with his eyes. "Actually, it's a nickname."

"For what?"

He winced, shaking his head. "You don't want to know."

"That bad?"

He grinned.

"I'll see you around," I said, as Ben walked away.

"And I'll see you," he replied.

twelve

That afternoon, I had a plan. The minute the bell rang, I would run through the main hall, then sneak out the back where the seniors parked. I'd call for a ride once I was far, far from school. There was only one thing that could ruin the plan, and that thing was Trey.

I'd filled my bag with everything I'd need to take home before the last period, so I wouldn't have to stop by my locker. All I wanted to do was get away from here. The last bell sounded, and it was like a starting gunshot. It took me less than ninety seconds to traverse the hallways and throw open the back door to the school ... to see Trey perched right at the corner of the lot.

He was standing in front of a ridiculously expensive black SUV, the bulletproof kind with rocket launchers in the doors. That was new. Trey had a truck before, and Jade's current car was something tiny and silver.

Someone was already sitting in the passenger seat. I was annoyed almost instantly. *Who the hell is that? What was he thinking, letting someone just ride in his passenger seat like that?*

It took a second for me to recognize Kayla. She was Gregory's niece and had worked in his shop. She'd also been Trey's girlfriend at one point. It didn't help that she was flawlessly pretty, the kind of girl who should do skin-care commercials or be on the cover of *Seventeen*.

What is she *doing here?* Students began rushing past me, all laughter and catcalls now that school was over. But my eyes were locked on Trey's, and his on me.

"I cannot *believe* she sent you to pick me up," Jade called out as she strolled past me. There was a moment where her hand brushed my arm, a move too soft and casual to be an accident. "The least you could have done was tell me you were coming," she added, her voice carrying across the parking lot. I guessed that was for my benefit. Jade and I couldn't be friends, but she still wouldn't blindside me like that.

Trey replied, too quiet for me to hear, but his eyes didn't leave mine. And then I watched them harden.

An arm slipped around me from behind, a one-armed hug that pulled me backwards. I tensed immediately, and tried to pull away. "Don't cause a scene now," Drew warned, amused as I'd ever heard him. He pulled my body close against his, and I resisted, but he was stronger. He smelled like pine needles and aftershave.

"What are you doing here?" I demanded. Jade glanced back, our eyes met through two pairs of sunglasses, and then she frowned.

"I'm driving him into a fit of rage," Drew said, as if it was the most obvious thing in the world. "Want to watch?"

Trey had gone tense, and now he wasn't even pretending

to listen to what Jade was saying. He turned to the side like he wasn't paying attention, but his head kept drifting in our direction.

I stopped struggling, something inside me enjoying the annoyance and anger on Trey's face. Kayla got out of the car, and she joined in the conversation with Jade.

The crowd between us swelled, and the next time they parted, I saw Trey getting in the car.

"You can let go of me now," I said, gritting my teeth. Drew's fingers had started rubbing against my shirt. It wasn't just Trey he was trying to provoke.

"You sure?" he whispered. "He might look again. And it's not really selling it until I start nibbling on your ear."

I did the first thing I could think of, which was to elbow him. But driving my elbow back into his stomach only had one effect: it really, really hurt. Drew didn't so much as exhale.

"Don't be so sensitive," he said, finally releasing me. Just as quickly as he'd grabbed me in the first place, he swung around, holding a large black helmet in his other hand. "Come on. I'll give you a ride home."

He gestured to a motorcycle—parked on the sidewalk, of course. I should have been thankful he didn't ride it right into the school.

"You have a bike?" I was understandably skeptical.

"Well," Drew replied after a moment, squinting up into the sky, "I do now."

Oh my god, he showed up to give me a ride on something he

stole. I closed my eyes and counted to five. I was still thrown off a little after seeing Trey in the parking lot.

"Y'know," I said, "I liked you better when I hated you."

"Relax," he said, interrupting my attempt at calming down. "I didn't steal it. It's a friend's."

"Braden!" Riley came running up, a couple of papers clutched in hand. "Drew," she said, stopping short. "What are you doing here?"

"Giving Braden a ride home," Drew said, glancing between us. Riley walked around him, putting him between her and I. She eyed the bike.

"Oh," she said, her voice getting soft. "I didn't realize you were still doing that."

Drew raised an eyebrow. "Doing what?"

She rolled her eyes. "Whatever. I still don't want to be involved, but this wasn't hard to find." She flipped the pages open. The girl from my vision was pictured at the top.

"That's her," I confirmed, pitching my voice for Drew.

"What do you mean, not hard to find?" Drew asked, flipping the top page over and looking at the second.

"Her name's Grazia Catling," Riley said. "She hit the *Seattle Times* this morning. Parents said she came to Belle Dam to see her boyfriend. After she didn't show up, he ended up calling her parents and—"

"They panicked," Drew finished, nodding.

"What did you say happened to her?" Riley asked, putting on her reporter hat.

"He didn't," Drew said, voice flattening. "Leave it alone, Riles."

"If this is a story, I just can't drop it," she insisted, regaining some of the fire I was used to seeing in her.

"This isn't some stupid story."

"He's right," I added. "You don't want to be involved in this stuff, remember?" I plucked the papers out of her hands.

She tossed a flinty look my way. *If looks could kill... well, it would maim a bit.* I would have expected a hard look like that from Jade, but not Riley. "You don't tell me what I can and cannot do, Braden Michaels. I'll have you know I've seen worse things in Belle Dam. If there's more to this than you're letting on, you can bet your sunglasses I'm going to figure out what's going. You're the *last* person who has any right to try and tell me what to do, so don't even think about it."

Drew and I looked at each other as the tirade just kept going. "I don't think she took a single breath during that," he said.

Riley whirled on him, but I cut her off before she could get started all over again. "Drew and I have to go," I said.

"No, I want to know what's going on with this girl. Who kidnapped her?" But Riley's voice trailed off as Drew and I headed over to the bike. He climbed on first, and then I duplicated his movements.

I'd never actually ridden on a motorcycle before, but I didn't want him to know I was nervous. "Does this friend even know you borrowed his bike?"

"He does now," he smirked, foregoing his own helmet. "Hold on tight."

"You are *such* a dick," I sighed.

thirteen

Drew dropped me off at the front gate, and I trekked up the long driveway to the house. With Jason still at work and the house staff wherever they went when I wasn't around, I had the house to myself.

The papers that Riley had pulled up didn't tell me much about Grazia, and nothing in the smidge of information I had suggested any reason why someone would want to kidnap her. Or kill her. There wasn't much more to find with a Web search. I was pretty sure Riley had already tried that, but it made me feel better to do *something*.

The text came in a little after dinner from a blocked number.

Meet me at Lucien's office. T.

The only T I knew was Trey. But why did he want to meet all of a sudden? Why there?

It could be a trick. Call Drew, make him go with you. But I pushed all the other thoughts down and grabbed the spare key Jason had for Lucien's office (the number of keys in his office was kind of terrifying). Making sure to take a jacket this time, I slipped out the back.

It took almost a half-hour for me to make it downtown. This late in the evening, Belle Dam was winding down. A breeze brought a bit of early chill to the fall air.

I hadn't been in Lucien's building since the night of his death. I held my breath in the lobby until the elevator doors finally opened.

I emerged onto the top floor of the building, the offices of Fallon Law. I left the lights off—I didn't want to draw any extra attention. I headed for his office in the back. None of the doors on his floor were locked, which I hadn't expected. Trey must have already arrived. The moon had the town lit up like some kind of spotlight, and I could see all the way across the bay.

At a casual glance, no one would realize that the room was unoccupied. Papers were still stacked on the desk, a pen uncapped and set to the side, and a stack of mail neatly organized. There was only one major difference. The giant painting that had covered the wall, a phantom Lucien looming over a young girl's body, was gone.

Part of me expected to see him working calmly behind the desk.

Trey coughed. "Took you long enough. Have a better offer?"

I searched the room until I found him standing in the corner, his arms crossed. "You'd be surprised how many enigmatic texts I get from emotionally crippled jerks every day. I had to choose between you and an illicit fishing-boat date."

"Then I'm lucky it's so cold out," Trey replied blandly.

"What was that, today? Why were you at school?"

"Cramping your style? Drew didn't seem to mind."

He wasn't jealous, was he? Of *Drew*? "Neither did Kayla," I replied evenly.

Trey pretended he didn't hear me. "I heard about the fight. Are you alright?"

I shook my head. Memories kept intruding. Talking to Lucien here, meeting Jason for the first time. The last time Trey and I were here. Pain. Agony. Lucien torturing me. Attacking Trey.

"I asked a question."

What? I shook my head, responding distractedly. "Just some friend of Jade's. I was too busy getting kicked in the ribs to really listen. He wanted a little payback."

"From you?" I swear I could hear him smiling.

I walked around the desk and looked out at the city. "Jade broke it up."

"That's my girl. Always getting involved when she shouldn't."

"Why are you being like this?" I asked quietly.

"You know why." The words were so quiet I thought I'd made them up.

"Then why did you ask me to meet you here?" I demanded.

His face was solid marble, and he didn't move. I don't think he was even breathing. "I've got a message for you. From my mother."

I waited, crossing my arms in front of me.

"She wants to talk."

I snorted. "That's not happening."

"There's a benefit Wednesday night." Trey's voice was crisp. "Suit and tie. Very public. You can talk to her there." It was like he thought I would actually show up.

"So, *you* can't be seen with me in public, but I can date your mom if I want?"

"She just walks to talk. No need for sweaty palms," Trey said slowly.

The idea of talking to Catherine two nights from now was insane. "Jason's never going to let me go to some benefit. Especially one thrown by your mom. He barely lets me go to school."

Trey's lips twisted upwards, but it wasn't exactly a smile. "Jason won't be there. He'll be gone on another one of his trips. A *curandero* crawled out of his hole and saw his shadow. Jason will want to wrap him up before my mother gets there."

"And Catherine's just going to let this one go?" I asked flatly. "Just so she can talk to me? Do I look like an idiot?"

He exhaled slowly. "I don't think you're an idiot, Braden."

An idea was forming in my head. Not about Catherine, but about Trey. "Why are you here? Why *you*? Anyone could have delivered the message. Did you lose your phone? Email?" I slid my hands into the sleeves of my jacket, bracing against the chill in the air.

Trey swallowed, his eyes skating over my head. "I was volunteered."

"Of course you were," I snapped. "But you could have

said no. Or sent me a message. We didn't have to do this in person."

He couldn't make up his mind. It was like he pushed me away with one hand, and with the other he pulled me in closer. I crossed the room.

Who did he think he was? Is it all a game to him? Make me feel something, push me away, then hit me with wounded, watery eyes. I could feel myself getting angrier, the thick coil of frustration and hurt that threaded through my every encounter with him.

But if he wanted to play games, fine. I'd play, too. "Tell her I'll be there."

His eyes widened, and he raised one of his hands like he was going to warn me off. That's when the tingling started in my fingers. I had about a two-second warning before it escalated. "Oh hell," I whispered, feeling the anticipation sweep through my body like a cold front.

Trey was instantly alert. "What's wrong?"

My mouth was still open, and I tried to answer, and then my jaw was stretching, spurred onto rapid growth. Bones growing longer, teeth sharper. Tearing against my flesh and gums, snapping like dead branches over and over.

Someone was screaming.

I hope to God it was me.

Ice crystals the size of pocket watches burst through my skin, fracturing and freezing me from the inside out.

"Braden, what's going on." He sounded scared.

Then the visions started, and I forgot there was anything outside of Hell.

She had been laid out on a sort of stone bench. I recognized her: the girl that was missing. Her dark tangle of hair was spread around her like a stygian halo.

Unconscious. Asleep. Maybe dead.

My eyes were open wide, but I couldn't move. The air smelled damp. I couldn't feel anything, like being in a sensory deprivation tank. I could see the girl, and smelled the air, and that was everything.

My sight was swallowed by another vision, a snapshot. *Woods. Panting. Agony a thousand fallen angels weeping bloody stumps feel like charcoal magma against the hundred burning stars so judgmental in sky silver and superior and renown. Pain, and something deeper than pain. Vanquish this weakness let it never be spoken of again.*

The woods cleared away, and all I saw was the girl again. Only this time, she was closer. Hands without bodies hold her aloft. Pressing her close to me.

"An offering," a harsh voice whispered.

Yes, I thought, with savage glee. My mouth tasted like sulfur.

¤   ¤   ¤

The first thing I realized was that my sunglasses were still on. Still blocking the light. Just like before.

The second was that Trey was blocking most of my city view, eyes wild, his hands on my arms.

The third was how much it *hurt.*

"Oh God," I managed to gasp, and then I was hunched over, making gagging sounds that definitely didn't sound human. My screams were so vast and deep they couldn't fit through my throat or past my jaws.

I saw fractions of the moonlit city and a pulsing wave of visions that had no intention of stopping. Hundreds of thoughts pounded into my skull. Memories from everything I could see, a view that stretched over the harbor and half the city.

Three people walked their dogs, one of them was sick but he didn't want to accept it. Someone was crying over a recent heart-break. She'd cheated, but it was his betrayal that was killing her. A mother checked on her children: loving one, merely tolerating the others. There was healing, and harm, and pain like night-mares writhing through the bones.

My skull cracked; pipes bursting under too much strain. Anything to relieve the pressure. Fingers in my brain, tearing out huge chunks to make room for memories that weren't mine, thoughts I hadn't had, and feelings I'd never experienced.

"What's wrong?" Trey demanded, sounding frantic, uncertain, and enraged all at once. "What is it?"

I gasped, suffocating under someone else's fury. Needles in my eyes grew warm, then hot, then scalding, as if they could burn the images before they appeared. I couldn't stop looking. There were memories *everywhere.*

Riley was still awake. She scribbled furiously in some note-book, copying notes from her laptop screen. Someone—her mother—was on the couch, a tiny sprig of a woman swallowed up in a giant pink bathrobe and rose-colored regrets.

"Too much." I couldn't do this. I was flawed and broken.

Trey looked over his shoulder, out the window, and the city view. Then he was pushing me backwards. I expected to hit the wall, but he stopped me before that happened. *Streaks of fire and volcanic issue so desperate to do something be a man and make things right.*

I heard something click. Trey had his hand at my side. He pushed me forward again, and I braced for the wall, but fell back into darkness instead.

The minute the door closed behind him, the cascade of visions stopped. I sucked in huge amounts of air, my lungs nearly bursting. Over and over again, like a man dying of thirst.

"Shhh," Trey said, one hand on my back. I realized I was sobbing.

The pain was different from the usual migraines. At first excruciating, with every passing second, I grew a little colder. The pain a little less. It was like everything burned, and then flare became frost. In its wake, my skin went numb.

I waited for the migraine to crest like it always did, but it never came. The cold soothed away the lingering pain until I felt nothing at all. My sobs became laughs, tiny choking sounds at first.

The visions had started coming whenever they wanted. I couldn't protect myself anymore. *If the sunglasses don't work, then I'm done. It's over.* The pain was worse than ever—my hands were still shaking. But in the aftermath, it faded faster.

The doctors all said that another episode would kill me. But this was the second time the visions had come, and I was still alive. Were they wrong? Or would the third time be the charm?

I flexed my arm, brushing up against Trey's chest. There were shelves on either side of me, and barely enough room to maneuver. *A closet. Trey dragged us into the closet.*

He moved, just a tiny shift, but it was like all the pieces came into alignment and our bodies snapped together. I *fit* in his arms.

"What was that, Braden?" He was whispering, his breath hot against my cheek.

The first thing that flashed through my head was my hand—Trey's hand—raising the gun and the shot that rang out. Lucien's body on the floor. How easy it was for me to murder someone.

No less than I deserve. That's what it was. Guilt and punishment and it still wasn't enough. I deserved worse with this. I shook my head, avoiding any answer I could give.

He shifted, pulling me closer and sliding his hand up to my neck, his thumb rubbing against my jaw. "I thought your glasses were supposed to protect you."

"The rules changed, I guess," I said with a bitter laugh.

"How? Why?" His voice got softer yet.

Whatever chill I'd felt before was gone. Now my skin, maybe even my blood, was on fire. I could barely think, my brain was so fogged. "I ... don't know."

"Are you okay?"

He needed to stop asking me questions. Each one dug

into the thorny tangle of guilt in my gut, excavating it a little further. Making it a little worse. "Trey," I whispered. I just needed—I couldn't—I didn't want to *think*. To worry if the next time would be the last. To remember what it felt like when my skin split apart. To remember how alike Jason and I really were. Trey was here, right *here*, and maybe for the last time.

I tangled my fingers in his hair, inhaling the smell of his cologne, woodsy and spice. I tilted his head forward, lifted my own face up, and counted victory when our lips met.

Trey kissed me, and for just a minute everything was perfect. Sparks crackled between us, a feeling like blue lightning racing across my skin to his, from his mouth to mine. My free hand snaked around him, pressing into the small of his back. His left hand grabbed at my shoulder, the fabric of my shirt bunching up under his fingers.

I traced my tongue against his lower lip, and whispered his name when he pulled away to draw in a gasp of air.

Never let this end.

Everything faded until there was only the pair of us, hidden in the dark. Nothing else mattered. Trey's mouth was on mine, and mine was on his, and it was exactly how it was supposed to be. I don't know how long we were there. I let my fingers run lines over the hard muscles of his chest, felt the quickening of his breath against my mouth.

Yes, I thought. *This is how it's supposed to be.*

"How scandalous," a dead man whispered in my ear.

The next few moments were chaotic.

I pushed Trey away even as I was whirling around, backing up into him and pushing us both out of the closet. Magic arced around us, throwing open the door while four tiny balls of light ignited above my fingertips. They streamed into the closet, spreading out to eliminate the shadows. Without even thinking about it, I was drawing on the wellspring power, the hidden cache underneath Grace's headstone.

"Braden?" Trey's voice was thick with something, his hands on my shoulders.

I couldn't catch my breath. It was like there were holes in my lungs, and all the oxygen was escaping out of them. *No. Nonono.* My body was telling me to run, to put as much distance from myself and this place as I could.

"There's nothing there," Trey said with exaggerated calm, one arm reaching past me, pointing into the closet. He was right—it was just a tiny walk-in closet filled with shelving units and a wall of filing cabinets stacked on top of each other.

There was no sign of Lucien in the cramped space, but I'd heard him as clear as if he'd been lurking over my shoulder like a guardian devil. His voice a sinister caress against my skin.

One by one, I let the lights from my fingertips die, returning the room to the silvery half-light of the moon.

"What's happening to you?" Trey asked. I struggled to think of something to tell him, some spin that would make it okay, but my mind was empty. His lips thinned, and he looked shaken. Hurt. "You're trying to come up with a lie, aren't you?"

He put several feet between us, his expression erasing what had happened between us in the closet. We were only a few feet apart, but it might as well have been as wide as the bay outside the harbor.

"Trey," I said, and then stopped.

"I thought it would be better, coming from me. I could do my duty and still convince you not to go." He touched his lips and shook his head. "But you're learning your lessons well, aren't you?

"Wait!"

Trey moved towards the door. "Don't show up on Wednesday. Please."

The rejection stung and it was several minutes before my heart and my head stopped pounding. Trey had pushed me away. Again.

fourteen

The idea of sleep never really crossed my mind. Between Trey, the visions, and Lucien's breath against my ear, I didn't bother. There was already enough rattling around in my subconscious, I didn't need to give it an outlet.

I curled up in one of the big chairs in the library. The more I practiced with Jason's search-engine book, the better I got at finding what I was looking for. Only no matter how many times I tried to work around it, there was nothing in the library about Lucien. Getting frustrated, I started looking through books that came up under "Thorpe family history" and "Thorpe feud" hoping there would be some mention of the family's demon heirloom.

Nothing on the shelves had been published after 1950, and the closest the books got to magic was some basic theory. *Jason must have a private collection*, I figured.

I nodded off somewhere around the time I was reading a first-hand account of when the evil Lansings blew up the first church in Belle Dam. By that point, I was too tired to dream. Almost as soon as my eyes closed, someone shook me awake.

"Unbelievable."

I grunted, shifted, and realized too late that I wasn't in my bed. My body uncurled and I stretched, feeling muscles groan in protest.

Jason stared down at his phone, his thumb moving casually. "I'll be back by Thursday."

I was still in the process of waking up, so I didn't realize what he'd said until he was already gone from the room. *Jason was leaving again. Trey had been right.* "Adios," I said softly.

It was still dark outside, but now that I was awake there was no going back to bed. I read about the feud from the Thorpes' perspective, and it made me sick. It also told me nothing about Lucien—the kind of demon he'd been, where he'd come from, where he would go.

Another family trait—the Thorpes took themselves way too seriously. And a few of them had a flair for the dramatic. One volume went into lurid detail on how Augustus Thorpe had "split the sky" and "cleaved the heart of nature with darkness."

This was what happened when the feud got out of control. I flipped to the last book in the stack and found myself engrossed almost immediately. It was about demons, yes, but the author clearly knew what he was talking about, rather than rambling about things he didn't. Finally, something useful.

I heard Drew's rumbling baritone before I even saw him.

"…course I know where I'm going. Don't think I don't know why you're following me…"

I noted the page I was on in *The Hastings Treatise on*

Demonography and Eldritch Genera and walked into the hall-way. Drew was being followed by a pair of Jason's employees. I waved the two of them off and went back inside.

"Can't believe I'm actually walking around in here," Drew muttered as he followed.

I smirked. "What's it matter to you? I'll be the one who has to explain to Jason why you're not on retainer yet."

"If he really wonders that, then he's dumber than Gregory." Drew said harshly. I gave him a look and he shrugged, but didn't elaborate. "What's with your maid? When I told her I was here to see you, she grunted and walked away. I almost followed her, until I realized she was going back to work."

"She doesn't like me much. Actually, I don't know if she likes anyone much."

He glanced around the room. "What is this?" he asked, glancing around the room.

"Well, when a mommy book and a daddy book tolerate each other and mommy doesn't have a headache..."

Drew snorted. "Cute."

Drew in a library. Not one of the most normal things I've ever seen. He looked at the shelves like they were animal cages at the zoo. Cages that had just been taken down, letting the predators go free.

"Library. It's where we lock up all those books before they start giving kids ideas," I said solemnly. "Very dangerous place to be."

Drew's eyebrow raised slowly. "It's about to be."

I rolled my eyes at the implied threat. "Research. I've

been trying to find out more about Lucien, but there's no handy *Idiot's Guide to Inherited Demons*."

He nodded, eyes going to the window. "What else?"

"I tried figuring out why the hellhound acted the way you said it did, but everything in here cites the same source. The one that says that hellhounds don't *act like that*. They don't fetch, and they never leave their victims alive. So now I've got this new book," I said, hefting the *Hastings Treatise* up off the table, "but it's all over the place and there's no index. So I can't be sure what I'm reading about until I actually read it."

"But you think it might have some answers?"

"Maybe," I said. Drew strolled over to the windows on the far side of the room, looking out into the tiny bit of grass we called a yard. "I'm meeting with Catherine tomorrow night," I added, tasting the words on my tongue for the first time.

Part of me expected Drew to overreact, so when he didn't, it caught me off guard. "I figured she'd hit you up sooner or later," he said with a nod. "So what's the plan?"

Plan? I was supposed to have a plan? Nothing was ever good enough for these people. "I was going to show up and talk to her?"

Drew looked at me over his shoulder. "And if it's a trap? Or if something happens to you 'accidentally' while you're there? What then? Sugar daddy's out of town, isn't he?"

"Don't call him that."

An eyebrow raised, and his smile turned mocking. "Why,

does it bother you?" He lifted his shoulders in a shrug. "I've said worse."

"Any sign of Grazia?" I asked, changing the subject. The last thing I wanted to do was to get Drew started on one of his homophobic rants. Because it was clear he wasn't homophobic, he just liked being a jerk and pushing buttons.

He turned and headed back for the door. "I'm going for a run," he said, without meeting my eyes. "You want to come with?"

I hesitated. "So that's a no."

Drew exhaled. "Obviously," he said under his breath. "Now do you want to come or not? Because being in this house gives me the jeebs. And I'm not in the mood to stumble upon one of your faux-daddy's pet projects."

"Stop calling him that stuff," I said, following him out of the room. "It makes the whole thing sound seedy and gross. And I have school."

"That's exactly why I'll bring it up as often as possible," Drew laughed. "Just skip. No one's going to care."

"I'll care," I said flatly. I sighed and trudged up to my room. School was the last thing I wanted to do, but at least it was doing something.

¤   ¤   ¤

I managed to get through the school day without getting punched or harassed, so it was a good day. However, as much as I tried to "accidentally" run into Jade, it wasn't happening.

Any time I got close, the crowd between us pushed her in another direction.

I waited to call her until it was dark. My day was spent *not* getting caught up on all the stuff I'd missed, and *barely* keeping my head above water on the stuff we were doing now. I still hadn't gotten anywhere with the research, and while I'd made a dent in the homework packet, it wasn't fast enough.

I figured that, by waiting, at least I'd catch her when she wasn't with a crowd of minions who would happily kick my ass. I was a bit mistaken. Jade didn't answer the first three times that I called. I pushed down the sense of hurt. I didn't think she'd just ignore my calls. I texted her instead.

Meeting your mom tomorrow night at the fundraiser.

The fourth time I called, she answered on the first ring.

"Esme," she said, her voice nearly drowned out by the sounds of fervent partying going on in the background. "What are you doing?"

"Jade?"

"Esme?" she returned, in exactly the same tone. The sounds of the party kept wavering in intensity, some moments louder than others. I heard more than a couple of catcalls, and Jade's mutterings. I could just picture her trying to find a quiet place to take a phone call in peace.

"Really? I have to be an Esme? You couldn't have pretended I was Trey or something?"

"You sound positively crabby," Jade said, with teasing warmth. She was enjoying this. At least one of us was.

It shouldn't have surprised me that my invitation got lost

in the mail. But once again, I couldn't help but think about what my life had been like before … in that first week I'd come to town. I'd probably have gone with Jade, and the stories we'd have on Monday would be hysterical and ridiculous.

All of a sudden there was silence on the other end of the line, and Jade's voice was firm. "I'll be there in ten minutes. And you're officially on my shit list for this." After a moment she added an affectionate, "Idiot."

It's technically not sneaking out when there's no one home to sneak away from. I just left. Autumn was in full effect, and it was frigid outside. I huddled into my sweatshirt and waited in the dark, but I didn't have to wait long. Jade pulled up in the same car Trey had been driving when he picked her up from school.

"Please tell me that was some sort of stupid ploy to make me miss one of the few decent parties this year," she said, the minute I got into the car.

"Afraid not."

She sighed. Tonight she was wearing a black dress with tons of gold jewelry; her blond hair slicked back with only the pink streak left to dangle free. I wondered if she'd started wearing darker colors to contrast the near-whites Catherine always wore. "Why would you even *think* about talking to my mother, let alone see her in public? She practically despises you. No, wait. I'm pretty sure she *actually* despises you."

"She despises Jason," I said, and Jade flinched even though there was no one around to hear us. "I think she just *loathes* me. For now."

"Either way," she said, waving a hand, "you're not exactly

going to be Facebook friends, now are you? So why tempt fate? And why isn't he stopping you anyway?"

"He's out of town again," I said. I instinctively grabbed my door as Jade put the car in drive and started back down the side road. Forest blanketed us on either side, although in my eyes that was a lot of lumber that Jade could treat like a bull's-eye at any time. She wasn't known for being a cautious driver.

"Speaking as the defense's expert witness on cries for attention, don't you think meeting with my mother is a little excessive?" Jade took a corner too sharply, and I sucked in a breath, already white-knuckling it.

"She requested it."

"Of course she wants you there," Jade said, in a way that sounded suspiciously like she thought I was an idiot. "This is a woman that had two dud children. She wouldn't mind having a protégé to teach the family business to. And if it hurts Jason in the process, well, Christmas came early."

I almost told her that part of the reason I agreed was because Trey didn't want me to go, and I wanted him to worry. But what I said was, "I don't want her to think I'm afraid of her."

I got the side eye for that one. "Of course you're afraid of her. *Everyone* is. And if you're not, you've got emotional problems." She pulled her foot off the gas and eased into the far lane. "Set something on fire and save yourself the trouble. Trust me, you're a boy. Pyromania is normal for boys."

"I'm not setting something on fire, Jade." I could have always closed my eyes rather than watch her chaotic road skills, but somehow that was worse. I wouldn't have any warning before Jade drove us over a cliff with a far-too-casual "Oops."

She turned to the left, for once obeying the red light and stop signs. It wasn't that Jade was a bad driver, she just wasn't very good at multitasking. Being Jade Lansing was far too complicated for the average person.

"So are you going?" I asked.

She started to laugh. "Do you know how many boring fundraisers my mom goes to every year? I'd never have a life if I went to all of them. Besides, this one's at the Harbor Club. The food's terrible, the members are geriatric, and the music will be something from the string quartet oeuvre. Not my thing."

"Well, I have to go," I said. "I have to know what she wants."

"Because that worked out so well for you last time?" she snapped. "You think Catherine's going to tell you anything worthwhile?"

"She's working up to something. I don't want to get caught off guard again."

"Let Jason handle it, for god's sakes." Jade sounded almost angry. "That's what he's there for. They're supposed to toe the line until we're old enough to decide we hate each other and pick up where they left off. It's a perfectly good tradition you're trying to ruin."

"Like Jason wants me around anymore than she does?" I asked, laughing. "The only thing he wants is to win. He doesn't care who gets hurt in the process. It's all just stupid details."

"Thank god I don't have it," she said with a relieved sigh.

Neither of the Lansing siblings had the gift, not like Catherine or I did. They could have learned little bits and pieces, but they'd never be in the same league as their mother. Part of the cease-fire agreement was that Catherine wouldn't teach them anything about magic. That was one thing she'd actually followed through on.

"So what are you going to do? What's the plan?" she asked a few miles later.

I hesitated. "Go talk to her? Find out what she wants?" Underneath the sound of the car, I could hear a little strand of pop music coming from the radio, but nothing I recognized. "You know your mom. Tell me what to expect."

Jade pulled the car into a tiny lot. I realized with surprise that we were south of the town, near where Drew and I had tracked the hellhound a few days ago. "What makes you think I know my mom better than you do?" she asked. "No one really knows Catherine. Not even me. We all just see ..." her mouth piqued, as she gathered the words. "Whatever side she wants to show. It's all a mask."

Just like Jason. It always bugged me, how alike they were. "So she'll show me what she thinks I want to see?"

Jade shook her head. "Of course not. My mother's a smart woman. She's going to show you the side you won't expect." She started reapplying her lipstick, studying her reflection. "That's how we do things. Keep you off balance."

fifteen

I spent the next morning holed up in my room with the *Hastings Treatise*. My bedroom was as stark as it had been on my first night. I hadn't done anything to decorate, and aside from the stack of books on the desk and the book bag tossed around a chair, the room was devoid of personal effects.

To know the demon is to know the hunger, the book read. *True demons consume, corrupt, kill. They are baseless deities, surviving on misery and sacrifice. The nature of offerings plays a heavy role in the foundation of demonology. Much like the way one must open their hearts to God to receive his blessing, so too must the sacrifice be offered to the demon, the ritual satisfied.*

None of this was particularly helpful, but at the same time I felt that the more I could learn about demons and where Lucien came from, the better it might help me to deal with him when the time came.

I still didn't fully understand why I'd said yes to meeting Catherine tonight, or why I was even going through with it. But part of me was attracted to the idea of being reckless, of doing something that no one expected of me. Of being some-one other than myself, even if it was just for a few hours.

School was a blur that barely registered. I walked the halls, I pretended to pay attention, and I watched the clock. Anticipating just how stupid I was going to be tonight.

Once I was finally home that afternoon, I hunted down a trio of suits tucked away in the back of the closet. Jason had gone above and beyond in the clothes-shopping department. Or I should say, whoever Jason paid to go clothes-shopping went above and beyond. My room was already the size of a football stadium, and the closet was some sort of never-ending portal into oblivion.

But the fact that I had a suit worked out well. I'd need one. The fundraiser tonight—the one Catherine wanted to meet me at—was being held at The Harbor Club, Belle Dam's answer to the lack of a pretentious country club.

I fingered one of the suits' lapels, pulling it off the rack and laying it on my bed. They must have assumed I was blind. Everything in the closet was separated into outfits, instead of all the shirts being together, or all the jeans.

I pulled a bright-blue shirt down next, realizing that a tie and pocket square were already on the hanger as well. *Well that makes it easier.*

All I had to do now was get dressed, and then get a ride into the city.

¤   ¤   ¤

The Harbor Club was a gorgeous building, I had to give them that. Situated at a corner of the marina, the front of the building was all windows in order to take advantage of the view. The building itself was newer than I would have thought—all the buildings in Belle Dam had age on their side. Maybe it had just aged well. Or maybe someone felt that it just wasn't pretentious enough and needed a makeover.

I shifted again, glaring down at the hard black leather shoes I'd worn. They were a size too big. My feet kept sliding around as I walked. *Fashion is pain,* as Jade would say.

The thing about high-society events, from what I'd seen on TV, was that everyone was so self-absorbed that you could do almost anything under their noses and they'd never notice. At least, that's how I thought it worked.

This is a stupid idea, I thought, walking up to the front of the club. Now that I had actually arrived, nerves had replaced recklessness. *She could kill me with a dessert tray if she wanted.* What was I doing here?

The doors were white, inlaid with gold-ivy scrolling along the top and bottom. The interior was plush and expensive and overwrought. Everything was lit by crystal chandeliers and entitlement.

"Fascinating little gem, isn't it?" The woman who glided up to me nodded at the building like it was an architectural masterpiece. She wore a slinky black dress more suitable for someone twenty years her junior. Actually ... more like thirty. "You look a little out of place, dear. Waiting on your parents?"

I shook my head, glancing around to see a number of

people in suits and evening gowns making their way to the entrance. "Just taking it all in," I said, faking a smile.

She patted my arm and walked in front of me, linking arms with a salt-and-pepper haired gentleman a few feet away. She leaned in and said something to him, and they both glanced in my direction before heading inside.

Such a stupid idea. What had I been thinking? I didn't know the first thing about being at an event like this. Everyone here was three times my age.

At the entrance, I stood in a line as people started filing in. After a few seconds of focusing on first the floor, and then the molding above the door, I realized I was the only one in line without a gold and silver invitation in hand.

I cleared my throat as I passed the table set up to collect invitations. A woman in a bright-green dress and flame-red hair was seated on the other side, a clipboard, pen, and stack of invitations set in front of her.

She looked up at me expectantly when it was my turn, her hand held out for my nonexistent invitation.

I cleared my throat. "I'm … uhm, Braden Michaels?" I really hoped there was a list or something with my name on it. Although I wouldn't put it past Catherine to arrange something horrifically embarrassing for me. Like being physically removed from the fundraiser.

She looked blank, staring up at me from her seat for a long moment. The moment dragged on, and for a second I almost thought she was somehow stuck in time, frozen in that moment. And then I watched as recognition flared in her eyes, and her plastic smile widened. "Of course you are," she murmured.

The woman gestured to one of the attendants on either side of the inner doors and leaned forward, covering her mouth with her hand as she whispered something to him. All I caught were the words "needs" and "vision." The attendant glanced at me, then looked down to her and nodded.

"I see just fine," I said stonily. "I'm not blind."

The woman twitched, her hand snatched back like she'd just touched a hot stove. "Of course," she said quickly, "So sorry, Mr. Michaels. Please, go on in." She looked like she wanted to say something else, but she held back, mouth slightly agape.

Already I could hear whispers behind me. So much for keeping a low profile.

The fundraiser was held in the main chamber of the club, which was a two-story ballroom done up in all sorts of shades of white. The floors were polished marble, all browns and blacks, and art lined all of the walls. Ice sculptures were spaced around the room, conversation pieces of famous statues like the David and the Venus. It was far more expensive and elaborate than almost anywhere I'd ever been... but a perfect fit for someone who lived in Jason Thorpe's house.

At least in theory.

"Of course it's him," a balding, short man said as he stepped in my path. The woman next to him held a pair of champagne flutes in either hand.

"You shouldn't bother him," the woman said out of the

corner of her mouth, turning her attention to me and offering a polite, if slightly strained, smile.

"Nonsense," the man said, shrugging off her warning. "Braden, isn't it? I'm Paul Wyszewski, a friend of Jason's. And this is my wife Cheryl." Paul tugged one of the flutes out of his wife's hand. I shook his free hand, and nodded towards his wife. "So tell me," Paul continued, his voice taking on a conspiratorial tone. "Is Jason planning on showing up? Maybe stealing some thunder with a big check?"

They both looked at me expectantly. "Oh ... I ..." This was not what I signed up for.

"Let's say we leave the boy alone," a chilled voice interjected. My spine stiffened, and I turned, but it wasn't the Lansing woman I expected who'd appeared next to me. Jade was in a pewter-gray dress that shimmered in the candelabra's light. Sometime since last night, she'd done a number on her hair, going from the natural blond I'd recognized to an unnatural honey brown. Even the pink streak was gone.

"Oh, hello Jade," Paul blurted out, his face and his impressive bald spot going almost immediately scarlet. "Your mother's event is exquisite."

Jade's lips were thin, but she feigned a smile. "Of course," she sounded bored. "Aren't they always?"

"I ... I love what you've done with your hair," Cheryl said, glancing briefly at me before speaking. Did they expect us to devolve into some feud-like tête-à-tête right in front of them?

"Thank you," Jade said, looking away and sipping at her own glass of champagne. "If you see my brother and his date," she said significantly, her eyes never leaving Paul's, "be sure and compliment her on the flowers. She designed all the arrangements."

Trey had brought a date? A girl? Now Paul wasn't the only one growing red. "If you'll excuse me," I muttered, making a hasty retreat.

I stuck to the fringes of the crowd, but I was only looking for one person. *I can't believe he'd do this to me. Is this why he didn't want me to come?*

More and more people were pouring into the ballroom. I headed for the bar, which was directly between the dual staircases, ducking past a pair of older ladies in bright-green wraps who reached for me as I passed. More than a few mouths dropped as I darted through the crowd. *This whole blind thing is getting really old.*

I leaned against the bar once I arrived, sighing with relief. While I waited for the bartender to notice me amidst the crowd, I counted while I breathed.

"It's Braden, isn't it?"

Kayla stood next to me. Trey's ex. I don't know what it was about her that twisted something in my stomach, but I just didn't like her. She *looked* like a nice person. Especially now. She'd dressed up like everyone else, and she looked ethereal.

Her hair had been pulled up, a few wayward curls spilling out of the sparkling hair clips holding her hair back. Where Jade had gone for the gray and shiny, Kayla's dress was a stormy blue satin, a shade which I realized matched her eyes. This wasn't a girl who did skin-care commercials.

This was the girl who stole away the prince at the end of the night.

"Hi," I said, at a loss for anything more.

Kayla's smile widened a little, and I realized for the first time that there was something sad in it. *She looks more like an Ophelia than a Kayla.* Beautiful and tragic.

"He's not going to be happy when he finds out you're here," she said softly.

"He had to know I'd come."

She stared at me, and if anything, her smile got sadder. "Yeah."

"So he brought you," I said, in an effort to change the subject.

She nodded. "So he did."

"Good," I added, hoping she couldn't read the insincerity.

"I'd tell you to stay away from him," Kayla continued, in that too-soft, country girl way of hers. "But you wouldn't listen to someone like me." She ducked her head, tucking back an imaginary strand of hair. Her cheeks were pinker than they had been a moment ago. "You're not good for him."

She said it so simply—shy, but casual—that I almost didn't understand her context at first. It took a moment for the words to translate. Shock robbed me of a retort.

"There you are," came a warm voice I recognized easily. Trey swooped in between us, wrapped an arm around Kayla's waist and was already pulling her away by the time I'd recovered from what she'd said. "There's some people I should say hello to," he added, not quite looking at me.

I heard her sigh, but before she could say anything else,

I slipped through the crowd. A group of men at the end of the bar were talking business and "revitalizing the harbor district." I heard one of them mention Jason, and then there was laughter. I needed to get away from here.

I headed up the stairs and away from the crowd. If nothing else, it would give me the chance to watch what everyone else was doing, and pinpoint Catherine with a minimum of effort. I didn't want her sneaking up on me.

It turned out that the second-floor landing opened into a series of doors leading out to a balcony. Outside, there was a perfect view of the marina and the bay to the east. The sky had finally started to darken, as night prepared to settle in.

This was such a bad idea. But there was no running away now. I'd come here, and the least I could do was see it through.

The party continued on below me, as people from Catherine's circles swirled and glided around each other. It was like a hideous and vicious ballet. Their moves practiced, their pirouettes perfected, and each of them struggling to climb just another rung on her ladder. Whatever the cost.

My presence had to be a fascinating little spectacle to them. What did it mean, was Jason planning to show up as well? Did he send me as some sort of envoy? Or had I turned away from him, and allowed Catherine to drop me in her pocket. The air down below was practically electrified as gossip arced from one conversation to the next like bolts of lightning.

I saw Trey and Kayla on the dance floor, engaged in some sort of waltz as the tuxedoed string musicians played. He was laughing, his head tilted back just enough that I could see his earlier tension had melted away. Kayla was glowing, moving in perfect sync with him.

"They've always been so good together," Catherine murmured from my right, timing her appearance with the drop in my chest.

She was exactly as I remembered her, the type of woman that made her name on Wall Street or sailed up the corporate ladder. A woman with striking looks, instincts like a shark, and all the charm of a politician's wife. Catherine was the total package. It sucked that she a.) was evil, and b.) hated me.

"He did that for you, didn't he?" I asked, inclining my head towards the pair of them.

She smiled, but it didn't touch her eyes. "I think he did it for you," she said lightly. Her scarlet gown was muted up here, embers and magma whereas downstairs under the proper lighting it probably sizzled and burned. Seeing Catherine in red was a change—she preferred whites and creams.

"I'm here," I said quietly. My eyes never left him, even if he was having fun without me. "Tell me why."

"There's time enough," she replied. "All evening in fact. We want you to stick around. There are hours and more ahead of us."

If she'd wanted to hurt me, she wouldn't have invited me someplace public. But that modicum of safety only stretched so far, and still didn't explain why I was here. She wanted something. Until she got it, she was going to play with me like a chew toy.

The more I learned about the feud, the more I came to understand Catherine and Jason. They had employees and minions, but neither of them relied on anyone outside their inner circles. When it came down to the big things, the sensitive things, they did everything themselves. By hand. So whatever I was doing here, it was something that Catherine trusted only to herself.

"You're not in Mexico," I said, more to fill the silence than anything else.

Catherine's eyes lingered on the crowd beneath us. "Why would I be in Mexico?" she asked, with the first real smile I'd seen on her.

Jason thought she was after some South American witch. But she never left. Of course. It was part of the game. "You don't care about the *curandero*. You just wanted Jason gone for a few days. Why, so we could talk?"

Catherine took a sip of wine. "Bravo. You've finally caught up with the rest of the class."

"And rob you of the chance to gloat?" I asked genially. *Always play the game. Change the rules if you can, but never stop playing.* "I was raised better than that."

"You'll have to tell me about that sometime. Still such a mystery, aren't you?" she mused. A shrewd look, and then she turned to the balcony and gestured for one of the waiters. He stopped what he was doing without hesitation and made for the stairs.

I drummed my fingers along the marble railing, wanting desperately to keep watching Trey. But I didn't. Instead, I watched as more than one pair of eyes looked up at us, and the flurry of conversation stared anew. "Jason doesn't seem to think so," I said absently. If she wanted the verbal parry and riposte, I could indulge her.

"There's still time to change your mind, you know. My children have both been so devastated at the way you turned your back on them."

"Scolding yourself that they didn't immediately reach for a knife, then?" I asked. Neither of Catherine's children had her cold streak, not exactly. Catherine's was a shroud that never lifted, but Jade and Trey wore it more like a scarf, pulling it on and off as it suited them. Neither were cold-blooded enough to turn on me. At least not yet.

Catherine tsked. "And risk the chance of correcting their mistake? Jason's told you all sorts of tales, hasn't he?"

No, I wanted to say. *But my mother would have, if you hadn't killed her.* But I couldn't. Catherine couldn't know. "You poisoned me," I said. Pastries laced with magic, they would have almost been delicious if they hadn't nearly gotten me killed. They'd forced me to tell the truth, to spill secrets I would never have shared. Any number of them could have gotten me killed, if Lucien of all people hadn't interrupted.

"Oh, hush," she said, like I was telling some sort of out-landish tale. She was *amused* by all of this. "I loosened your tongue. Think of it as a party game."

"That's what they tell idiots who play Russian Roulette."

She inclined an eyebrow, a move that mirrored her daughter's perfectly, as if to say *touché.*

The waiter finally approached, and Catherine glanced in my direction. "Bring my guest a glass of the Berg, but wait to open the bottle." Her smile widened, just a fraction. "We wouldn't want Braden to think we've tampered with his drink."

"I don't drink," I said flatly. The waiter grinned, like he was in on a private joke, and hurried back down the stairway.

She sighed. "Only water, Braden. There's no need for all this lingering suspicion."

"I'm never going to side with you," I told her, feeling the need to lay my cards on the table. The point of this entire evening was to put me on parade. *Not only me*, I realized as my eyes dropped to the floor beneath us, where Trey was still dancing with Kayla. He dangled on his mother's apron strings. Did he even realize that's why we were here tonight?

She was playing with me, like I was just some little bug that she could squash at any time. The water came back with a tray, a wine glass full of ice, and a frosty blue bottle. He undid the cap and poured the water into the glass, handing it to me.

"There now," Catherine said, sounding unnaturally warm. "That's more like it."

I held the glass, but didn't actually drink from it. I didn't care what she said—I wasn't going to trust any of the food or drink laid out here.

"Did you know that Ben Franklin was the one who said, 'three can keep a secret if two are dead.'" Catherine tilted her head to one side. "And now the lawyer has been quietly retired. How curious."

Catherine wasn't stupid. She knew Lucien's disappearance was more than the stories said. But the fact that she kept the knowledge to herself bothered me. Why wasn't she using it to press her advantage? "Maybe he stopped being indispensable," I said.

She raised her wine glass to that, then took another sip. "Still. I've always found murder to be so … messy. It says something profound, don't you think? Men turn to murder when they cannot take the advantage any other way. You might even say it is the lowest form of negotiation."

Acid dissolved the thin scraps of calm I'd managed to collect, leaving only a sprawling mess of nerves spilling out everywhere. "Trey told you."

Catherine inclined her head, eyes glittering as she stared down below us. I had a feeling she was looking for her son. "Do you really think you can keep secrets from me, Braden? Nothing happens in this town without my knowing."

"I *happened*. I *happened* a lot, actually." I smiled and faced her. "Lucien strung you along, too. He moved against both of you, and neither one of you was perceptive enough to see. He even tried to kill your *son.* But you knew that was going to happen, right? Since *nothing happens without your knowing*."

I might have imagined it, but I thought her hand tightened on the glass.

"You can ask Trey. He'll tell you what happened that night. Lucien wanted him dead almost as much as he wanted to use me."

"Yes, and I'm still so interested in what makes you so special."

I almost swore, realizing I'd said too much.

But Catherine didn't notice. She exhaled slowly, her eyes hooded. "I see Jason's arrogance has rubbed off on you. You almost died killing the lawyer. Which makes me wonder if it was all hype." Her voice had dropped down into freezing temperatures.

"Continue underestimating me. I'm counting on it." It was a bold move, to challenge her so blatantly. "I'm done here."

I left her then, and took the stairs back down. As I slipped through the crowd, one person after another tried to catch my attention, my arm, my eye. But I sailed past all of them and right back out the front doors.

Night had fallen during my conversation with Catherine. I spent several minutes trying to control my breathing. My blood was singing, and I felt like I'd just come face to face with a predator and lived.

Belle Dam at night was beautiful, especially the view I had of the harbor. I could see distant lights across the bay— another town, probably. I bet it was easier over there: no need to worry about feuds or witches, demons or hellhounds.

That was stupid, I thought. *Challenging her like that. She's going to come after you. You know this.*

A hand yanked at my shoulder and spun me around. Someone screamed like a little girl, but it definitely wasn't me.

sixteen

"What did you say to my mother?" Trey demanded, trying to catch his breath.

I shook loose from his hand, some part of me knowing this would happen. Trey had tried to warn me away, but now he couldn't let it go without a confrontation.

"Careful," I snapped, holding my hand up in warning. "Someone might see."

"What were you thinking?" he seethed, his face tight and eyes wild. "*Were* you even thinking?"

I straightened my suit jacket and glared. "What were *you* thinking bringing Kayla like that?"

Trey blinked, momentarily caught off guard, but his eyes quickly narrowed. His tone turned spiteful. "You didn't think to invite Drew? He's always got his hands on you. But there are leash laws, so you'd probably have to tie him up at the door."

"You're such an ass." I turned my back on him. I didn't get more than a few steps away before he called after me.

"What did you say to her?" I could hear him coming. "You need to tell me. Did you threaten her?"

I tried to put as much distance between us as possible. Trey, however, had other ideas. He caught up with me and blocked my escape. "She just bolted out of her own party. I need to know if something happened, so I can stop this before it gets out of hand."

My shock was so great at first that I couldn't speak. "You think she left her party so she could *put a hit out on me*?"

Actually, I should probably be worried about that myself.

"We need to get you home," he said, reaching for my arm.

"I don't need you to try to protect me! I can take care of myself!" Why did we keep having this argument?

He looked at me like I had said something completely schizophrenic. "Do you think this is some kind of game?"

At that instant, I really wanted to punch him. I took a moment and gathered myself, and then said with exaggerated calm, "You think your mother might have put a hit out on me. And you still think Jason's the villain in all of this?"

There was a stubborn look on his face that would have told me all I needed to know, if it wasn't for the troubled look in his eyes.

"You know she didn't invite me out for tea," I continued, my words sharp. "You're not dumb enough to think this was a social call. Do you really think I'm having *fun*?"

His eyes blazed. "Then why *are* you here?"

"Because you asked. That's why she sent you." I said quietly, losing hold of the fire in my head. I felt washed out, like all the energy had been sapped from my body.

Trey took a step back, looking like he'd just been slapped. "I told you not to come," he whispered, confused.

"She was expecting me. And she might have taken it out on you if I didn't show."

"Braden, I can take care of myself. You don't need to protect me. You can't keep doing—"

It started in the middle of the sentence, looming over me like a tidal wave that had just started to crash when it froze solid.

It wasn't a vision this time. At least not at first. A second, new kind of gravity pressed in on me from the sides, trapping me between ground and sky and holding me tight. A boreal wind curled over my fingers and trailed along my flesh. Ice crept through my veins like a criminal, spreading roots and expanding along my bones.

Underneath the coating of ice that covered me like a second skin, I could feel it in the distance. Magic. A lot of magic. The ice in me protested, wavered, as I moved one foot in front of another. A second set of ice-born instincts urged flight. Demanded it.

Each step was a fight, a struggle to resist the strange gravity pressing down on me. Sweat formed on my skin, instantly freezing and digging down into flesh. But I pushed forward. And again.

Someone was talking, I could hear it in the beats between, when the sheets of ice in my head cracked and screamed their way apart like symphonies composed by mad gods.

"Another." The square of grass lined with perfectly sculpted trees and flowerbeds that knew nothing of overgrowth or abandonment. Small-town Americana. How utterly pedestrian. Prodigal

sons and daughters skulking under shadows like carrion hoping for a meal. Scavenge and be sated. *"You know where to send them."*

Just like that, the cold fled past me, like a specter in the night. I was off and running before I'd even fully recovered. *The square.* Whatever it was, it was happening at the town square. It was like a beacon, and I couldn't help but chase it. I could feel the hollow ache inside of me, resonating there.

"Where are you going? What's going on?" Trey had stopped following me, his voice getting farther and farther away.

I felt like an animal hunting down prey. *It might be the hellhound.* I didn't care, the threat didn't even slow me down. I had to *know.*

Somewhere on Lake Street I'd shrugged out of my jacket, and as I turned the corner onto Spring—which lead directly to the downtown—I cut diagonally through someone's front yard and kicked off the hard leather shoes as I ran. My heels were going to be a mess of blisters in the morning as it was, and they were only slowing me down.

The feeling of magic was already fading away by the time I sprinted across the street and into the square. Cobbled paths, fountains, flowers. Everything looked normal. *All it would take is one look. One look to find out exactly what happened here.*

But I didn't invoke the power of the witch eyes. Ever since the frozen visions had started, I didn't trust myself. I thought that exposure was supposed to be fatal, but this was ... not. Were my powers just expanding or changing?

"What the hell's going on?" Drew appeared from the opposite end of the square, barely winded. He jogged over to me, his eyes scanning the perimeter around us. "And why aren't you wearing any shoes?"

I started pulling at the tie, unable to unravel it and finally settling for pulling it over my head. I tossed it to the side while I undid the top buttons. *Relief, oh that's nice.* I was never wearing a suit again for as long as I lived. "You felt that?"

Drew snorted. *Of course he felt that.* For other witches, feeling the presence of magic was a lot like closing your eyes but still knowing there was a light on in the room. For a Shifter like Drew, it was an actual sense. They could smell the magic.

"Was it them? Hellhounds?"

His nose wrinkled up and he looked to the sidewalk before shaking his head. "No burns on the concrete," he said, gesturing to the paths. "You're the witch. Can't you figure out what it was? Or who?"

I shook my head, trying to feel out the square. Nothing jumped out at me, and I'd never really learned to decipher magical energies. No need, when the witch eyes had always done it better than I could have on my own. It was easier to look and be filled with the *knowing*. It was a painful brain download, but it was always exact and precise. "You're sure it wasn't someone summoning a hellhound?" I asked. Drew's concern tensed, lines fracturing his forehead.

"What is it?" I asked, immediately on alert.

Drew shook his head slowly, glancing at me. "You don't smell that?"

I inhaled again, but all I got was a hint of the ocean air, and some late season floral smells. I shrugged.

"It's like … wet dog." A silver haze like some sort of aura wavered around him, but Drew didn't shift. He just kept breathing in through his nose. "It's too strong," he murmured. And then all at once, he was off like a hunting dog that had picked up the fox's scent.

If Drew hadn't dropped out of high school, he probably could have gotten a track scholarship. Or maybe an Olympic tryout. Even pushing myself as hard as I could, blood pounding through my chest and my muscles burning, within a matter of seconds he was half a block ahead of me. *At least he's wearing shoes.*

Drew darted across Spring Street, nearly jumping at one point as a car came swooping down around a corner, almost running him down. He never got so far ahead that I couldn't still see him, but halfway down Spring Street I had to stop. There were *two* dark shapes in the distance—one to the south and one to the west—and I wasn't sure which one was Drew.

It was the sound of yelling that made the decision for me. I headed west, and watched the blob I was chasing disappear behind a curtain of pine trees. I gained a second wind, my feet slapping against concrete as I bolted down the sidewalk. Finally, I caught up to the pine trees, and veered to the left.

There was a fence next to the pine trees. I slowed, tried to catch my breath after stopping next to the rusty black iron bars. I leaned back, resting my head against the cool iron as

I waited for my lungs to fall back into my chest and do their job.

That's when I saw the scarlet-eyed creature hanging from the top of the bars.

It was a strange, mottled color. All dark greens and blacks with spiny protrusions on the shoulders. It looked like someone had crossed a monkey, a porcupine, and a teacup poodle. And then they took all the leftovers and made this thing.

It opened a mouth full of fangs and grinned down at me.

At first, I thought it was some kind of hallucination, or vision. Nothing that tiny and disturbing could be real. The drop of thick saliva that slid between its teeth and plopped down on my shoulder like a sticky, slow-motion raindrop convinced me otherwise.

"What the fu—"

The thing's mouth widened, revealing a second row of teeth in the back, and then it screeched. Spittle flew and I caught a whiff of its breath. Like fetid, rotting animals throwing a house party. From beyond the gate, I heard additional screeches, varied slightly in pitch almost as though they were answering a call.

I scrambled around, sliding my butt down onto the sidewalk and turning at the same time. The creature continued to hang there, watching me with large eyes.

"Any day now," Drew called roughly from the other side of the gate.

I climbed to my feet, keeping my eyes on the creature. It hung from its hind legs, and as I watched, it started to swing back and forth. Like this was nothing but a game. *Some kind of demon, but I've never heard of anything like that.*

The front gate wasn't much farther. I ran from the demon, giving the fence a wide berth. The peeling black iron of the gate crumbled in my fingers as I threw one side open. Moonlight illuminated what was a modest graveyard. Drew was thirty feet away, the light seeming to collect on his skin. Trying to shift.

But every time the light slid up his arm and his body started to contract, one of the little monsters leapt from the shadows. Drew could dodge one, maybe two, but there was always a third that managed to drag its claws along the changing skin. The quicksilver light was cut neatly in half, and faded immediately. The monkey demon things chittered in glee every time.

"A little help?" he snarled, throwing one of the creatures over his shoulder where it disappeared between two large cross monuments. It bounced up almost immediately, leaping to the top of the cross and wobbling there.

"What are they?" I called. Maybe if I knew what they were, I would know what to do. Another one launched itself into the air at Drew, spreading its arms and legs like it thought it would float on the air. He snatched it and slammed it into the ground.

I closed my eyes and started drawing the magic in, feeling the wellspring's magic soothing all the jagged pieces inside of me. I felt *connected*, a part of everything. All the moisture in the air, seeping down onto individual blades of grass, deeper and into the dirt and tree branches extending so far below us.

Two of the creatures slammed into my legs, in the spot right behind my knees, and I dropped. My concentration shattered as I slammed into the ground.

The fog started rolling in, thicker and thicker by the moment. I heard, but didn't see, the gremlins scampering away.

"Braden!" Drew snarled. *He should really work on his impatience.*

What could I do? I didn't know how to fight things like this. Even when we'd confronted the hellhounds before, it wasn't like I was whipping up fireballs.

I hadn't even gotten back on my feet when two, or three, or five hundred of those little fuckers pounced on me. It was like they knew all the right pressure points to hit. One foot was swept out from under me at the same time as another knocked down my arm—the only thing keeping me semi-vertical. I ended up sprawled on the ground, feeling cold, wet sliminess soaking into my clothes.

I looked up and saw Drew being swarmed over by almost a dozen of the creatures, nearly invisible under their black and green exteriors.

The fog continued to intensify.

Two of them leapt off of tombstones in the distance, screeching as they approached. But as they neared the fog they balked, reaching out with hesitant claws to brush up against the cloudiness. It was like they'd never seen fog before.

Or they were afraid of it.

The fog had gotten so dense, I could barely see the perfect row of headstones in front of me. As it continued to advance, the creatures fell back. One of them stared at me. Pointed, batlike ears flat against its head, he bared his teeth at me and scampered away.

That's when *he* appeared.

It was hard to see him at first. The fog billowed out from him, thick like cloud cover that nearly managed to drown out his all black attire.

The hairs on my arms stood up as I felt the magic surrounding him. It was like an electric current, and I could feel stray bits of energy humming against my skin as it soared towards him. He looked down at me and sighed in exasperation.

"Where are your shoes?" Uncle John asked, sounding tired and bemused.

SEVENTEEN

Uncle John was really here. Standing in front of me, like we'd never been separated. Like this was any other time that he had to step in and rescue his wayward nephew.

He extended his hand, and I gripped it, almost afraid that he'd turn out to be another vision. But he was solid. Stable.

"The fog will disorient them," he said, "But that's all I can manage. They can't stand cold. Can you handle that?"

Cold? I shook my head. "No. I mean … I don't think—"

He grabbed me by the shoulders. "You can do this," he said, determined and confident. "I taught you how, remember?"

"I can't even concentrate," I said, trying to pull away. But Uncle John wouldn't let me go. "They know whenever we try to do something."

"We?" He asked, but shook it off just as quickly. "Concentrate!"

The chittering of the demons got suddenly louder, and

I heard a strangled cry that sounded so desperate and inhumane that I shivered.

His fingers dug into my shoulder blades. It was like the floodgates suddenly opened, and magic was spilling over his fingers and into me.

I closed my eyes, and felt the magic clinging to my breath, my bones, and the blood that was still rushing through my system. I was a part of it. And I could feel all the things that *weren't*.

There were more than a dozen demons, I could sense that much. They felt like sewers and grime, like the kinds of things that would bubble over in a landfill. I didn't know what they were exactly, but I could *feel* how alien they were. Demons, even if they were the pint-size versions.

Most of them huddled on top of a lump; pulling, scratching and prodding at their prey. I could feel Drew, too, collapsed and throbbing underneath them. Something was wrong with him, he felt... pressured. Like he was a soda bottle someone kept shaking up. Any moment, the sides would split and he'd explode.

I had to help him.

John was right. I could do this. Everything inside of me had been freezing over for days. I had ice to spare. There wasn't anything to even *think* about. I dug down, feeling the ice inside of me that kept crackling towards the surface. Ice, that had kept me cold when Jason frustrated me, that kept me company when Trey pushed me away.

My fist was clenched, and I opened it and raised my hand in a fluid motion. Instantly, a gale formed from behind me, a storm of air and frost and anger. It surged out of nowhere, and everything I felt went into it. The wind rushed past me, a desperate whistle against my ears.

This time, the ice settled against my skin, it didn't tear through it. I could feel it inside of me, some glacial well of frozen, static power. As the feeling spread through me, everything seemed to quiet. Even the things inside that I didn't know were screaming.

With the pulsing force of the tempest tearing away the fog, it set all the creatures on edge. They stopped in their torment, their merriment. *Playing with their food,* I realized.

I forced the magic to harden, to grow cold and stoic and to pull the moisture from the air.

"Think of snow," Uncle John whispered in my ear. "Remember that winter with all the ice? How many times did you fall down?"

But his words fell on deaf ears. I couldn't listen. Didn't want to. Everything inside of me was quiet, silent, and still. I'd never felt like this, it wasn't like some sort of high, it was an emptiness. Everything inside of me that ached, the places where all the bruises and feelings lingered iced over. Trey, and Riley, and everything with the feud and Lucien, it was all just walls of ice. I couldn't feel anything. I couldn't hurt. It felt *good.*

I liked this. I wanted this to stay. Cold. Untouched. This time, the feeling of ice and frost didn't tear through my skin. This time, it came easily.

The torrent of wind blew away the traces of fog, and sparkled in the light. Shards of ice, thin and sharp like arrows, swept across the graveyard. The dozen or so demons had appeared again now that the fog was gone, piled high on top of Drew's body.

With the first wave of ice carried by the wind, the demons started to scatter. But they weren't leaping away quite so nimbly, or running with as much speed, either. When one of the ice arrows managed to strike, it tore across the demon's skin like it was paper, shredding away the top layer and revealing something dark and tarlike underneath.

Amused chatter turned to shrieks and cries of pain as the demonlings scattered. The ice chased them like a plague, tearing through their bodies like paper. Chitters of amusement turned to cries of pain as they fled.

Once they were gone, I lowered my hand. All at once the wind died. Even the chill to the air rose and vanished, like a balloon we'd released.

Drew was sprawled on the ground, and from a distance I couldn't tell if he was still breathing. I started forward, completely forgetting that Uncle John was behind me, and ran to him. Every few seconds his body spasmed, like he'd been struck with a defibrillator.

His skin hummed and glowed with silver light. It pulsed like a heartbeat, strongest around his arms and chest, and nearly invisible around his head and feet. But it vibrated, like some kind of electric field.

"Drew?" I shook him, but he didn't move.

I heard Uncle John approach from behind. "Is he still breathing?"

I put a hand on his chest and leaned forward, scared for

a second that he might not be. That it was too late. Riley's words rose in the back of my mind. *"It's dangerous to be your friend, Braden. They all get hurt."*

But his chest rose. Slowly.

"He was trying to change. And those things kept attacking him. He couldn't finish."

"They're called *mokoi*," John said. "Dog spirits. They're descended from one of the trickster demons. They interfere with magic."

I cleared my throat, resting my hand on Drew's chest. There had to be something I could do to help. Drew got hurt because I couldn't handle a couple of monsters on my own.

"Drew?" My voice sounded hesitant, and I tried to summon up some of that ice I'd felt before. "You have to change." Authoritative.

But if Drew could hear me, he didn't feel like listening. Big shock.

"Braden—" John started, but I never gave him the chance.

I raised my fist and slammed it into Drew's chest. It was a move based on instinct, and the moment it connected, something happened. The sound of the blow struck like a judge's gavel, a gust of power slipped out of me, and the next thing I knew, I was swallowed up into the visions.

Agony and pieces missing, the whole lesser than the sum, everything seething anger cherry-red rage.

My prison—and it is a prison—of cobbled stones and archaic air, I slumber here and dream of murder. Of how their bones will twist, and blood will fount, and I will drink up their fears and the whispers of lives unlived.

They've promised me sacrifice. But nothing will undo this memory of shattering, as I was broken so will I always in some way be broken.

They will pay.

Gasping for air, I came back to myself. The vision faded, leaving behind a wash of fatigue that would have made me fall if I wasn't already on my knees.

"Kid? You okay?" John's voice was reassuring. Worried.

It was happening more now. I had to figure out what was causing the visions. They were about Lucien, I was certain. They were also useless—nothing I'd seen had helped me so far.

"I'm fine," I said, and then I focused on Drew again. He was still unconscious, he wasn't spasming as much, and his breathing had improved. But he *was* still in trouble. I leaned down, and whispered again, "You need to change."

This time he must have heard, or understood. Because the silver glow surged forth and swallowed up his body. I expected a wolf—since that was the first thing I'd seen him shift into, but when the glow diminished there was a pit bull sprawled on the ground.

Drew the dog got up and started running towards the street. Halfway there, he stopped and turned just long enough to make eye contact before he kept going.

"Never actually seen one of them transform," John said, letting out a low whistle. "I see you're making friends with the locals."

I whirled around, momentarily forgetting I was

exhausted. "Where have you *been*? I've been calling you! I almost died!"

It was like I slapped him across the face. Uncle John reeled back, his eyes wide. "Braden, I—"

"No," I railed. "No! Where were you? Even if you couldn't be *here*, you shouldn't have left me alone!"

Any trace of emotion dropped off his face. "You were the one who left," he said slowly.

Now I was the one who felt like he'd been slapped. "I *had* to come. He would have killed you. I didn't have a choice."

John shook his head. "We always have a choice."

"No," I said, seeing it clearly for the first time. "You left me here. I came back to find out the truth, and you washed your hands of me."

"Who's telling you this?" John demanded, stepping forward. "This isn't you, Braden."

I took a step back. "I almost died. He almost killed me. And instead, I—" I choked off, turning away.

"What's going on with you?" he asked softly. "And what was that back there? Something's wrong, isn't it?"

I hesitated, part of me wanting to confide in him. To tell him about Lucien, and the visions, and the girl. That maybe he'd be able to help like he used to when I was young and had a nightmare. That he could understand what I was going through with Jason. But before I could make a decision—to tell or not to tell—we were interrupted.

"Braden!" Trey shouted from somewhere outside of the graveyard.

Oh crap.

159

I turned back to my uncle, my thoughts strangely calm. "You have to go. He can't know you're here." Already, I was trying to figure out how to make that happen. Sneak John out the back somehow. But what was Trey even *doing* here? Why now?

John blinked. "Who is it, Braden?"

I shook my head, pushing John in the other direction. "You have to go. He's one of *them*. A Lansing."

He looked over my shoulder, but didn't resist when I started moving him in the opposite direction. I felt a whisper of magic, tickling and irritating against my skin. The edges of Uncle John blurred, like a camera out of focus.

"We'll talk soon," he promised, and despite the now clear night, by the time he was only a few feet from me, I'd already lost sight of him.

He needs to show me how he does that, I thought as I headed for yet another bad encounter with Trey.

eighteen

Even with my sunglasses on, I was blind the moment I walked out of the cemetery gate. Trey was parked in the middle of the road, his headlights flaring into me.

"Turn off your car," I snapped, taking the opportunity to close the gate behind me and compose myself. This night was just one incident after another. Through the haze I finally saw him, half out of the car. "What are you doing here?"

The car shut off, and I saw clearly again. He was still fully dressed, buttoned up and professional. But there were little things, like the way the tie's knot hung just a little askew, and faint little creases and rumples in his collar. He wasn't as put together as he appeared.

"That's my question." He closed the door, then leaned against it. "What happened?"

Twenty minutes ago, we'd been fighting outside the Harbor club. Now it was like the argument never happened. I looked down at my throbbing feet.

Trey saw the look, and reached in through the open window.

"Must have been in a hurry," he said, pulling out the shoes I'd abandoned.

"How'd you find them?"

"I was motivated," he said, with a grin that made me shiver.

I'd lost my shoes in someone's yard. So he must have followed me. "Are you planning to dress as a creepy stalker for Halloween?"

"You're still going as a pain in my ass, right?"

I didn't return his smile. I couldn't handle another argument right now. Especially since all I wanted to do was go home and sleep for about a million years. "I'm fine," I said, voice clipped.

Trey didn't take the hint. "Tell me what's wrong."

I rolled my eyes. "I'm tired, and I've had more than enough manipulative Lansings for one day."

He tossed the shoes towards me but didn't make any move towards leaving. "Come on," he said, nodding to the car. "I'll give you a ride home."

I stared at him in shock. "Are you high? I'm not getting into a car with you." I shoved my feet back into the shoes, and ... then I hesitated. Looking down both sides of the street, I didn't see anything that was familiar. Was this even the street I'd come down?

"We should talk," he said from behind me.

I closed my eyes. "You always want to talk," I muttered. "But you never actually say anything with meaning."

Surprise quickly turned to hurt. "Braden ..."

Now that I'd dredged it up, examples kept piling up in

my head. "You say we have to stay away from each other, but you won't stop *following me*. You say we can't be together, but you keep *kissing me*. And then tonight, you knew I was coming here, so you brought a date?"

The quick-fire retort I expected never came. I turned to see him staring at me, his jaw working but he couldn't pull together a defense. As quickly as my anger had come, it faded, and we stared at each other.

"I'm trying," he said finally, his voice nearly broken and almost too low to catch.

I wrestled with myself, knowing I should walk away right here. "You can drop me off at the Harbor Club," I said. A different kind of headache was forming behind my eyes. This wasn't some sort of migraine. It had Trey's name all over it. Without saying anything else, we got into the car. I focused on the view out of my window, trying to ignore the way my stomach seized when I smelled Trey's cologne mixed with something floral.

He pulled into the street, and started driving. I could see him wrestling with something, and I waited. Instead of taking the quickest way to the harbor, Trey cut across one of the housing developments and down onto one of the circuitous forest roads that skirted the city.

"You keep trying to paint my mom as the villain, but Jason's no saint, either," he said. I was about to open my mouth to agree with him because I knew neither side of the feud was innocent, but Trey just kept going. "If she knew about you, knew what Jason *did*, she'd have every right to freak out. He always planned to bring you back here and use you against her."

"You know I don't want that," I said, trying to calm him down. His face was getting redder and more agitated, and as a result we were accelerating. A lot. Every curve we took got tighter and tighter, pressing me first left, then right. "Trey, the road…" As the fog got thicker, visibility diminished, but he didn't slow down. I don't know what he was trying to prove.

"My mom didn't have anything to do with Lucien. That was all Jason. He would have killed me."

"I was there," I snarled.

"You keep trying to make this *so simple*, like Jason's the hero and my mom's the villain." He sounded so controlled, like his car wasn't inching its way towards 100 miles per hour.

"She didn't want me here tonight so I could join her book club. Half an hour ago you thought she was going to have me killed!"

"She's on edge," he said tightly. "The last time she let her guard down, the Thorpes tried to kill my father."

No. John *tried to kill him.* "She *did* kill my mother," I snapped, focusing everything I had into smothering the rage that had been stoked.

But it was wasted because my angry words slid right past him. "That's a convenient lie," he said thoughtfully. "It makes sense. Anything he could do to make you hate her more. Can't you see that he's using you?"

Acid rose in my throat, coating my words. "Can't you see that *she's* using *you*? You think you know everything," I hissed. I was like a geyser that could blow at any moment. The pressure in me just kept rising. "There *aren't* any good guys. Why—" But before I could finish, I doubled over as my stomach tried to strangle me from the inside out. Crushing pressure, like a corset pulled bone-crushingly tight spread out from my abdomen, inciting a revolution my insides were only too happy to join in on.

The pain washed through my body, cracking and shredding its way to the surface. I think I gasped, but it was only to empty my mouth for the screams that were building. My vision iced over, everything washed out in pale blues and greens.

"Stop the car," I managed to say. But he didn't. I saw him touch my arm, but I couldn't feel it. The pressure, the pain, it was still building. It had to go somewhere. Anywhere. I had to get rid of it.

"Stop!" I screamed. A pulse swept out of me, carrying away everything inside that had been building up. *Too much feeling, too much hurt, too much humanity to take.* Just like that the engine, the lights, the entire dashboard; they all went dark.

My vision cleared. The steering wheel had locked up, and no matter how hard Trey tried it wouldn't budge. We were still hurtling down the coastal road, only now the car was out of control.

"Braden!" Trey struggled with the brakes, lifting his entire body off the seat to push with his legs. When that didn't work, he tried to throw the parking brake back, but it refused to move.

I felt like I'd run some sort of marathon. It hurt to breathe, my *lungs* hurt, and no matter how hard I tried, I couldn't catch my breath. But the pain was gone. Again.

"Braden!" His fingers caught in my shirt, and he tried to shake me.

The car's still moving. You're going to crash. There was a presence in my head. Like a voice, but etched out of hail-stones.

We were quickly losing road and a wall of trees was drawing closer.

You can stop the car. You remember that day. The bus, barreling down Washington, and the demon princess. My second day in Belle Dam, and my first near-death experience.

"We're going to have to jump," Trey shouted. But when he tried the door handle, it moved uselessly. The locks were electric, or frozen. We were trapped.

You can get it right this time. I didn't question the voice in my mind. It was a solid voice, something separate from me but still *me*. It was what winter would sound like, if winter could form words.

I already knew what it wanted. The trees were getting closer. Five hundred feet.

I grabbed hold of the magic, almost more than I could even picture. I twisted it into thick ropes and rubber bands, and felt it burn against my skin as it slid past me.

Three hundred feet. The interior of the car started to glow. Out of the corner of my vision, I could see Trey's face filtered through sapphire blue. The magic continued to weave together, crystal cords and diamond strings.

One hundred feet. Trey threw one of his arms in front of me, pushing me back against the seat.

I knew what I'd done wrong the last time. I'd reacted on instinct, and the spell hadn't formed properly. Now I saw how the spell was supposed to go. The way the forms curved—the way they should have all along.

"*Now*," I whispered. Power snapped out of me like a bow and arrow, the plume tethered to my chest. I felt the world hum a melody.

The car was swallowed into sapphire and the sound of rushing waves.

¤   ¤   ¤

"Does the boy know? Is he aware of what is to come?"

It took four labored breaths before I could answer. My voice, which once enflamed the hearts of the truly desperate, was now a choking rasp. To be humiliated was to be human. But I am not that. Never that. Even at my most graceless, I am so much more than this cage of blood and bone.

"He sees more than you think." I knew it in my innermost essence. We were bound, now. He had tasted the power primordial. My power. It called to him. Soon it would call to me.

"And you will remember our bargain?" Some part of me knew that voice. It wasn't something I'd ever heard before, but I could feel it against the back of my neck. Whispers against my teeth.

It grated to have to strike such a bargain. I, who was once a being of rages and grace, as fluid as quicksilver and existing everywhere I was worshiped. To have to bargain, and bargain poorly. As devious as the witch had been, in this she had chosen wisely. To ravel what she had so meticulously unraveled was not my way. But I had no choice. The Paths were closed to me.

"Agreed," I said, sinking back down onto my bed of stone. "Bring me another. I must be restored."

¤　　¤　　¤

We were alive.

The light faded slowly. There was a noise coming from somewhere, a staccato clicking. My breath came harsh, but I was still breathing. I looked to my left. Trey's head was thrown back, but his chest rose and fell. We were okay.

Better yet, the car was okay. We hadn't crashed. None of the windows were broken, the car wasn't wrapped around a pine tree, and I didn't think I was suffering from whiplash. We were on the side of the road, liked we'd parked here on purpose.

Trey's arm was still pressed against me, only now my hands were wrapped around his, holding on as if for dear life. The cab was frigid—frost had formed along all the windows, and I realized the chattering sound I heard was my teeth.

"Are you okay?" He shifted, groaned, but he sounded unbroken.

I gripped his hand tighter in response. The ice, the visions, something *was* wrong with me. I could have killed the two of us. But as quickly as the panic raced up my spine, the urgency and the worry vanished. *All that matters is that we're okay,* I told myself, and if my thoughts were tinged with a hint of frost, I didn't notice.

All at once, the car came back to life. Trey didn't try to take his hand back, instead he leaned towards me as he fiddled with the heat, turning the fans on as high as they would go. I closed my eyes and pulled my hands closer—and by proxy Trey's hand—and gripped them tight against my heart.

You could make him love you. Strip away all those pieces that make him so stubborn and loyal, the winter voice inside me murmured. *Make him burn with passion until he combusts. So pretty when they pop.*

I shook my head, focusing on the warmth of his hand and the heat from the vents.

He squeezed. I opened my eyes to find him watching me. "You like to make things difficult, don't you?" His playful sarcasm only made my stomach twist harder. It still didn't change anything between us.

"I don't know what happened," I said. And that wasn't enough, not nearly enough. "I'm sorry."

His mouth flared, a flash of vitriolic emotion across his face. "Sure you don't," he said. "You've learned how to keep your secrets, haven't you?"

That wasn't it! I didn't know how to convince him otherwise. I squeezed his hand and tried to put as much earnest feeling into my words as I could. "I trust you, Trey."

His response was immediate, and full of bitterness. "You shouldn't. My mother—I know I should—and sometimes she's wr—but I just can't."

I let him ramble, cycle through a dozen different thoughts,

the one and only time I've ever heard him struggle with his words. *Was Trey starting to doubt his mother?* It could just have been my own wishful thinking.

I forced my fingers to relax, to release the white-knuckled grip I had on him. When I pulled away, I could almost see my fingerprints imprinted on his skin.

He pulled his hand back and put the car into gear. In the glow from the headlights, I saw the muscles in his jaw flex and his mouth pinch down into a tiny slit.

Once we were back on the road, Trey respected the speed limit. Neither of us spoke as he drove us back into town. I don't know what he expected from this little side trip. Whatever it was, he was leaving disappointed.

Belle Dam looked shy and embarrassed as we drove back into town. Houses were closed up, lights were off, and even the streets were empty. Trey drove with a purpose now—no more side-street adventures and detours. We were heading straight for the waterfront.

He slowed once we saw the hint of circling red and blue lights near the harbor. I knew before the police cars came into view, before the crowd outside the Harbor Club, and before the tears that it had happened again. I knew what we had missed.

Another girl had been taken.

Nineteen

Through traffic had been suspended, so Trey simply pulled to the side of the road. Still without speaking, we both jumped out of the car and headed for the crowd huddled outside the club. Two police cars, a fire truck, and at least two ambulances blocked the street.

The muttering started before we even reached the crowd. A few people went so far as to point us out, and what started out as a few discreet whispers soon became a mob of gossip.

"Isn't that ..."

" ... can't imagine Catherine will be happy ..."

" ... son will be so disappointed."

A sudden pressure at my back made me jump, only to realize that Trey had rested his hand against my spine. That only enflamed the gossips more. The crowd parted as we approached, like we were suddenly lepers.

Catherine in her scarlet gown was easy to pick out of the crowd once we were close enough. She was standing near, but not next to, the huddle of officers. Almost like she was their supervisor.

She sighed upon spotting us. "Really, Gentry? Are we doing this *again*?"

Trey's hand dropped from behind me. "What happened?"

Catherine glanced towards the officers, after barely looking in my direction. "There aren't any leads so far."

"Leads about *what*?" he asked tightly.

Finally she turned towards me. She stared, and I hesitated, afraid to blink. She seemed to be puzzling something out.

"It seems I really have underestimated you," she said finally. Catherine turned to her son. "Kayla is gone."

"Kayla?" Trey whispered.

"What do you mean she's *gone*?" I demanded.

Her eyes were cool on mine. "The girl stepped outside for a bit of air. Her purse was found near the street, the contents spilled out across the concrete."

I could hear the restless buzzing around us. "The police are looking into it, Gentry. I have the *utmost* faith in them." Catherine said, once again glancing at me with a look of consideration. *What was suddenly so interesting about me?*

"Trey," I said, but when I reached out to touch him, he stepped out of reach.

"No. This is my fault." His head was shaking, his eyes focused on the ground. "I should have been here. But I left. She was here all by herself."

"Nothing is your fault," Catherine whispered harshly, glaring at her son. "You couldn't have known something like this was going to happen."

Trey looked up at her. "Did you?" The question startled him almost as much as it startled her. Trey was the good son, the *loyal* son. The fact that Catherine let her surprise show at all told me how rare a moment this was. Had he ever questioned her like this before?

She turned back to me with thoughtful eyes. "A bold action tonight, yes?"

I couldn't figure out what she was talking about. I'd missed some part of the conversation, clearly. Was she suggesting I was involved? Or was she commiserating about her own involvement? I took a half step back, and then told her honestly, "I have no idea what you're talking about."

Help came from a surprising source. "Leave him alone," Trey said, standing up to his mother. "He was with me. He couldn't have done... what you're implying."

"Someday you'll stop wondering why the strays keep biting the hand that feeds them," Catherine sighed, her mouth tightening. With that, she turned on her heel and clacked away, off to go make nice with the lingering officers of the law, no doubt.

Trey turned to look at me, his arms crossing in front of him. His eyes were cold and reddened. "You should go."

I didn't even try to protest. I turned around and left.

You keep playing into their hands, the cold voice disclosed. *And now he has another girl.*

¤   ¤   ¤

I left Drew a voicemail later that night, figuring he was still scratching at fire hydrants and burying bones in town.

"Another girl disappeared tonight," I said. "Kayla. I think she was taken just like Grazia was. Call me when you get this."

There wasn't a proper vision this time, only flashes. It had been like a tease—just enough to get me to the square and in pursuit of the demons. But it wasn't all pointless. I'd learned something. Lucien had a partner—he'd struck a bargain with *someone,* and he wasn't happy about it.

Even though the voices had been so clear in my vision, they'd started to fade and warp as soon as I was back in my own head. I knew one of them had to be Lucien's, but I couldn't say for certain if the other was even a man or a woman.

Was Catherine helping him? I'd seen her approach him about switching sides. She could have brokered a deal with him. But what did she get out of it? Lucien had known that he was getting the poorer end of the bargain. What would Catherine have asked for that would have upset him so much?

I curled up in my bed with my copy of the *Hastings Treatise,* and tried to skim through, looking for a mention of *mokoi,* but I fell asleep before I'd so much as cracked the book open.

When I stumbled downstairs the next morning, Drew was already in the kitchen, helping himself to my pancakes. Another mountain of breakfast foods lined the table, in case I'd forgotten that I was supposed to eat my weight in batter.

"I think I'm wearing your nanny down," Drew confided. "She almost smiled this morning."

"No she didn't," I snorted. The woman was incapable of levity. "And she's not my nanny."

He looked at me in confusion. "She's not the one who burps you after every meal? Wow, that makes our last conversation really awkward then."

I rolled my eyes. It was too early for Drew's brand of humor. I went straight for the coffee, hoping it would wake me up faster.

"You want to tell me what that was last night?" he said, in between shoveling a half-dozen pancakes in his mouth.

I shrugged. "Demons."

"Isn't it always?" Drew's silverware continued to clatter against the plate as he sawed and shoveled. He was treating breakfast—*my* breakfast—like it was yard work. He very pointedly waited for me to elaborate, but I held off, enjoying the brief respite.

"They're called *mokoi*. They create some sort of interference, messes with powers. That's why you couldn't change, and I couldn't finish a spell."

"But you did," he pointed out.

I squirmed, not wanting to admit I'd had help. I poured a cup of coffee and sat across from him. I almost gagged at the plate of sausage links in front of me, and swapped them for the plate of waffles. "How much do you remember?" I asked carefully, as I drowned my plate in a sea of syrup.

"I remember you standing around while I did all the

heavy lifting," Drew said through a mouth full of food. I looked anywhere else that I could.

"Heavy lifting? Is that what they call getting beat up by a bunch of little Chihuahua demons?" I hesitated a moment. "You don't remember anything else?"

The fewer people who knew Uncle John was back, the better. If word spread that the bastard Thorpe had returned after all these years, the town might institute an early curfew and close the post office by noon. I wondered if the school practiced "black sheep" drills the same way they practiced tornado drills.

Drew shrugged and drained half of his coffee. "So you killed them?"

"Scared them off." I focused on my breakfast for a few minutes, trying to plot the best way to explain what else had happened. Lying. It would have to be more lying. "They're in some of my demon books. Scared of the cold."

"I've never heard about anyone stopping a demon by starting a snowball fight," he scoffed.

"Anyway," I said, raising my voice slightly, "Then you wouldn't shift. You kept having these ... seizures. Spasming, I guess."

Drew's chewing slowed, and his fork hovered above the plate.

"So I did ... something." I still didn't even know what I'd done. Punched him. Jump-started him. "You kept trying to change but you couldn't, I hit you, and there was this surge of magic, and then you were okay."

I turned back to him when I heard his fork drop down

onto his plate. He was staring. "Don't go getting hearts in your eyes," he said abruptly. "It's not like I owe you or anything."

He had caught me off guard. "What? I wasn't!"

"You were totally having a moment and getting all misty-eyed." Drew smirked. "Freak."

"Glad to see you're still a dick," I said under my breath.

"Finally get tired of wasting all that food?" Drew asked with a raised eyebrow.

He nodded towards my plate, and I looked down. I didn't even remember starting it—hell, I could barely remember the last time I'd eaten anything—but I'd very nearly licked the syrup from the plate after devouring the waffles. "Huh," I said. "Guess my appetite is back."

"So what now?" he said, standing up from the table. "You think it was Catherine? Didn't those things seem a little ... passive for her?"

I hesitated, remembering the way she'd looked at me last night. "I don't know who it is."

"Not a lot of options, are there?" Drew walked to the coffeepot, pouring himself a second cup. I followed his example, finishing the rest of mine. "How many Belle Damned can whistle up a murder of demons at a moment's notice?"

"That's a murder of *crows*," I pointed out.

Drew shrugged affably. "Still sounds right. But anyway, how many are we talking? You and Pops. Catherine." He let the moment hang in the air before he casually added, "And your mystery friend from last night."

I choked on my coffee.

"Don't," he said, holding up his hand. "You know you're a terrible liar, right? Does it just slip your mind? Because it's like you're not even trying."

I sat there, helpless, any and all words strangled in my throat.

"Fine, don't tell me. For now." Drew gave me the once over, then quirked an eyebrow. "You're not actually going to school like that, right?"

I looked down at my sweats and T-shirt. "I ... hadn't planned on it?" School didn't start for another half hour. I had nothing but time.

"Well, you better hurry up," he said. "I'm not waiting on you all day."

I moved on instinct before I pulled up short. "You're *not* taking me to school."

"Of course I am," he said, beaming at me. "Odds are Gentry will be there, dropping off kid sis, and nothing would annoy him more than seeing me first thing. Besides, you still have secrets to share."

"I have research I need to do."

He shrugged, as if that part wasn't important to him. Then again, I couldn't really picture Drew studying. "So do it at school. I slept through half my classes. I'm sure it'll be fine. You'll still have a book open, so you're halfway there. In the meantime, I know a guy that can probably help. It might take some time to get him to meet with us, but he's got an ear to the ground."

I crossed my arms in front of me. "You know a guy. On

whose side? Is he going to go running to Catherine the minute I walk away?"

"Possibly," Drew said offhand. "Matt's an entrepreneur. He'll follow the money."

"We need to *pay* him?" I didn't know the first thing about paying off an informant. Was that part of Belle Dam preschool?

"He might let me call in a favor," Drew said. "He doesn't exactly work for cash. We'll have to bring some gifts, too. Price of doing business with him."

"Like what? Babies?" I hesitated. "We're not bringing him babies, right?"

He snickered but didn't answer right away. He walked out of the room, and I was forced to follow after, shouting, "Right, Drew? *Right?*"

twenty

There wasn't a scene when Drew dropped me off, despite his very best effort. We pulled into the back parking lot, and neither Trey nor Jade was anywhere to be seen.

"I'll see if I can turn anything up on Kayla," Drew said, as I climbed off the bike.

"Ask Riley. Maybe someone around here knows something," I offered.

"Why don't *you* ask around?"

I snorted. "No one talks to me. Or even around me. There's a cone of silence that follows me from class to class. I wasn't feeling paranoid enough, so it's *fantastic*."

Drew just rolled his eyes and drove off, and I went to class.

The only demons worth the classification as such, I read during homeroom, *are the Riders at the Gate. They who ride the storms into frenzy, who break men with bargains and gifts, and those who blind the eyes of Fate. The Riders, of which there are seven, are the true Demons of the world. As such, the world rejects them, forcing them to weave their insidious tidings far from the Gate.*

Those who blind the eyes of Fate…that sounded like Lucien. I flipped ahead, hoping for more about the Riders, but within two pages the book was digressing into legends of drowned behemoths and sacrificial altars.

I looked for Riley during lunch, skipped the cafeteria and went straight for the newspaper offices. Unfortunately, this was the one day a year she wasn't in them.

I stepped into the room, but there was no sign of her. "Riley?"

"Oh, hey Braden." It took me a second to place Ben. The "friendly face" who didn't mind being seen with the school outcast. He carried a pair of trays into the room, giving me the eye. "Are you eating in here with us?"

I looked around at the empty room. "Us?"

He smiled. "Riley's supposed to be meeting me. You know she gets all twitterpated when it comes to layout." He set both of the trays down, taking the one loaded with fries and liquid cheese for himself. "I know they're so bad for you, but I can't get enough of 'em."

"So she's supposed to be here?"

Ben nodded. "Any time now. Apparently she mocked up some pages and can't wait to show someone." He leaned over the table and pushed a stack of pages out from in front of the chair. "You can wait if you want. I don't care."

"Uhm, thanks."

"So, you read the article?"

"Huh?"

He looked down at his plate, a fry still aloft in his hand. "Nothing," he replied quickly. "Just a stupid article in the paper. I thought maybe that's why you were here."

"Riley wrote an article about me?" That wasn't good.

Ben squirmed in his chair. "It wasn't all bad. Just talked a bit about how lenient the office has been about attendance this year."

"And they talked about me specifically?"

"No," he said. "But most people figured out who she was talking about."

"I was in the hospital, though. Riley knows that."

He looked at the fry still clutched in his hand, made a face, and dropped it back on the plate. "It doesn't mean anything. You know how it is when someone gets pissed off. They talk about it. Riley just covered it for the paper, that's all."

I opened my mouth to respond, but what was I supposed to say? *No, it was totally fine because my cursed supernatural vision is what landed me in the hospital, and I'm not entirely better yet but at least I'm not dying on the daily.*

"So why are you here? If it's not about the article."

"Riley was looking into that girl that disappeared. I just wanted to see if she found anything." I don't know why I didn't lie. I wanted to.

"Wait. You mean Grazia?" Ben suddenly piped in.

I flinched, caught off guard.

"I know Grazia," he said simply. "The girl that took off, right? She used to go here."

"Here, like Belle Dam High?"

Ben nodded. "It's no big deal, she's probably halfway to

Vegas. She's a dreamer, y'know. Grazia always wanted to be a star."

"They don't start manhunts for girls that go to Vegas," I said.

"Guess we don't know the same kind of girls," Ben said. "She was a pageant baby. Her parents would do anything to sell her out and make a few bucks. That's why she wanted out so bad. When they moved to Seattle, she almost stayed."

"Stayed with who?"

"Her boyfriend. She and Billy were two of a kind. He walked around like he was a drama god. Dropped out of *Romeo and Juliet* his senior year after Grazia moved away." He shrugged. "He would have made a terrible Montague anyway. Brooding is a thinking man's sport."

"So you knew them pretty well?"

"More or less," Ben said, leaning back in his chair and lifting the front legs off the ground. "I mean, I watched them. Y'know."

"Like in plays and stuff. Right."

A beat passed before he said, "Yeah, exactly."

What's that about? I shook my head, looking up at the clock. "Does she normally take this long?"

"She's a girl," Ben shrugged. "Grace was never on time either."

The hair rose on the back of my neck. "What? Grace?"

He looked at me in surprise. "Grazia, I mean. She was always talking about changing her name to something more American sounding. Grazia means 'grace' in Italian."

Her name was Grace, too. That was too much of a coincidence. Grace was the witch who'd trapped Lucien in Belle Dam in the first place. She was one of the first Lansings who settled the town.

"I've—I've gotta go," I muttered, pulling myself up from the table. "Thanks, Ben. I appreciate it."

"Thanks for what?"

But I didn't answer him as I left the room. Once the door closed behind me, I tugged a thread of magic to me and concentrated on visualizing Riley in my head. "Find her," I whispered.

The effect was immediate and unexpected. When John had showed me how to use the spell, it always manifested as a tiny ball of light. Nothing appeared for me. I scratched the back of my hand, waiting.

Maybe she left the grounds. The spell might not work if it doesn't have proximity. The itch in my hand wouldn't go away, even with the scratching. It only made it worse. I looked down and my eyes widened. A welt rose up off my hand, like the needle in a compass, except that the top of the skin was blue.

My hand throbbed and burned, but when I moved it, the direction of the needle moved, too.

"What the hell is going on?" Even if I had screwed up the spell, *this* shouldn't have happened. A mystical frostbite compass? Who'd even heard of something like that?

If you don't follow it, it might never go away. The thought made me shiver. I set off down the halls, hoping it really was taking me to Riley.

The closer I got, the less the compass needle itched. But

it was still turning my skin blue, and if there was an extra hustle in my step, it was because I didn't want to lose my hand due to some botched spell.

The longer I was in the halls, the darker the welt on my skin got, and the more pronounced it became. My hand was ice-cold, and I could barely flex my fingers. But finally I stumbled on a closed classroom door. I hesitated, knocked, then as the irritation got worse and I was desperate to keep scratching, I pulled the door open. Riley was curled up on top of the bookshelves that doubled as a window seat, picking at a bagged lunch.

"How did you find me?" she asked, her voice devoid of emotion.

I held up my hand, wondering how I was going to explain, when I saw that the icy compass was gone, along with any trace of the welts. *Thank God I still have my looks. The Belle Dam beauty pageant judges would have taken off if I had a rash like that.* "Uhm—magic?"

"Of course," she snorted. Riley knew about my magic, so at least I didn't have to lie to her. "What?"

Ben had been carrying two trays, right? So why was Riley eating alone? "Weren't you—never mind." I still wasn't used to this new, abrasive Riley. "You heard about Kayla last night?"

She slid off the counter, her lunch forgotten. "You think it's related, don't you? Someone's taking girls? Are they stupid? Her relationship with Trey alone; they know Catherine's always had a soft spot for her."

"All I know right now is they're both gone, and I think—

well, I don't know what I think yet." I changed directions. "Grazia means Grace in Italian. As in Grace Lansing. Then a friend of the Lansing family goes missing, too? It looks like a pattern to me." Lucien was just the sort to play games and manipulate. This was exactly his style.

Riley picked up a pen and started clicking it. "Do you think someone's trying to send you a message?" Her eyes widened. "Do you know who did this?"

Riley had said she'd gone to Lucien's office that night, after Jason had come and collected me. That Lucien's body had been there, she'd seen it with her own eyes. "You were there," I said slowly. "That night. Did you see anything? Did someone come and help him?" I pictured the way we'd left the office—with everything slightly askew but still surprisingly neat considering the showdown that had occurred. The magical energies hadn't done much damage. Lucien's body by the desk, with the hole where his eye should have been. Empty. Still.

I flinched, feeling frostbite coursing up my spine, an icy heat that crackled in the spaces between vertebrae.

"You mean Mister Fallon?" It was like Riley could sense the frost, because her voice suddenly could have frozen water. "He … was there, on the ground. I knew, even before I walked into the room—I knew he was dead."

"Did you see anyone? Did someone come for him?"

She shook her head, like she could shake the memory right out of her mind. I wished it was that easy. "He was just dead." And then she looked at me, and somehow she knew.

If it was possible her face got even more pale. "He...was dead, Braden." A heartbeat. Her voice wavered. "Right?"

"I..." But I didn't know how to answer that. Or how to tell her anything. I'd gotten so good at keeping secrets, at not telling anyone the whole story. *But Riley doesn't want to know*, part of me spoke up. *She said you're dangerous.*

Normal people accept that once someone's dead, they're dead. But Riley definitely wasn't normal, and she knew as much as anyone about Belle Dam's dark side.

She grabbed my wrist. "You're saying he's alive? Again?"

"I don't know," I said quietly. It was true. I wasn't sure *what* Lucien was right now. Hobbled. Broken. "I think so."

"There's got to be something," she muttered, reaching down into her bag to pull out a bright magenta laptop. The backside was covered in a plethora of stickers, which didn't surprise me in the least. However, the size did. The thing was easily as big as a Gutenberg Bible, and probably weighed about the same.

"What are you looking for?"

"Gregory's files," she said absently, waiting on the computer to boot up.

There wasn't a part of this conversation that hadn't completely confused me, one thing right after another. "What are you talking about, Riley?"

She looked up, her forehead creased with annoyance. "Last month while you were busy confronting Gregory, I changed his passwords. Then when I got home, I downloaded everything he had on Belle Dam." The screen lit up, and pulled her away.

"I know that. But what are you looking for?" One minute, Riley couldn't stand me, and the next it was like the story was all that mattered.

"A door that's not a door," she said absently, intent on the screen. "Go away. I'm busy."

"Riley." Seconds passed, but it was like she really couldn't hear me anymore. I raised my voice. "Riley!" Still nothing.

I finally gave up, turning back the way I'd come. "Let me know if you find something," I said quietly.

I spent the rest of the day trying to read through the demonography while being discreet, but it wasn't exactly easy. I almost got caught several times and had to adjust my plans in classes where the teachers liked to circle the room while they lectured. Those were the worst. At least when I was growing up, if I wanted to read a book about demons, Uncle John would have left me alone. Here, they weren't so accommodating.

Uncle John. *Why was he here?* I didn't even know how to get in touch with him—the only phone number I had was for the house phone in Montana. It had a long cord, but not *that* long.

Drew pulled me out of class five minutes before the last bell. The teacher didn't even flinch, seemingly unfazed by the glowering dropout at the door, or the fact that I got up and left without a word.

"Did you hear something?" I asked quietly as we walked out the back.

Drew handed me a helmet. "Just that Grazia turned up

this morning, drunk off her ass and wandering around the marina."

I almost dropped it, recovering at the last second and pressing the helmet against my leg to hold it steady. "What happened?" I demanded. "Is she okay?"

"She's in the hospital," Drew said, the bored monotony of his tone at odds with how sharp his eyes on me were. "Till she went all *Girl, Interrupted* on them and got herself a fashion-forward straightjacket for the trouble."

"Drop me off, then. I need to see her."

He shook his head. "Whoa there, space cowboy. They picked her up a couple of hours ago, while you were daydreaming about blond-haired mama's boys. Let them get her settled, and get some drugs pumping before you go and ruin her day."

"You don't get it, Drew. He might have *done* something to her. He probably did. But I can't do anything about it until I figure out what."

"Listen," he said, voice hard. "You need to take a breath. If you're right, and he did something, it's not going to change anything if you give her a day to settle down. They don't lock people up in the psych ward for having the sniffles."

Knowing that Drew might have a point and admitting it were two different things entirely, and I wasn't going to give him the satisfaction. I needed to see this girl and figure out what Lucien would have done to her, and why he let her go after all the trouble of taking her in the first place.

It didn't make any sense. Or at least, it didn't make any sense to *me*. But I was still trying to figure out what Lucien's endgame was all about. But maybe Drew's informant could help with that.

After he dropped me off, I went straight for the library. Where there was only one reference to the search for "Riders at the Gate."

When the First Ones shattered paradise, cleaving the Garden in twain, so did they carve light from dark: bestowing the powers of choice into the spirits of men. The Riders at the Gate, separated forever from the world, retained their power but gained impotence, unable to feed their diabolic hunger. They were the first demons, the progenitors from which all lesser species were birthed. They are eternal, unchanged, subject not to the whims of eternity.

Was Lucien one of these original demons? Was that why he didn't die when we shot him?

And if that was the case, how was I supposed to stop something that wouldn't die?

TWENTY-ONE

The next morning, I didn't go to school. Drew didn't ask any questions when I told him to pick me up on the far side of the property—close to the hellhound-burned concrete he'd pointed out.

"Surprised you didn't ask Lansing to chauffeur you around," he said, after pulling up on the motorcycle. "Unless his baby blues are too good for honest work."

"Careful, your jealousy's showing," I said casually. "And speaking of honest work, didn't you *steal* this?" I climbed onto the back and put on the helmet he offered.

An eyebrow lifted. "Feel me up all you want on the way over. I don't mind." Drew didn't wear a helmet himself.

"I need to go to the hospital." Normally, Drew would have a clever retort for that. But not today. We sped through the back roads leading to downtown, and headed away from the peninsula.

The hospital was a midway point between the town and the rest of Washington. I remembered the drive home with

Jason had been long, but I had never seen the building from the outside before.

It was a stark white, like a tower, and surrounded on three sides by a forest of Douglas firs. The road circled the property, and as we followed it, the forest opened up to reveal a second building that was as long as the first was tall, right next to and hidden by the tower.

We parked in visitor parking, and walked into the lobby. "Psych is on the fourth floor," Drew said without hesitation.

I eyed him, the question on my lips, but I forced my mouth closed.

It didn't matter, because he answered it anyway. "I spent a weekend here once," he said, lips quirking upwards. "It happens."

"Voluntarily?" I asked, because my control is good, but it's not superhuman.

I heard him chuckle as we waited for the elevator. "Does it matter? Everyone healed eventually."

That made the elevator ride incredibly awkward. We listened to Muzak and Drew even hummed along. "You know they're not going to let you just walk around," Drew asked, once the doors opened again.

"I already thought about that," I said, striding confidently towards the desk. I waited for one of the nurses to look up. "I'm from Jason Thorpe's office. I'm here to see the Catling girl."

It was almost like magic itself, the way that Jason's name made things happen. The nurse didn't even question me, she gave me a nervous look and nodded. After a few moments typing behind the computer, she gestured for us to follow her deep into the heart of the ward.

"We told Mr. Thorpe that we'd call if there was any change," the nurse said, as she rounded a corner.

Jason had already been here, or sent someone else. He knew something was going on with Grazia. Maybe he even knew about Lucien. I kept my face expressionless. "This is just a follow-up. I'm doing what I'm told, that's all." After a moment, I added, "You know how it is."

The nurse's smile bloomed, and she nodded. She understood about doing what she was told. And she knew what it was like when those orders came from someone like Jason Thorpe.

"She's in isolation for the time being," the nurse confided as she swiped an access card and into a hallway with another door not ten feet in front of us. Another swipe, and we passed through the second door and into what I assumed was the isolation area.

"At first, Dr. Raymonds thought she was just traumatized, but now, he's not so sure. He thinks she's a danger to herself."

We turned to a new hallway as the nurse continued chatting about Grazia's care. Halfway down, a dark-haired girl in shoes that Jade would have killed for stomped into the hall from one of the patient rooms. Her eyes went right for me, and her mouth curved into an enigmatic smile.

"So she's here until they decide otherwise?" Drew piped up to ask. His attention was solely on the nurse, he didn't even notice the girl. But I did.

I know her. The feeling was intense, and I understood what people meant when they talked about déjà vu. This girl was familiar in some way that I couldn't explain. I knew her, but I was just as sure that I'd never seen her before today. I knew how it sounded when she laughed and that she never left her apartment in less than four-inch heels.

But as we continued down the hall, the girl walked away from us and further down the hall, slipping out of my head just as quickly as she was slipping out of sight. Just before she disappeared down another hallway, her hand lifted up, fingers waggling and eyes sparkling in my direction.

"Who was that?" I asked, when I finally found my voice.

Drew and the nurse turned to me, but the hallway was empty except for the three of us. "There was ... a girl," I mumbled.

"Now that's an interesting twist," Drew said under his breath in a chuckle.

The nurse stopped us, her lips parting slightly. "She's still asleep. So don't expect too much." She's stopped us in front of a room halfway down the hall. *The same room that girl came out of. Who was she? And why was she here?* I looked at Drew, but he was too busy getting his flirt on with the nurse. Or trying to, at least.

The door was propped open, and I peered inside. The patient, Grazia, was strapped down to the bed.

"She doesn't know where she is," the nurse said, stepping to one side to allow us to enter. "Most of the time she's docile. Nearly catatonic. Then for brief moments, she falls into these ... episodes."

"What kind of episodes?" I glanced at Drew, who had his eyes trained on Grazia.

"She becomes ... feral," the nurse said, thinking over the wording for a few seconds. "Do you know what I mean?"

"Angry," Drew said. "Or ferocious. Like a wild animal." There was something in his voice, a familiarity mixed with frustration. Both of us walked into the room, but the nurse remained in the doorway.

"Yes, well," she glanced at the girl and shivered. "I have a daughter a few years younger than her, you know. It just ... "

It was obvious she didn't like being here. I cleared my throat. "It's fine. We'll only be a few minutes." The nurse nodded gratefully, and headed back down the hall.

"She smells wrong," Drew said, circling around the bed, his forehead wrinkled.

The smell was the least of it. "There's a teenager strapped down and drugged halfway to Narnia," I said. "It's a whole hell of a lot of *wrong*." There was something in the air itself, the room felt heavy and pressured. It was like the girl was exhaling something denser than carbon dioxide, like the air was soaking up the trauma she'd been through.

"It's like ..." Drew scrunched his face up, but he didn't follow up with anything.

"Grazia," I whispered, moving to the edge of the bed. Her eyes were open, and she stared up to the ceiling, but it was clear she wasn't seeing it. How many drugs they were pumping into her?

Grazia Catling was an exotic beauty, but right now it was hard to see. Her hair was limp and oily, her skin pale and bruised, and her chocolate eyes empty. In the visions and glimpses I'd had of her, she was a girl who embodied life. She was vivacious, living by extremes and snatching every ounce of experience out of life that she could. That is, until she came back to Belle Dam, and ended up a broken shell strapped to a hospital bed.

"She looks so tiny," I said, because I'd seen her active and in motion. Here, when she was so still like sleeping, it was like something had deflated in her.

"If you're going to do something to help, you'd better do it quick. The nurse is going to check on us sooner or later," Drew said, positioning himself at the door. "I'll try to stop her if she heads this way."

I looked at him in surprise. What did he think I was going to do exactly? "I don't—how do I even know if I can do anything?"

"Be the ball," he said, taking himself way too seriously. "You might not get another chance."

I hate you, I thought, and not for the first time. I thought something would jump out at me when we showed up. That maybe she'd be conscious and I could question her. I hadn't expected her to be so ... still.

"It's okay, you're going to be fine," I whispered, sitting at her bedside. I didn't know if it was true, but lies were easy now.

Her hand was relaxed into a loose fist, and I clasped both of my hands around it. The minute our hands connected, a door opened, a dam burst, and the sky shattered. Something like white noise and terror flooded through her hand into me, up my arm and lodged in my throat. My mouth opened as wide as it could, my jaws straining.

I screamed, the kind of shriek that was all lung and diaphragm, but my vocal cords were paralyzed. Nothing came out. A funnel of wind howled through Grazia and into me and then expelled out of my mouth.

"What the hell are you doing?" Drew grabbed my other hand, trying to pry me loose. "What's wrong?"

Listen, the winter voice said. The need to scream died like the wind sometimes does, casually and without care, and I tightened my grip on her wrist. I closed my eyes, ears straining.

The world around me twisted, background sounds faded away, and suddenly it was clear. I wasn't listening for a specific sound, I was supposed to listen for the *lack* of one—the hollowness.

I opened my eyes and leaned over her. Everything took on a darker hue, like the world was suddenly cast in shades of blue. Her dark eyes were open, and I stared into them. *The eyes are the windows to the soul.* But like her eyes, Grazia's soul was empty.

It was like the world I saw through the witch eyes. Those visions were always active, ever-changing landscapes. People were never just one thing, they were like mercury, always fluctuating between several states of being.

She was a girl of crystal, with a void where there should have been color and life and spirit. Something had cleaned her out—drained her—and left an empty husk behind. She was like the ice statues at Catherine's event. Completely transparent.

I whimpered, only once, before the ice soothed my concern. *Be rational.* Yes, rational. I had to look at this with a clear head.

Lucien hadn't just taken the girl's future. He'd stolen *everything*. But the nurse had said she was prone to rages. I looked, but couldn't find a source for her actions. The thing that was responsible.

"What's going on?" Drew whispered, his voice harsh against my ears.

I held up my hand. *Just wait*, it said.

Lucien had fed on this girl, drained her of everything that made her human and functional, and then cast her aside.

He was going to do the same to Kayla.

I released the girl's hand, blinking several times as the icy wash of my vision cleared, and colors became bright again.

"What'd you see? What'd you do?" Drew looked over my shoulder. "Nothing's happening. Are you sure it worked?"

I shook my head. "She's ... not there anymore."

Drew frowned. "Then where is she? What happened to her?"

The hunger consumed her, the winter voice said.

I nodded, agreeing. Drew's eyes narrowed and his frown deepened. "Braden?"

"She can't tell us anything," I said. I knew I should feel repulsed at what Lucien had done, horrified at how the girl's life was essentially over, but I was detached from it all. Like a doctor would have to be. *It's only logical.* "There's nothing I can do for her. Unless we can find Lucien and figure out how to stop him."

"I believe I can help with that," a man in a suit announced as he breezed into the room.

Drew pinched the bridge of his nose, having moved past the bed and putting himself between the new arrival and me. "Braden, meet Matthias Sexton. He runs that club Downfall."

Matthias was a dark-skinned man, and I watched as he brushed a hand against the shoulder of his suit, smoothing it down. If the two weren't so physically opposite, I would have called him Lucien's twin. Something in the way he held himself, his neck and head poised like a predator. Something primeval in his cold, amber eyes.

Demon eyes.

I turned to Drew. "This is your contact? A *demon*?"

Matthias threw back his head and laughed. "Oh, how I miss the old hypocrisies. Aren't you just precious?" He had a deep voice. Soothing. The kind of voice that could lull you to sleep even while he was prying your soul out of your body.

"Be fair," Drew replied. "I thought I'd have time to prep you on the way over there. How was I supposed to know that now the city offers demon delivery? They should be putting that on the brochures."

"Are you insane?" I snapped at the Shifter.

Drew shrugged. "Depends on who you're asking, I guess. Unless you're asking a psychiatrist."

"I miss the days when psychiatry was all exorcisms and leeches," Matthias sighed fondly. "I miss the leeches."

This was some kind of joke, right? I took a deep breath, trying to hold onto my calm. "Remind me never to drink at your club," I said dryly. His *club*. "Wait, you were the one Trey was meeting that night, weren't you? He wanted something from you."

Drew exhaled. "Picking a side without even hearing the counteroffer? I'm surprised, Matt. You're not normally so rash."

Matthias sniffed. "I care not for Thorpe or Lansing. My interests lie elsewhere."

"So then why were you meeting with Trey?"

"My dear boy," Matthias laughed, "if you still think Belle Dam is the town that Grace Lansing's feud built, then you haven't been paying attention."

"Then what is it?" I challenged.

"I suppose that depends on whether you're Hansel or Gretel," he said, cocking his head to one side, studying me. "And if you recognize the oven before you stumble into it."

"Christ, we get it, you're enigmatic and smug!" Drew snapped. "Fast forward through all the self-indulgent crap already."

Matthias examined his fingernails. "Did you bring it?"

Drew pulled a taped-up envelope out of his back pocket and tossed it at him. Matthias caught it with his free hand, never once looking up from his cuticle examination. "All the sandalwood I could find," Drew said.

"Sandalwood?" I caught a brief sharp smell that I recognized from Gregory's shop. Uncle John had never been one for burning herbs. "Why does he want sandalwood, exactly? Does he run a demonic candle shop in his spare time?"

"Oh, I like this one already," Matthias grinned, leaning forward. He extended a hand. "Please, sit. Stay awhile."

"This isn't your office," Drew said, looking pointedly towards the bed. "Show some respect."

Matthias's eyes flickered to the girl. "Such a shame," he murmured, but the words were empty pleasantries. The only thing demons were sincere about was how utterly insincere they were.

"Do you know where he is?" I demanded.

"Oh, I know where a *lot* of people are," Matthias said, coolly amused. "The problem lies with which one you're looking for today."

I started to say something, using choice words that I'd learned from Drew, but he cut me off. "Lucien Fallon. Do you know where he is or not?"

Matthias pulled back the sleeve of his suit, glancing down at the thick, gleaming, silver watch on his wrist. "The things I know about Fallon could fit inside a very small, very arrogant volume."

"That's not very nice," Drew chided. "Don't your kind stick together? Bridge club? Support group? Demons Anonymous has a ring to it."

"It's a wonder anyone laughs at your jokes," Matthias said, shaking his head. "As to where he ended up, who can say? If I were a superstitious man, I might believe..." he trailed off.

"You're a demon," Drew said, his voice short. "You're

seventy percent superstition, thirty percent pain in the ass. Just tell us what you're trying to build up to."

"With all these magicians slinking back into town, the city is rather crowded, wouldn't you say?" Matthias plucked at some lint on his sleeve, then smoothed the fabric back down. "Maybe one of them is keeping him tucked away for safe keeping."

"Magicians? You mean witches?" I glanced from Drew back to the demon. *How did he know about John?*

"Human words," he said. "Do you know their meaning?"

I looked to Drew and gestured towards the demon. "You can punch him if you want. I won't stop you."

Drew looked like he was seriously considering it.

"You don't know anything at all, do you?" Matthias asked. "You call those with magic 'witches' as though they were the originals. But time and blood dilutes it down until you're but a fraction of what you were."

"And what were we?"

His eyes gleamed as he sneered, "You were *worthy*."

I stepped forward, unsure of what I was going to do but knowing it was going to be bad. My legs moved under their own command, and the icy ire clawing up my chest supplied thoughts of controlled violence: shoving him against the wall, breaking his face, his legs, his will. *Do it. Hobble him. Show him what it means to be worthy.*

"You owe me, Matt," Drew said, placing his hand on my chest and pushing me back. Then he braced against me, when it was clear I had no intention of backing down. "I've done you favors before."

"As I recall, you've gained as much as you've given," the demon said, gripping his chin in his hand. "I'll humor you. Your little witch fascinates me."

Just as suddenly as it had come on, like an winter squall, the winter voice and its rage melted away. For a moment, I was lightheaded, blood rushing to my head.

"Jonathan Thorpe slinks back into town and darkens Belle Dam's doorstep for the first time in a decade just as Lucien vanishes into the night. Those two were thick as thieves once upon a nightmare. I'd start your search there," Matthias offered.

He thought John was helping Lucien? There was no way. Matthias's eyes were trained on me. He was looking for something, or waiting on a reaction. He knew I was a witch, and he likely knew I was living at Jason's.

"You think Johnny Boy's involved?" Drew scoffed. "That's good for a laugh." Off of my curious look, he explained. "John's the Thorpe family screw-up. If he's hiding Lucien, we'll find him before dinner."

"Jason never mentioned him," I said evenly.

Matthias shrugged, but his eyes never left mine. "You asked for my help. I'm only telling you what I know. He must have a good reason for such a momentous return, don't you think?"

A new voice answered for the both of us. "I do."

I turned towards the door to see Trey standing in the frame. His eyes locked on me, and he said in a too-calm voice, "Braden? A word?"

twenty-two

Trey didn't just walk out of the room, he walked halfway down the hall before he stopped and whirled on me. "What were you thinking? Don't you know what he *is*?"

"A demon," I said, crossing my arms in front of me. "I know. It's not like he bothered hiding it. Don't treat me like an idiot."

"A demon." He wasn't repeating me, his tone was full of disbelief. "You think that's no big deal?" Trey made a move like he was going to grab my arm, but he stopped himself. His voice grew strangled. "Don't you—Why would—He can—" Then, "I'm going to *kill* Drew."

"It's not like I'm inviting him to eat lunch with me all week. Drew thought he might have some information."

"Did you touch him? Did he touch you?" Trey reached for me, again, but this time it was nerves, not anger, that prompted the motion. Still, he caught himself and dropped his hand. *He won't even touch you now,* the winter voice murmured in satisfaction. My skin throbbed like a sunburn that had just peeled away, like I could feel the ghost of his fingers on my skin.

"Of course not!" I clenched my hands into fists, trying to pretend I hadn't noticed the slight. "Why is that such a big deal?"

"All he has to do is touch you, and you're an open book to him," Trey said, exhaling his aggravation. "Drew didn't bother telling you any of this?"

"Drew didn't know he was going to show up. We came to check out—"

Trey cut me off. "Yeah, I figured that out that part. You need to be more careful! Demons like Matthias or Lucien, they have their tricks. Matthias touches you, and he learns secrets you'd never say out loud. Why do you think I asked you to stay away from Downfall?"

That made sense, at least. "Then why were you there? Why would you meet with him, if he's so dangerous?" I bit down on my lower lip, and Trey's eyes dropped, following the motion.

"I . . ." he trailed off, and then swallowed abruptly. "My mother wanted to ensure that Matthias was planning to remain neutral, and if not, to steal him away before Jason claimed him." He swallowed again, then looked back to the room we'd come from. "But I think that might be a moot point now."

"He's only here because Drew paid him. He's not working for Jason." After a moment, I followed it up with, "I'm not either, you know."

Trey looked unconvinced. In fact, I'd never seen him

look so uncertain. His arms came up, one hand holding his elbow while the other covered his mouth in a light fist, his thumb tucked under his chin.

The silence unnerved me. "Drew and I are trying to figure out what they did to her," I said, gesturing towards the room. "Maybe we can figure out where they were keeping her, and then we can..."

Trey wouldn't look at me, but he nodded. "The nurses said she's catatonic. You think that's what they're going to do to Kayla, too?"

He'd made it clear that he didn't want to touch me, so I pushed down the instinct to rub his arm, hug him, whatever. "I'll find her," I promised. I didn't have the first clue about where to start, or where to look, and the fact that I was making the offer to find Trey's ex made my chest hurt.

"It's Lucien, isn't it?" he asked quietly. I flinched, and as soon as it happened I cursed myself. Trey nodded to himself. "I thought so. The way you were acting in his office, and those questions you asked about him."

It was too late to lie, and it didn't even faze me that my first instinct *was* to lie. "He was...haunting me," I said. "Or whatever the not-a-ghost version of haunting is. I thought it was all in my head at first. It started with the dreams, but then it started happening when I was awake."

"And you didn't tell anyone."

"I told Drew," I admitted. "But only because he was there for one of the episodes. The hauntings stopped when the girls were kidnapped. "

"You could have told me." But there was a weariness to

Trey's tone. Like he knew that would never happen. "You should get back, before Drew starts humping one of the nurses." But there was no real heat in the insult.

"You can't have it both ways," I said quietly, looking up at him. "You need to decide what you see when you look at me. Either you see *me*, or you see Jason's pawn. But you can't keep flipping between the two." Before he could say anything else, I hurried back into the room.

A stalemate of sorts had occurred in the room in our absence. Drew remained by the door, acting almost like a security guard charged with keeping everyone inside. Matthias had drifted to the far side of the room and calmly stared out the window, hands clasped in front of him.

"I told him I wasn't going anywhere, but he seems to enjoy playing the enforcer," Matthias called over his shoulder.

I rolled my eyes. Once Drew realized that Trey wasn't far behind me, he came around to my side and dropped an arm around my shoulder. "Now, now, Gentry. You had your chance," Drew taunted.

I shrugged out from under his arm and shot Drew a warning glare. "Not the time."

Drew rolled his eyes. "Anyway, the Grimm thinks he can offer some insight."

"Grimm?" I asked.

Drew turned to me, his tone warmed significantly. I couldn't tell if he was doing it to make Trey jealous or if he was just really into the topic. "Matthias," he clarified. "Once upon a time, he used to be a real boy."

"Demon," Matthias corrected absently.

Drew continued: "Back in the old days, some priests livened up their Saturday nights by dabbling in ceremonial magics. Me, I'd be watching ultimate fighting, but it takes all kinds, right? Anyway, these crazy kids figured if they could whip up a demon and bind it to the Lord's work, they'd be providing a holy service. Reforming a demon, making him act as a guardian over the church and all its—people."

"Parishioners," Matthias said.

Drew waved it off. "So when some of those silly rabbits built Belle Dam a shiny new church, they brought Matthias along for the ride. Until someone set it on fire—"

"—it was stone," Matthias cut in witheringly, "fire would have been useless. It was an explosion–"

"—fine, then it was an explosion," Drew said, rolling his eyes. "*Anyways*, the building got blown up, but enough of it survived that Matthias can't go home, and he's still not a real boy—"

"—demon—"

"—demon anymore."

"You try my patience, Armstrong," Matthias nearly growled. "The moral of the story," he said, his voice smoothing, "is that until further notice, I'm at your service."

"Yeah, you seem real servile," I said. Behind me, Trey snorted. "Do you really think I'm going to trust you?"

"Stop playing games, Matthias," Trey said, trying to restore order.

I headed for the chair at Grazia's bedside. Almost in sync with my motion, Drew deftly moved to the end of the bed, as though blocking Matthias from getting close to me, even though the man hadn't moved from the window.

In all the blustering and irritation, I'd almost forgotten that there was a girl here. "If I can fix this, I will," I promised her quietly.

"We're going to have a conversation about this later," Trey said from behind me, his voice dangerous. I looked back to see him glaring at Drew.

"I'm *quivering* with excitement," Drew deadpanned.

Matthias looked up, clearly amused. "My referee services are always available."

"Shut up, Matthias," the boys snapped in stereo.

I took Grazia's hand again, trying to ignore the playground antics going on around me. I drew power from the wellspring in the cemetery, felt it streaming invisibly through the city to me, settling around me like an invisible shroud of power and chill. I fashioned spells of seeking, remote viewing, translocation, and everything I could think of, but every last one of them failed. Wherever she'd been, whatever had been done to her, magic couldn't punch through the veil that had hidden her. It was as if the past several days didn't exist at all.

When I finally sat back in my chair, my spine was stiff and groaning, and the light in the room was different. Brighter. *How long was I out of it?* It hadn't felt like more than a couple of minutes.

Trey stood right behind me, his hand on the back of my chair. Drew had taken up a spot on the wall, arms folded in front of him. Only Matthias was in the same spot I'd left him—the corner by the window—I don't even think he'd moved.

"He covered his tracks," I said, standing and trying to stretch some life back into my limbs.

"Almost like he knows what he's doing, instead of fumbling around a hospital room," Matthias supplied.

"Shut it, Matthias," Trey said.

Matthias glanced at him, his eyes considering. "It's interesting, the pair of you being in the same room together," he said, eyeing Trey and I one at a time. "After all, the Thorpes and Lansings haven't gotten along in a *very* long time."

"Do you have a point?" I asked icily.

"Just an interesting anecdote, that's all. Especially now that Jonathan Thorpe has reappeared after all this time."

I stiffened, but Trey's reaction surprised me. He stared at Matthias, cocking his head a bit to the side. "You're normally a lot more subtle. Did my mother put you up to this?"

Trey was questioning his mother again? Where had the world gone wrong? "What is it?"

"He's putting a lot of cards down on the table," Trey said thoughtfully, taking a step forward. "And Matthias is never one to share something for free if he could charge you for it."

"And you're not normally one to think for himself," Matthias said pleasantly. "I suppose we're all growing as people."

"At least some of us *are* people," Drew said, pushing off of the wall.

"So either you really want to tell us something about John Thorpe, or you're trying to stir up trouble between the two of us," Trey continued. "So which is it, Matt?"

The demon shot him a withering look. "It's *Matthias*."

Trey held up his hands in apology. "Touchy. I forgot how sensitive your kind get about names."

"Says the boy who hides his pretention in a nickname. You understand the importance of names, don't you Gentry?"

"Is face-punching still on the table?" Drew asked. "Because I'm bored."

Matthias turned his glare on Drew before turning to me. "Lucien arranged a meeting with John Thorpe a few nights ago at Downfall. We have," he paused a moment, searching for the right word, "*private* rooms for select clientele."

Trey's expression hardened. "And what were they talking about?"

"As if I would eavesdrop on paying customers," Matthias said with an apologetic shrug. His expression kept flickering between obsequiousness and smirking. Trey was right, whatever game he was playing, he was playing badly. "Lucien appeared, looking quite the worse for wear I must say, and they talked. Eventually they shook hands and left together."

"Why would he meet with Lucien?" Drew asked me. I initially shrugged, then I realized all three of them were watching me. Like I would suddenly have all the answers.

I shook my head, trying to organize the facts in my head. Fact: John wouldn't, or *couldn't*, tell me why he was back. Fact: he was creeping around Belle Dam like a stalker. Fact: he'd shown up at the cemetery at exactly the right time to save the day. Everything that had happened since he'd returned was at odds with the John I'd always known.

Is that what he's counting on? That John is just some face-

less Thorpe that he can tarnish and blame? Whatever Matthias thought he had, he'd better hope he kept the receipt, because it was faulty. A month ago, I might have taken his word at face value, but now I knew better. Never trust anyone from Belle Dam implicitly. Everyone had an angle.

So the question was: what was Matthias's? And more importantly, what was John's?

John wouldn't turn on me like that. But the winter voice countered, *Wouldn't he? Are you sure? There's so much he's kept from you.*

Was it all to make some arrangement with Lucien? Was that what he was really after? There had been something in the vision, something that Lucien had been thinking about bargains, and how he'd gotten the worse end of the deal this time out of need. Had John figured out what happened, and then snuck back into town to take advantage of Lucien while he was down?

"How long has he been back in town?" Trey asked, a struggle evident on his face. "Did you know?"

"Here's a thought. Let's not discuss this in front of the D-E-M-O-N." Drew suggested. "Are you done here?" he asked me.

I nodded, and without another word went into the hall. Instead of heading back the way we came, I went in the other direction. The way I'd seen the dark-haired girl take when I arrived. I could hear Trey and Drew following me. No one bothered saying goodbye to Matthias.

"You should have told me," Trey said.

"So you could have run to your mother?" I asked, before lowering my voice. "You *know* why I can't do that."

"He tried to kill my father."

"And you pointed a gun at me," I said. "Right before I hijacked your brain. This isn't about the feud right now, Trey."

"I take it the couples counseling hasn't been going so well?" Drew interrupted.

"Shut up, Drew," we said together.

But it wasn't enough for Drew. He sauntered over, dropping his arm around my shoulder and pulling me close. "I'm absolutely devastated you kids couldn't work it out."

Trey went from conflicted and uncertain to positively red in the face. His fist clenched.

"Don't worry, I'll take good care of him," Drew said.

Speaking of people who failed at subtlety. *Teach him, like you would any other mongrel,* the winter voice whispered. *It will only hurt for a moment, but the lesson will chafe for a lifetime.*

"Stop." I turned and pushed my fingers against Drew's chest, five points pressing into hard muscle. I felt my fingers go cold and saw him wince. When I pushed forward, he moved back, until I had him up against the wall. "All of the creepy flirting and the suggestive comments: they stop now. If you're only here to taunt Trey, then leave."

Drew, to his credit, didn't show that he was in any pain. But as my fingers got colder, I could feel that chill passing to his chest. It took an age for him to react. When he finally nodded and I pulled my hand away, the tips of my fingers stuck to his shirt, tiny spots of ice and cold frozen into the fabric.

He met my eyes, or at least as close as he could get. For a moment, I thought he was going to hit me, but then Drew smirked. "I've got a wart on my foot you can freeze off later, if you want."

"Come on," I said quietly, "you can drop me off at school. Maybe I'll find something in that book."

"You're going to school?" Trey asked, a moment of amusement at seeing Drew backing down replaced by more uncertainty.

"Do you have a better idea?" I said, not bothering to look at him. "I'm still supposed to be getting an education, remember."

Drew rubbed his chest, but he didn't protest. "I'll meet you down there."

By silent agreement, we waited until Drew found the elevator and headed downstairs before we continued the conversation. I flexed and released my fingers, trying to chase away the chill that had settled in. "You can't tell her John's back."

"I have to."

"If she goes after him, I'm going to have to stop her," I pointed out. "And that's time away from finding Kayla and Lucien."

"Maybe he's not the man you think he is. You heard Matthias. He wanted you to know about that meeting."

"John raised me," I replied. "I know him better than you

do. He wouldn't be working with Lucien." The winter voice tried to lobby a protest, but I shoved it back down.

Trey hesitated, his eyes searching. "Are you okay? You're ... different."

I shook my head and felt the ice numbing all the aching parts inside of me. It made me stronger, less emotional. Stronger. "I'm good." I said.

He didn't look convinced. "Are you? Good, I mean. You just threatened one of your friends, and while I can't say I hated it, that's not the Braden I thought I knew."

Nothing you do is good enough, the voice whispered. Privately, I was starting to agree. "I'm what I have to be," I said, and left him there.

twenty-three

"So. John Thorpe."

Drew let the words hang while he handed me the helmet.

"John Thorpe," I repeated. "Do you have a problem with that?"

He shrugged, his lip raising in a momentary sneer. "What's another Thorpe? But if he's trying to fly under the radar, he needs to know he sucks at it."

"Matthias is trying to tie him to Lucien," I said. "But I don't know why."

Drew was watching me. "And?"

I shrugged. "I can't even get in touch with him."

Riding on the back of Drew's motorcycle was a lot like sitting on top of a really fast washing machine. The one Uncle John and I had used to throttle the floor, trembling and shuddering as it spun.

"Why'd you want to come here?" he asked, putting his feet down as the bike finally stopped. I stared at the school building. My first day, Belle Dam High had seemed too impressive—too much to handle. And now, only a month later, it had become an annoyance.

"I needed someplace to read," I said, pulling off the helmet and then trying to finger-comb my hair. It was probably useless, anyway.

Drew laughed. "You could have just gone home, y'know. Or to the library or something."

"The worst I have to worry about here is kids who want to beat me up, or the ones who want something from me." I handed him the helmet back, and grabbed my bag. "Other than that, no one's interested in what I'm doing. Anywhere else I go, I'm Jason's ward. Everyone's interested."

"Well, whatever."

"Hey, wait," I said, after he'd already kick-started the engine. He waited, looking at me evenly. "Why are you helping me? Really?"

Drew, who never gave a straight answer when a sarcastic one would suffice, grinned. "I really, *really* want to get invited to your Sweet Sixteen."

He started to pull away. "I'm seventeen, dick!" I called out before he'd left the parking lot.

I stayed in the library for most of the day, but as dense as the demonography was, I didn't make much progress. I waited through the bells and the after school activities, only leaving when the building was a ghost town.

The walk home gave me time to think. Dark was already starting to settle by the time I reached the property line. I walked alongside the stone wall that marked the front half of the Thorpe property, my hands shoved in my pockets.

The wall led to an overdramatic iron gate that never closed. The wall and the gate provided an illusion of security, one that was really unnecessary. Just being the Thorpe house was more of a deterrent than the wall itself.

Finally I caught sight of the lamplights that designated the end of the driveway. Pulling in to Thorpe Manor was like stepping back in time a hundred years. Old-fashioned lanterns hung on either side of the driveway entrance, leading to a long, manicured path to the house.

I cut behind the first lantern and beyond the open gate.

"Braden," a shrouded figure called from behind me. From just inside the wall.

I narrowed my eyes. In the dim evening light, from behind my glasses, it was impossible to see him clearly. But once I turned, he stepped into the lantern's light.

"What are you doing here, Uncle John?" I demanded, whispering as if Jason could hear me all the way from the house. On instinct, I moved into the shadows, away from the driveway entirely.

"I had to make sure you were okay," he said, following behind me.

"*Now* you show up to check on me?" I walked in the shadow of the wall, as far from the driveway as I could. The trees were bent and skewed, growing up and over the top of the wall instead of straight. The ground seemed level, but I wondered what had happened to change their nature. Trees were supposed to grow up, not over. *Nothing in this prison ever grows right,* the winter voice whispered.

"Of course I'm not okay," I said, hardening my voice. "You have no idea, you just show up like it's no big deal."

Uncle John raised an eyebrow. "Take a deep breath," he said, calmingly.

"*Everyone* knows you're here," I snapped. "It's only a matter of time before Matthias or someone tells Catherine that you're here." I just hoped that it wouldn't come from Trey.

He looked surprised for a moment, but it turned out he was more concerned for me than for himself. "You've been to see Matthias?"

"He came to see me. He said you met with Lucien."

"You know that's not true." This new, serene Uncle John was disconcerting. "I have to keep a low profile."

"Then why tempt fate? Why keep showing up like this? If you'd given me a phone number, some way to reach you..."

"Braden," he said, holding up his hand. "Calm."

"A demon is kidnapping girls I know," I whispered furiously. "The same demon who would like nothing more than to cut my eyes right out of my head. Calm's been off the table for two months now!"

"I know things seem out of control," Uncle John said, "but that's all the more reason to keep it together. Now tell me what's going on."

"Where have you been?" I demanded.

"Tell me what's going on," he said, his voice softening.

I did. Because letting John take the lead was familiar. Easy. I didn't have secrets from Uncle John—he knew exactly who I was. I told him everything.

It would have been so easy to beg him to take me away,

to vanish into the night and never spare another thought for Belle Dam, but there were too many strings tied to me now. If I left, then whatever Lucien did to the girls would be my fault. Whoever he hurt would be my fault.

As I finished telling him what had happened, I realized I was shivering. Had been shivering for awhile now. Uncle John gave me a strange look, then made a flaring motion with his hand. The air around us began to warm by degrees.

"That is … a lot," he said finally. "I understand why you're concerned."

The first flames of anger were just being stoked in my cramping stomach when I pushed them down, wrapping myself in winter armor. "That's all you have to say?" My words could have cut diamonds.

"There is not a lot *to* say," he replied, choosing his words carefully.

And then I remembered the *geas*.

Before he'd fled Belle Dam, my uncle had gone to Lucien for help. Or Lucien had intercepted him before he could leave. Either way, a bargain had been reached. John would raise his nephew, me, far from Belle Dam and Catherine's reach. In return, Lucien would keep his enemies at bay. All it would cost was his ability to talk.

It wasn't like he lost his voice. But Lucien wanted John to keep his past a secret, *to keep Belle Dam's secrets*, for reasons I still didn't understand. The binding was called a *geas*, and it was a thing of demonic power. The *geas* kept him from talking about the town where he was born, the people he'd grown up with, or anything useful.

There was no telling what secrets John knew that I didn't, but he couldn't help me. The dark compact forbade it.

"I wouldn't know where to start. Taking the girls like that sounds like there's a ritualistic component to what is happening, but I couldn't speculate on why," he said.

"Then why did you come?" I was still angry, still frustrated with him and his helplessness.

He looked surprised. "How could I not? I never should have let you stay in the first place."

I shook my head. "You were right. This is where I belong."

He was quiet for a long moment. "You've changed," he said. It wasn't surprise in his voice, but resignation. "Jason must be impressed."

"Hardly," I said. "What good is a weapon if it doesn't work?"

"He said that?"

"It's true," I said. Anyone else, I might have let it go at that. But this was Uncle John. "I *feel* different. Like I'm already cracked, and one good push and everything will shatter."

"Braden." John said my name like he used to—with a hint of exasperation and fond affection. "No one can break you but you. Don't you understand that?"

I opened my mouth to respond, trying to summon up something witty and biting, but nothing would come out. I stood there, trying to force something out. Anything. Sarcasm wasn't what came out, though. "I killed someone," I whispered. "I didn't hesitate. Pulled the trigger. Bang."

"I know." It was all he had to say. All he could say.

"Why are you here?" I asked again. I felt like no one would answer me lately unless I kept repeating myself. "What's going on, Uncle John?"

"Nothing you need to worry about," he said, taking that back-off tone I recognized from my childhood. He pulled something from his pocket and tossed it to me.

I fumbled for a second, but ultimately caught the small black phone.

"In case of emergencies. My number's programmed into it. And there's a couple of spells on it, in case you're in trouble."

Enchanted cell phone? I hated to admit it, but that was kind of cool. "Can I get on the internet with it?"

He shot my another annoyed look. Then the look changed, and he just looked ... sorry. "You're going to be okay. I'll take care of it."

I looked down for a second, willing myself not to feel anything. It *hurt* to feel things. And I couldn't afford to hurt right now. I pulled the cold around me, drowning myself in the numbness surrounding the winter voice.

By the time I looked back up, John had disappeared.

twenty-four

Thursday was gray and unhappy. Or maybe that was me. I'd burrowed so far down into the bed, I could barely get back out. I fumbled for my glasses and made my way to the window.

"Contemplating your escape?" an unamused voice came from the doorway. I turned to see Jason, dressed more casually than I'd ever seen him before. He'd turned in the three piece suit for a black, ribbed turtleneck and a pair of jeans.

"Considering going back to bed," I said, wondering about the change. *Maybe he's skipping work. Does Jason even know how to skip work?*

Jason rested his hand on one of the bedposts, rubbing the smooth wood with his thumb. He flashed a smile that didn't sit right on his face, balanced precariously like a spoon against a nose. It vanished a moment later. "And how is school?" he asked, his voice awkward.

Either Jason had turned over a new leaf or this social call was a ruse. I tried to finger-comb my hair into shape. "What do you want?"

No response. I turn away from the window, and saw him staring at me. I stared back, waiting. *Do you ever wonder if he fears you?* the winter voice murmured. I pushed it down. Now was not the time to think about how Jason felt about me.

"Well?" I demanded. One did not demand things from Jason Thorpe. But I didn't care anymore. I couldn't be bothered with tact. The fastest way through this conversation was to cut through his awful attempts at parenting.

"Have you seen him? Jonathan?" he asked, a terseness in his voice. But if Jason expected me to flinch and go pale, he was sadly mistaken.

I shrugged it off. "He's a liar. It's all he does," I said. "He left me here and gave Lucien every opportunity to manipulate me. Why would I care?"

"Surely you *care*, Braden," Jason said. I could tell that my retort had puzzled him. "Jonathan has a great many enemies here. More than you know."

"Then he shouldn't have come back," I said. "Maybe that's the trick. You should never come back. Never go backwards. Never give the past that much hold over you."

"Someone's feeling fatalistic this morning. Is that how you really feel?"

He wanted something from me, and he wasn't getting it. Far from it, I think I was only worrying him more. *That is excellent*, the winter voice said.

"What do you want from me?" I said, standing across the bed from him. "I'm here. I leave every morning, and come back every night. I could disappear any time I wanted, but I don't. But don't ever fool yourself into thinking this means anything. If you want to spend time with your son, go visit his grave. I'm not yours. And I never will be."

The words caught him off guard. Jason didn't ever let his walls completely down, there was always a mask in place, but briefly something hidden splashed across his face. A moment of weakness, or vulnerability. Was it—concern?

You don't have time for this. He's trying to weaken you. "I have to get ready," I said, looking pointedly towards the door.

"We'll figure out a way to help you," Jason said. He wasn't listening. "There are still some reme–"

"Stop!" I commanded. He did. "You can't fix this. No one can. There isn't a training manual for the things I can see. There aren't even legends about it. There's just me. And the ghost bitch who set all this in motion." Jason's eyes widened, but I couldn't stop. "So stop feigning concern. Put the parenting façade away for another week."

When Jason didn't take the hint—for the second time— I brushed past him and went into the hall.

You're wrong, you know, the winter voice continued. But it wouldn't go on. Wouldn't tell me what I was wrong about.

¤   ¤   ¤

Riley was lying in wait when I walked through the front doors. Any other day—especially lately—I would have been happy. But now was not the time for a sassy teen reporter. I turned on the phone John had given me, and tried the only number in the Contacts list. There wasn't a name attached, just a star.

"Where have you been? I've been calling you for hours," she demanded, matching her pace with mine once she realized I wasn't going to stop. I'd walked in on the middle of a class change, and the hallways were full of people.

The phone went to voicemail. I hung up. "I'm busy, Riley," I said, as if that'd be enough.

It wasn't. "That's great, but what have you found out about Lucien? Because I've been doing some research, and I think…"

"Riley, stay out of it. This isn't a game."

"Hey, you came to me, remember."

The next thing I knew, something hit me from the side and slammed me into the row of lockers. Pain washed up my arm and down through my hip. Carter towered over me, wearing his letterman's jacket like it meant something.

"You told your sugar daddy I beat the shit out of you?" Carter demanded. "Huh?"

"I don't have time for this," I said, struggling to free myself.

"Oh, you've got time, you little shit. Admit it, you ran to Thorpe and cried like a little bitch, didn't you?" Carter's face was getting redder by the second. It was almost purple.

Riley flashed a quick look at me, and then to Carter. "Did something happen, Carter?"

"Yeah," he said, his eyes trained on me. "Something did."

"And you're not worried what's going to happen now?" I asked, my voice like iron.

Clearly Carter wasn't much of a thinker, and the consequences of his actions didn't occur to him very often. "Screw you."

"I. Don't. Have. Time. For this."

When he threw another punch, as I fully expected him to, this time I was ready. My hands moved faster than my brain, directed not by electricity and neurons but by frost and ice. I caught his fist in my hand, gripped it tight. My fingers crackled, growing tight and cold.

Carter's eyes widened, but I wasn't done yet. I took a step forward, caught his other hand before it could punch me, too. "You're a bully," I said quietly. He couldn't say anything at all. The ice in my hands had spread past his finger bones and into the wrists and from there the forearms—ice that had also frozen his tongue.

It slid through his veins and plundered through the jumbled mess that was Carter's head. I saw his boiling anger directed at a thousand sources: the parents who were constantly fighting around him, the coaches that wouldn't stop riding him, teachers who kept raising the bar.

All of his weaknesses and imperfections rolled out in front of me like a red carpet. I saw a thousand different ways to break his spirit, no two ways the same. I saw what drove him, what pushed him to find an outlet for his rage: a father who drank too much and mocked his son for letting a "blind faggot" make a fool of Carter and his friends. Something his father, under the haze of dark liquor, claimed would never have happened in his day.

He thought I was an easy target. But Jade didn't look at him in wonder the way he'd thought. And then word got around, and his mother took the fall. Her position at the school was eliminated, and god knows his father can't support them all on his own.

In another life, I might have had sympathy for him. I might have felt *something*. Now all I wanted was to finish it.

"You think that because my eyes are broken, that it makes me weak." I leaned forward, and for a second, I thought I could smell his fear. It was like something off the grill, seared and fragrant. "I could tear you apart," I whispered in his ear, "teach you how it feels to really suffer."

I pulled away. "You struggle to be mediocre, but you're not even that." And I released him, pushing him away from me. He fell into a sprawl on the ground, staring at his hands.

Where my fingers had grabbed him, the skin was tinged with blue.

"You'll never be anything more than you are now," I said, and turned away. A nameless member of the crowd laughed, which sparked a couple of snickers. Riley stared like she'd never seen me before. She looked horrified. "What..."

I looked away, and when I turned back, she'd vanished into the crowd.

¤ ¤ ¤

"I always thought Goliath was a cocky little twit," Jade announced over me.

I'd found refuge in a corner of the library with the *Hast-*

ings Treatise, searching for anything else I could find about Lucien.

"He started it," I replied absently.

Jade looked fantastic as always. She usually dressed in whites and creams, so the monochromatic grays threw me off for a second. The black pencil skirt, a hint of white blouse hidden underneath a gray jacket. She looked like a print model, like always, but today it was different.

"Everything okay?" I asked, finally meeting her eyes.

"I talked to my brother."

I flipped a page. "And?"

Jade hesitated, and then finally blurted out, "Are *you* okay?"

"I'm fine." Flip. "Did he tell you what happened?"

Jade shook her head. Maybe that was a good sign. If he wasn't talking to Jade, maybe he wasn't saying anything to Catherine. "I heard about Carter. They took him to the hospital."

"Did they?" I responded coolly.

"What's happening to you, Braden?" she asked, her eyes honed on me, her voice quiet. Jade never did things quietly. There was always a flourish, a drama, to everything. "The nurse said he's got frostbite."

"You weren't so concerned when he was trying to break my ribs," I said. "You waited until I was nearly unconscious before you stepped in, if I remember right."

Color stained her cheeks, and her mouth tightened. "I stepped in the second I found out what was going on," she said. "Don't rewrite history to make me the villain."

"You're not the villain, Jade." I flipped another page. "I'll leave that to your mother."

She didn't react right away. Well, at least one Lansing wasn't too wrapped up in family loyalty to see the truth.

"You were the one who wanted this cold war," I said, turning away from her. "So maybe you should leave now."

Jade opened her mouth, but the words caught in her throat. Her head tilted slightly, and she looked at me with thoughtful eyes. Perceptive eyes. Jade didn't have the thrill-seeking gene like Trey, but she was every bit as perceptive as her mother.

"We're still friends," she said quietly. "That didn't change."

I stared at the words on the page, struggling to say something that wasn't harsh and hollow and insensitive. But the shell I'd covered myself in was thick and unyielding. Finally, I looked up, intent on saying something like "I know" or "me too." But Jade was already gone.

¤   ¤   ¤

"So where is he?" Hours later, Riley hovered over me. I was still in my chair, and no one had made me leave yet. "I've checked his condo, his office is all weird, and every phone number I tried has been disconnected. None of the other aliases he's taken up are doing anything, either."

The librarian had wisely chosen to leave me alone. I could see her stroll by every half hour or so, as if just to remind herself that I was still here, still hiding out. Other than that, no one had bothered me for hours.

I'd found another section on the Riders, and for a moment I'd been ecstatic, but the reference was brief.

Demons must bow before the rules of binding. It is an essential part of demonic nature that they are creatures who can be bound, who must obey their captors. All of them, from the black dogs that sired the hellhounds, to the Riders themselves, must abide by the ancient compacts.

Which told me why Grace's plan had succeeded—she had bound him and he couldn't break free by himself. But that wasn't anything I didn't know already. And it didn't tell me how to stop Lucien.

"I asked you a question," Riley repeated, her hands on her hips.

My stomach growled, but all the same I couldn't eat. "I told you to stay out of it."

"Like you're staying out of it?" she scoffed. "He has to be hiding out somewhere. I mean, he's still in town, right?"

"Lucien's gone underground, Riley. If he doesn't want to be found, he won't be." Underground. Grace had buried his power in the earth to shield it from his view, maybe he did the same. Wait. "What did you say, about his office being weird?"

Her eyes were hooded. "I figured that was your doing. It's all … off-kilter. I couldn't wait for the elevator to get back up. I had to go down the stairwell."

"Was it like a 'I don't want to be here' vibe?"

Riley shook her head. "More of a 'you've seen enough horror movies to know this is bad' vibe. I assumed you did something so people wouldn't go there anymore."

"No," I said thoughtfully. "I didn't." Whoever did it had to have acted in the last couple of days. There was nothing like what Riley mentioned when I was there with Trey.

"You think he's going back there? Or maybe he's hiding out there and I missed it?"

"Stay out of it," I said, trying to sound firm.

"I need to find him, Braden. You don't understand."

She *needed* to find him? "Are you insane? Lucien's a monster. Maybe even more of one now. He's not some interview you need to line up for the paper. This is serious."

"You wouldn't understand," she said stubbornly.

"Yeah," I snorted, "I wouldn't. You can't look at me but you suddenly want a demon as a new best friend? Nice." I closed the book and stood. Riley jumped backwards immediately.

My heart thumped once, and I forced it to harden. Forced myself not to feel. If I didn't look her in the eyes—didn't see the fear there—then everything would be okay.

"There's no story, here, Riley. You have to leave it alone."

"Lucien being alive changes everything," she said urgently, but I pushed the back door open and slipped back into the hallway before she could finish talking.

Underground.

Maybe there was something to that.

twenty-five

Riley wasn't exaggerating. The offices of Fallon Law were still as empty as they'd been all week, but there was something in the air now. It had a heaviness to it that I'd never seen before, similar to Grazia's hospital room. A room filled to the brim with something intangible. But there was also a current and a chill, one I'd felt before. Like invisible eyes watching, no matter where I went.

Like a haunting.

I didn't have a lot of experience with ghosts, but I knew the signs. It took energy for a ghost to become visible, or manifest. But once they managed that, they were nasty pieces of work. Ghosts absorbed ambient energy wherever they went. When they remained in a place for too long, the temperature dropped and the air took on a hum like there was a surplus of electrical equipment.

Why was something haunting Lucien's office?

All of the lights were on. A stack of papers from the secretary's desk had been knocked off, spilling out all over the floor. Everything on top of the desk had been moved around, patches of flawless wood grain next to a film of dust that must have taken months to accumulate.

"That's everything," a little girl's voice called out from the inner office. She appeared in the doorway and froze at the sight of me. The same evil little princess with an unknown agenda.

She put her hands on her hips and scowled. "You're not supposed to be here!"

"I missed my bus," I shrugged. Had she been trying to find something, or get rid of it? "But there was no one to push me into the street, anyway."

"I'll push you out a window," she threatened.

Was she working for Lucien? It would certainly fit. Lucien wanted me to be scared, to trust in him, and having me attacked so soon after arriving suited his purpose. Gregory had been the one to collect the research on Lucien in the first place, so it made sense to get him out of the way.

"I don't think anyone's pushing anything out of a window. Defenestration is such a drastic act, don't you think?" A Latina girl dressed in black sauntered past me and dropped a leather gym bag on the secretary's desk.

It was the girl from the hospital—the one who'd come out of Grazia's room just before we entered. Tall, maybe even taller than me, she was almost too much fashion for Belle Dam. She wore a tiny black dress over black leggings and a striped gray blazer with the sleeves pulled up.

Maybe she's a lawyer? She might have been old enough, but all I knew for certain was that she was older than me.

"Stay out of this," Princess commanded.

"Mmm, I don't think so," the girl said. She tossed her hair out of her eyes and flashed me a smile. "Well, aren't you cuter than advertised?"

"Oh. Uhm. Huh?"

The dark-haired girl shook her head. Her smile could have powered the whole city. "No time for that now, hot stuff. And cut out all that flirting. You'll make a girl blush." She canted her head and turned back to her purse.

"I—huh—who?"

"Hanna Downing!" The girl in black pulled a small mason jar out of her purse and unscrewed the lid. Princess looked alarmed all of a sudden. "Oh, sorry. Hanna *Elizabeth* Downing, I summon you."

Princess stomped her foot, eyes flashing. "I'm right here!"

The woman shrugged. "Formalities," she offered like it was an apology. She turned the mason jar over slowly and shook, dirt sifting out until the entire thing spilled all over the somewhat clean carpet.

The effect on Princess, or Hanna as she was apparently known, was immediate. The girl who was solid and real only seconds ago flickered in and out of sight. She vanished only to reappear on top of the dirt particles. One of her legs was on the ground, I noticed, the other raised a few inches, not actually touching.

"Are you serious?" Hanna demanded, scowling down at her feet. "You're a real bitch—"

"Kids," the woman said over her shoulder, looking back at me. "Can't take them anywhere. Be a dear, and start lighting the candles around her." She grabbed one candle at a time and pushed them at me.

"Who are you?" I managed, even as I started taking the candles from her. Hanna was busy ranting with the kind of language that even I don't use on a daily basis. It might even have made *Drew* blush. "You were at the hospital, right? I saw you."

"And I saw you," she said with a twinkle in her eye. "She has to manifest on the grave dirt. Unless there's not enough." Hanna was still ranting, and the woman cut her off with a sharp, "Hey! I could have used half. Then you'd be standing *en pointe* and *really* uncomfortable."

"Okay, who the hell are you?" I asked again.

"You can call me Elle." She pulled a bell and a tiny glass vial out next.

Hanna laughed. "Didn't answer the question," she sing-songed. Then she made a face.

"Come on, light the candles. There's a good boy." I felt like a beloved pet, but I did what Elle asked me to, anyway. *Another witch,* the winter voice murmured. *This is dangerous.*

Like I needed the reassurance. I lit the first candle with the lighter she provided, and looked up at her. "Are you the *curandero*? The one Jason went looking for?"

She gave me a speculative look, grinning. "I'll be who-ever you want, handsome."

Elle was like the girl version of Drew, except instead of insults and slurs, she was flirty and bright.

There was only one conclusion I could draw. She couldn't be trusted.

I lit the second candle, then stepped back and waited. Elle gave me a disgruntled look, but a tiny flex of power and a wave of her hand, and the third candle ignited. "Staying on your guard," she said. "I approve." She sprinkled a bit of whatever was in the vial into each of the candle's flames, and set it back in her bag.

"Let me out of here!" Hanna hollered, but at least now she couldn't stomp her feet.

"I'm afraid I can't. You've been interfering in all the places you shouldn't," Elle said, lifting the bell up and ringing it once. The clapper struck the side, and a resonant tone washed over the room. That was the only way I could think to describe it. The strange heaviness of the air, the chill, the bell's chime sliced through all of it. "Bells can disperse dark magic, did you know that?"

I realized after a moment that she was talking to me. "Is that why churches—"

"—ring them so often? Makes you wonder, doesn't it?"

Hanna was still flickering in place, unable to stay completely solid. "You are such a bitch!" the six-year-old hollered. "I can't believe you'd—"

Elle rang the bell again, drowning out the end. "I banish you, Hanna Elizabeth Downing. Return to your slumber. Cling to the world of the living no more. Strike no more bargains with the darkness."

The ghost girl screamed something unintelligible, a channel for her frustration and rage. The flickers became slower and slower, and she was visible less and less. Until Elle rang a third time, and the girl vanished entirely. Without her, the pressure in the room eased up even more.

"Weren't you lucky I showed up when I did? Alone in an office building with a ghost? You've got a wild side, boy."

I crossed my arms and took a few steps to the side, until most of the desk was between us. No one in Belle Dam was nice for no reason. Not even new imports. "Who are you?"

She tucked her hair behind her ear and started blowing out the candles. "I was offered a job, and I took it. I'm a bit surprised to see Jason's son is so grown up and handsome, though." Her eyes crinkled. "I'd pinch your cheeks, but word on the street is the boy has a temper."

I gaped. *Jason had told her? Why would he do that? He said secrecy was the most important element we had going for us now.*

She didn't seem to care that the candle wax needed time to cool. Everything got shoved back into her purse. Except for the smell of burning in the air, it was almost like she'd never been here. "Ugh," she said, looking down at her bag. "Dust." She ran her finger along the edge of the desk as if to prove a point.

"So Jason sent you here? To take care of the ghost?"

She seemed to think that one over for a second. "I'm a problem solver. If it's not a challenge, I'm not enjoying myself."

"And the hospital, you went to see Grazia."

"What was left of her. I was too late to do any real good. But luckily for *you,* I tracked Hanna down before she could do any more damage."

"Who was she working for? Was it Lucien?"

Elle glanced at one of the pieces of artwork on the wall, and caught a hint of her reflection, which she used to play with her hair. "I thought that much was obvious. Didn't I hear she tried to kill you once upon a time?"

I nodded. "When I first got here."

She spread her hands, as if that solved everything. "There you go, then. Demons love to strike back-alley bargains. I'm sure whatever he promised Hanna was worth its weight in gold."

Something wasn't right. Icy fingers tickled at the back of my neck like a warning. I scrubbed my hands back there, trying to ease the feeling. "So you know about Lucien. Jason knows about him?"

Elle gave me a funny look, watching my hand against my neck. "Oh," she said softly. "I didn't realize. I'm so sorry."

"Didn't realize what?" Instincts I didn't completely understand were screaming warnings.

"Does Jason know? Does *anyone*?" I was the one with the special eyes, but Elle was looking at me like she saw something under the surface. Something no one else had noticed.

"Know what?" I could feel my heart quickening. *End her, end her now. Quickly, while her guard is down!* With the winter voice, it wasn't fight or flight. It was *strike first* or *strike hardest*.

She bit down on her lower lip, weighing her response. "I know what you're carrying inside," she said.

I pulled the cold around me like a shield, and concentrated on drawing the power towards me. "You're not working for Jason," I said flatly. "Who are you?"

Her tone grew softer, more calming. A therapist's voice. "Who I am is a person with information. I need you to listen to me."

"I'm done listening."

Silence filled the room. I got the sense that she was waiting to see what I did next. I tried to push back against my instincts, not willing to lash out at her yet. Maybe she was a threat, but maybe this could be salvaged. She reached out, grabbed my hand. "It was hard on you, wasn't it? Thinking you killed him? And now you find out he's alive again."

I was caught off guard, so much so that at first I didn't feel her fingers tracing against the skin of my palm. Her hand was hot, or mine was cold, either way her skin tingled against mine. The curling serpent inside of me eased, and the urges to silence her stopped. The winter voice grew quiescent, almost sleepy.

"He's broken, but not forever. There are very few ways he can rejuvenate himself. Lucien needs an act of restoration." There was no humor in her tone, now. She was all business.

"How do you know this?"

Elle shrugged. "I read a book once. How many girls has he taken so far?"

"Two. Wait, how did you know he was taking girls?"

"I told you. Act of restoration. It's a ritual of three parts. The girls must be offered as a sacrifice, the old ways being what they are. The first needs to have a spark, a life that loves life. From her, he'll take it all: drain the fire and leave nothing behind." *Grazia,* I realized. Elle continued, "You'll recognize the second. You've seen it before. He'll take her future.

But the last is the most important, and only a true sacrifice will do."

"So whoever he takes next—"

"—is going to die," she finished, nodding. "Fallon is a manipulator. He'll choose people that will hurt *you* if he can. As retribution."

"Who *are* you?"

"I told you. I'm a mercenary." She flashed me her crooked grin, but now it didn't reach her eyes. I didn't like the way she looked at me now, too much knowledge in her eyes. "All this information makes a nice debt, wouldn't you say? Once you get that demon out of your system, of course."

She dropped my hand, and it flopped to my side. I looked down at it, realizing after a moment that there was a delay between trying to move my head, and my head actually moving. Then my shoulder dropped. Then my knees.

"What . . . ?" My mouth was numb, my question slurred.

"Sorry, lover," Elle whispered, "but you've got a plague slumbering inside you, and power is a problem."

I struggled to stay standing, but once one leg dropped, the other was quick to follow. Whatever she'd dosed me with spread quickly through my limbs, leaving a pleasant haze behind. I couldn't hold my eyes open, and the dark took me.

twenty-six

When I woke, the office was empty, the lights were off, and the sun was going down.

She drugged me. I groaned, climbing to my feet and holding my head. *Who the hell was she?* More questions. She wasn't working for Jason, that much seemed clear, but then who sent her to take care of Hanna? Catherine had a lot to gain by sending the ghost after me, but Elle had known that Jason was my father.

There's another witch in Belle Dam. That couldn't possibly end well.

I made it into the elevator and pressed the button for the lobby, then sank back down to the ground until the doors opened again. Whatever she'd done to me had the effect of a really good nap. I was invigorated but still loose limbed and laid-back.

That all changed when I walked out into the lobby, and my phone vibrated in my pocket.

"Where've you been?" Drew demanded, once I picked up.

My response was flat. "Roofied."

"Right," he drawled, sounding either annoyed or stressed. "Where are you?"

"Lobby of Lucien's office building."

"What are you doing there?"

I sighed. Seriously, he wanted a play-by-play? "Princess Barbie Psycho Killer turned out to be a ghost. Some woman I've never seen before showed up and used witch fu to banish her. She warned me about Lucien and then magically roofied me. Oh, and I have the plague."

There was silence on the other end of the line. "Was that supposed to be in English?"

"What do you want, Drew? You called for a reason, right?"

"Riley's demanding to know what we found out about Lucien. You suck at talking people down," Drew said dismissively.

I rubbed at my forehead. "What do you want me to do? Lock her up somewhere?"

"She's not going to give up on this," Drew insisted. "We need to talk some sense into her."

I laughed. "Talk sense into Riley. There are so many problems with that sentence, I don't even know where to begin."

"Well, you better find a place," Drew said, unusually dogged. "Because she's serious."

"She's always serious." I stopped. "What's the deal with you?" Drew rarely got worked up like this.

He hesitated. "You know what? Get your head out of your ass, junior. Riley may not have weird magic eyeballs, but at least she goes after what she wants. And right now, she's got Gregory's contact list. People like Matthias are on it. She's going to start ringing up every bit of dark spawn she can unless someone stops her."

I think there was an insult buried in there somewhere, but the idea of Riley getting friendly with Belle Dam's darkest was definitely a bad idea. "Fine," I said. "What's the big plan?"

"She's at the school. We'll talk to her. Together."

¤   ¤   ¤

It was full-on dark by the time we arrived at the school. The front doors were unlocked; meaning someone, somewhere, was still in the building. "Are you even sure she's still here?"

"She's in the newspaper room," Drew said. "I talked to her half an hour ago. She'd ordered Thai and planned on an all-nighter. Something's got her all worked up."

"She found out he was still alive," I said, realizing that was when things had changed. Since Lucien had "died," Riley had been strange and aloof. But now that she knew Lucien was alive, something had changed.

More questions. Why did it make a difference to her? Why did she suddenly think that Lucien being alive was a good thing?

We headed through the halls, our footsteps echoing strangely. A school without bodies was like walking through an abandoned beehive—a place of motion and angst, suddenly still and complacent. A whole lot of combs without any honey.

A perfect analogy, the winter voice whispered. *You could harvest them, you know.*

I shivered, and the voice slunk down under the surface of my thoughts like a shark waiting for another meal.

Riley was in the office just like Drew had said. A trio of Styrofoam coffee cups were perched on the edge of her computer desk, all perilously close to falling onto the floor. She jumped when we came in. With the lights dimmed and the hall lights washing us out, I'm sure we could have looked like anyone.

"What are you doing here?" she asked, a little breathless.

"Braden's going to talk a little sense into you," Drew said, staying by the door. He sat on one of the desks, propping his foot against the chair.

I'm going to talk some sense into her? On top of being a dick, Drew was also delusional. "We're going to find Lucien. We'll stop him. So whatever's motivating you, we'll take care of it."

Riley's jaw was set. "It's not that simple."

"It is," Drew burst out, because apparently "me talking sense into her" came with bonus commentary. "He's kidnapping girls, Riley."

"There's a few hundred girls in Belle Dam."

"But there aren't a few hundred girls that are friends with *me*," I pointed out. "He's going after people that he knows are going to get a reaction."

"You didn't know the first girl," Riley pointed out, strangely triumphant. "Grazia doesn't even live her."

"No, but Lucien was the one who sent me after Grace Lansing in the first place. That's how all this started. And Kayla? She used to go out with Trey."

"I can't. Sorry, but I'm not going to let it go," Riley said, her jaw set. "If you won't help me, I'll figure it out on my own."

"Why do you care?" Drew exploded, pushing himself away from the desk. "This isn't your world, Riley. You're just a girl with too much time on her hands."

Riley was so startled that it looked like she was going to cry. There was a pause, a hanging moment where it seemed like tears were going to spill before she pulled herself together. "I care because he's going to kill me," she said, in a faint voice. "And then he's going to kill all of you."

Drew and I looked at each other. "Explain." Drew crossed his arms in front of him, and went to stand in front of the door.

"When I was seven," she started, then stopped. "When I was seven, my dad left. Drew, you remember. He just . . . took off one day."

Drew nodded. "Your mom lost it. Quit her job, and then everything went to hell."

Riley turned to me. "She used to be a nurse. Then she started drinking. Telling me my dad left because of me, that I was responsible."

"What's this have to do with Lucien?" I asked. I had a bad feeling.

"I'm getting to that," Riley said. "Just go with me. My mom's always been ..."

"Annoying," Drew supplied.

She shrugged. "Sure. Annoying. Anyway, she got worse without my dad. And then one day, at school, this man showed up."

Of course. I knew this story. I'd seen it, in my dream. "Lucien."

Riley nodded. "He talked about my dad at first, then it got freaky."

"How old were you?" Drew asked.

"Eight? Nine?" Riley's eyes were unfocused, her forehead showing a crease. "And it was weird, but I kept thinking how nice he was. I mean, he was saying all this creepy stuff, about my dad and my life. All this weird stuff, but he was just ... he was *smiling*."

"He told me I was lucky, that Dad going away was the best thing that could have ever happened to me. His smile was so ... nice, y'know? I trusted him. He told me about how we were going to move, and when Mom would quit drinking."

"Jesus," Drew whispered.

"And then he told me, like it was the most casual thing ever, that he'd kill me. If *he* ever died, I'd die. And so would everyone I ever loved. He wanted me to know so that I'd be afraid. That I'd spend years remembering him and being so scared I couldn't sleep at night." She looked confused for a second, holding up her hand. "And then he held out his hand like this," she extended her pinkie, "and his smile was huge. He was practically glowing. And he said, 'pinkie swear.'"

It was the pinkie swear that really creeped me out. Lucien threatening a kid didn't surprise me in the slightest. But to follow it up with the kind of oath that little kids hold sacred, *that* was horrific.

"Why the fuck did you never tell me about this?" Drew demanded.

"Because up until a couple of years ago, you didn't even believe in the boogeyman. And later…" Riley was quiet for a minute. "He was right. Just like he said, we moved. Then mom got sick, right on time, and then she was sober."

"You should have told *me*," I said. "Maybe I could have done something." *Like not killed him.*

"Yeah, but I didn't know he was going to *die* that night." she said. "That's why I went to his office. I had to see it for myself."

"Then you saw his body, and you realized that he was telling the truth," I said, finishing the story. "And you realized if the rest of it was true, that meant the threat was, too."

Riley nodded. "But now he's not dead," she said, voice wavering a bit. "He came back, and I'm still here."

"Jesus," Drew said again.

My pocket started vibrating, preceding the ringing of my cell phone. "Yeah?" I said, after flipping it open.

"Braden?" Jade's voice on the other end was shrill, panicked, and almost unrecognizable.

"Jade?"

Drew whirled around at my tone.

"Braden?" She repeated my name like she couldn't hear

me, like our connection was only one way. "He's not answering his phone! I don't know what I'm supposed to do!"

"Jade, what's going on?"

"What's going on?" Drew demanded, pressing into me.

I pushed him back, motioning for him to be quiet. He had superhuman hearing. I just had the regular old kind. "Jade? What's happening. Tell me what's wrong."

"Gentry told me about them, but he never said they were so big!" My skin went cold, and not from the ice inside of me. Jade was terrified. "They're circling the house. They burn the concrete, just like he said!"

Hellhounds. Shit. "Where are you?"

"Tricia's house. We were planning—"

"—I know where that is." Drew interrupted. He was already moving for the door.

"Jade, we're coming," I promised. I fumbled in my pocket, tossed the spare phone John had given me to Riley. "Call Trey. Text him. Do whatever it takes to get him on the phone. Tell him Jade's in trouble. Tricia's house."

"Braden—" Riley stared at me in surprise.

"Do it!" I rushed out of the room, and had to run to keep up with Drew who was nearly flying down the hallway. "Jade, we're on our way."

"Braden!" Jade's voice was choked with panic.

The call dropped in the middle of her scream.

TWENTY-SEVEN

I redialed Jade twice before we got to the bike, but she didn't pick up.

"It's on the far side of town," Drew said, not even bothering with the helmets. By the time I caught up with him, he'd kick-started the engine. One-handed, he grabbed me and lifted me over the bike and onto the seat behind him. And then we were off.

I nearly dropped my phone, but managed to press it against my stomach and wrap my free hand around his waist. "How long?" I shouted.

The wind sheared off Drew's response, but I gathered that it wasn't good.

There are things you could do, the winter voice whispered silkily. *Violate the natural order. Bring it to pass.* And like a door unlocking in my mind, I saw what it was talking about.

It wasn't easy to draw on the power while we were moving so fast. But the wellspring power came to me even still. The night wind tore at me, slicing through my sweater like it

250

wasn't even there, but the chill rolled right off my skin, as the power rolled in.

"What are you doing?" Drew shouted. But I couldn't respond.

I couldn't see the odometer, but I was sure we were going nearly a hundred miles an hour. Drew was weaving through traffic as much as he could, but there were too many cars. It wasn't about *if* we got into an accident, it was *when*. Even heightened Shifter senses could only do so much.

I drew more and more power, feeling it curl up from harvest crevices and furrowed ground. My fingers itched with it, intangible smoke and sorrow on the tip of my tongue.

"Clear," I whispered, feeling the power lancing out of me, funneling it down the crowded street. One by one, the cars shifted left and right, engines cutting out entirely, leaving a center strip two lanes wide for us to travel on. I caught glimpses of drivers behind the wheel, perplexed by vehicles that had seized control and parked themselves.

We started going even faster, but with the roadways clear, we swept out of the city in seconds rather than minutes. Drew headed for the mainland, skirting the highway exit. Before I knew it, we were turning down a forested road, houselights shining faintly in the distance.

Out here, away from the center of town, homes were few and far between. We passed only a handful of houses in the half-mile drive down the paved road. Huge walls of trees blocked the rest of the city from view, only a narrow sliver of the coast was faintly visible in the distance. Isolated.

"It's over here," Drew called over his shoulder.

But I didn't need him to tell me, because even before we pulled into the driveway, I could feel it. Something twisted. Raw. A dark kind of power that reeked of rotting. The house was set back from the street, far enough that we could barely see the lights. But about three-quarters of the way there, the wall of trees on either side suddenly gave way, and there was a clearing.

In that clearing was the picture of Americana. A two-story house, two cars, a shed. Even a basketball hoop where father and son presumably played together. And a large yard with at least one visible oak tree. A yard that, under normal circumstances, would look warm and inviting.

This yard, however, was littered with hellhounds.

Not so Americana after all.

"You never take me anywhere nice. It's always demons, demons, demons, with you," Drew said, a slight hitch in his voice.

"I hope you get eaten," I hissed. The last time, there had been four hellhounds. I'd boxed them in while Drew killed three, and the last one I killed on my own.

Hellhounds were dogs raised on demonic steroids. Bigger than wolves, they were thick and stout creatures that looked like they could get hit by a semi and walk away. Their fur was coarse and spottled, and even at their best they looked mangy and unkempt. In some spots, the fur was almost spinelike and sharp, like it had been grown out of razors and battle axes. They were, in effect, really ugly. It was almost a selling feature: something that ugly *had* to be lethal.

The yard was the size of a basketball court with the house

dead in the center. There were well over a *dozen* hounds in the yard. This was more than just a pack. It was an armada.

Drew whistled, a low sound. "How about I take the three on the left, and you can have the seventeen dozen on the right."

"Now's not really the time for jokes," I growled.

He looked offended. "There's always time for sarcasm."

A few of the closest hellhounds had turned at our approach, but the rest ignored us. There was no straight line to the house, and no chance of getting the girls *out*.

"Something's not right," I murmured, climbing off the back of the bike. Drew followed a second later. The hellhounds were just … waiting. All of them, standing at attention like they were waiting for a signal to attack.

Hellhounds were an aberration. The legend said that a warlock once summoned a dark spirit, trapped it in the body of a dog and set it loose. The hound had been beholden to its master, but demons and spirits are crafty creatures. The hellhound sired a litter of pups, tainted with its own demonic essence. These pups adapted to magic; resisted it.

They had also become completely consumed by the spirit's rage, and its obsession with killing. They were meat suits with only a single purpose—kill.

"Look," Drew said, pointing up. The curtains in one of the second-floor bedrooms were pulled back, and Jade's frightened face appeared. On the ground, one of the hellhounds growled in response.

"What are they waiting for?" I whispered to myself. The tingling sense that something was wrong was only getting stronger. But even the winter voice was silent now, and I was on my own.

"I think we need—" Drew broke off in midsentence, grabbing the front of my shirt and throwing me to the left. I was airborne for only a second, and then gravity was pulling me down. I threw out my arms, bracing myself as I felt the air displacement of something extremely large and extraordinarily angry hurtling through the spot where my head used to be.

I heard Drew snarl, his voice changing to something more guttural midway through.

By the time I was standing again, Drew was gone, and in his place was a very large, very irritable looking grizzly bear.

"Next time, use your words," I told him. And then the battle began in earnest.

I was already summoning more power to me, drawing from every source I could feel all over town. That was all the indication the hellhounds needed to know that the game had changed. Hellhounds could sense magic, just like Drew, but to them, it was salt in a wound. It infuriated them.

Without even thinking, I threw an invisible field of hardened air around me. Tight, stable magic. *Okay, that'll buy me a minute.* I really needed to start planning ahead for these things.

I squeezed my fist, gripping the magic tight. If I'd had more time, I would have invoked the elements to strengthen it, or bound the field in defensive sigils, but things were too chaotic right now.

There also wasn't any point. The hound leapt again and tore through the shield like it was a paper banner.

I dropped to the ground. "Damn." The hound just barely sailed over me. Hellhounds adapted to magic. I'd always assumed it meant *individual* hounds adapted to magic. The hounds I'd used the barrier on last time were all dead and banished. These new hounds shouldn't be immune to the spell, but they were. It must have been some kind of cellular memory.

It would have been fascinating if it wasn't also terrifying.

I caught a glimpse of Drew, wearing his bear form, and realized quickly why he'd gone for the big and slow grizzly instead of a faster, more agile option, like a wolf. One swipe of his paw and two hounds were instantly bowled over, deep-clawed grooves in their sides.

The hounds weren't focused on the house anymore. Great for Jade, not so great for Team Witch. "Crap, crap, crap," I panted, trying to scurry backwards without looking like a total coward. The fact that I scurried, though, might have lost that battle before it even started.

Can't do the same trick twice. Sure, that'll be easy. Even I rolled my eyes at the excessive sarcasm of the thought.

I whipped the magic I'd collected out, spun it around, and allowed it to gain speed and ferocity. Between one moment and the next, it became a gale force of wind originating from the palms of my hands. But air along wasn't going to stop the hounds. In midstride my movement changed, and I exhaled even as I clapped my hands together.

Air became a torrent of water like a rogue swell torn

straight from the ocean. I pulled the magic back again, afraid of letting the power dissipate, and touched it to the core of my power, the part of me that had been freezing for weeks. The temperature dropped sharply, and liquid became solid.

Three hellhounds were caught in a block of ice bigger than the monstrosity that Trey called an SUV. I could feel their anger pumping blood through their corrupted hearts. I could feel them struggling, but the ice refused to break easily.

A snarling interrupted my all-too-brief reverie. Drew had shifted into something smaller, more lithe. I wasn't sure what at first until I saw the hind legs shoot out, cracking a hound right in the face. A donkey. I could have laughed. Except there was another hellhound bearing down on me, boxing me up against the giant ice cube I'd just created.

Ice wouldn't work again. Defensive shields wouldn't work. There was nowhere to hide until I thought of a better plan.

Break the sky. You remember how.

What did that even mean? The winter voice wouldn't explain.

The hound advanced, and I skirted back, just the way it intended. Drew had taken the shape of a wolf again and was busy taking on, damn, four of the hellhounds at once. *Pull it together.* I didn't need to be rescued. In fact, wasn't that one of the points I'd made to Trey once upon a time?

I focused on the ground in front of the hellhound and narrowed my eyes. The magic flooded down, into the soil. I let it seep, only for a second, and then I pushed it away.

"Move," I whispered, feeling the spell shape itself to my words.

Underneath the hound there was a sudden rumble, almost like a crack, as six tons of dirt compressed. The grass underneath it began to sink, first slow, then progressively faster, until an entire section of sod tore away from the rest and the monster went tumbling down into the darkness.

Sweat beaded down my temples, but I held the dirt away for another heartbeat before releasing it. The dirt expanded, like a spring that had all of its tension unleashed. Where the hound had been was now just a small patch of brown, the sod top swallowed up somewhere down below.

An animal's cry pulled me away from my minor victory, and I saw Drew, now in the form of some kind of cat, darting away from a trio of hellhounds. They were getting smarter. Maybe they adapted to fights, too.

Two of them broke away from their pursuit of Drew and started for me. Another pair appeared at the fringes of the forest, They were toying with us, and I was running out of tricks.

Shatter them. I can show you how. You can save him.

I looked back to the block of ice, at the hellhounds frozen like bugs in amber. Then I looked at Drew, back to the grizzly. We were overmatched. *Yes*, I answered.

I gave myself over to the winter voice.

The next few moments blurred together, and my perception shifted and narrowed. It was like watching firsthand as someone played that game Mousetrap, a series of chain reactions that the eyes couldn't help but follow in wonder.

First my fist clenched, then it punched at the air. The magic that had formed the ice shattered like it had been struck by a giant hammer, along with the hellhounds inside of it. My hand opened, pulled both ice and power back towards me even as it melted. For a second, the yard was dazzled by a cloud of mist, and then the wind shifted and the water was gone. And so were the hounds that had been inside.

But that was only the first stage. I could *feel* things building.

I drew in more and more of the power, felt it rip through me in sickly sweet gasps. Energy coursed through my veins and burned against my skin. It was familiar and foreign all at the same time. I'd never tapped into magic like this.

That's when the pain started.

It hit with the force of every migraine I'd ever had growing up. Every migraine. Combined. It was harder and worse than any pain I'd ever felt before. There were no visions, but I don't think I would have noticed them anyway.

My vision completely washed out into agonizing white. My blood felt like it had somehow caught on fire, and it raced through my system, igniting everything as it spread. Faster and faster. Electricity crackled along my fingers.

But somehow, my body was holding on to the magic, even if it was by the fingernails.

The power spiraled out of me, the way it had the night I'd tried to summon the dead. I could feel it crackling upwards, a geyser of power.

Break the sky and be it done.

The geyser pierced the clouds and infected them, turning the sky virulent. Wind rose into a howl, the clouds grew heavy, and a storm was born in moments.

Yes.

Thunder cracked so loudly above us that my body shook with the force of it. Rain came down in sheets. Coughing, sputtering, I rolled onto my side, and my vision cleared.

I could still feel it, the magic. It coursed through the storm, spiraling and circling, drawing strength and power. Then it struck down. One bolt, then a second. But even these lightning strikes were not the endgame. Lightning struck to the north, to the east, to the south, to the west. And then a massive bolt struck so close that heat coursed over me, a blast of fiery air that burned my skin red on contact.

I felt the last bolt strike, and the moment it started to ground, the lightning... split. It struck seven hellhounds at once, igniting them with the true power of a storm. It coursed through all of them until each was nothing more than ash.

I kept my eyes closed, focused on breathing in and out. The sound of padded feet came closer, and for a second my mind assured me that the spell hadn't taken care of the hellhounds after all, that it had missed one.

But the sound of paws soon became harder, less graceful footsteps.

"You alive?" Drew asked, towering above me.

I opened my eyes long enough to assess that he was in one piece. His jeans were torn in a few places, which didn't make much sense because Drew the animal didn't wear jeans.

But it looked like the wounds he took in one form were replicated in another, and his clothing suffered for it.

Wordlessly, I held up my hand. He gripped it, pulling me back to my feet. I wobbled. Weebled. But I managed to stay upright.

I heard the car coming up the driveway before Drew did, which surprised both of us, I think. "Trey," I said tiredly. Drew turned around, watching the black SUV crawl up the driveway.

"Probably wonders if he got the right house," he said.

I looked over my shoulder, at the dozen or so hellhound carcasses littering the lawn. The lightning had left them charred piles of darkness. A pungent, ugly smell caked the yard, and in a few places the grass still smoked, embers of fire turning to ash.

"Pretty sure he'll figure it out," I replied.

Trey was alone, which surprised me. But not as much as the wicked looking machete knife he pulled off of the passenger's seat and brought out with him. It was the kind of blade that a steak knife dreamed of becoming someday. It was bigger than a cleaver, but not quite broadsword size.

Drew whistled. "How many box tops did he have to turn in for *that*?"

"Where is she?" Trey demanded.

Wordlessly, I pointed towards the house.

"She's okay?"

I closed my eyes and focused my senses, not sure what I was doing yet when Drew interrupted. "She's fine. Scared, but fine. She's busy taking care of her friend and keeping away from the windows. Other Girl had a meltdown so Jade gave her some Xanax until she blissed out."

"You can smell all that from out here?" Trey asked skeptically. I have to admit, he wasn't the only one thrown off.

Drew shot him a withering look and raised his hand, revealing his cell phone. Then he shook his head in disgust at the both of us, and turned away.

Some of the tension went out of Trey's shoulders. He set the knife down on top of the car, then turned to me. "What happened?" he asked quietly. "All Riley said was that Jade was in trouble and that you two went ahead."

"Hellhounds." That was really all that needed to be said.

Trey's eyebrows raised, and his lips parted. "That explains it."

I gave him a curious look, noticing as I did that Drew still had his back to us. Were he and Jade still talking? *Aren't they supposed to hate each other?*

Trey looked at a point over my head. "Kayla came home," he said. "Doctors say she's fine."

Kayla had been found? "They took her to the hospital?"

Trey nodded. "She's fine. Exhausted, doesn't remember anything, but fine. They're sending her home."

Elle's words echoed in my head. Kayla wasn't alright, but how was I supposed to tell Trey that the doctors were wrong? That she might never be all right again. Lucien had fed on her future, the same way he'd fed on countless girls before, leaving a shell of a girl with no more potential.

"You said that explains it," I looked back up into his eyes. "What'd you mean by that?"

"Isn't it obvious? Trey said. They're only holding one girl at a time. Kayla got taken, and Grazia showed up on the docks the next morning."

"And now that Kayla's back, they needed a new victim," I said. Something still wasn't right. Drew appeared at our side again, his phone gone.

Trey nodded, and for a minute it was like nothing had changed. "Are you okay?" he asked, his tone terse and his jaw flexing.

I nodded. "Drew and I took care of them."

"Sure did," Drew agreed with an amused drawl. "We make quite the pair."

I was going to fire back with an irritated retort, but before I could, Trey had stepped forward, his hand brushing through my hair, pushing it off my forehead. He lowered her voice. It was like Drew didn't even exist to him for the first time ever. "And you're okay? No weirdness? No visions?"

My mouth went dry, and my stomach twitched with butterflies. "No," I said breathlessly. "I'm fine."

Trey's grave expression lightened a bit. "I was worried. Riley said…" he trailed off, looking off to his left, but not quite looking at Drew. "Riley just said there was trouble."

"If you two are going to start eyefucking, will someone please find a hellhound to tear out my throat first?" Drew remarked caustically.

"If only it was that easy," Trey said under his breath.

The moment didn't last.

"Guys," Drew began.

"Lucien's not going to stop," I said. "He'll have something in mind, since he didn't get Jade. We have to find him."

"We will," Trey promised.

"Guys!"

The front door squeaked open and interrupted. Trey and I both turned, although he didn't drop his hand. Jade poked her head out, still as pale as a sheet. "Is everything—"

That was when Drew surged forward, his expression dark. "Stay inside!"

I knew what was going to happen just before it did.

Trey reacted instantaneously, seeing Drew as a threat to his sister. All he saw was Drew making a run for Jade, and reacting. He threw his arm out and clotheslined Drew across the chest. Trey still thought he was some kind of rabid animal, and Drew's sudden movement did nothing to help his cause.

The Shifter went down, and immediately leapt back to his feet. They began to circle each other, all in the span of a few seconds.

I looked at Jade, and she hurriedly slammed the door and disappeared inside.

"What's wrong with you?" Trey snarled.

"Turn. Around." Drew snapped back, biting off each word with a level of self-control I didn't know he had.

I didn't need to turn around, though. That's because a moment later, the hellhound behind me growled, the deep rumbling interspersed with the *mokoi's* heinous chittering.

twenty-eight

"Next time we save the day, we're not waiting around for them to regroup," Drew snarled, dropping into a defensive position.

"Yeah, yeah," I muttered.

The problem with having a house in the middle of a clearing was that it was surrounded on almost every side by thick forest. At least another dozen hellhounds poured in from between the trees.

We were nearly surrounded. Only now, there were tiny, monkeylike creatures climbing tree branches, claws deep in the trunks, or even in a few cases riding on the backs of the hellhounds.

"Can you get them out of here?" I asked.

Trey shook his head. "There's no way." He'd parked on the far side of the clearing, by Drew and me.

"I hate my life," I said to no one in particular. "Drew, focus on the hellhounds. I'll try to deal with the teacup demons."

"How are you going to do that?" Trey had followed

Drew's lead, and dropped into a defensive position. He swung the knife a few times, testing it in his hands. I had the feeling this wasn't the first time he'd used it.

"This is just like—" Drew began.

Surprisingly, it was Trey who finished his thought, "—that night on the beach. With the bonfire."

As if tonight wasn't insane enough already, the two mortal enemies shared a fierce grin and a moment of ... something. Amusement?

What the hell? "I don't even want to know," I muttered. "Drew, shift. Before the *mokoi* stop you like last time."

"I'm not a pet," he grumbled, glaring at me over his shoulder.

"Who's a good girl? That's right, you are." I nudged him in the shoulder and pointed to the hellhounds. "Kill." Drew muttered something offensive under his breath, but within seconds the silver blurring spread up and down his arms.

"Are you sure ..." Trey gestured to my eyes.

I smiled. "I'll be fine, Trey." I'd become a phenomenal liar. "Are you sure you know how to use that?" I asked, nodding at the weapon.

He nodded. "Stay close. I'll keep you safe." Trey's arrogance over his abilities aside, the sentiment was cute. Worrying, but cute. I took a quick assessment of the demons—the hounds and the *mokoi* were evenly dispersed. Organized by someone with an attention to detail.

I had a theory, but it would have to wait until I dealt with the demons. Again.

There has to be a better way to deal with them. Just like that, something came together. I didn't know if it was my own idea, or some seedling from the winter voice, but it was there, and brilliant, and probably completely stupid.

"This might take a minute," I said, warning Trey. He nodded. It was risky, but it had taken an incredible amount of power to kill just one hellhound last time. I couldn't just kill one or two, I had to shut down the link that was powering them.

The silver light stopped shining in the corner of my eye, signaling that Drew was fully changed. As long as he could keep away from the *mokoi*, who had the power to seriously screw up his abilities, he'd be fine, too.

I withdrew my focus from both of the boys, and reached out for the magic. Wellspring power swelled under my grasp, rising up through the earth. My skin tingled, feeling the diamond strength that had become my own personal store of power.

After that, I reached out for the ambient magical energy that existed all over town. Belle Dam had its history of witches and magic, but underneath all of that was a shade of the truth. Because people believed, secretly and in the dark of night, that became more true. More real. Magic was stronger in this place than anywhere else I'd seen. More power was there for the taking. So I took.

The top of my head buzzed and the pressure inside my brain increased. My skin hummed, tuned to some frequency that couldn't be put into words. I had never used this much magic before—but somehow I knew this would work.

The hellhounds advanced. I heard the raucous chatter of the tiny demons as they jumped back and forth, and I could feel them heading for me. A few minutes ago, I had agitated the sky in order to bring down lightning on the hellhounds. Now I had a different goal in mind.

I poked at the storm, pushed and prodded and taunted it into a fury. My thoughts whispered profanities at its edges, turning graying clouds back into the thick, swelling darkness that had rained down upon us once already. I stole the warmth from the air, adding it to my store of power. A fierce wind was born as warmth and chill split themselves apart.

I took the warmth and taught it to be silent and stoic. Warmth became water, and water became moisture, until the clouds were soaking with it, simply desperate to unleash their fury down below.

But it wasn't enough. Never enough. I circled, and spun, and drew the storm in tight, until parts of the city that went to sleep under a bank of clouds would awaken to an empty night sky.

This time, I wasn't just conjuring a storm. Lightning alone wouldn't cut it. The problem wasn't just the demons, it was the person summoning and controlling them. So I conjured up a blizzard. It took everything I had, and other things beside, but I threw everything I had into it.

And this was only stage one.

I opened my eyes to a slasher film. Trey had thrown himself in front of me as a tiny army of *mokoi* jumped and played with him, their dark eyes gleaming. Two or three or maybe even more *mokoi* had already fallen under Trey's weapon, which confirmed his skill with a knife. Maybe I shouldn't have been underestimating him.

He spun again, and my mind was made up. Trey didn't attack any of the *mokoi* themselves, he sliced at open air. The joking, playful jumping of the demonlings could not be anticipated. But he did. They were leaping and rolling so fast that by the time they landed they were already in motion again. But somehow, every one of Trey's swings made contact, striking not where the *mokoi* were, but where they would be.

It was like plucking a fly out of the air with chopsticks. Possible, but so totally improbable. But I watched Trey do it once, twice, three times. It wasn't dumb luck, there was no way.

"We need to hold them. Just for a few minutes," I shouted. Trey nodded sharply, but kept his ground. I stayed out of his way.

There weren't just *mokoi* to worry about, and Drew couldn't take on the hellhounds all by himself. We were just lucky Trey hadn't tried taking one.

That's when I saw three of them gathering together, like a conference of monsters before they decided to attack. They had been starting to circle around, waiting until our attention was focused totally on the demonlings.

"Eff my life," I said, turning around and backing up until Trey and I were back to back.

Above me, I could feel the storm churning. Magic leapt from cloud to cloud like lightning gathering the nerve to strike.

It would start soon.

This was big magic: bigger than anything I'd ever even *pondered* before. This wasn't the kind of thing that Belle Dam could sleep through, either. So much magic in the air, a storm slamming down on them, a lot of people were going to wake from a dead sleep. Jason and Catherine. Lucien. Countless others who had a glimmer of ability. They'd start looking for the source of the storm. They'd come for us.

But that was only if the hellhounds didn't kill us all first.

"You got this?" Trey shouted, then immediately pulled away as the knife went snick-snick. Another demon fell to the ground in several pieces. Trey was building himself a nice little pile.

In that single moment of distraction, one of the hellhounds leaped. I didn't think, just threw out a chain of magic, wrapping it around him like a leash and then yanking hard to the side. The hound slammed into one of the oak trees with enough force that the clearing was pierced with an audible crack that echoed.

The second leapt, and I repeated the process. Only this time, when I threw the hound towards the wall of trees, I tied the chain. With one makeshift magical leash in place, I repeated on the third, then back to the first, and then started winding the chains together. As hard as I could make it for the trio to escape. The end result was that when one pulled, another one was yanked backwards.

I looked up to the sky. "Come on," I muttered. "Hurry up already." But it was still clear.

"Jesus, they just keep coming!" Trey yelled, hacking and slicing away.

I chanced a look at Drew to confirm that he was still alive. The other side of the clearing was awash in silver light—Drew didn't stay in any one form for more than a few heartbeats, first an elephant, then an inky black jaguar, and then into housecat, of all things. A calico-Drew darted under a pair of *mokoi* that had jumped into his path, and then scampered right between two of the hellhounds as fast as you please.

A flurry of sparkling caught my attention, and I looked up. At last, it was finally snowing.

Snow fell in a way it never had in Belle Dam. In seconds, the sky was simply coated with white, as the approaching blizzard swept over the woods around us. For about a circular mile, for right now, it was like Siberian winter had come to visit.

The winds I'd crafted, strong pulses of force that swept in a vaguely clockwise direction brought the temperature down in seconds. Fall weather descended below zero in less than a minute.

"Are you doing this?"

I shifted enough that I could turn to Trey, and shouted an affirmative.

The *mokoi* had changed tactics. They could feel the cold coming, feel the blizzard on its way. Their frenzied taunt-and-attack system crumbled, and they began to scramble. Every tiny demon for itself.

But that was the second purpose of the gale-force winds

I'd summoned. They cut off the outside world, left us to this tiny clearing and the dozens of demons inhabiting it. The *mokoi* couldn't flee, because they couldn't get close enough to pass through the winds.

So the storm raged.

The demons, collectively, began to slow. Then they stopped. It was more than just cold, or snow, or even hail. It was the storm itself, a blanketing emptiness. Demonic power had summoned the tiny little demons here, and the storm dragged *it* down, too. It attacked the energy of the summonings, coated it in ice and dragged it down.

The hellhounds whimpered, feeling something go wrong but powerless to do anything. Something that they weren't prepared to handle. The *mokoi* struggled more, as they couldn't handle the temperature change. They were creatures of warmth, weak creatures used to comfort. They never had to struggle.

They never had to suffer.

I tapped into the power of the blizzard, an elemental force as great or greater than any magic. It was like an engine powering the spell. The snow was never allowed to settle on the ground—it fell, but the sweeping winds kept picking it back up before it touched the ground and melted. The sky was a whiteout, and even though Trey was only a few feet away from me, I couldn't even pick out his shape anymore.

Everything should be like this, I found myself thinking, as my body relaxed in the cold. Everything else was muted underneath the cold, and nothing else mattered.

I fed the power of the storm into the demons, tapping

into the power that had summoned them here. The last time, I'd overpowered a hellhound by plugging it in to a much, much stronger source of magical energy. This time, I needed to find the original source.

With the demons nearly slowed to a halt, that left me free to try. I tapped into the shadowy, toxic power that had summoned the demons, drawing them out of wherever they existed when they weren't here.

Charged with the storm's fury, I traced the spells back to their source. I felt myself moving faster than sound and swifter than air as I followed the trail. The spells were still chained to the hellhounds, a link that kept them from simply being unraveled. We could kill the hellhounds, or destroy them, but under normal circumstances we couldn't send them back. Not when there was a stronger link already in place.

The trail led me through the city, and part of me lit up with focus. They would lead me back to Lucien, and I could finally stop this once and for all. I could finally stop *him*. Before anyone else got hurt.

But then we were descending through the city, down past blacktop streets and sewer lines. I couldn't see where the path was taking me anymore, deep through the city's underbelly. We could have been going anywhere.

Except when the cavern opened in front of me, we weren't anywhere. I knew exactly where we were.

I just wasn't expecting what I found.

TWENTY-NINE

The cavern was something between Prohibition hideout, storm cellar, and cultist's dream vacation. Each of the walls was different—different materials, different sizes, different angles. The oldest parts were ancient brick, red and gray and black, evenly spaced between crumbling mortar that looked like nothing more than ground-up bones. Newer walls, or at least newer finishes, spread out here or there: half-walls and angles full of plaster, evidence of disappointing renovations and unfulfilled ambition.

The lights flickered in patterns that seemed strange at first, but then I saw the wall of candles. Someone had stolen their decorating motif from a church. There were probably over a hundred. It was a fire hazard waiting for a spark.

The flickering of the lights also revealed the circle etched into the floor. Etched wasn't the right word, though. For most of the cellar, the floor was a solid looking, single piece of concrete. But right here, in front of the candles, there was a circular patch of... something else. It was dark like obsidian, and just as reflective, but even just looking at it, I felt strange.

It was reflective, yes, but it was a sort of possessive reflection. Like once your image fell onto the dark mirror, it wouldn't ever let it go. And standing at the tip of it, wearing his trademark black suit, was Matthias Sexton.

"It took you long enough," Matthias said, his eyes trained on my invisible form.

"Is this the part where I look surprised?" I asked. My spirit was here, but not my body. So I wasn't sure how it was I could speak, but the demon didn't seem to have any trouble hearing me.

He crouched down carefully, and pulled a handkerchief out of his pocket, and dabbed at the obsidian, wiping away a spot. "I'd never make the mistake of underestimating you. That was Lucien's folly. But then, he never learned to adapt."

"And you did?"

He rose back up, inclining an eyebrow around him. "Lucien needed minions who could go out while he could not. This is not my battle. You and I are not enemies, boy."

"You've been helping him. You're just as guilty."

Matthias exhaled slowly. "And here I was hoping tonight's episode would have forced you to step up your game and start paying attention. You still have no clue what's really going on, do you?"

The winter voice brought forth everything it knew about him. Images that surged forth, like the witch eyes, but different. Ordered instead of chaos. Structured instead of random. It was like pulling information directly from an encyclopedia. The winter voice read it aloud to me.

The Grimm was one of the first demons to walk the streets

of the city-trap, bound into the bedrock of the first building con-
secrated to the Holy Lord of the Bound and Fallen. Grimms are
old, some of the oldest of the Rider-progeny, and effective when
tethered. They hold dominion over the dogs and curs, and know
a man's heart with only a touch.

The widow-witch Grace hobbled him, shattering the church
he was constrained to protect, leaving only a pair of stones left in
the foundation. As long as those stones remain, so he remains. As
troublesome as the demon was, I could not grant him the release
he sought. Someday, he might be necessary. Someday, I might
have need of him.

Pray that day never comes.

Matthias flicked his wrist, and the bank of candles went
out. I felt the link that I'd followed back here start to unravel,
and as it snapped, I was torn from the city back to my body
in the clearing.

¤   ¤   ¤

"What the hell?"

Trey was spinning around, his knife still poised for fighting. I could see the gooseflesh covering his skin, the shudders
of a cold that had passed in my absence. The blizzard was
gone, dissipated, and the demons along with it. Matthias had
banished the demons back to where they belonged.

"It's over," I said, wavering.

Trey was there before I could fall. My knees gave out,
and the adrenaline high of channeling so much power
through me washed away, leaving me empty and wiped out.

I heard the knife strike snowy ground, abandoned the instant I fell.

"He just let them go," I said, grabbing his arms with what little strength I had.

"Shh," Trey said, pulling me close.

The temperature was turning back to normal, but even as wiped out as I was, I could feel movement in the sky above us. Elemental magic was reacting with the weather, as a storm front of magical impossibilities reacted against the natural weather pattern. Things were in flux.

One doesn't antagonize the natural order without consequences, the winter voice murmured, caustic and amused.

I couldn't worry about the weather right now, though. If something was set into motion, then I'd have to deal with it later. "He just let them go," I said again, as if I could make Trey understand through simple repetition.

"Who?"

"Matthias. The demons…they were all because of him." I wondered about the connection. If Grace had broken him, trapped *him* in Belle Dam the same way she'd trapped Lucien, then why did she use hellhounds to guard her grave?

"I'll kill him," Trey breathed.

"He's not the problem right now," I reminded him. "Lucien is. We have to find him."

Trey didn't back down, but he did pull me closer. His arms tightened around me. "He went after my sister, Braden. There are rules. I can't just let him attack my family and not *do* something."

"They thought that way after my mother died, too," I said, and Trey flinched. But he didn't pursue it further.

Drew was curled up underneath one of the trees, in wolf form. The silver sheen spread over him, and as I watched, his shoulders widened and his muzzle retracted. His body elongated and became more human ... all except one of his legs. The transformation got almost all the way through, but as the leg wouldn't shift out of its wolfen form, the entire process reversed.

Drew whined, getting up long enough to circle around and lay back down again. Even from this distance, I could see a mat of red on one of his hind legs, and the limp in his steps. One of the *mokoi* must have done this.

"Stop!" I shouted, as I saw the silver sheen starting to spread again. Trying to change too much had almost killed him the last time. "Wait!"

Even though the wolf was probably half the size that Drew normally was, it was about twice as intimidating. Ice-blue eyes narrowed at me, and for a second my body reacted in typical fight-or-flight. Angry wolves were completely different from angry hellhounds.

"Remember last time?" I pushed, trying to collect my thoughts. My brain was still a little jumbled from all the magic. "Give it a minute, Drew."

"Last time?" Trey asked.

"He almost died," I said, lowering my voice. Not that it mattered. Apparently wolves hear very well. Drew growled, and I gave him a dirty look. "Well, you did." *I'm having an argument with a wolf. Not my finest hour.*

Trey looked me over. "Are you okay? Other than the collapsing. None of them hurt you, did they?"

"I'm okay," I said, finally starting to extricate myself from him. Standing on my own two feet, that sort of thing. But I couldn't give up the contact entirely, and slipped my hand into his while I surveyed the clearing. With the return to a normal temperature, most of the snow was melting off, though the ground was now thoroughly drenched.

By morning, there wouldn't even be any evidence of a blizzard. Assuming the weather held out.

But something was still bothering me. "He was expecting me."

Trey turned back to look at me. Jade had appeared on the front porch, and Trey was cautiously waving her forward. "What?" he asked, startled.

"Matthias," I said. "He was expecting me." I squinted, trying to remember what I'd seen. "There's tunnels ... or a subbasement under Downfall. He was down there. He'd summoned the hellhounds, and he was just ... waiting. To see if he needed to summon more, I think."

"But you're sure he stopped. That he won't be summoning more?"

I shook my head. "No, I felt him shut the connection down. It would take him awhile to summon that many demons again." Matthias was here because Grace had a thing for hobbling demons. Was she his test subject? To see if it would work? "We have to go to Downfall."

Trey looked surprised. "Wait. What? Why?"

I was speaking, but it was like I'd taken a back seat in

my own head. Suddenly, Lucien wasn't nearly the threat I'd thought he was, and all I could concentrate on was stopping Matthias. He was a loose cannon. *A traitor.* "He needs to be put down. We can't have an errant demon running around starting fires when we're trying to fix what's broken. We destroy whatever parts of the foundation are left, and Matthias goes back where he came from."

"Just like that."

I nodded. "Just like that."

Trey pursed his lips, his eyes focused but thoughtful. "You can't just go around blowing up buildings," he said gently.

"No," I corrected. "Not the building. Just part of the foundation. A few bricks. They built the warehouses on top of the remains of the church. So we just have to go down into that basement, and we can get rid of Matthias once and for all."

"I thought you were focused on Lucien. On stopping him."

"I am," I said immediately. "I mean, I was." But once the idea of removing Matthias had occurred to me, it just kept looping through my brain. Lucien's threat was growing smaller by the minute, while Matthias's was increasing exponentially.

Trey's eyes narrowed. "Are you sure you're okay?"

My voice picked up speed. "Don't you see? Jason was trying to buy up property down by the harbor. I think he was trying to buy Matthias's loyalty. A demon to replace the one he lost." *No, this isn't right. That's not what I mean.* But my thoughts were quiet, and my mouth moved before I even knew I was saying.

"He didn't lose Lucien. He went rogue."

"We can worry about Lucien later," I said, my hand waving dismissively.

"What the hell's going on?" Jade called, running over to us. "Those were—were—"

Trey looked at me, then at his sister. He dropped my hand, then grabbed her by the shoulders. "You're okay?" he asked intently.

"Yeah, we're fine." Jade's eyes were showing white all around, and her skin was an unnatural shade of white. It took a lot for the tanned and toned Jade to look pale. "Gentry…"

"Everything's going to be fine," he said. "We're going to get you home. And then we're going to make sure they never come after you again."

"Make sure *who* doesn't come after me?" Jade asked.

But Trey wouldn't answer her.

"You think they're really going to give up? Just like that?" Drew came sauntering up, moving gingerly. He wouldn't let himself be seen limping, but it was clear his weight was shifted strangely. I could almost see some of the tension in his face.

"Matthias walked away. For now. But we have to stop him." I said. I was forgetting something. Or there were pieces I hadn't put together yet.

Trey gave me another one of those inscrutable looks, and pulled me away from the others, off towards the tree line. "What's going on with you?"

"Nothing!"

"I'm taking you home," Trey decided. "Jade's okay now, and the threat's gone. But you're acting strange."

"I'm fine," I insisted. *Am I?*

Over his shoulder, I saw Jade and Drew still facing each other. Jade bit her lower lip, Drew saying something I couldn't hear. Whatever had happened between them in the past, they never actually spoke anymore. There was always Trey or Riley to run interference. So now, when it was just the two of them, and I saw them watching each other, I realized something. They stared at each other with a hunger, like they couldn't get enough. Quite the opposite of two people who claimed to hate one another.

Trey noticed I was looking away from him, and turned. I grabbed his shirt and pulled him towards me just as I saw Jade pulling Drew to her in much the same manner.

He held me without complaint, probably thinking that I needed the comfort. But I was busy trying to figure out why my head felt so funny, like it had been lined with tiny bits of bubble wrap. Things that should have been sharp, dagger-like thoughts were bubbled over. I couldn't even summon up a trace of the anger and misery that had been plaguing me lately.

Stop Matthias, the winter voice urged. But as the last of the adrenaline trickled out of my blood, my body sagged, and exhaustion clung to me like a second skin. The winter voice strategized. *Rest first. Regain your strength. Use it to break him.*

"I need you to take me home," I said, parroting Trey's words back at him. "Right now."

I got another look for my trouble. "Okay."

"I'll take him," Drew said, having disentangled himself from Jade while we were talking.

"*I'm* taking him," Trey said. "Jade, you can ride in the back."

Jade huffed, but she didn't argue. Surprisingly, neither did Drew. Trey led me to the passenger side, and I hated how hard my hand gripped at his. I needed to hold onto *something*. Otherwise, I would suffocate inside my own head.

"You're okay," he whispered.

For now.

thirty

I barely remembered making it into the house and into my bed. There was just a hazy memory of Trey in the driver's seat, saying something lost in fog. When I woke the next morning, the house was even quieter than normal. Impressive, since the Thorpe manor made mausoleums look cacophonous by comparison. No one came to wake me up, even though the clock at my bedside innocently suggested I'd slept through half the morning, breakfast, and the start of school.

"You still sleep like the dead."

It was only because of the haze of sleep still clinging to me that I didn't immediately recognize it was John in the room with me. "Leave me alone," I muttered, dropping back down onto the pillow.

John. John was here. Here *in Jason's house.* I bolted back up to a sitting position. "What are you doing?"

"He put you in the east wing," John mused. "That's curious. I thought for sure you'd end up in his old room, or maybe mine. Somewhere he could keep an eye on you." He casually moved around the room, taking it all in. As if he was just another visitor, and not a fugitive.

"Uncle John!" This was bad. Dangerous. Someone might have seen him. It was already becoming an open secret that John was back in town, but to actually come into the *house*?

"Jason left this morning with an overnight bag," John said, moving towards the window and pulling back the curtain. "Take it easy."

"You keep telling me not to worry," I said furiously, "but people keep finding out you're here. You *suck* at undercover."

At that he smiled, the faint twist of his lips that meant he was trying to be serious, and I'd surprised him. I knew almost every expression that John's face could make, I'd seen them all a thousand times. *What did I say? What's so funny?*

"You need to relax," he said, still staring out the window.

That was when it dawned on me. "You *want* them to know you're here," I said in wonder. "You want them talking."

Another quick flash of a smile, before it descended into a lighter version of Jason's normally dour expression. "No need for you to worry about that."

"Are you kidding?" I was out of bed in a flash. "*Jason* knows you're here. He's probably got people on red alert if you come back to the house. You have to go!"

John's inscrutable expression remained, and he didn't pick up my urgency. "My brother and I have already had words," he said carefully, "which might have had something to do with his choice of luggage this morning."

"He left town because of you?" I asked. "Why?"

John inclined an eyebrow. *I keep my secrets close*, the gesture said.

"This is crazy," I said. "You have to leave. Once Catherine finds out, she'll come after you. Trey already knows; it's only a matter of time until he tells."

"Gone for a couple of months and suddenly you think you know everything," John said, still at ease. This didn't make any sense. John hated people. He hated being cheerful and positive. He crossed the room, and stood in front of the mirror hanging just behind the door. But he didn't look at himself: his reflection watched me.

Maybe it was just you he hated, the serpent's voice in my head provided. *Now that you're gone, his life can begin again.*

"What do you think you're going to do? Kill Lucien? I tried that."

"There is always a bargain to be made," John said under his breath. He cleared his throat, and raised his voice. "Jason said you were troubled. That Lucien's death was hard on you."

I scoffed. "I wouldn't take anything Jason said at face value."

"Oh, I know very well how to react to the things my brother tells me." His eyes kept staring into me. I shifted, and turned away from his reflection. "But in this instance, I think he was right. While he may not be a fan of *having* emotions, your father is very perceptive when it comes to recognizing them."

"Don't call him that!"

John feigned surprise. "What? Your father? However

285

much of a failure he is at it," and there was a particular note of pride when he said that, "he is still your father."

See? He never wanted you. He couldn't be more glad to be rid of you.

"Braden?" John turned away from the mirror. "What's wrong?"

Thought after thought fluttered to the surface, a thousand things I wanted to say, or scream, but none of them were just right. "You couldn't tell me the truth, I get that." And I did—I understood the nature of the *geas* and how John couldn't have told me the truth even if he wanted to. "But you could have prepared me. You *had* to know I'd come back here eventually. It was inevitable."

He collected you like his thirty pieces of silver and fled like a coward under the cloak of night. You were nothing more than the price of his freedom.

"There was only one person who thought it was inevitable."

I hated him. Hated the way he had to *think* so hard just to answer me. The glib, serene smile that was foreign on his face. "I'll take the fortune-telling demon's word on this. I don't like it, but I saw it for myself. He had a hundred different strings that he could pull to recover me. And *you should have made sure I was ready!*"

I knew I sounded belligerent, but I couldn't help it. The words came out carrying venom I didn't expect. But the more I thought of it, the more the anger soaked into my thoughts. It was like there was an entire cavern inside of me, filled to the brim with rage and grace, and it couldn't help but ease through any crack it could find.

"If it had been up to me, we would still be at home," John said. But whether that was an explanation, or an apology, I couldn't tell. "I would have protected you."

"You would have *died*."

"You don't know that."

"Did you really think that Lucien was just going to forget about me? You *knew* I was different. You're not stupid, you had to know. Lucien helped you escape because it kept *me* safe. Safe until he came to collect me."

John blanched. "Braden, I never—I—" but whatever he wanted to say, he couldn't get the words out.

"You were happy to get rid of me," I said. The words just kept pouring out, half-thoughts that had never fully formed, and feelings I'd never cast to light before. "You were scared of me. Jealous. Every day reminding you that you were your father's least favorite, the runt of the litter, the one my mother never looked twice at." Things were spilling out so fast, I didn't stop to think where they came from. "The only thing you ever succeeded at was failing. You were grateful for the excuse to run, happy you never had to wake up another morning in the town that laughed at you."

"Who are you?" He was deathly calm, but he looked like he'd aged twenty years in a matter of seconds.

"You never wanted me to control the visions. You *wanted* me to die. Because I was everything you were never able to be. You had to try to sleep at night knowing I was the Thorpe everyone wanted, that I was the only one that Jason would ever acknowledge as an equal. You could practice and plot for a hundred years, and still never measure up. That's why you never begat children of your own; deep down so terrified that they too would surpass you."

I had to stop to catch my breath, winded after the explosion that had come out of me. My chest was heaving, my heartbeat a drum solo that nearly had me splitting out of my skin. It was just like before, during the fight with Carter. Except this time I didn't need to touch him to see the soft spots in John's soul. They sang out to me, like a martyr begging for purpose.

"You're not my nephew," John said, his hands clasped in front of him. "So I'll ask you again. Who are you?"

"You don't like what you hear, and I'm not your nephew anymore?" I sneered. "You really are a Thorpe, aren't you? Just like Jason. One toy breaks, and he's off searching for another. No skin off his nose."

"You're still his son."

"I'm his *nothing*! I'm a failed plot that cost him twenty years of his life. Only I couldn't die quietly, and I didn't have the decency to waste away in silence."

"Who are you?" he asked again, this time his voice ringing off the walls.

"You know exactly who I am," I snarled. "I'm exactly what I have to be. You know, I couldn't get away fast enough? Anything was better than watching you hold me back."

"I could tell something was off the other night." Even though I'd pressed at half a dozen buttons that should have had him curling up on his side, John stood his ground.

The cold fury inside of me hesitated, unfamiliar with prey that didn't split apart at the seams and collapse under the weight of their frailties. John was resilient, like a break-wall against the storm. "There's nothing you can use against me that I haven't come to terms with. It's true: I ran, and I ran for all the wrong reasons. I earned my infamy. I know the minds of demons, I know their tricks. I will never be his victim again."

"I..." But the winter voice provided nothing. Something buried deep inside of me was rising, and the winter voice *recoiled,* slithering deep down where light couldn't reach. I stared at John, the well of fury draining like someone pulled the plug out of the bottom of the bathtub. I still felt like I could explode at any moment, but now it was because there was too much inside of me—a feather's weight more and I would burst.

John's face softened, just a tick. "One time, you must have been five or six, you didn't want to go to bed. Said you were going to hold your breath until I changed my mind. And then, when that didn't work, you said you weren't going to wear your night goggles and you didn't care what happened."

I didn't recognize the memory. I shook my head, trying to pull the fractured pieces of my feelings together. I was angry...wasn't I? Ten seconds ago, everything had been clear and crystal, and now my head was floating, the blood coursing too hot and too fast.

"What did you do to yourself?" John asked. He brushed the fringe off my forehead, his hand warm against my head.

My breath hitched. I'd become so used to letting the words

come out on their own that now in their absence, I was at a loss. The numbing agent in my blood retreated, and it *hurt*.

"I—I—" But once the floodgates opened, there wasn't any room for words. John pulled me close, and I sobbed into his shoulder, tears that burned my ducts and scoured across my skin.

I cried for everything I'd done since coming to Belle Dam, the lies I'd told, the people I'd hurt. I cried for the fact that I'd shot someone, for the knowledge that I could take a life in the heat of the moment. Everything that had been pushed down, bottled up, or frozen underneath the winter voice, I let it out.

"It's okay," John whispered, stroking my hair like he did when I was little. He was even just as gruff as he was when I was younger, as though consoling a child was too much for him, but he couldn't help but do it.

"How long has this been going on?" he asked, releasing me slowly.

I shook my head. Ever since I'd come to Belle Dam? Ever since I killed him?

"You can't run from what you're feeling, kid. Even if it sucks. Trust me, I know better than anyone what … your home can do to you." His cadence changed halfway through, like a skipped record. Still bound by the *geas,* John couldn't offer comfort without a cost.

"I know that's not you," he added, tapping my chest. "You're still the same boy you were at home. All they can try to do is make you forget."

It took me a minute to find my voice. But Uncle John

was right—I was still the same person I'd been in Montana. The same person who'd run away in order to protect him. "You have to go," I said. "You can't stay. It's too dangerous."

He smiled, the rare smile that was as much *no worries* as it was *trust me*. "I've only got one errand left."

"And then you'll go?" I pushed. "Please?"

John looked at me sternly and sidestepped the question. "You have to fight—" but the rest of his words were drowned out in white noise and a piercing tone like an angel scratching a blackboard on the head of a pin.

My legs buckled, but he caught me.

"Do you—" But again, the words were swallowed up in light, sound, and static. Things happened, he moved and motioned with his hands, but I could barely even see him, the noises were so loud.

I covered at my ears, as if that would help.

"Just one more stop," he promised, sitting me down on the edge of the bed. It took me a minute to get my bearings together. It was the winter voice, I was sure of it. I could feel it in the back of my head: a low, warning hiss. When the sound had finally died, and my body felt like my own again, I looked up, but John had left.

There was a stack of something on my desk that wasn't there yesterday. I crossed the room and picked it up. It was one of those Word-a-Day calendars, only this one was filled with sayings. John must have left it for me.

April 17th. The man who speaks the truth is always at ease.
—Persian proverb.

thirty-one

Storms raged the rest of the morning and into the afternoon. I didn't even consider leaving the house, not when monsoons kept sweeping in, and then vanishing as quickly as they began. The confrontation with John had scared me, and the onus of the winter voice had me rethinking all of my actions over the past few days. Actions I knew on some level were wrong, but I couldn't be bothered to care. Until now.

The winter voice had stayed buried ever since, and I used the relative lucidity to remember what I was supposed to be doing: looking for Lucien.

My phone rang while I was in the middle of some old-school dowsing. I'd spread out a map of Belle Dam onto one of Jason's no doubt priceless work desks and had tied a string around a smooth piece of quartz. The theory was that the quartz would spin until it detected what I was looking for, where it would drop on the map and reveal my destination.

In practice, it was the world's worst game ever.

"Where are you? Are you okay?" Trey asked, when I

flipped my phone open. I dropped the quartz on the desk and gave up.

"At home. My alarm never went off, and no one's here anyway. Jason must have given them all the day off. Where are you?" It was weird to think that we could have anything resembling a casual conversation, considering some of our angst-ridden arguments of late.

"Jade and I are coming over then. You're sure Jason's gone?"

"You're with Jade? And yeah, I'm sure."

Trey's voice was grim. "After yesterday? I'm not letting her out of my sight."

"So what's so urgent? Why risk coming here? I can meet you out behind the property."

"It's too out in the open," Trey said. "If Lucien makes another move on her, I don't want to be in the middle of nowhere."

The connection started to break up, static reminding me again of the winter voice. *How much was me, and how much was you?* I wondered, but got no reply.

"We'll be there soon," Trey promised.

Soon was relative, as they didn't show up for almost an hour. The storm had finally broken, giving a few minutes of peace when they jumped out of Trey's car. I held open the front door, waiting to usher them inside.

"I always expect Frankenstein's Castle, not *Architectural Digest*," Trey said, studying the foyer. Jade looked at me and rolled her eyes.

"Pretty sure this is a violation of some sort of treaty," I

said, still uncertain about having the pair of them *in Jason's house.* So far today it had been his wayward brother, and now the Lansing heirs. Jason would probably have preferred I just trash the house with a party.

"It is. You're going to have to pay us two goats and a handmade wreath," Trey responded blandly. He crossed to the far end of the foyer, and peaked into the sitting room. Or was that the drawing room? Whatever, it was pretentious and barely used.

"He was worried about you," Jade said softly, once Trey was out of earshot.

"You're okay?" I asked, forcing myself not to look after him.

She shrugged, the only hint that last night had taken a toll on her was in her eyes. Her flawless façade was perfection as always. "Not exactly the way I wanted to spend the night. I'd been planning a Ryan Gosling marathon and watching Tricia eat the majority of the ice cream." She sighed. "Of course Belle Dam had other plans."

"We're not going to let anything happen to you," I promised.

Jade didn't say anything, and I turned back to her to see her biting her lower lip. As soon as she realized I was looking, she turned away.

"What?" I asked, but Trey came back before the conversation could continue.

"Any idea what he's going to do next? He's not just going to give up or anything, right?"

I shook my head. "No, he still needs one more. And he

wants it to be someone that hurts me. Or maybe us," I said, looking at Trey. "Since you were there, too. That's what I've heard, anyway."

"And it has to be me?" Jade asked.

I hesitated.

Her expression was nervous. "I'm not the only person you're close to."

"Call her," I said immediately, my stomach twisting into knots. *Such an idiot, she* told *you this was going to happen.* My thoughts were tangled up in thorns of anxiety, a fresh wave with every new piece. She'd told me straight out. *"It's dangerous to be your friend, Braden. They all get hurt."*

"What?" Drew sounded annoyed when he picked up on the second ring, and I looked at Jade before answering. She shook her head again, her expression growing tense.

"Do you know where Riley is?"

"Considering her gold stars in attendance, my guess is whatever Advanced Placement for Dummies class she has in the afternoons," Drew replied, but his tone was guarded. "Why?"

"She's not in school," Jade said, as though we were all on the same wavelength. Her thumbs flew over her phone. "No one's seen her since yesterday."

"Is that Jade?" Drew asked through the phone, sounding suspicious. "Where are you? Is Golden Boy with her?"

"He came over to the house—" I started.

"—I bet he did—" Drew snorted.

"—and she's been with him all day! Now, what about Riley? Have you seen her since last night?"

"I took her to school this morning," Drew said. "She didn't say anything about leaving. You tried calling her?"

"Jade did."

"That's good, she'll pick up if Jade's calling." The unsaid part of that sentence being *she might not if you called her.*

"With everything that happened with Jade last night, I forgot about Riley," I admitted. "But Jade's right. If he wants to hurt me, she's not the only target."

"I'm on my way to her house," Drew said a moment later. "Remind me to kill her later." There was a startled pause, where we both realized what he'd said. He cleared his throat awkwardly, and added, "Sorry."

It was the gravity of the situation that kept me from commenting. Drew Armstrong, who had one of the filthiest mouths I knew, apologized for something he said? Somehow, that made things even worse.

"He's going by her house," I said, tucking the phone back into my pocket a few seconds later. I looked to Jade. "Still nothing?"

She shook her head. "I've called her twice, left a voice-mail, and sent a couple texts. I'm waiting to hear back from a couple of people I know from journalism, see if she showed up today."

"Try that Ben kid, I think they're friends," I said, picturing the preppy kid in my head.

Her face contorted for a moment. "Ben Chapman? Really? I didn't know that."

I shrugged. "I don't know his last name, but he mentioned her a couple of times.

Jade shrugged a *whatever* and went back to texting.

"You said you forgot about Riley," Trey said, leaning against the stairway banister. "Something happened before she called me last night, didn't it?"

"Long story," I said, exhaling slowly.

"So why'd he leave her alone if he knew she was in trouble?" Trey asked, almost like he couldn't help himself.

I'd hoped that the tentative cease-fire that had occurred in the aftermath of the demon fight would have carried over, but it looked like old habits were hard to break.

"I don't know," I said, because as much as I'd never admit it out loud, there was some truth to what Trey was saying. Drew was crazy overprotective, so why would he leave Riley on her own?

My phone rang a minute later. "House is empty," Drew said. "Doesn't look like anyone's been here since this morning."

"Where the hell are you, Riley?" I said under my breath. "You don't think she found out something about Lucien and didn't tell us, do you?"

"Knowing Riley, it's possible. I *knew* I shouldn't have left her alone. But she insisted. Claimed she had a deadline and she'd kill me with a cafeteria spork if I didn't let her go."

"So where've you been all day?" I asked.

"Staking out Matthias. For a demonic co-conspirator, he's got a taste for buddy comedies. He's been at the theater all day. It's kind of creepy, not gonna lie."

Matthias watching movies like a normal person? "He knows someone's watching him," I said, the only explanation that made sense. "So he either wants an alibi, or he's messing with you."

"All I need to know is that Riley's not with him. And if he's busy, that means he wasn't conjuring up a dog park full of demons to go grab her. I'll be there in fifteen." Drew hung up on me before I could get a response in.

I looked at the Lansing heirs, shrugging helplessly. "He'll be here in fifteen."

"Oh, fantastic," Trey snapped, throwing up his hands. "Just what we need."

"He helped save me last night," Jade pointed out softly.

While they talked, I headed back to the far side of the room, to the desk that held the map and the bit of quartz. I concentrated on Riley and tried to repeat the same scenario as before. But still, the quartz spun and spun, never locking down on a single spot. I dropped it in disgust.

"Right," Trey said, finally responding to Jade's defense of Drew. "I haven't forgotten."

"Are you sure?" she asked without any real heat.

I took a seat at the bottom of the stairs, and told myself it wasn't only because Trey was leaning against the railing. I just needed to sit. To think. "She's been obsessed with Lucien, and finding him, but how would she even know where to look?"

Drew said he'd be here in fifteen, but he made it in ten. He swaggered through the front door like it was his house, not mine.

"Anything?"

He got three simultaneous headshakes in response.

"Can't you just," Drew gestured dramatically. "Y'know?"

"Already tried," I said, openhandedly waving towards the desk to the rear. "Where would she go?"

"She wouldn't have gone anywhere by herself," Jade said suddenly, who'd shifted her position since Drew walked in so that her brother stood between the two of them.

I don't get her, I thought, and not for the first time.

"You can't know that," Drew said dismissively.

"I know how you think everyone who isn't you is a complete moron," Jade replied immediately, "but Riley's not stupid. She might have gone somewhere to do research, but she wouldn't have put herself in danger without some sort of backup. Most of which is currently *in this room*."

"Fine," Drew said grudgingly. "I suppose you're right."

That's when it hit me. "Wait. John gave me a magic phone." I almost slapped myself in the head, how could I have forgotten?

"Is that some sort of euphemism?" Jade asked, raising her eyebrows.

Drew barked out a laugh. "There's my girl."

Jade's expression cooled. "Drew, I'm going to put this as delicately as I can. Not your girl, never going to *be* your girl. You could never afford me."

Then Trey was the one who laughed. He'd been fairly quiet since Drew walked in, but it was like his sister's condemnation was enough to stir him back to life. "Magic phone? Explain," he said, turning to me.

"He didn't give me much more than that," I said, but I hurried back to the desk and the map. "But if it's spelled,

I might be able to pick up on it. I know what John's magic feels like—almost as well as I know my own."

Sure enough, it only took me seconds to feel out the traces of John's magic through the quartz. This time the stone smacked down on the map like it suddenly weighed a hundred pounds.

That can't be right. For more than one reason. Why would Riley be at the high school now, if she hadn't been there all day? And the stone had landed exactly where it had the last time, when I'd been sure that the dowsing hadn't worked.

"She's … at school."

"Good enough for me," Drew said, reaching for my elbow. "Come on, you can ride with me."

"He's not going with you!" Trey said immediately, coming to my other side.

"You just going to leave baby sister here all alone?" Drew asked, his eyebrow raised insolently. "What happens if this is another trick?"

The truth of it hit Trey right in the face. His eyes went wide, and his skin paled and flushed in equal measure. He stared at me, looking hopelessly lost. "I … "

"Don't be a fuck, Drew," Jade said, the condemnation somehow sounding worse coming off of Jade's crisp voice. "You can't leave me behind, and you two aren't going by yourselves. Problem solved, we'll all go."

I shook myself. "I don't think—"

"Argument over," Jade said firmly, and headed for the door.

thirty-two

My heart wouldn't stop thudding in my chest—I was sure Drew could feel it hammering against his spine on the ride to school. I was shivering by the time I climbed off the back of the bike. Trey pulled up a few seconds behind us.

The city was eerily silent, punctuated only by the sound of Trey's car doors slamming shut. Belle Dam had tucked itself into bed, snuggled up to its ignorance. As if I needed the reminder that we were on our own.

It was in the air almost from the moment we'd approached the school. I wasn't the only one who noticed, either. Drew's nose was scrunched up, like we'd driven to a landfill or compost heap. Jade's eyes kept darting around, trying to lock down something she couldn't quite see. And Trey was tense and taut, looking as severe as I'd ever seen him.

"He's here," I said. There was demonic power in the air, pouring out of the school like gas. Riley wasn't alone. But had Lucien already taken her? Or was there still time?

I was the first one through the doors. The hallways at the front of the school were all dark. The three of them were still by the door, moving so slowly. Jade had her arm wrapped around her brother's, her lower lip caught between her teeth. Trey had grabbed the knife from the night before, which gleamed against the street lights shining in through the glass doors.

I was already at the front hall, waiting for them to catch up. *What's taking them so long? We don't have time for this.*

The main hall of the school was blocked off by a pair of doors that were perpetually left open. As I crossed over the doorway, taking my first step into the main hallway, the air was thick. Not thick like muggy, but thick like pudding. I *felt* the air resisting me as I pushed through, and it wasn't until I emerged on the other side that I realized.

"Oh, hell," I whispered.

The doors behind me slammed shut. Metal shrieked against metal, and I nearly leapt out of my skin. Lunging back, I pushed the bar in, but the door wouldn't budge. The locks refused to disengage. The air was charged with something electric and dank. The heating vents died, the buzzing of hallway lights faded, and it was as if everything held its breath. Waiting.

"Braden!" Trey pounded on the other side. Through the tiny window running up the middle, I saw the three of them, with Drew bringing up the rear. Something was said between them, I couldn't hear what, then Jade jumped out of the way. I watched the two boys count, and on three the pair launched themselves at the door.

I could have told them it wouldn't work. They fell back,

the combined impact barely shaking the doors at all. The doors wouldn't open until Lucien wanted them open.

He wanted to separate us. He wanted me weak.

But we don't always get what we want.

"Lucien!" His name echoed off the walls, bounced off of lockers and up the stairwells. The lights flickered in response. From inside the rows of lockers framing either side of me came hollow noises, like aluminum cans being scratched by tiny claws. Or small monsters, nursing their way out of the darkness.

He was toying with me.

"Riley!" But she didn't—or couldn't—answer. I tried to convince myself that she was fine—that Lucien wouldn't hurt her until he absolutely had to. Some part of me knew Lucien's process, and knew that he wouldn't hurt Riley unless he could do it in front of me. It wasn't just the pain he caused that he relished, but also the pain he'd leave behind.

I turned back to the three of them. "I'll be fine." They couldn't hear me, but my meaning was clear enough.

Trey's jaw had locked, and he stared through the window like he could force his way through, if only he wanted it badly enough. Drew looked down, his expression turbulent. Only Jade was truly upset: I saw the emotion in her eyes. This might not have a happy ending, and Jade knew that. I never gave her enough credit.

Drew said something on the other side of the glass, pointing emphatically to somewhere behind Trey. Their faces lifted, and they disappeared from my view.

I couldn't wait around to see what they were up to. My

footsteps sounded like gunshots as I half walked, half jogged down the hallway. I kept expecting him to pop out of every corner. To emerge from every shadow. Each time I passed a doorway, I hesitated for a second. Waiting to see if this was the one he was hiding in.

"You're hiding now?" I called. "Am I really that scary?"

The lights flickered again. Behind me, they went out entirely. Every strip of lights I passed went out the moment I was out of range. He wanted the shadows to keep nipping at my heels, I supposed.

Riley screamed, somewhere in the distance. The sound crawled against my skin, making my hair stand on end. *She'll be okay. She has to be okay.* My pace picked up, and the fluorescent lights popped loudly, going out as I passed under them. My pace quickened, now a fight to stay ahead of the darkness.

I should have taken a weapon. Brought something with me. We'd used the gun last time, and maybe that hadn't worked out so well in the long run, but it helped in the heat of the moment.

Lucien appeared behind me before I reached the end of the hallway. Some part of me just *knew.* I stopped running, and turned back to the wall of darkness that had been nipping at my heels. It was like he'd always been there, waiting for me. He had Riley in front of him, his hand around her throat and wearing her like a human shield. Lucien's inhumanity was obvious, now. His skin was cracked and segmented, broken up almost like a snake's scales. Black and green rot appeared in the crevices, patched together like some sort of Frankenstein monster. His face was even worse, the scales and demonic essence underneath had consumed half of his face.

The sacrifices were supposed to be healing him, but were they faulty? Was he like me, broken beyond repair?

The bullet hole I'd put through his skull was gone, the eye healed. Only now it was a solid black, except for the iris, which was an unnatural, cornflower blue, like a ring tossed in the center of a pool of ichor.

"Let her go."

"You have become such a disappointment," he breathed. Unlike the rest of him, his voice was just as I remembered it.

"Everything's going to be okay, Riley," I said. Her neck was stretched and exposed, her head thrown back and scared eyes tracking me, doing everything she could to alleviate the pressure of his hand against her throat.

"Will it? Are you sure?" Lucien's fingers gripped her tighter, and I watched as Riley's eyes go white all around as she tried to lift herself up even more.

"Leave her alone!" I started forward, but Lucien raised his free hand, his index finger shaking at me.

"No, no, no. I've been waiting for this little chat of ours. I would hate for things to end prematurely."

I froze where I was. "Then let her go. And we'll talk." I held up my hands, showing that I wasn't armed. "There aren't any guns this time."

"Funny boy," Lucien hissed. His demon eye regarded me with something like consideration. "But I made this little girl a promise." His eyes on me, he leaned forward. His teeth slowly started to close, as though he was going to start nibbling on her ear. "Unless you can make a better offer."

"What do you want?" This was part of his plan, I realized. Making me some kind of offer. He had something in mind. Some plan that I was still crucial to.

Lucien smiled. I hated it when he smiled. "I went to a lot of trouble to keep in touch. Have you misplaced our conversations already? Those Thorpe traditions I told you about."

My stomach sickened. How could I forget? "You want me to kill him? Jason?"

Lucien inclined his head, as if patiently awaiting my response.

I tried to consider the possibilities, to see the situation as Lucien would. Killing Jason would leave Catherine victorious, and the feud essentially over. I could never replace Jason, nor would I want to. And Lucien *wanted* the feud to escalate: he wanted war in Belle Dam. For things to escalate until chaos consumed us all.

"That's not it," I said, shaking my head. "That's the last thing you would want."

"Someone's been paying attention after all," he whispered.

"Then what *do* you want?" I looked again at Riley. Really looked. I didn't think he'd done anything to her, but it was hard to tell. She was utterly, completely silent. *Did he do something to her already?*

"I WANT WHAT WAS STOLEN FROM ME," Lucien suddenly roared, composure be damned, his face green and red fury. His cornflower iris expanded as his pupils shrank in rage.

I remained very still, like an animal in the eyes of a predator. Lucien was unhinged. Something hadn't gone according to plan, I just didn't know what.

"Ahem." Lucien made a show of loosening his nonexistent tie. He swallowed. "That was ... regrettable."

"You have my friend. I'm willing to talk."

Lucien's posture changed, his stance shifting towards Riley, as if he just remembered that she was in his possession. "But she's had years to prepare. I even gave her fair warning. Beyond fair." The corners of his cracked lips turned up. "How many people can know the details of their death?"

"Why her?" I asked, my eyes narrowing. "You knew this would happen. But why *her*?"

"The hurt her death will cause you, not to mention her destiny snipped out so completely. There are many factors."

No, I thought. *There's something more there. Some reason Lucien wanted her dead.* But why Riley? Intrepid girl reporter that she might be, she wasn't much of a threat to something like Lucien.

"I'll stop you," I said. I'd never been so serious in my life.

Lucien's good eyebrow raised. "Is that so?" he rasped. The split in the skin of his hand slipped, and something green and alien pulsed through. At first, I thought it was pus oozing out of the crack between demonic flesh and human skin, but then I realized what it really was, and I stepped back.

Thank god I hadn't eaten anything this morning. Because there, between the flaps of skin that made up Lucien's hand, in the green space where his demonic essence shone through, there was an *eye*. An eye in his hand, flat against his skin, like it had always and would always be there. The eye matched the demonic eye on his face, black with a cornflower ring.

I couldn't stop staring at it. And then part of me wondered if there were eyes everywhere, hidden beneath his human cage. I almost started heaving right then and there.

Lucien looked down, to see what caught my eye. "You've seen worse," he said, sounding pleased with my discomfort. "I even suppose you've done worse. So squeamish. If only Jason and Catherine could see their exalted weapon now."

"They'll come after you, once they realize you've gone rogue," I said, hoping that it was true. If Jason and Catherine could be made to see reason they would, at least. Although whether or not they would cooperate was a different story. "They'll never trust you again, not after what you've done."

"Do you think I fear them?" Lucien's demon eye rolled in its socket. "And who's to say I've even *gone* rogue. I've prepared for this, just as I prepared for a hundred other outcomes. There is *always* a contingency plan, little boy. That is the benefit to eternity."

"You tried to kill me, and you tried to kill Trey. That's powerful motivation. They'll come after you. Destroying you won't even be a challenge to them."

"And yet they're nothing like you," he said scornfully. He traced his fingers along Riley's neck, and she stiffened. "Pretenders to a throne that belongs to you alone. They dress up in Mother and Father's clothes, but they will always be lacking. They are not fit to wash your feet, nor will they ever be."

"Let her go, Lucien," I said to the ruined, lizard-cracked skin that was once Belle Dam's most renowned lawyer. I had to keep control of this conversation. Lucien's tangents only proved that his death was not without consequences.

"Witches and *warlocks*," he spat, as if he had not heard me. "As if those words hold any meaning. They are spawn."

"Then what does it mean?" I asked, unable to help myself.

"In the old days, they were hedge witches, scrambling to perform a fraction of the feats that the sorcerers could do merely by snapping their fingers." He snapped his fingers, his sneer widening. "Some say angels first taught man to wield the power primeval. They would be mistaken."

If not angels, then that meant... "You did. The Riders."

Lucien inclined his head. "So we did. We created *you*, the sorcerers. But human blood is weak, and your offspring too frail to wield the true power. In a dozen generations, there might be *one* true birth, and only then if the stars align."

Sorcery. Was that it, then? "Then how am I here, Lucien?" If I could just keep him talking. Maybe I could figure something out. Some way to save her.

"You were the most likely outcome, obviously," he rasped, disdain dripping from his voice. "A century of pruning your family tree, pairing one generation with the perfect mate."

"So the witch eyes..."

He waved his hand away. "A birthright, I've told you before. Only I'd forgotten how unpredictable they make you." His lips tightened, threatened to crack apart. "Free will, so frustrating. How I despise *choice*."

"A birthright that's killing me."

"You could have struck a bargain," he said silkily, the smoothness of his words at odds with the broken, scaled oozing of his skin.

"I don't want your power," I said. "I'll manage somehow. Jason will find a way." Neither of us believed me, but it didn't matter.

"Warlocks," he sneered. "They twist a mind here or there, or unravel a secret. Theirs is the power of parlor tricks. You, my boy, you are descended from ones who raised up plagues. We taught you to shatter mountains and to raze whole worlds with storms that would not end. We made you gods." His eyes were dismissive. "You chose to be forgotten."

"Until Grace." There was something there. Something had changed with her.

His expression grew colder. "Enough of this," he spat. "The bitch caught me off guard once, but you are no more her heir than she is," he said, shaking Riley. "The time for games is long since past."

"Then let's talk about agendas," Uncle John said, his voice echoing down the dark hallway.

thirty-three

John came in from behind the demon, down one of the darkened side hallways that splintered off from the main. "What are you doing here?" I half asked, half whispered.

"It took you long enough," Lucien said caustically. "Disrupting my schedule, yet another Thorpe family trait I loathe."

John's eyes were locked on Lucien. His boots thudded against the tile, a hard kind of sound. Like a heartbeat. I turned back to Lucien, and he mockingly bowed, gesturing my uncle forward.

"This was your last errand? To see Lucien?" I asked. What was he *doing* here?

"Enlighten the boy, Jonathan," Lucien said with a smile. "He wants to know the master plan."

"Is that the game, then? Try to turn us against each other?" John looked to me then, and it was familiar and foreign all at once. He'd always been *John*—flannel and jeans and all. But now his graying black hair was slicked back, like his brother's. And he was dressed all in black. Like his brother. He looked like a funeral director. Like his brother.

Lucien's head dipped. "Doesn't he have reason to suspect you? The boy is smart enough, I'm sure he's wondered about the timing of your return." His slow smile built, filling with smug satisfaction.

"I'm done letting you manipulate my family," John said.

"Dear old Jonathan, you cast off your family a lifetime ago."

"Braden is my family," he snarled.

"Technically speaking," Lucien said thoughtfully, "I am the one who brought him into this world. And we share a nature and power. I would say my claim is stronger."

Pressure started building in my head, like clouds of gauze were being stuffed into it. "I—I told you already," I said, struggling to find the words. "I'm nothing like you. John's right. *He's* my family."

Lucien rolled his good eye. The demonic one stayed trained on me. "Family loyalty," he sneered. "As if either of you ever appreciated the Thorpes a day in your life." He looked down at Riley, yanked her up enough that her heels left the ground and she struggled to gain some sort of balance.

I heard her squeal.

I reacted without thinking, even while John was shouting, "Stop!" I drew power to me, instinctively drawing from the store of power under Grace's monument. The pressure in my head increased, just enough that I didn't stop to think about what I was doing. I reacted.

The power flowed into me, and out through my outstretched hand. I wanted him to stop, but more than anything I wanted him to *hurt*. As the power flowed it hardened, snapped apart and forged together, link by link, until a chain like seething sunsets and melancholy blue shot out from my fingertips.

The spell chain whipped out from my hand, straining towards him. Lucien held up his free hand, complete with reddening scars and burn lines … and the spell sank into his skin.

I blinked, thrown off even as the spell continued to surge through me and out of my control. The speed picked up, intensified, and Lucien's cornflower-blue eye glowed. Faster and faster, the concealed power flew out of me and into Lucien like it had always belonged there.

Which it always had. The cemetery power had been his power once. *Idiot,* I thought, even as a grim sense of satisfaction frosted over a corner of my mind.

Lucien smiled, and I swore I could see bits of skin knitting itself together, hiding the hint of black and green monstrosity underneath.

"Enough!" John's hand sliced through the air, and silver and green energy cut through my spell. The conduit between the demon and me shattered, and the kaleidoscope of power slunk back down into the earth.

Lucien snapped the fingers of his free hand, and the gravity in the room intensified a hundredfold. My body suddenly weighed several thousand pounds, and even though I struggled, my knees quivered and I dropped to the ground.

"Don't try to get involved now," Lucien snapped at John,

his grip on Riley loosening. "I overlooked your return, but don't *ever* think to cross me. You know what he is. And you know to whom he belongs."

"Braden doesn't belong to you." John took another step forward, his forehead slick with sweat. He was fighting Lucien's demon-gravity, but it was a losing battle.

"That's not what you thought ten years ago," Lucien said, his voice suddenly silky. "As I remember, the thought of raising your brother's whelp was once a punishment, was it not?"

"Things change," John said.

Lucien arched his head a bit to the side, adjusting position like he was a cell phone trying to find the hot spot and get a signal. He opened his mouth again, and a voice broadcast itself from his throat, though his lips didn't move.

"I'll do anything, Lucien. Even take ... him." My uncle's voice emanated from the demon's mouth. The level of disgust in his voice was unmistakable.

Everything I'd said to him at the house came back in a rush. *Was I right? Did he truly hate me all this time?*

John looked at me, his eyes pleading. It was all the proof I needed that Lucien's words were true. "Things were different then, Braden."

"He didn't come back for your forgiveness," Lucien said, his mouth twisted cruelly. "He came for mine."

I looked up then, looked right into my uncle's eyes. I stared at him, so similar to his brother that it was obvious once you put it together, even though they were so totally different. John liked flannel and fast food, and Jason was three-piece suits and a personal chef.

I inched forward while Lucien's attention was on John. *If I can just.* But the demon's sneer faded, and he whirled on me.

"Oh no," he said, his sneer growing even wider. "Not again. This time, you will not get in my way."

His grip twisted and his hand skittered up her jaw, past her ear, and tangled itself in Riley's hair. His free hand grabbed her wrist, and he ... pressed in on her. It wasn't like his hands sank into her skin, but his fingers disappeared against her skin like camouflage. His hand and her hair turned the same inky shade of midnight, and stars began to swim against his skin.

"No! Riley!" There wasn't even time to think about it. I tore off the sunglasses for the first time since the hospital. Dying wasn't important. Not anymore.

I reached for her, catching the edge of her sweater between my fingers. Lucien pulled her back, but I held on. We each had an arm in our hands, like she was a wishbone getting ready to snap. I opened my eyes, as wide as I could, trying to force the power of the witch eyes, but nothing happened.

Nothing.

Happened.

Wrong. Unnatural. The minute the glasses came off, my head usually exploded with thousands of voices, melodies, images, sensations. They would come surging forth and swallow me up. If I could hold myself against the tide, I could use the power. If I couldn't, the power swallowed me up.

But this . . . *nothing*. It wasn't right.

My head throbbed, pressure from the inside out, like a shaken bottle, but I didn't lose my grip on Riley.

Something was in the way. Something that had worked where Jason had failed. It was like the front of my head had been filled with cotton, or layers upon layers of cellophane, blocking the power of my visions. It was smooth and hard, like glass or maybe diamonds. But in places it was soft like packed snow.

No! You'll die! You cannot do this! the winter voice shrieked. It came from the blockage, a wall that had gone up piece by piece. Layer by layer. The pressure intensified. It built and pressed until I was sure my forehead was going to crack apart, anything to relieve the screws drilling into my brain.

And then, just like they always did, the witch eyes tore through the winter voice, the wall around my eyes, and the demonic link that had grown in place.

One second the wall was like diamonds and snow, and the next it was a giant sheet of paper. My visions punched one hole through, and then another. Tiny little holes that spiderwebbed out like gunshots through a glass mirror. Into the gap, an image struck just before the entire thing came tumbling down.

Silver fire burns against raging amber crystals where bugs trapped golden echoes once walked these grounds there shall never be too much darkness roses rife with decay taste like demon

against your lips wash it down with hypocrisy and devil's brew.
She will see, and shatter, and…

" …everything will change," Riley whispered, her eyes opened so wide they looked twice as large as they were, her eyelids straining.

My fingers gripped her icy skin and something passed over me and through me. The winter breath of Lucien's demonic power collapsed underneath the bone-burning heat of the witch eyes. We were two magnets, attracting and repelling each other in equal measure. And caught between us was Riley.

I couldn't move, my feet were part of the floor, my hand was part of her hand. I could see across the gap, and Lucien was frozen, too. Bound.

His eyes, trained on the east, burn with sun flares and deceit. Something was torn from him.

I face the west, bound in chains of ice and apathy. Something arced out of me like lightning.

And her sightless eyes reign down upon the south, and were she to command the mountains to fall, they would do so under the weight of her truth. Everything converged on Riley. In her. Lucien's power slithered up against her soul, and the power my curse smashed against it, tempering it like a blade. Again and again, our powers collided, stopping him from tearing away her future by striking iron with a hammer. Changing her.

Changing us.

And then she spoke.

"Bound and broken, lying fallow on the ground, yet he begs for mercy." Riley's voice was deeper, echoing on a register beneath or above reality. It was the scream of angels as they fall, and the shriek of devils as they die. She continued, "The heir will come, and fires will rage in his wake. The darkness will know him, and he will be fostered with desolation."

A cornflower-blue sparkle in Riley's eye caught my attention, and as I focused on it, a surge passed between us. I saw what she saw, a vision I'd seen once before.

Trey and I, connected hand to wrist. All around us, behind us, beneath us, Belle Dam was burning. Wherever my gaze fell, fires raged. Eyes that had battered me all my life now brought ruin to everything they saw.

Lucien was splayed on the ground in front of me, either begging forgiveness or favor. My vision expanded, seeing the rest of the street—the bodies cut down as they tried to flee. People I knew. People who knew me. There hadn't been any mercy for them. Nor would there be any for the demon who made me this way.

The vision ended abruptly, and Riley's head dropped against her chest. When I tried to pry my fingers off her arm, I saw my reddened fingers, and the flash of pain igniting when I moved. My skin was sunburned and starting to blister in a few places. Lucien flinched, trying to pull away as well, though his fingers were blue and black.

Riley sank to the ground. It was like everything that was *Riley*, every color and memory and image that made up her being, had been shredded and torn apart, then stitched back together until it resembled a Surrealist painting. What emerged was something different. Something new. A girl from far beyond the pale.

My eyes, unshielded, returned me to my home. A crashing, shrieking, cacophonous melody of simple pains and history bled into the walls and lockers of the school.

Things I never wanted—be better—sapphire chords amidst the dank, sandlike grains ember misery, can you believe this hallway is a bog—be stronger—quicksand misery drags me down world of unnatural rotting smiles—be smarter—no one trusted—be hotter—the stink of corruption burns rumors gliding through the halls not like birds but mosquitoes—be deadlier—when they find out saccharine emptiness freak slut whore.

"What did you do?" Lucien was on his hands and knees, much as I was. He coughed and panted, struggling to pull himself together. "WHAT DID YOU DO?!"

I don't know. I could barely hold the thought together. Visions continued to freight train through my head, thousands and billions of snowflakes that crashed into me, lighter than feathers but harder than steel.

He yowled in a voice that wasn't human—sounds I don't think even animals could replicate. Dips and cadence to the screech made me realize it was a language. Even in his strange tongue, frustration and terror were obvious.

I tried to crawl forward to check on Riley, but the only part of me that worked were the tips of my fingers, and they had already been scalded once tonight.

Lucien's fingers crackled against the ground. Only it wasn't his fingers making the noise, but the tiles themselves. Lucien's hands pressed so hard against the ground that tiles cracked like mirrors, spiderwebbed faults spiraling around his fingertips.

Another scream of rage. He tried to push himself up, but

his arms gave out and he rolled over it. Lucien lay there, better but still somehow broken.

The visions faded, and I embraced the silence. No secret voices. No hidden words. The winter voice was gone, Lucien's influence on me eradicated.

John crouched down next to me, slipping the glasses over my eyes. His hands were cool against my skin, a steadying presence.

My head throbbed, and waves of red on the horizon. Even through the shield of the sunglasses, the glare of lights was too much to handle. I had to get up. Had to force myself to be okay.

"Shh," John said. His hand rested against my temple. The soothing gesture abruptly turned harsh as his fingers stiffened and knotted in my hair.

My eyes widened and I lurched up, trying to stop the sudden pain. John's back had spasmed forward, his other arm thrown to the side. Behind him, Lucien had regained his footing. His fingers dug into the skin of John's cheek, forcing his muscles taut like an electric shock.

"I will be restored," Lucien hissed.

"John?" I grabbed at his hands, my mind furiously trying to pull itself together.

John didn't respond, his eyes staring blankly above me.

"Do it now," Lucien said. It took me a second to realize he wasn't talking to me, but to the cell phone propped against his ear.

My teeth started to vibrate as something swept up from the ground beneath us.

Black clouds of power started pouring out between the seams of tile in the floor, and created a wall between John and me. It pulled him in deeper, closer to Lucien, while it pressed me back, cold and burning against my skin at the same time. The smoke continued to billow forth, getting thicker and thicker until it swallowed both of them up.

When it dissipated a few moments later, they were gone.

thirty-four

"Braden!" The shout came from a far corner of the school, echoing its way to me. They were still so far away. Footsteps clattered down the hall, and I winced when everything was bathed in light again. With the demon gone, the lights had returned. Like it was as easy as flipping a switch.

The tingling sleep faded from my skin, even though my mind had continued to race. Lucien had John. Lucien was going to kill him. It went without saying that the next stop on his agenda would be to come after me. Especially now, after whatever it was that I'd done to him and Rilcy.

Riley. Was she okay? As soon as I remembered how to sit up, I'd check on her.

I could feel all my fingers and toes, so that was a good start. I tried flexing my fist, squeezing several times in wasted effort. My hand laid at my side like discarded meat. It took a minute to realize I was trying to move the wrong hand—sure enough, when I turned my head I saw the other balled up in a fist.

I wriggled against the ground but couldn't manage to get

vertical. Trey and Drew finally appeared at the end of the hall, far too late to pull the white knight routine. Jade wasn't far behind. Blood rushed to my head, a fog swept through my thoughts, and everything went vague.

Something had just happened. Hadn't it? Trey dropped down to his knees in some sort of weird baseball slide, gliding the last few feet to me. His eyes were wide, and he was panting.

Something had happened.

He spoke, but everything was weird. Fuzzy. My head was full of clouds, my stomach was in knots, and I was freezing.

" ... think he's having a stroke," someone said.

My head snapped back, my face alight with pain. Someone had slapped me. Drew pulled his hand back, his palm a twin to the imprint against my cheek. I clung to the pain, feeling my head start to clear.

"Now he's not," Drew said, with far too much satisfaction in his voice.

"Touch him again," Trey dared, his eyes narrowing to dark little slits.

"I don't think she's breathing," Jade called from somewhere behind me.

Drew disappeared from my sight. In a rush, everything started to come back. Lucien had been here. He'd come for Riley.

"Braden, what happened?" Trey had me steadied, halfway sitting up. His eyes were trained on me, his face pale.

"You know what happened," Drew snapped, "Fallon lured him in here and attacked Riley. The idiot walked through the

323

front door all by himself." Shoes squeaked against the tile. "She's alive, case you were wondering."

Every second that passed, my head cleared a little more. "Lucien had help," I said, trying to pull myself up into a standing position.

Trey wasn't having any of that, though. "He's gone. We've got you. Everything's okay." And then quieter. "You took them off, didn't you?"

I nodded, even though my brain was on fire. It squiggled around my head a little, but luckily it didn't seem like it was going to fall out. I forced the issue, putting myself back on my feet and away from Trey. That didn't work out so well, as the moment I was supporting my own weight, my legs had other ideas.

Trey's arm swept around my waist, and I grabbed his shoulder. It was the only thing that kept me upright.

"He had help." The words taste like chalk and bad medicine against my tongue.

"Riley needs a doctor," Jade said, looking up at me.

I looked down at Riley, her hair still scattered, finger marks visible on her throat. The doctors would ask questions, especially when the bruising started. Her eyes were still half open, though it was clear she wasn't seeing anything at all.

"What happened to her?" Jade asked quietly, biting her lower lip.

Her eyes were still the same, unnatural blue. Demon-eye blue. Maybe I'd stopped Lucien from feeding on her, but now she was nothing more than an empty husk—I hadn't saved her. Not really. My stomach twisted. Just looking into her eyes, seeing the new color there, was enough to make me want to vomit.

"We have to get you both to the hospital," Trey said.

"No."

"You're going to the hospital," he insisted. "You can barely stand!"

"He had help. Someone used ... it." I just couldn't figure out what *it* was for a second. I should know this. There was a word, a word that meant exactly what the thought in my head meant. I could *see* it in my head, I was sure of it, but walls had come up and swept any number of things away.

Drew looked up at me. Jade's hand was on his, and that was weird for some reason. "It? You mean magic?"

I nodded. Magic, of course. "Yes. Uhm, that." I could still feel it, the hum of it in the air. Lucien hadn't vanished through his own power, someone had summoned him. Demonic power couldn't be sensed, normally, but magic could. Magic left a resonance in the air, spilled over power that dissipated slowly.

I couldn't have made him vanish like that. The amount of control it would have taken was insane. And there weren't many other suspects. "Your mom," I whispered.

Last week, Trey's defense would have been immediate. "You're sure?"

"Who else?" I had never heard Jade sound so caustic before. Her voice was a blade. "This is *who she is*. She doesn't care who she hurts."

"I can find her," I said, exhaling. I reached up, my hands settling on the curve of my glasses. Catherine had used magic. If I used the witch eyes, I could see what she'd done, find out how she'd taken him.

Trey's hands clamped down over mine. "You're going to the hospital. You can barely stand."

"I can do this," I insisted.

"The fact that your legs almost gave out was a total coincidence, right?" Drew asked, but for once, the rampant sarcasm was toned down.

I steadied myself on Trey, but his hands stayed pressed against my head. Holding my glasses in place.

I turned to him. "She needs to see a..." I stopped, fumbling for the word that had rattled free from its place in my head. I could picture one of them in my head. Lab coat. Stethoscope. Why couldn't I come up with the *word*? "A..."

"A doctor," Jade said quietly.

"That," I said, snapping my fingers.

They were all staring at me now. Jade's forehead knotted up, and she gestured under her nose. "Braden..."

I touched my own nose. My fingers came away red.

"I'm done arguing," Trey said, his eyes narrowed. "You're coming whether you like it or not."

"No... Lucien has my uncle. I can't—"

But Trey disagreed. He bent down, a hand coming around the back of my knees like he was planning to scoop me up into his arms. That was his mistake. My body ached, my head was throbbing, and I was pretty sure I was almost spent, magically speaking. But his guard was off, and so was his center of balance. I tucked one of my legs behind his and shoved, and sent him tumbling down.

"Take Jade and go to the hospital," I told Drew.

"And you?"

I pulled off my sunglasses. Instantly, the world was a tempest. Through a thousand shades of orange and a sonata of screams, I said, "I'm taking back what he stole from me."

It had been magic that stole Lucien away, the proof was right in front of me. A haze of crystalline pegs, orchestrated into a spell so complicated, and so powerful, that even the witch eyes needed time to digest it all.

The way magic really looked to my eyes always made it seem so simple. The truth was that for most people, spells were complicated and hard to channel properly. For me, a spell was just a matter of arranging no more than five or six parts, into the right spots, like a puzzle. This spell was different. This was more like a three-dimensional puzzle with about fifteen thousand different pieces.

My goal was to copy the spell and follow it to wherever Lucien had disappeared to. Only now I wasn't so sure if I could pull it off. A very, very quiet part of me wondered what I'd be walking into, but I pushed it down.

There was no need, though. The spell had required so much power and been so complex that it was almost perfectly preserved. The tiniest nudge, and power flared up and repeated the spell. One second I was looking at Drew and Jade, and the next I was falling apart.

It wasn't as bad as it sounded. Everything that I was broke down to the tiniest essence, and I was swept down a dark tunnel. It was like the opposite of dying and going into the light. I went into the dark. Flashes of deep purple lightning arced through the black, just enough to emphasize how much deeper than night it was.

Coming out the other side was jarring. I was underground, or something close to underground. It was a hall, like the Harbor Club I'd met Catherine at, only this was old. The walls were crumbling brick and iron sconces hung off brackets every few feet. The ceiling was high—too high for just another basement. This was someplace new. Someplace old.

Things came together when I saw a rectangular stone on the other side of the room, set up like an altar, with my uncle sprawled on top of it. John's eyes were closed.

It took my eyes a few seconds to recover from the spell, but the moment they did, the subterranean hall expanded.

Murder by torchlight divination entrails broken dreams hearts and eyes smell like ossuary spices laments for the old worlds the Paths no longer open to blinded eyes and caged animals. Ancient words crippled when Latin was young burn against the tongue, for thine is the kingdom, flames for the spirit, and shadows ravenous with contemptuous rage.

"What the hell?" Trey breathed from behind me. He'd followed me through the spell. I turned, suddenly scared that I'd brought *all* of us through, but it was only Trey and me. I turned back towards the altar, and at its head, saw the demon.

Lucien looked as bad as I felt. He had cracked hands pressed against the sides of the altar, holding himself upright. Barely. Across from him, as I knew she would be, stood Trey's mother, Catherine.

Her outfit was particularly out of character. A thick cashmere sweater, solid black when Catherine only ever wore white, and jeans. Even her hair was pulled back. Soccer mom, not a warlock mom. She stared at us, her mouth parted in an uncharacteristic expression of shock.

Correction, she was staring at me.

More specifically, she was staring at my eyes.

thirty-five

"No!" Catherine whirled on Lucien. "What game are you playing?" It only took one look: for a flicker of confusion to be replaced with recognition, and swiftly shoved out of the way as fury settled in. This was it. Catherine knew.

People were born with brown eyes, or blue eyes, not eyes that constantly shimmered and changed colors from one moment to the next. My eyes were a kaleidoscope neon sign that proved the truth of Grace's legacy. My power, my curse. Catherine knew the legends of the Widow Grace better than anyone.

Trey stepped in front of me. "Mom? What are you doing?" The deferential tone he might have taken before was gone, replaced by suspicion of his own.

"I told you the boy was necessary," Lucien said, his broken eyes flicking towards me. "You know what you needed to know and nothing more."

"You're manipulating me," Catherine said hotly. It was almost funny, coming from the woman who had literally half the town eating out of the palm of her hand, who wove agendas into every word and manipulations into every event. To be manipulated herself must be the ultimate betrayal.

"The boy is necessary," Lucien snarled. "Everything else is irrelevant."

"Mother?"

But Catherine had no eyes for her son right now. Her focus was on me. "This is what you've been after all along," she spat, her finger jabbing towards me. "He's been the goal all along, hasn't he?"

Lucien dealt with her like a lawyer. Patient. Calm. "He serves a purpose, just as I will. You will have what you seek. I could not have done this without you."

"You should have told me," she said, her cheeks stained red. "This changes everything." She pulled back the sleeves of her dark sweater like she didn't want to dirty the material. "The boy isn't a tool. He's a threat. To all of us."

"The *boy*," Lucien said, "is not your concern. You were brought into this for very specific reasons. Don't think to violate our agreement now. The contract is binding."

Catherine's blue eyes flashed like sapphires in the light. She'd rewritten the laws of time and space, pulling Lucien out of thin air. Her power was incredible—but I knew this already. If it came down to a confrontation, could I even hold my own?

She didn't seem to hear him. She stepped down the first stair, the heel of her boot striking stone with an audible, and ominous, clack. "I should have known. The sunglasses. The excuses." Finally, she hammered her gaze in on her son. "Did you know?"

Trey stood tall, his jaw tight. "What are you doing here?"

"Of course," she sneered, pulling his unspoken answer from the air. Her disappointment came down in waves. She and Jason were more alike than I'd ever realized.

"You knew what Lucien was doing?" Trey continued. "You knew about the girls he was hurting? You knew about *Jade*?" he demanded.

For a moment she looked taken aback. "Jade?" She turned to her left, as though she were going to address the monster behind her, but she thought better of it. "Jade is fine," she said, coming to some decision by herself. "And soon you will be, too."

"Forget your son," Lucien called out. His voice echoed darkly against the high stone walls. Something was stirring in the air, intangible and invisible to even me. But I could feel it gathering. Demonic power.

Catherine glared down at me. "You think you can come here, steal my son? Steal my birthright? My legacy?" She sneered. "All because Jason Thorpe gave you a father figure you never had?"

There was a moment's pause before Lucien corrected her. "*Father.*"

The room froze. Her shock only lasted a moment before her eyes turned calculating on me. I could see her running through the clues: the age that Jason's dead son would be now, the power at my disposal, the secrecy involved in my arrival to Belle Dam.

Her thoughts were written across her face. *Jason smuggled the child out of Belle Dam, it never died after all. He planned this, a plan seventeen years in the making.* Her eyes studied me, trying to find the traces of *them.* My parents.

She'd left me alone for the most part because as an outsider, I was a mercenary she could steal away eventually. She'd probably been confident that with the right price, or the right offer, I would turn on Jason. But that would never happen if I was a Thorpe by blood.

And on top of everything else, I saw the flash of embarrassment pass across her face, realizing that she'd been played from the moment I stepped into town.

I had approximately two seconds before Catherine made her move. Two seconds wasn't a long time: especially when an enraged witch decides the world was better without you in it.

The only thing that saved me was the thing that almost killed me on a regular basis. Without the shield of my glasses, I saw what Catherine was doing.

A small beam shot from her hands like some sort of laser. It was melted gold and glittered like diamonds, impossibly small like barbed wire or fishing line, and sharp enough to cleave individual molecules of air apart.

Trey stood in front of me, but the beams of gold light arced around him like homing missiles. Great for him, not so great for the home team.

I'd drawn in my magic the moment I'd felt Catherine doing the same, careful not to draw anything more from the wellspring. Even still, her spell sliced through every defense I threw up; everything John had ever taught me. In half a second, I'd created a half-dozen shield spells—some meant to resist, some to deflect. But Catherine's spell tore through each of them like shark's teeth.

She's got a lifetime of experience, how did I ever think this was a good idea? I can't fight her, she'll wipe the floor with me. Every defense, every reflection I tried was useless. Which meant that Catherine must know all the same spells.

Oh shit. Oh shit. Oh shit. I grabbed Trey, who was oblivious to what was heading our way and shoved him to the ground. The spells might not be targeting him, but I didn't want him caught in the crossfire. I landed on top of him, rolling onto my stomach as I climbed back up to my feet. I stared into the spell, and focused my power.

Catherine's spell was deadly, that much was certain. *Silver must be done cold rage must be given. Lacerate cut slice rend hack sever.* But it could only cut what it could touch. I saw as much as the parts of the spell unraveled themselves in front of me.

Her spell dissolved under the power of the witch eyes, but it just kept coming. I wasn't expending any of my magic anymore—I had to rely solely on the witch eyes. My eyes kept pulling the spell apart by the threads, but Catherine's spell just kept coming, like thread pulled from the spool.

I could only hold off something I could see—every time the spell dipped left or right and I lost my focus on it, it crept a little closer. Something Catherine seemed to realize as well.

Her witch wire started to move erratically. Gouges were sliced into stone and hunks of rock split in two as it crept closer and closer. I could barely follow it, losing a second here, or two seconds there. The delays kept adding up, and the spell came closer. I took a step backwards, only to brush up against the wall. The snaking spell kept gaining ground, and I couldn't stop it.

What am I supposed to do? How am I supposed to do this? But there was no one else in my head to answer.

Trey threw himself in front of me, arms outstretched. The spell had gotten *so close* that I thought he was a goner, and I screamed. I grabbed the back of his shirt and tried to move him out of the way. But he was stalwart, frozen in place. Like a statue, or some kind of guardian angel.

Catherine's eyes had unfocused as she directed the spell, but with Trey there, *undeniably there,* she couldn't ignore it. Her eyes registered her son, and she let out a little gasp. The spell vanished as panic washed over her face.

"You're just going to *kill* him?" Trey's voice was judgmental and cruel. "Who are you?"

I grabbed the back of his shirt, trying to control myself. "You idiot," I whispered, my voice thick. And then the image of the spell hitting him caught me full in the face, and I spun him around, feeling his shirt.

But there were no tears, no wounds. Catherine had stopped the spell in time. "You're okay," I said, filled with relief so strong it choked me from the inside. He pulled my hand from his shirt, linking his fingers with mine.

"Enough of this," Lucien demanded. I'd almost forgotten he was here. He was poised over John, holding a knife against his throat. "You have an obligation here, Catherine, and killing the boy won't alleviate what's coming."

I could barely hold my own against Catherine. I *wouldn't*

have if Trey hadn't interceded. I couldn't hold her off, challenge Lucien, *and* save my uncle all at the same time.

It wasn't possible.

Catherine was still staring at Trey, half in shock and half in something that I couldn't decipher. Anyone else, I might have described it as shame. But Catherine defied weak emotions. Even her tears would be icy.

"I'm going to kill him," Trey said under his breath.

"I'm going to help," I replied.

He looked over his shoulder at me and grimaced. Our hands still linked, we stepped forward.

Just like Lucien knew we would.

I didn't see the threshold until we crossed it, a simple line in the dirt. But that line was part of a spell, and it snapped into place the moment we tripped over it. Magic, and the demonic power that was its opposite, writhed together in harmonic chaos up and around us. Thick cables of power spun while the ground itself literally glowed. Rust and raspberry-red power clashed against cerulean and steel blue as a circle spiraled into being around us.

A binding circle.

"I knew you wouldn't be able to help yourself, of course," Lucien purred. "And why not? Hearing your screams as Jonathan dies..." he sighed fondly. "I couldn't help myself, either."

"What is this?" Trey whirled around, looking at the incandescence of the circle. Tiny little sparks floated up like fireflies, each a different shade. The circle was drawing on an enormous reservoir of energy—I couldn't tell where it was coming from, but I could feel the immensity behind it. Magical words and symbols had been etched into the ground, and now they blazed with golden light so bright that I could barely read the simplest of them.

This was bad. More so than usual. To start, the binding circle was a powerful spell—it had taken Uncle John weeks to build one that wasn't even half as powerful as this. What was worse is that the witch eyes should have torn the spell to shreds by now.

I stared into it, even trying to force the visions. Every time something wobbled, as though it was going to shake loose, invisible shadows oozed down and held the circle together.

I reached out, almost desperate, and felt my hand touch something that was electric and glass all in one. A solid wall that hummed and pulsed with energy. And more stable than concrete.

"I do enjoy seeing the arrogance torn from his face," Lucien said, in an aside to Catherine. "Now, finish the preparations." The two of them focused on the altar, suggesting that there was more to Lucien's restoration than simply assaulting the victims and stealing from them. There was some kind of ritual involved—a ritual that might buy us a few minutes.

"It's a binding circle," I said to Trey, licking my lips. John had taught me about them. He'd tried to train me for something just like this—and this time I didn't have my power to fall back on. "It'll hold us here, and anything I try to do to get us out will just bounce back on me."

"And there's nothing you can do?" he asked.

I shook my head, but then I stopped. There *was* still something I could do. It might not help much, but the first thing John had taught me was to look for the flaws. The weak points, where the spell wasn't as strong.

I crouched down, forcing my eyes to simply read the spell in front of and all around me. Lines appeared to me, skewed, slanting scripts of something that wasn't English, but was a language all the same. Scraps that I could read. Most of it was broken up, hidden by the demonic power that was also fueling it, but I learned a little.

None of it was good.

"We can't force our way out," I said, lowering my voice. "I wouldn't know where to start. They've done this before, they knew all the loopholes to cover to keep us in here." And then a thought occurred me. "To keep a *witch* in here." I looked at Trey speculatively.

"What does that mean?"

I didn't answer, but a smile graced my lips. Finally, something was going my way. "You have to break the circle from the outside," I said, pointing to the ring of golden symbols surrounding us.

"Me?"

I shoved him as hard as I could. The binding circle was meant to hold witches in. It didn't say anything about normal people like Trey. Only there had been a giant, cosmic screw-up somewhere, because Trey lost his balance, tumbled towards the side of the circle, and then bounced right back off.

Something that *should* have only happened to a witch.

My jaw dropped, and as my brain tried to put everything

together, I struggled to keep perspective on the situation. "You're a witch?" It was only half a question.

Trey had regained his balance almost immediately, and he shot me a strange look. "Of course I'm not. What the hell just happened?"

I pointed to the binding circle around us. "You might want to tell the circle that, because it's saying you are."

"I'm not a witch," he insisted, dropping his own voice so that his mother and Lucien wouldn't overhear. I wondered, but didn't say anything out loud. There were times when Trey moved, when he *reacted,* where he almost seemed superhuman. Like fighting off the *mokoi,* or the night we ran from the hellhound, and he appeared out of nowhere to catch me before I fell.

There was a quiet thump, and then a pressure of something against the side of the binding circle. My eyes went immediately to the altar, but it was empty. John was gone. My heart dared to leap in my chest. Somehow, John had gotten free.

Lucien and Catherine hadn't noticed yet. They faced us, their backs to the altar. They hadn't noticed yet. Catherine looked at us thoughtfully. "This wasn't supposed to happen. He could harm Gentry."

Lucien barely spared me a glance. "He won't."

"I don't know how far I trust your assurances," she said. "What's this about my daughter?"

He waved a dismissive, broken hand. "Distractions. Nothing more. And he won't hurt your son." His tone grew scornful. "He *loves* him."

Trey nudged me, gesturing with his head. To one side of the room, dusty footprints crept towards us, one appearing after another. John had hidden himself under a veil. I still didn't know how we were going to handle both Catherine and Lucien, but John would have a plan.

"Lucien!"

I flinched, my head whipping towards Catherine. Lucien had twisted at her shout, his body moving in segments like a screw.

"Hurry," I hissed, but I should have saved the effort.

A crack of thunder shook the room, a sonic pulse that nearly dropped me to my feet. Catherine held her hand out imperiously, like a Queen about to condemn a man to death.

Whatever the spell was that she'd used, it swept over John's veil and revealed him less than five feet from us. It had also driven him to his knees. He wavered, nearly falling over completely, and spat blood out of his mouth.

"We don't have time for this," Lucien spat. "Everything's in place. Do it. Now."

Catherine's mouth twisted. Her eyes were trained on John, who was on his hands and knees. "He tried to kill my husband. My children could have been in the car." Her voice was softer than I thought Catherine could ever manage. But though I noticed it, I couldn't fathom where it was coming from. Was she having second thoughts?

"Do it," Lucien hissed.

Catherine grew more resigned, but her eyes hardened. Eyes that said she'd do this without losing a minute of sleep. That moment of hope had crystallized and shattered. No, this wasn't happening. It couldn't. I threw myself against the side of the binding circle. "NO!"

Catherine spread her fingers, the tips pointing at my uncle. A fraction of the torrent that was holding the circle up splintered off from the whole, drawn to her will. Black and purple motes of light hesitated around her fingers, like fireflies that had gone rogue and spread darkness instead of light.

John was still trying to get his bearings. Still trying to pull himself back up. He looked up at me, our eyes met. Held.

Catherine's voice. "I offer him. A sacrifice."

I threw myself against the circle again. Bounced off the side. Trey caught me. He tried to hold me steady, but I fought. "JOHN!"

Catherine made a fist. The motes flared into colors muted with darkness: dusky purples, muddy reds, decaying greens. Then the spell, a cloud of ichor and stain, spilled forward. It swept over John like a shroud.

"JOHN!"

It wasn't like any of the euphemisms they used when someone died. The light in his eyes didn't die, and he didn't shuffle off the mortal coil. One second he was alive, and the next...

He simply... collapsed.

He didn't move again.

thirty-six

I was six years old.

There weren't any sunglasses when I was six. It was swim goggles. Swim goggles all day, every day. I was never allowed to take them off unless Uncle John was there.

I'd missed some eye crusties when I woke up. It would be okay, it was just for a second.

My finger slipped up under the green plastic and scrubbed the corner of my eye. But there was more than one crusty there, and I got too excited, rubbed my eye too hard.

The goggles slipped.

By the time Uncle John found me, I was flat on my back, everything in my room was destroyed, and there were cracks in the ceiling plaster. Cracks that looked like a hand with claws. Cracks that plaster never seemed to fully cover.

I slept on the couch every night until I turned ten.

¤　　¤　　¤

One morning when I was nine, for no reason I can remember, I'd forgotten that my eyes were time bombs. I was frustrated with something, Math probably, and I ripped the sunglasses off my face in a moment of pique. Maybe I'd seen someone on TV do it, or maybe I just thought it would look cool.

Uncle John didn't think it was cool. Probably because I started screaming bloody murder and by the time he got me into town, I'd started convulsing, and then stopped just as he pulled up in front of the doors of the hospital.

When I woke up two days later, he towered above me like a sequoia tree. Huge. As soon as he realized I was awake, he started yelling, saying all kinds of things. But underneath, I saw his fear.

He'd feared it was over. That I'd never wake up.

¤ ¤ ¤

"I don't want to."

John was tucked into the corner, flipping through the Sports section of the paper. I think he secretly liked these hospital visits because the hospital carried all the big papers. He could read six different sports sections and still have time to read Sports Illustrated.

"Of course you don't," John said absently. "But you're going to do it anyway."

"They're going to put me in one of those machines. What if something happens, and I get stuck inside? What if I'm claustrophobic and never knew it?"

John sighed and folded up his paper. There'd be time enough later, *I could almost hear him thinking.*

"It's just an X-ray, Braden," he said. "Just keep your eyes closed, and you'll be fine. The doctor thinks he might have figured something out, but he needs the X-rays to be sure."

"Doctors are always saying that they might have a solution."

The technician came into the room, and despite another five minutes of pleading, John let him take me away.

I was back fifteen minutes later, although now John was trying to read underneath the emergency lights in the corridor.

"What happened?" he snapped, looking at me.

The technician was the one who answered, though. "I don't know what happened! We walked into the room and the machine just… I've never even seen fire that color before!"

John looked at me, and in his eyes anger gave way to concern. "Are you okay?" he asked gently.

¤   ¤   ¤

I was drowning.

Rage, denial, and grief were waging a war to see who was going to come out on top. Right now, rage was winning. But grief wasn't going down without a fight.

I don't know if it was just an accident, or they'd intended it that way, but John's body was turned towards us, his eyes frozen somewhere between pain and surprise. *No. There was some mistake. It was a trick.*

Trey had his arms around me, but I was screaming so loud I couldn't hear what he tried to say. The binding circle continued to pulse around us. Catherine dropped her hand, her expression sickened.

I'm going to kill her.

I don't know if I actually screamed it at her, or if she just knew it was coming, but she looked over at me. Flinched.

Trey kept a tight grip on me, but I kept trying to pull myself away. As if breaking free from him would somehow get me out of the circle. I couldn't handle him touching me right now. He needed to not be touching me.

This was my fault.

Lucien was ecstatic. He stood by the altar, full of satisfaction as the power of the sacrifice flowed into him. I could *feel* something coming together—like two halves of a zipper coming together again.

This was the last. The one he needed the most.

"I told you this day would come," the demon whispered, and his voice carried like his mouth was right against my ears. "Just because the vision wasn't yours doesn't mean it wasn't true. Consider this the price for killing me."

The vision that had started it all—the one in the convenience store. The reason I'd fled and come to Belle Dam in the first place, to save him. Save the man who raised me. *It was real? Always real?* No. He'd planned for this: killing John. One way or another.

Lucien's dark laugh pierced my thoughts. It sharpened something inside of me, feeding into everything I was feeling and polishing it until it was razor fine.

Like the night in Trey's car, a power was building inside of me. My anger and my pain were calling out. I could *feel* things shifting inside of me, making way for something new. My soul was shoved to a dusky corner, every available inch given over to new sources of rage and power. Something was coming together, a new power that was familiar and foreign all at the same time.

"What's happening?" Trey's voice was soft in my ear, surprised and filled with wonder.

Blue light began to fill in the circle, a kind of light that had texture and shape. It grew, and spread, until we were bathing in sapphire. My body tingled, like electric currents skipping along my skin.

I could still feel things I could only sense. *Powers* in the air and stone, stirring in response to something. The oldest of spirits, woken by preternatural vibrations, scurrying far from here like animals fleeing before an earthquake.

The curse of the witch eyes, the power I didn't completely understand and couldn't even begin to control, bled over into my rage. Something clicked into place. It felt like until this moment, I'd only ever been partially complete. Integral pieces had been missing, but now all the hollow places were filled with anguish and wrath.

Something aligned, and everything that I was came together in one fluid movement, as if reality had to jerk itself suddenly forward to compensate. Everything I was had become part of my power. My voice was no longer my voice.

Now it was something more.

I screamed, putting into it everything I was, everything I *used* to be.

The blue light grew brighter and thicker and *warm*,

bulging at the sides of the containment spell. *Arcs like lightning jealousies fester tear it asunder the source of power taste like old money sacrifice and bitter copper black smoke vain clouds of ozone fury.*

The spell strained, trying to contain everything that I was now, but it lasted only seconds. The binding circle collapsed, its magic and demon power instantly consumed into the blue light, absorbed and strengthening around us like a funeral shroud.

The scream died on my lips, and inside the room, the pressure intensified. My ears popped. Trey's grip on my shoulders tightened.

A hush settled over the building. Catherine and Lucien both looked shaken. They could feel it building.

I sucked in another breath. In the aftermath of my scream, while my lungs burned with the need for oxygen, a hush settled over the building. Everything caught its breath, but it wasn't over. This was just the calm.

It started as a buzz, quiet at first but quickly becoming high-pitched and deafening. Louder and louder, until I could actually see the air vibrating in response. I sucked in a breath and watched the explosion expand from inside me.

The walls shrieked.

Gravel vibrated off the concrete floor.

The candle flames first dropped until they were so small they were barely sparks, and then surged upward into foot-long tapes of fire. The pressure in the room continued to grow until the air was so thick it pressed down on everything.

The magic needed release. It needed to ignite. It was everything inside of me, and something new as well.

I was a bomb.

I broke the world.

There was one solid, concussive blast that shot out from around me in every direction. The walls, the ceiling, the entire structure exploded under the weight of the growing cacophony. White light swallowed everything, and Trey and I were thrown backwards. We landed together, limbs entwined but not broken.

Time passed. There was so much energy in the air it was hard for me to figure out where it ended and I began. It was like being in a sensory-deprivation tank.

Open sky stared down on us. My eyes swam in the stars, and slowly my mind came back. I pushed Trey off of me, a hitch in my breath.

"Trey?" I shook him. "Trey!"

It seemed like forever until I saw his chest rise and fall. Alive. He was alive. That was twice he'd terrified me. I climbed to my feet and looked around.

The building was gone. The ceiling above us had been completely destroyed, with no trace of rubble. Nothing to indicate that it had ever existed. The floor was cracked and ruined, looking like an earthquake had torn the ground asunder. The majority of the brick walls had collapsed and shattered, unleashing a landslide of dirt. Whatever this place had been, it was now simply ruins in the earth, a hole we'd fallen down into.

Outside in the night, I could see limbs of trees, strange

and wrong. It took me a minute to realize that they were the roots, the trees knocked down and torn out of the ground by the explosion.

In the center of the room between where Lucien had been and where we'd been trapped, there was a … disturbance. It reeked of magic and power, the edges crackling like fire. The air around it shimmered like the edges of a curtain that had—at last—been torn free and fluttered, tattered and violated. It was shaped like an open doorway, revealing order in the face of chaos. Offering a peek into some other world. A room of white stone and lanterns hammered into the wall.

A piercing breath cut free from the world inside the portal, sprinkling me with bits of snow that melted quickly against my skin. It cut through my shirt, leaving goose bumps in its wake.

Tear the fabric rend the veil walk the Paths that cannot be walked only shattered violated renewed in sparkling silver moons in transition darkness truncates the light strips the essence bare like children born blind blissfully walk crawl run towards desolation.

The visions struck briefly, but hard. A portal—some kind of path to another world or place. The power I'd used, it had torn something. Split the world apart and revealed a world behind the curtain.

I took a step forward, hesitating. Was this a hallucination, like the demon-tainted visions of Lucien I'd had before? Was it even real? But as I crossed into the stone world, the ground felt solid. As real as I, then.

The hour is upon us, a voice whispered into my mind. A

woman's voice, cool and hard. It had more presence than the winter voice had—a real voice, instead of one born of stolen power. *Linger no more.*

"Who are you?" I asked, but there was no answer. The room was empty. Everything was made from the solid white stone, but it was small. Like a prison cell.

I took another step. "What about the others? Trey and Lucien? Catherine?" A red knife cut through my stomach, just saying her name.

The voice remained silent.

"This is a bad idea," I muttered. But I went through with it anyway.

thirty-seven

A staircase was set into the wall to my left. I headed up.

I climbed. And climbed. The walls and the stairs were flush and sharp, without a trace of wear and tear. Everything was pristine, as if I was the first to ever walk up these stairs.

The staircase circled the building—it wasn't until I'd gone up about two hundred steps that I realized what I was in. A tower. Just as quickly as the thought settled in my head, it was replaced by something better. *Not a tower. A lighthouse.*

The only thing that kept me going was adrenaline. There had already been too many fights, too many struggles tonight. I barely had the strength to make it up the never-ending stairs.

But eventually, I reached the top, and emerged into the lantern room—the top of the lighthouse where the lantern was kept. Unlike the rest of the tower, there were signs of wear and tear up here. A circular wall and ceiling covered only half of the room. It looked like the top had been struck by a wrecking ball, or some kind of giant. The stones at the edges were scoured and broken and through the wreckage a restless, purple sky was visible.

Above me, I saw an open sky brimming with strange stars. A ring like Saturn's, pale yellow and stretching half the sky, though there was no planet at its core. There were things only visible in deep space: mint-green galaxies and violent, violet clashes of red and blue nebulae. It was an aberrant sky, the kind of starry wonder that Picasso might have painted, if Picasso went to demon clubs and visited otherworldly lighthouses.

Across from me, just inside the ruined edifice was a woman. She faced the open night, hands clasped in front of her as if in prayer. She wore an old-fashioned gown, white sleeves that came to her wrists, and a skirt that teased the floor. Head covered with a lace veil, she didn't acknowledge my presence.

She didn't need to. I'd seen the veil before. She could have stepped right out of the pictures I'd seen of her, those photographs taken over a hundred years ago.

"Grace," I whispered, my voice half a question. "Is it really you?" I asked, my voice growing fainter. "Am I—did I—"

"He slithered through his prison for a lifetime." Grace's voice was strange.

She spoke like a worldly woman: clear, crisp, and thick with culture. A woman who had absorbed everything in her travels—not a frail recluse condemned to a small-town existence.

"Did I die?" I could barely get the question out. The last

thing I remembered before stepping through the doorway was the blast: had it been the final straw the doctors warned me about?

"A century. The entirety of a man's thread. And now you dangle freedoms in front of him like choice meats."

"Uhm ... what? Is that a no?"

"You draw breath and reek of fear and useless emotions," she said with disdain. "Death is not as kind a mistress as some, but she would not leave you so debased."

So I was alive. Maybe. But then, how was I here? And where *was* here? Was I in the past? Had I somehow traveled back to Grace's time? There was hope blooming inside of me for the first time in days. She could help me! She knew more than anyone how to deal with the witch eyes. How to deal with Lucien.

"How desperate an animal you are." Grace kept her vigil at the cusp where the wall once stood. Past her and the rubble of the wall, I could see a small, railed gallery, like a widow's walk. But Grace remained inside. "Even now, you scramble for order in the chaos you brought to pass."

"Desperate? What are you talking about?"

The wind surged outside, a hollow winter sound. I could see the sky full of flakes, but none of it passed the widow's walk. Even though half the building was exposed, nothing crossed the line of rubble where walls once stood. There was a truce between lighthouse and winter, it seemed. Winter did not so much as stir the hem of her dress.

"Play not the fool with me. You swell with contagion, aiding the Rider at every pass. You were meant to hobble him, but instead you chose to salve and bandage his wounds. Actions that could no longer be tolerated in good conscience."

My body was telling me to flee: run now, and run fast. But I didn't listen. "The Rider," I said slowly.

"The light that blinds the eyes of providence. He that man calls Fallon."

Maybe it was the blast, or the night's events catching up with me, but I was struggling to piece together what was going on. "I was trying to *stop* him."

There was a sound like tapping. I moved to the side, seeing the baton slapping her open palm. After a moment, she flicked her wrist, and as the baton opened, I realized what it was: a fan. The surface shimmered in somber reds and electric purples. The colors swirled constantly, hypnotic and disturbing. It must have been a trick of the light, but it looked like there were things *slithering* inside the paper, like a nest of serpents was hidden in the folds.

"Can, can you help me?" I took a hesitant step forward, instinct warning me not to get close. Warning me of danger. Questions and pleas fell from my tongue one right after another. "Help me stop him. Tell me how to control the visions. How did you survive for so long? How can I keep them from using me? Please, I need you."

"Stop him?" She whirled on me, eyes blazing. In that moment, I understood the instinct to flee. Grace's eyes were *actually* blazing. The irises were rust-colored magma, shining through the lace, and casting her face with a seething glow. "You wish to cut his thread? That it is so easy, to erase a primordial creature from the books of life?" She slammed the fan against her wrist, then pointed it at me. "Long after this world has cracked and shattered, he will continue to gnaw on the pieces; ever will he scavenge. "

"Please," I begged, raising my voice. "He's hurting people. Killing them."

The fan flicked dismissively. "Death is the eternal equalizer. In all things, balance."

Hope wilted in my chest. Grace was not my savior. Once, I thought I could summon up her ghost to find answers, but I realized now why that was never to be. If I was alive, then so was she. Over a hundred years since her disappearance, and she still lived. I looked around the lantern room, my curiosity stirred. "Where are we?"

A humorless chuckle. She turned away, back to her vigil of the storm coming in on the bay. "You know a lighthouse when you see it, boy."

"That's not what I meant." There was a lighthouse in Belle Dam, but it was safe to say we were not *in* Belle Dam anymore.

"So of matters of inconsequence, he sees true," she mused. "How apropos. Would that you have seen the devil slithering in your belly with such clarity."

"Have you been here all this time? *How*?"

"Do you really think I would hobble the demon and then trust his captivity to the ages?" Grace took a half step forward, as if testing the boundary keeping her from winter. "The lighthouse acts as my bastion, as it has ever since we sought it out."

"I don't understand. What do you mean, you sought it out?"

She turned only slightly, enough that I could see her face in profile, and the curve of her lip underneath lace. "Why else would we grow a town on blood-stained earth? We were foolish children who sought the lighthouse. Our castigation was deserved."

That didn't make any sense. Grace was part of the group that first settled Belle Dam. She had gained a reputation as the one responsible for the design of the town. "Wait, are you saying the lighthouse was already *here*?" I demanded. "But I thought *you* founded Belle Dam."

"I did," she replied. "But there was a lighthouse before there was a town. We sought it out, thinking it was the answer to secret desires we dared not name."

"Then who built it?"

She raised a hand, fingers splaying slowly. "Sands lost in time. Questions even we scholars and witches could not answer. But we came, and settled, and in time I designed the trap you call town. When the lighthouse passed from one world to the next, another came to be built. This," she said, sweeping her hand around her, "is the original. Timeless and tucked in worlds between. We have much in common." There was a hint of melancholy in her voice, a touch of humanity that I'd not yet seen in her.

I thought I understood. "You're trapped here, aren't you?"

Scorching eyes spun around to pin me down. "Dig

deep and find a civil tongue, or I will rip it out of you," she growled. I had no doubt that she would do it.

I backed up several steps, the instinct to flee becoming a shriek in my blood, overwhelming my thoughts. *She'll destroy you, she will. She's not like Lucien. She has no use for you.* A litany of thoughts—reasons why I was expendable—circled in my brain.

"I meant no offense," I offered, fear rasping my voice.

"You *are* an offense," she muttered. "A thief, sneaking in during the night and taking powers not meant for you. Stealing that which was not yours to steal."

"I didn't ask for it," I said. "And I didn't steal it. If I had the choice, I would have picked the life without glasses or veils, without nearly dying every time I see something I shouldn't. I wouldn't have the witch eyes at all."

"And just to spit in fortune's eye," she went on without listening, "you infected yourself with demon taint. Nursed at a power archaic; growing dark with infernal vigor."

"I couldn't have known...!"

"Couldn't have known." She barked out a laugh. "You drew on it. Felt your soul icing over and begged it to quicken. You took what was offered and the cost be damned. More readily than any bargain between demon and man before. Is it any wonder that misfortune follows you so boldly? Light the pyre for your sins and be it done."

"And you were any better?" I snapped. Fear had masked over the tumult of emotions that had begun to surge long before the lighthouse, but anger was the quickest to return. It reminded me of where I was—of *why* I was here. A truth that

Grace had glossed over in all her talking. "You created a town to trap the demon and left the people there to suffer under him. He came for *you*, Grace. You don't get to judge *me*."

She hissed out something in a language I didn't speak, but I knew profanity when I heard it. "Mine is a power that demanded I wed sacrifice and take it to my bridal bed. Watching as it crippled, then killed, everyone around me." Her burning, coal eyes tracked me as I circled the room, piercing through the veil she wore. She sneered. "Do *not* speak of things you do not understand."

"You aren't the only one who suffered. My friends could have died tonight, because of me. My uncle—" I cut off.

"You understand nothing," she snarled. "But be at ease, wicked little creature. For the audience I grant you now. Just as I opened the way to you, now I will bring it to the close." Grace's eyes were hard rubies, and her anger was still palpable. "I had hoped your frailty would tear you asunder. But alas," she sighed with mocking regret and stood tall. "Once again, I must wrest fortune from the hands of demons."

"What are you doing?"

"You have tasted the power infernal." Her words carried their own gravity, as if she was passing judgment. "You allow the blight called Fallon to twist my power, to sup on it." There wasn't an ounce of pity in her eyes when she looked at me, despite what she said next. "Your death will be swift. Such is the essence of my mercy."

The hellish light that gleamed from Grace Lansing's eyes doubled, tearing the veil from her face, and a mountain of power slammed into me.

Jason's laser-sharp focus, Catherine's passive control. Even Lucien's dark, smokelike energy was nothing compared to the onslaught of Grace's eyes. My shoes squeaked on the marble tile, as inch by inch her power pushed me back. I stared into the maelstrom, but my power was a pebble next to her volcano.

Blue light flickered around me, flared, then blazed. The same power that had come to me in the car with Trey, and then again in the binding circle. Sapphires and oceans and blueberries right off the vine. It grew stronger and brighter, and somehow stood against the scarlet light pouring out from her. The more intense her force became, the stronger my own grew to resist her.

"You would dare," the witch snarled, "raise my own power against me? This place is inviolate. Sacrosanct."

As the light around me grew stronger, my movements slowed, then stopped altogether. Where our powers met, brilliant flashes of purple and violet exploded out like fireworks.

Grace shifted, taking slow and deliberate steps. I kept pivoting to keep her in front of me. I'd circled half the room before I realized what she was doing, but by then it was too late. She'd circled me around until my back was to the open sky. "You walk with devils." The fan baton was back, and pointed at me.

"I should die, because I made a mistake?" I shook my head. "I thought you'd have all the answers. But you're not even human anymore."

"I am the only sentinel this lighthouse has," she responded

gravely. The tip of the baton began to smoke, turning a shade of ember that matched her eyes.

The pressure on me increased, and I slid back an inch. The sound of winter fury grew even harsher behind me. I was dangerously close to the edge of whatever shielded the lighthouse from the storm. There was no doubt that the second the outside wind caught me, it would fling me from the parapet.

Sweat beaded across my forehead. The intensity of her power raged, the temperature continued to increase, and I sweltered under the assault.

"You punished him by binding him to the town," I managed to spit out. My feet slid back another inch. "Everyone he's hurt. Fed on. You're the one to blame."

Her eyes widened.

"Belle Dam suffers for your pride," I snarled. The more anger I felt, the more *anything* I felt, the stronger the light around me pushed back. My feet gained traction against the marble floor.

"Your mewling does not concern me," Grace said, trying to regain her composure and her advantage. The tip of the baton caught fire, a thick, golden flame almost a foot high. "I knew one day another would come, cursed with power tied with demon strings. But I had hoped you'd not be so soft."

Something about the way she said that. "You knew there would be another like you?"

How her eyes managed to burn and yet be so cold, I could not understand. "I've seen the threads of providence, I know the paths the demon wanders. Desperate for his freedom. Why else would I pit my blood against that of savages? Your *union* will bring only doom. It has been seen."

The feud. She started the feud because of *me?* "You saw the city burning," I said slowly. "Lucien begging for mercy." The vision.

"And the monster you become in his wake," she confirmed. "The alignment of Thorpe and Lansing will make the constellations themselves shudder and collapse."

The maelstrom died, but a ruby star hung between us still. As casually as flicking away lint, Grace moved her wrist, and the tiny ball of molten red light struck me full in the face.

Trey and I stood on the streets of Belle Dam, and all around us, the city burned. But our hands were not linked, fingers waffled together. My hand was on his wrist. Proprietary. His head was down, eyes sunken and vacant. But that didn't matter, because he was mine.

My eyes were different: no longer the constant shimmer, or even the azure light they'd become: now an awful, writhing violet. The kind of violet that spoke of madness and misfortune.

Lucien was prostrated below me, my boot on his neck, but my attention was elsewhere. In the distance, hanging above Belle Dam like a phantom juggernaut, was the lighthouse, impossibly tall and dividing the sky like it was the city's own Tower of Babel.

It was more than a lighthouse. It was a ladder, reaching so far from one world that it crested into the next. Even though I couldn't see, I could feel them: *clawing down from the apex and up from the base, reaching for this world tucked perfectly in between. The Riders, some of them so massive that they required a dozen bodies to carry the whole of their essence. All of them, coming for this world.*

Coming because of me.

Lucien still begged for mercy, but mercy was a word I knew no longer. I had become a twisted thing, consuming the powers of the wellsprings, sloughing off the harsh human emotions I needed no more.

I was not Nero, to fiddle away while the world burned. I would light the fires myself.

And then I would smile.

"No," I gasped, as the vision faded. The vision she'd *put in my head.* "That's not real! It's not!"

"That it *could be* is enough," Grace said. "You've proven yourself to be weak. That you will take any corruption, so long as its sweetened with a dash of power. You are a plague."

"And power is a problem," I whispered to myself.

"So it has always been," she agreed, inclining her head.

Stars swam on either side of me, pinpricks of light that were growing more and more bold. I wouldn't be *that.* Couldn't be. "You did all of this on the off chance that I met Trey? That it would lead me down the path to that vision?" Knowing where I could head, *seeing it,* made it real in a way it wasn't before. "You pull strings as well as any demon. Lucien was right all along, humans make the better demons. And you're one of the best."

With a snarl of rage, Grace whipped her other hand forward. All at once she was directly in front of me, and she thrust her arm forward.

Her hand was taut like a claw, and *melted* through the skin of my face. My body exploded into white light and pain. The agony was everything. Her fingers dug through vein and cord and tissue, brushing against my brain and the top of my mouth from the wrong side of my skull.

The worst pain was my eyes. They were doused in napalm and covered in fire ants. Lightning burned against my corneas and mace leaked out of my tear ducts. The visions stopped plaguing me, but only because all I could see was Grace's fingers rummaging through my eye sockets.

I'd screamed when John died, but the sounds coming out of my mouth now were something else entirely.

She pulled her hand back, and I could feel the sound of something tearing away.

Oh god, oh god, she ripped them out of my head. They told me the Lansings would do that, tear the witch eyes right out of my head but oh god she ripped them out of my HEAD!

I didn't think it was possible for me to scream any louder, but once again I was proven wrong. It lasted for a moment before the wind was knocked out of my chest and I couldn't make *any* sounds. Something struck me, so big and with so much force it was like being scooped up by the same giant that had knocked in half of the wall and roof. I flew back and up, out of the lighthouse and into the heart of the storm.

My body had forgotten how to scream, but that didn't stop me from trying.

I screamed all the way down.

thirty-eight

I was still screaming when I hit the ground. The floor of
Lucien's lair, just as I'd left it. My hands cupped my face. I
could feel blood trickling down my palms. My eyes had been
replaced by twin suns; the pain relentless. Nothing existed
outside of me.

There was nothing but the pain. The pain, and my
screams.

Hands appeared on my shoulders, pressing me down. I
tried to roll left, or right, to even remember *which* was my
left and which my right. The hands held me down. My heels
dug into the ground, and I thrust myself up, trying anything
to free myself, to move away from where I was.

Let me die let me die let me die let me die. I forget how to
speak, but everything inside of me wanted only one thing.

The hands kept me down. And slowly, the pain broke up
into smaller parts: white-hot agony, throbbing bass torment,
and screaming anguish. The liquid gold sloshing around my
empty eye sockets cooled by degrees.

"It's okay. Let me see."

I didn't recognize the voice. Not right away. The sounds replayed a dozen times in my head before I even recognized that they *were* words, and another dozen before I could attach a meaning. I tried to keep screaming, but nothing would come out. My voice had run out.

"Braden, it's okay. Let me see." The voice was more insistent this time. There was definite panic underlying the words.

My hands were frozen over my ruined eyes. I couldn't have moved them even if I wanted to. Fingers circled around my wrists, and then tugged. Gentle at first, then harder.

"Jesus," I heard him whisper. "Where's it coming from?" His fingers ran against my skin, but he couldn't find what he was looking for.

I almost lost it again right there. I could feel myself, right at the edge of some precipice, ready to fall off at a moment's notice.

This isn't happening this isn't happening this isn't happening this isn't happening.

Fingers grazed my ruined skin. My hands tightened into fists and I would have whimpered if I could have made a sound. He pulled my hands down, away from my ruined face.

Trey started saying things, whispered words that had no meanings but were carried on sounds meant to be soothing, caring.

"Can you see anything?"

I shook my head, something burning against my cheeks. *Why would he ask that? Was he taunting me?*

"Braden, I need you to open your eyes for me. Please"

Fingers roamed over my skin, pressing and pulling and almost scraping against my cheekbones. "It's not yours, is it?" Panic in his voice warred against frustration.

What was he talking about?

"Open your eyes!"

Seventeen years of reflex flew out the window. My instinct had always been to shut my eyes at the slightest provocation—to avoid the ravaging visions. But Trey was so insistent, I didn't think twice. I opened my eyes, and almost immediately slammed them shut again. Too bright. Too much going on.

Too much *everything*. It took me seconds to reconcile *I'm blind* with the image of Trey, covered in dirt and leaning over me, beautiful and perfect and *visible*.

I opened them more cautiously a second later, tears leaking out the sides. Trey's hands were dipped in red, and I looked down to see that mine were a matching pair.

But I could see them. The drying, sticky red staining our fingers, the dark of Trey's jeans. Even the concrete floor underneath us.

"What?" I whispered.

I touched the ground, half to make sure it was real, and half to assure myself that this wasn't another dream. My eyes still burned, but now it was embers instead of flame.

Trey leaned in to me, his eyes locked on mine. "You're okay," he said, half to himself. "I thought..."

But I already know what he thought. Because I'd been thinking the same thing. "She attacked me," I whispered.

"Clawed her fingers through my skin and ripped them out."
I shook my head. "I was so sure."

He was looking at me strangely, still. Like something still
wasn't right. "There's no one here. Whatever you did ... it
knocked us all out." He squinted above us, at the empty
night sky. A circular hole had appeared in the clouds above
Belle Dam. Whatever I'd done had reached up into the
atmosphere, too.

"It was so real. She was going to kill me." I grabbed his
arm, squeezing. "She wanted me dead!"

"It's okay. She's gone. We're the only ones here." Trey
rested his forehead against mine, his breathing quickened.
"You're okay."

I reached up, trying to touch my skin again. The blood
was still wet against my fingertips. My vision was still blurry,
everything painted in watercolors instead of high definition.
Even Trey looked lumpy and skewed.

"You're not bleeding," he confirmed. "But I don't know
where it came from."

It had been real. The blood confirmed it, at least to me.
"But I can still see," I said, my voice full of wonder. How was
that possible?

"I don't know."

Slowly, things started coming back to me. A knife surged
through my heart when I remembered what had led me to
the lighthouse. What had happened to John. I struggled to
my feet. Trey was there every step of the way.

The room was as I remembered it. Shattered and broken
apart at the seams. Like the aftermath of a bomb. The altar

had been broken apart at an angle, like a sword had sliced through it from the right down to the left. John's body had been thrown back, but now his head was tucked against the ground, hiding his eyes.

"What was that, Braden? What did you do?"

I shook my head. I felt empty. I couldn't have whispered up a candle flame, let alone half of the things that I'd done tonight. Every muscle in my body hurt, and everything else was tenderized, like someone had smashed into every inch of my skin with a meat hammer.

"Where are they?" I asked, realizing now how rough my voice sounded. It was thick and scratchy, and I would have killed for some water.

But I had to find the two of them. Catherine and Lucien. I had to stop them. Somehow.

Cruel laughter echoed down on us.

He was silhouetted by lights from somewhere in the distance, so I couldn't see his face, but I didn't need to. Lucien stood at the edge of the pit we were in, something large held over his shoulder in a fireman's carry. It took me a second to recognize the limp blond hair trailing down from the body.

"That was unexpected," he called down to us. "Maybe you have a bit of Grace in you after all."

I surged forward, rage pushing its way past everything else that was going through my brain. All I knew was that I wanted to make him hurt. I wanted to tear him apart. I would improve upon what Grace had done and create a whole new dictionary to cover what I'd do to him, when words like *torture* and *punish* and *anguish* wouldn't do anymore.

"I'll kill you!" My voice was so thick with hate that it wasn't my voice anymore. I reached out to my power, to draw forth the same magic I'd used to free us from the binding circle.

Already my mind was spinning with all the ways I'd make him suffer. A demon couldn't die but I could make him pay. I *would* make him pay. For everything he'd done, and everyone he'd hurt. I wouldn't be like Grace, striking from the shadows and then hiding from his retribution.

I would make him suffer, and suffer daily.

I reached for the magic.

And nothing happened.

Not a damn thing happened.

"What?" I focused my senses, feeling for the magic that *had* to be there. It was always there. I'd unleashed enough power tonight that the spillover should have been intense. Residue of everything I'd done, and all the power central to Belle Dam besides.

But there was nothing but emptiness.

"Braden?" Trey was standing next to me, and he was concerned. "What's wrong with your eyes?"

From above us, Lucien's snarl was immediate, and his reaction just as swift. "What?" he snarled, and just as the word was leaving his lips, the power that was like black sand swept around him, and suddenly he was in front of us, his hand inching towards my face.

I flinched back, stumbling and falling down onto the

ground. Trey was on top and in front of me in an instant, putting his body between the demon and me. But Lucien wasn't interested in any of that. His eyes were narrowed on mine.

"How—it shouldn't—this was never a—" The demon stretched out a curious hand, his eyes flitting back and forth erratically. Only now I knew, he was scanning futures. A thousand, perhaps a hundred thousand threads, each just slightly different.

"Useless," he muttered. "Ruined! Everything!"

The grainy power swept around him again, and he was gone.

That's when I realized what had happened. Things didn't just look out of focus … they looked flat. My eyes weren't just blurry.

They were normal.

I reached for my face hesitantly. "She…"

The witch eyes, the curse that had ruled my entire life, the powers that had *defined* me … they were gone. That had been what Grace had done. She hadn't ripped out my eyes. She'd ripped out my power.

"I'm normal." I kept touching my face, like it would cease to be real.

Trey understood. He knew how much I'd wanted this, how hard the power had been on me. But he also knew what it all meant. And what not having that power would mean for me. He pulled me to him, and wrapped his arms around me, whispering words into my hair.

Uncle John was dead, and I couldn't avenge him. Catherine had more reason than ever to hate me. And Lucien was restored, while I was now useless to him.

I had been crying for several minutes before I even realized I *was* crying. Even then, I couldn't be sure what I was crying about. If I was mourning the only family I'd known growing up. Or the albatross around my neck that was suddenly gone.

There was a scream of absolute rage from somewhere far in the distance. Trey pulled me tighter to him. I wasn't the only one who was suffering. I had been crucial to Lucien's plans. The witch eyes had been his skeleton key to unlock the demonic essence that Grace had torn out of him. Without it, and me, his confinement would continue indefinitely.

"Good," I whispered.

It wasn't enough, but it was a start.

thirty-nine

It took us some time to climb out of the basement. I wouldn't have made it without Trey. Pushing me, in some cases pulling me, whatever it took to get us over the side of the wall and up the ruined devastation.

"I think we're near the lighthouse," Trey said, squinting into the distance. I don't know what he thought he'd see in the middle of the night, but he seemed satisfied enough. "Back where the original Lansing house used to be."

I didn't say anything. I was concentrating on keeping one foot in front of the other and not collapsing onto the ground.

"I think it was the chapel."

A chapel. Of course it was. It was fitting and profane.

Trey climbed over one of the fallen pine trees, then turned to grab my hand and pull me up and over. We were just starting to clear the fringes of the blast when Drew found us.

The ground for fifty yards around the chapel had been riven and shattered. All around us, a circular section of the forest had been absolutely flattened and shoved down. The only thing left of the chapel building we'd been in was half of the basement and the foundation. There wasn't any sign of anything else, not even debris.

As if my night hadn't been weird enough, the impossible started happening. Drew and Trey agreed on something.

"You need to get checked out," Drew insisted.

Trey took the more casual, but firm, response. "We just need to make sure nothing permanent happened."

Normally, I would have argued. I would have pushed them away and done what I needed to do. But the fact was I didn't have the strength to even mount a resistance. "But someone needs to get Uncle John."

Trey nodded sharply. He took a deep breath. "I'll … be right back." He exchanged a hard look with Drew, and then looked pointedly down at me. Drew took up a spot just to my right, his arms crossed in front of me. Like a bodyguard, I thought drunkenly. A shape-shifting bodyguard.

I watched Trey walk away from the clearing, choosing his steps carefully as he tried to navigate a path. I could barely keep my eyes open, but I refused to pass out. My body was trying to mutiny, and waves of exhaustion kept slipping through, crashing through my limbs, lulling me towards sleep.

"What's he doing? He looks nervous," I asked, looking up at Drew.

"Calling your old man," Drew said. "Can't imagine why that would make him nervous. Last time he just talked to one of the ass-kissing sycophants."

He was calling Jason? "What?"

Drew arched an eyebrow and looked down at me. "You're an idiot, Thorpe."

"Don't call me that," I said weakly. I wasn't a Thorpe. Not really.

"Someone has to clean up this mess," he said, crouching down next to me. "Collect the body, talk to the cops about what happened to Riley, and generally keep the serfs out of grown-up business."

"But why's *Trey* making the call," I asked, confused. My eyelids were getting heavier by the second. "Jason hates him. He hates all of them. Why didn't you call?"

Drew smirked. "Don't be an idiot. You know why he's calling. For the same reason he jumped through that portal thing after you."

I didn't have it in me to argue. "Where's Riley?"

"At the hospital. Jade's there. She'll call if anything changes."

It was while I watched Trey, with one hand gesturing emphatically while he spoke, that it really hit me.

John is dead. He's not coming back. Adrenaline had held me together up until this point, but the simple, quiet acceptance tore through any insulation I'd built up. *He's dead.* It was an angry, red wound that ran through the entire length of me.

When Trey came back, the boys traded positions. Trey came up to my side, reaching out to put his hand on me, and I instinctively shifted away. I saw the twist in his expression, and then I looked away quickly.

It's too much. I can't.

Eventually, Jason's entourage of black suits showed up, but he wasn't with them. *Obviously not,* I thought. *He left town after talking to John.* Despite urgings from both Trey and an exasperated Drew, I didn't get back on my feet until the men pulled John out of the pit. They treated him like he mattered.

It was important.

On the way to the hospital, I was quiet. Trey drove. He started to say something, and I quickly turned up the radio to ear-blistering levels. Heavy guitar, deep throbbing bass. So loud I could barely think. I liked it better that way. It was easier without having to talk or touch. I just couldn't. Not yet.

¤   ¤   ¤

When we finally came through the emergency room doors, we were late to the party. There was a flurry of activity going on inside, with nearly every visible cubicle occupied.

"Not exactly a welcome wagon, is it?" Drew asked at my side.

Trey had a pair of sunglasses in his glove compartment, and putting them on covered over the worst of the blood. They were big and bulky, and something told me they were probably Jade's. I tried wiping off the blood in the car, but it had already dried, and the parts that didn't just smeared.

The sunglasses *also* helped, because my eyes were still sensitive to the light. That didn't change with my new condition.

The spotlights and glow of the emergency room signs was enough to make my eyes water, even through the lenses.

"There must have been an accident," Trey said. He left my side and hurried forward to work his Lansing charm and get some answers.

Drew gave Trey's departing figure a sour look. "Real master of the obvious, isn't he?"

"A month ago, he was trying to kill you," I said quietly. "Besides, at least he's a master at *something*. Sarcasm isn't exactly a trade skill."

"You should see me debate," Drew said easily. I saw him side-eye me, clearly waiting for my reaction, but I sank down into one of the waiting-area chairs instead. His bluster faded and he dropped down next to me. "You okay? Any dizziness, nausea? Anything like last time?"

"Last time I got wheeled in on a stretcher," I said. "I'm just tired." I couldn't help but worry about what else was going on in Belle Dam tonight. Had there been another incident? Had I set something else in motion, the way killing Lucien led us here?

I tried not to think about it, but the list of people hurt because of what I'd done kept growing. Grazia would never act or dance again. Whatever had been in store for Kayla was gone, stolen and devoured. Riley. John.

Everything that had happened was because of me. They'd all been hurt because of the feud, and the feud started because of me.

"I'm going to get a nurse," Drew said, unconvinced.

"Trey's already doing that," I replied. And sure enough,

I could see Trey at the nurse's station, turning and pointing back towards us before he gestured towards his eyes.

Great. More doctors. The selfishness of the thought hit me, then. There were people here who were really hurt, maybe dying. And I was feeling bad because I'd have to see another doctor, and deal with another exam.

Things could be a lot worse.

Drew had his head cocked to one side. He was doing that listening trick again. The one where he had weird Shifter hearing. "There was an accident on the highway. They're still not sure what the cause was, there's been a lot of different reports."

I released a breath. A car accident. That was mundane. It wasn't hellhounds or magic, then. "Is everyone—"

Drew didn't give me the chance to finish. "There's a couple of serious cases, but I don't think anyone died." He waited a moment, then shook his head. "He asked how serious, but she deflected."

Just as our conversation ended, a fresh wave of action began at the ambulance entrance. The doors, which were on the far side of the ER, opened and another fresh batch of patients and medics started swarming inside.

"After I get checked out," I said, leaning in towards Drew as the noise level increased, "I want to go check on Riley. Where is she?"

"She's up on the fifth floor," he replied absently, still trying to eavesdrop. The louder it got, the harder for him to listen, apparently. "I think Jade said it was 521? We'll go up with you."

I settled back and waited. As I figured, with the new rush of traumas, everything in the ER that was non-critical, i.e. *me*, was left to sit tight. Trey remained at the nurse's station, dealing with one harried woman after the next. He glanced back at me, and my heart squeezed in my chest. *At that angle, and in this light…* Just for a moment, I'd seen something of Catherine in his expression. Thinking of Catherine twisted the knife in my gut again, thinking about John and the way the men had to carry him out.

"Useless," Drew muttered a few minutes later. He got up and strode for the nurse's desk, presumably to team up against the busy nurses.

The moment the both of them were distracted, I walked out of the ER and headed for the main hospital wing. I kept my head down and prayed the boys would stay occupied long enough for me to find an elevator.

With every step, I expected an angry yell and for someone to grab me by the arm and spin me around. But I made it to the elevators without even being recognized, which might have been the first time in weeks. There was a hazy reflection of me in the stainless steel doors, but as far as I could tell, the sunglasses hid most of the blood.

I walked through the halls like a zombie. I had a passing familiarity with the hospital, so navigating my way around wasn't difficult. But I went out of my way to avoid anyone else—I was afraid that someone would try to stop me, or send me back down to the ER.

I started concentrating on the room numbers as I went down the hall. 515. 517. 519. I was so focused that I didn't notice the man coming out of Riley's room until he was right in front of me. He pressed his hand against my chest, pushing me back just enough to prevent us from colliding.

"Sorry," I muttered automatically.

Fingertips brushed the hollow between my clavicles. A voice I knew responded with relish, "No apologies necessary, my dear boy."

Matthias wore one of his trademark black on black suits, though he'd foregone the tie for once. He looked down at me with a pleased smile.

Matthias touches you, Trey's voice said in my head, *he'll learn secrets you'd never say out loud. That's his gift.* I looked down, at the fingers pressed against my skin. Fear and revulsion welled up inside of me, and I stepped back hurriedly, even though it was too late.

His smile widened at my reaction. "All our cards on the table," Matthias confided, nearly bursting with the demon equivalent of joy. The deep timbre of his voice echoed down the hallway, and made me wonder. "You have been a *very* busy boy, haven't you?"

He knows everything. At times, the weight of secrets I was keeping made me feel like Atlas, struggling to hold on. But to have my secrets stolen like this? It wasn't right. The only consolation that came was that Catherine already knew the biggest of my secrets. I was already screwed.

"Don't think this changes anything," I said.

"Oh, tonight has changed a great many things," Matthias said with a laugh. "My condolences on your loss. Had I known what Jonathan was to you, I might have—"

I grabbed the front of his shirt and shoved him back. He already knew my secrets, there was no reason to avoid him. Matthias slammed against the door, and he *laughed*.

"As far as I'm concerned, you're just as much to blame for that," I snarled.

"Jason really should teach you some manners," he said, his smile growing. He pulled his shirt from my grasp, and smoothed out the new wrinkles. "But then, he never had many, either. The only difference," he said, eyes speculative on me, "is that he had the juice to back up his threats. You don't."

"Why are you here?"

He inclined his head. "I'm thinking about becoming a candy striper. I've been told I have the legs for it."

"Stop trying to be cute. You're not."

"Aren't I? Maybe it has to do with your approach. Like a rabid dog."

"Speaking of dogs, you sent the hellhounds after Jade." I narrowed my eyes and faked a sympathetic tone. "Trey's going to be gunning for you now. Catherine too."

"*Demon*," he said, sounding bored, as he gestured to himself. "Have you learned nothing? I'm a better ally than an enemy. The way your night has gone, you should start plugging the holes in your little crusade. Because that ship is sinking fast."

"You know what I am."

Matthias stroked a finger down his jaw. "But are you *still*, is the question. Better to ask if I know what you *were*."

"You said yourself, you knew better than to underestimate me. Don't make that mistake now."

He gave a slight nod, as if to concede the point. "Tell me, does Lucien know? Has he even the slightest clue that she's out there, patient as ever?" There was *glee* in his voice.

I kept my face blank, giving him nothing. But I was curious. "You don't feel an ounce of loyalty to him, do you?"

Matthias threw back his head and laughed. He looked entirely too pleased with himself. "Demon," he said again, as though that was an answer that made sense. "I wonder if he even realizes the game he's been playing all along. Ah, well. What say we keep that our little secret for now?"

I studied him. "You've been playing both sides all this time." And then another thought. "Were you *waiting* for this? Did you know she was out there?"

Matthias avoided the question, tilting his head just a tick. "Oh dear, and the blood on your face? You've already got enough on your hands, don't you think?"

There was more to this than just what Matthias did or didn't know. He'd said before that there was more than the feud to Belle Dam. More than just Thorpe versus Lansing.

I thought back to all the things that didn't add up. The ghost that had tried to kill me and the girl in Lucien's office, the one with the unknown allegiance. "The witch? The one who swept in to banish the ghost at Fallon Law. You hired her, didn't you?"

"Finally, he starts asking the right questions," Matthias said under his breath, his smile starting to widen. "There may be hope for you yet." He turned to look back at the door he'd just left.

I reacted instantly. "Stay away from Riley."

"Or you'll do what exactly?" He leaned into my space, our noses nearly touching. "I'm not intimidated by your Daddy's influence, and you have no power without him. Remember, boy: I am Grimm, and as of now? You are *nothing*."

My hands clenched into fists.

"I felt what you did to the girl. Lucien isn't the only one walking blind, is he? If you could see the things you've set into motion..." He moved back, but his hand hovered, and for a moment I thought he was going to tap me on the nose. Instead he turned and headed in the opposite direction.

"You need a shoulder to scheme on, you know where to find me," Matthias called out over his shoulder as he sauntered down the hall.

¤   ¤   ¤

Riley was asleep. Or she was sedated. It was hard to tell, and I didn't know how to read the medical chart outside her room. They'd put her in a private room. I wondered if Jade had any influence on that, or if there was some other reason. But since visiting hours had ended hours ago, it wasn't like I could just ask the nearest nurse.

She looked like a little kid, swallowed up in a bed that was too big for her. It was hard to see the girl I knew because asleep like that, she so strongly resembled the little girl from my vision. Her hands were bound to the sides of the bed in thick cuffs—*was Riley a danger to herself? Like they said Grazia was, with the rage episodes?*

I didn't understand what had happened to her—how Lucien's power had intersected with mine, or what it meant for Riley, caught between us.

Her breathing was slow. Things around her hummed and beeped, keeping her vitals ... vital. The hall lights were enough to keep the room from total darkness, allowing me to find my way to the bedside chair.

I sat with her. Her hand was right in front of me, tiny and open, palm facing the sky. But I couldn't touch her. I didn't deserve to touch her. *I'm sorry, this is my fault.* But my lips wouldn't form the words.

The only thing I *could* offer were empty promises and lies. Grace had taken any hope of Riley's restoration away when she tore the power out of me. *And maybe that's a good thing,* my traitorous mind supplied, *look at all the good your power has done so far. Look what it* could *have done.*

Maybe Jason would find a cure, but I wouldn't hold my breath. I couldn't even begin to describe what had happened to Riley. Matthias implied that he knew *something* about what I'd done, but what would it cost to find out? And who would be the one to pay?

I'll do whatever it takes. More empty promises. I didn't have much left to offer. Would he even bargain with me?

"Long miles from home. She has everything she needs. Three moves from checkmate." Riley's eyes opened, staring at the ceiling.

I stood, biting my lower lip. "Riley?"

Her body tensed, and for a moment it looked like she was floating off the bed. But it was only her head and neck, straining up off her pillow, reaching for something I couldn't see. With her arms braced at her sides, it was the only motion she could make.

"Checkmate. Checkmate. Burning, ashes. All falls down." She fell back, her eyes already closed. For a second I was terrified that she was dead, that this was one last sputter before her flame went out, but the monitors continued to beat steadily. If something were wrong, there would have been an alarm.

I felt Drew approach before I saw him. Maybe it was his exasperated huff or some lingering sense of magic in the air. I turned, saw him leaning against the door frame.

"C'mon. The doctor is in."

I turned back to Riley, wanting to say anything. To apologize, to beg for forgiveness. Something important. But nothing I could say would be enough. "I want—" but my voice cracked and splintered, and Drew was there to pick up the pieces.

"She knows. C'mon. We'll come back."

I will, I promised. Because right now, that was all I could give her. Drew clapped his hand on my shoulder, and wouldn't let me look back.

¤   ¤   ¤

I ended up seeing the same doctor I had the last time I was here. A pair of nurses escorted me to an exam room set apart from the rest of the ER, and on their way back out they dimmed the lights for me.

Half an hour later, I'd gone through the doctor's exam, a series of questions that no longer applied ("How is your migraine right now?" "I don't have one." "You don't ... huh. Are you sure? You always have a migraine after an episode."), and a nurse that came in and cleaned most of the blood off of my face. He talked about sending me for a MRI or a CAT scan just to be sure, but because of the accident that it would be a few hours.

Drew stood against the wall the entire time, brooding but silent like the perfect bodyguard. Jason would probably hire him and give him a raise right off the bat. Or threaten to kill him. Jason was touchy, so it depended on his mood.

I left the exam room and ended up sitting at one of the benches, staring at a sign that explained fire procedures. In the event of a fire, I was to remain calm before anything else. Then, I should walk calmly and quietly towards the fire exit, helpfully diagrammed at the bottom.

Drew moved off to a corner of the hallway, head dipped as he talked to Jade. I couldn't hear what they were saying, and I didn't try to listen, either. I studied the escape plan, and the diagram, and tried to find some order in the chaos of my night.

Trey showed up a few minutes later. I could tell he'd been working himself up to something. He held out his hand—*Catherine held out her hand, black and purple motes of power hesitating against her fingertips*—and I flinched. I scooted back on the bench, keeping space between us.

Trey didn't notice at first. "What did the—"

I held up my hand, stopping him. "Stop."

I caught him off guard. He looked down at his out-stretched hand, perplexed, and then at me. "Braden?"

I focused on the floor. Stared a hole through it. I probably couldn't do that anymore: destroy something just by looking at it.

"Please," I said. "Don't."

Trey was understandably confused. "Don't what?"

There was too much going on in the room. Too much happening. I'd never noticed how much room Trey took up: he stood there, but it wasn't just him. There was also his mother, his family, his *expectations,* and the weight of all the things he needed, pulling at me and taking what little I had left. There was so much, and so little of me, and all the air was pushed out to make room, and I couldn't breathe and there was no space and he kept coming closer and there was no air—

I ran for the exit. Automatic doors whooshed open, and I ran. I kept going for the entire length of the hospital, afraid to stop.

Catherine at the restaurant. At the Harbor Club. In the basement just before she…John's eyes. That arrogant moue she always made. Disapproval flashing in her eyes.

I hunched over, opening my mouth and sure that once I started throwing up, I'd never stop. I gagged, and thought for sure that with every heave, this would be the part where I actually vomited, but nothing came out.

Once the retching stopped, I struggled to breathe, to

force deep and even breaths. Once I was sure I could breathe again and my stomach was under control, I pulled myself back up.

Drew had followed me, of course. He hung back, just out of my line of sight, giving me the illusion of being alone. But he was silent, and silence on Drew was so loud and distracting, I could barely think. I longed for the days when there wasn't a line he wouldn't cross, or a cruel remark he wouldn't make. Not being an ass was just too dignified for Drew.

"I don't know if I can go back in there," I said. "He wants... and I can't. Not right now."

"You have to talk to him," Drew said grimly. "You owe him that much."

"Since when do you care what I owe him? You hate him."

"It's not that simple," he said. "You know that. So does he."

I asked a question I'd wondered about sometimes, but never thought to ask before. "Do you ever think about him? Your dad?"

Drew surprised me, ready with an answer. Like he'd known all along it was coming. "Not often."

"Do you ever think about revenge?"

That answer took a little longer. "Sometimes," he admitted. "I've done some things that I'm not proud of. Tormented them a bit. Jade could never figure out why so many birds kept crapping on her car." He chuckled at the memory. "But not what you're talking about. We're smarter than that."

"Are we?" I mused.

"Well, you are," he conceded. "You know how it would end."

"And if I don't care?"

Drew looked at me, and in the gentlest voice I'd ever heard him use, he said, "Gentry would. Jade, too."

Et tu, Armstrong?

I turned and went back the way I'd come, back through the automatic doors and into the hospital proper. Trey stood almost exactly where I'd left him, like he'd been frozen in place until I was ready to deal with him.

"Not here," I said, still refusing to look at him. It was easier if I didn't. I headed for the cafeteria, the only place I figured would be deserted at this hour. Trey fell in line behind me. The tightness in my chest eased a little when he didn't argue. Maybe this wouldn't be so bad.

The cafeteria wasn't empty. A single man in green scrubs sat at one of the tables near the coffee machine, hands wrapped around his cup. "Leave," I said, striding past him until I reached the center of the room. Behind me, I heard Trey say something, either turning on the charm or following my lead. Either way, I heard the man's sneakers squeaking for the door.

And then we were alone.

He started to speak, but I cut him off. If I let him, he'd take control of the conversation, spinning it out of control and twisting everything I said. No, I couldn't let it happen like that.

"My uncle's dead." It tasted like betrayal on my tongue to say it out loud.

Trey stopped what he was about to say and hung his head. "You know I'm—"

I kept going. "When my mom died, John couldn't handle it. You'd think it would have been Jason, but it makes sense: he's too rigid and controlled. But John wasn't. He had to do *something*. Someone had to hurt as much as he was hurting. So he went after your dad."

"Braden—" Trey's face was white, like he knew where this conversation was leading.

Every word was chosen with deliberate care. I could control myself only so long as we followed the script in my head. "I mean, he tried to *kill someone*. It wasn't like he tripped and fell onto murder. He set out to kill someone. He made a choice. I never thought I would understand that. But I do." I looked at him then, at the blond hair and blue eyes he inherited from his mother. "I'm going to kill her."

"Please," he said. Was that *please, don't?* Or *please, stop?* But I couldn't stop, I don't know what he wanted from me. I was barely holding it together as it was, I couldn't stop to think about what Trey wanted.

"It's not just that," I said. "Lucien's been in my head for weeks, messing with how I feel, and what I feel. But he never really broke me down. He never made seriously think about killing someone."

"That's because that's not who you are."

"That's not who I was," I corrected him. "I'm different now."

"You're not," he said, his tone softening. "I know it's hard right now, and I know you can't—"

"She's your mother," I said. "You should go. She'll want to know you're alright."

He looked shocked. "I'm not going back there. All this time, I believed my mother when she said that Jason was a threat, and we had to take care of ourselves. But you have to know, I don't agree anymore. Not with what she's done."

I shook my head. He wanted this to work out so bad, but he needed to accept that it couldn't. I already had. I'd been accepting it since we climbed out of the pit. Tonight had drawn a line in the sand that couldn't be erased, and Trey and I were more divided than ever. "That doesn't change anything. I look at you, and I see *her*." I couldn't look at Trey without thinking of Catherine and the way John looked as he dropped to the ground for the last time.

He looked like I had punched him in the face. "Braden!" His voice was softer now, pleading. "I'm not—"

"John died because of *us*," I said, putting the final nail in the coffin. "Because Lucien was so scared at the thought of us being together that he'll kill anyone he can to tear us apart."

Trey tried to be resolute. "I'm not going anywhere. I'm not leaving you."

I nodded. "I know. I am." I took off the sunglasses, looked at him with my ordinary eyes. "Goodbye, Trey."

When I turned and walked away, he didn't follow.

¤   ¤   ¤

Somehow, I ended up in the hospital chapel. It was empty, and quiet, and tucked back into a corner of the building far from everything but the gift shop. Even though the sign outside the door proclaimed its function, the room itself looked like a patient's room that had been converted at random.

There was a cloth-covered altar on the far side of the room, and three rows of pews, but the room was otherwise unadorned. No crosses, no candles, no smell of incense hanging in the air. Everything I came to expect from a church, and none of it was present.

"I thought that was you," a pleasant voice said from the door.

I turned, not recognizing the boy at first. "Hey," I said cautiously.

He smiled and stepped over the threshold. "Ben, remember? From school? Riley's friend?"

The slightly creepy one. Right. "Now's ... not really a good time," I said, trying to figure out why he was talking to me in the first place.

"I was coming back from seeing a family member and I thought I saw you get off the elevator," Ben went on like he hadn't heard a thing I'd said. "So I followed you and here you are."

"Here I am," I said awkwardly. "Didn't visiting hours end forever ago?"

He made a dismissive gesture with his hand. "Visiting hours should be more of a guideline than a rule."

I didn't say anything in response. Maybe if I stopped talking, he'd get the hint and go away.

"Hey," he walked closer towards me, eyes narrowed in concern, "are you okay?"

"I'm fine." I looked away.

"Because you've got a little—" he made a gesture towards his face.

I mirrored the move, wiping at the skin by my ear.

Ben shook his head and grinned. "You're not getting it," he said with a little laugh. The next thing I knew, he was right in front of me, sharing the same air. He reached out, a tiny little napkin or scrap of cloth in his hand and scrubbed at my skin. "You just had a little blood," he hummed. The napkin disappeared into his pocket when he was done. "And now I do."

"What?"

"Elle said it would be easy, but she didn't say how easy," Ben said to himself. "One more thing," he said, leaning close. "Ask Jason what really happened the night your mother died. The truth is so much better than the fiction."

"Braden?" Jade appeared in the door of the chapel, framed in light. "Who are you talking to?"

I flinched, and turned back to Ben, to figure out *what the hell he was talking about*. But Ben was gone. Not like *left the room* gone. Like *vanished into thin air*.

I sank down into one of the pews. "I think something bad just happened," I said. "Again." Too much had already happened. I couldn't even deal with this now. What did that mean? Ben had been working with Elle? And how did he know about my mother?

Were they both working for Matthias? Why would he want my blood?

"I know," she replied. But Jade assumed I was talking about the normal bad that had happened tonight. Not something new. After a few moments of thought, I decided not to correct her.

"Jason won't be home until sometime tomorrow night," she said. She didn't sit in the same row as me, but moved to sit one behind. Like we just happened to arrive at the chapel at the same time, but we definitely weren't together. Maybe Lansing habits were hard to break. It was like the movie theater all over again. "Whatever it was that he was doing, he said it couldn't be dropped. He said he had good news, though. He found who he was looking for."

"He told you that?" I asked, surprised.

"I think he realizes that loyalty isn't always about blood," she said. "He never kept me from visiting you last time you were here, remember? He could have."

"I'd forgotten about that," I admitted.

Jade smiled softly. "I'll take you home later. We can make a sleepover out of it. He just wants to make sure you stay in the house. Just in case."

"You talked to him?"

She shook her head once. Not her then. Trey. Of course.

We were both quiet for a long time. The chapel must have been soundproof because it was like there wasn't anything outside of this room.

She didn't apologize. She didn't try to defend her mother. And she didn't push me. "What was he like?" she said finally.

Uncle John defied description. I opened my mouth half a dozen times, but each thought contradicted the next. He was impulsive and boring; caustic and gentle; demanding and relaxed; funny and serious. He was the reason I'd come to Belle Dam in the first place, thinking I could protect him.

Somewhere along the way I'd forgotten that.

"He was my family," I said slowly. "And I don't think I ever thanked him. I was … horrible to him the last time we really spoke. It was," I hesitated, "I wasn't myself. And I said things. Awful things."

"Everyone fights. Especially with people you love. But that doesn't change what your relationship was," Jade said. "People are complicated. On some level, we all know that. Just because you had a fight doesn't mean he changed how he felt about you." Her eyes were focused on the altar, and even though we were talking, I got the feeling that she was very far away.

Was she thinking about Catherine? Of the two, Jade struck me as the more unforgiving Lansing sibling. That helped as much as it hurt.

"He came back for me," I said. "Everyone's going to say it's my fault."

"Everyone knows who's fault it was," she said. But she didn't push the issue by trying to convince me. She didn't push me at all. She was there, a solid, reassuring presence at my back. Exactly what I needed.

I found myself telling her stories about my childhood. Like the time that John had taken me to a county fair in the middle of nowhere, and I'd somehow become best friends with a goat. Or the time I'd snuck out of the house to attend a football game and ended up being chased through a cemetery by the Homecoming court.

For a little while, I smiled even through the ache in my chest. The stories made me forget about Catherine and the feud, and Jason's mysterious errand. Matthias and his scheming. Grace and her betrayal.

Since I'd come to Belle Dam, I'd learned to lie like a professional. I'd put my friends in danger. I'd gotten my biggest wish at the worst time. I'd killed a man. I'd gotten a man killed. I hadn't been smart enough, or strong enough, to deal with the consequences to my actions.

John had come back because he was afraid. Afraid of what would happen if I let the city corrupt me.

And just like everything else in my life... he wasn't wrong.

But I didn't know where to go from here.

THE END

ACKNOWLEDGMENTS

As always, to my rock star agent Ginger Clark, who accepts my tendencies to relate everything to America's Next Top Model and only judges me a little. I cannot convey how deep my appreciation runs for everything that you do.

To everyone at Flux, especially my editor Brian Farrey, Marissa Pederson, Steven Pomije, Ed Day, and everyone who has made this journey possible. Thank you all so much.

Gretchen McNeil and Karsten Knight have listened to more than their fair share of randomness on my part, and it's appreciated. Dear, sweet Tiffany Schmidt gave me Guster, read more versions of this book than almost anyone, and listened to me whine when I thought I'd never get through it.

Thank you to Saundra Mitchell, who made *"I marky wif mah red marky!"* a part of my daily lexicon, and Rachel Clarke of Fiktshun who has been a fabulous cheerleader and didn't mind the teasing. And to the rest of the ladies of TS: Susan Adrian, Linda Grimes, Emily Hainsworth, Victoria Schwab, and Courtney Summers, thank you so much for the daily support.

*Read on for a sneak peek from the first book in
Scott Tracey's forthcoming new series,* Moonset.

ONE

*"Moonset, a coven of such promise. Until they turned to the
darkness. Their acts of terrorism fueled by dark magic nearly
destroyed us. But we fought back. And we won."*

—Illana Bryer (C: Fallingbrook)
From a speech
given the night Moonset was captured.

There were 245 students involved in the riot. What had started
as a minor altercation between the basketball and track teams
had devolved into a literal kind of class warfare. Freshmen against
juniors, girls against boys, art kids versus burnouts, 4-Hers against
everyone.

The town's entire full time police force, all three of them, had
been trying for the better part of an hour to re-establish control.
Reinforcements had been called, the rest of the school had been
evacuated, and I found myself in the principal's office with my sister, only two days shy of winter break. We'd been so close this time.

We sat in silence: Jenna examining her nails and touching up
her makeup; and me leaning against the window, afraid to peek

between the blinds. The view overlooked the front quad, and today it offered a glimpse of madness. I don't know how she'd managed it, but the entire school had lost it an hour ago.

These things tended to happen when Jenna got bored.

She favored me with a sullen, annoyed look. I didn't have to say anything, didn't have to sift through old frustrations and new accusations until I knew the words I wanted to use. One look, and Jenna saw it all on my face. She always did.

"Calm down, Justin," she said after I'd closed my eyes. "It's no big deal."

"Getting kicked out of school is a big deal, Jen."

"The first time, maybe," she mused, "but you've had enough practice by now. You're a pro." This was school number seven, and I definitely should have seen this coming.

Jenna and I were unaffectionately known as "the twins." It was how people introduced us, talked about us, traded stories about us. Like we were really a single person split between two bodies. It never failed that the minute Jenna crossed the line and got hauled in to a principal's office, I was right behind her. Our fates had been superglued together for our entire lives—especially in situations that involved buzzwords like "vandalism of school property," "suspicious fires" and "criminal charges."

Seven schools in three years. We'd almost made it through an entire semester, and I'd gotten lazy. I forgot what Jenna could do with just a few whispered words. Riots were the tip of the iceberg. Fitting that Jenna's rap sheet was the size of Antarctica.

To be fair, not all of the expulsions were her fault. One of them was our brother Malcolm's, and a few others were for reasons we didn't fully understand.

Our lives were just a tad complicated.

I looked around the room, but the precarious stacks of paperwork on the desk were definitely a theme in this office. Every available surface had something on it. Even the lampshade was littered with blue Post-its.

"Bailey's going to be crushed," I pointed out absently. How does anyone find anything in here? There's too much paper-work—and too much bureaucracy—for one small-town principal. I couldn't even think of his name. It wasn't Reynolds, that was the last school. Jeffries, maybe?

"She'll get over it," Jenna said, keeping her words light. Bailey always got her heart crushed when we moved. She threw herself into every new school as if it would be the last. It never was.

"Don't you think we're running out of schools," I said tiredly. This was an argument we'd had a thousand times.

"We haven't even tried Europe," she fired back. Her fingers tapped restlessly against the wooden arm of the chair. "I hate wait-ing. Where is he?"

"I apologize if cleaning up your mess has inconvenienced you in any way," the principal from behind us. I turned just in time to see him pushing a wiry blond boy into the room and then closing the door. "I can only imagine the kinds of delinquency I'm keeping you from, Miss Bellamont," he continued.

The blond boy was the last of our siblings, Cole, and his arrival with the principal meant nothing good. Cole tried to saunter in only to nearly trip over himself. He ended up lunging for the back of my chair, trying to keep himself upright.

Somewhere after Seattle, he'd finally grown into his ears. When we were kids, Cole was the kid with giant Dumbo ears dwarfing the sides of his head. Now they were barely notable, although he still hadn't hit a decent growth spurt. He was the shortest boy in the school.

"What'd he do now?" was quickly followed by how could he possibly make a riot any worse? "What'd you do, Cole?" I asked, already wishing I didn't have to ask. Things went from bad to worse so quickly around us I should have been expecting it.

Jenna was more acerbic. "You got caught?"

Cole had the decency to look ashamed. I pretended it was because he'd helped start a riot and not because he'd gotten caught. "I just wanted a good seat." A few seconds of silence went by, and he continued. "And maybe I was egging some of the football jerks on."

"You were shouting out quotes from Gladiator and trying to tear your shirt off," the principal said dryly. He was a red-haired, mustached man who I hadn't talked to since we'd enrolled.

"I just wanted to know if they were entertained," Cole said, blushing a little, before he caught a glimpse of Jenna's waspish look and his voice died.

She and I traded a look. "Can we get on with this? I'd like to deface my locker before the last bell," she said, as though she were on a schedule.

The principal sucked in a deep breath, and held it. I wondered who he was praying to. Buddha? Jesus? St. Jude, the patron saint of lost causes? Whatever god he was praying to, it wouldn't help. Jenna defied the power of prayer.

"I have put up with enough from you and your lot," he said, his tone icy.

Your lot. I could practically hear Jenna preening next to me. There was nothing she liked better than someone who tried to put her in her place. Especially when it was an adult.

I could see it all laid out in front of me, even before it happened. It wouldn't be enough for Jenna to embarrass the principal by making him look like an incompetent, she'd want a hand in embarrassing him personally. I chanced a look to my left. The anticipation was nearly killing her. There was more to come. What did she have on him? Alcoholism? Mistress?

"Now then," the principal said, exhaling. I could almost see

The Speech building up strength, rising from his gut as he worked through the preliminaries. The part about not quite understanding how things had gone so wrong. A whole subconversation about how we clearly needed things that Byron High could not provide. Principals, no surprise, rather enjoyed The Speech. The one that ended with the word "expelled."

But his joy was to be short-lived. An insistent knock cut off what he was about to say. "I told you not to disturb me," he shouted.

There was silence on the other side. And then a slower, insolent series of raps on the door. Jenna covered her mouth with her hand, but it didn't stifle the giggle. Not that she wanted it to.

The principal muttered something under his breath, and got up to open the door. "Marjorie—" he cut off, because the woman on the other side definitely wasn't the part-time receptionist that he expected. The woman on the other side was all business. She wore pantsuit paired with an emerald green blouse and a charcoal gray overcoat. Her thick, unnatural red hair hung down loose, almost as curly as Jenna's.

Cole's eyes about fell out of his head. Jenna and I exchanged a look, and without missing a beat she grabbed the fabric of his shirt, pulling him closer to us.

"Jeffries?" the woman asked in a deep, smoky tone.

I could tell that Jeffries wanted to hitch up his pants and start blustering. This woman—though she was only in her twenties—had him sized up in a second, and strode into the room, heels staccato against the floor.

Who is she? Jenna mouthed. I shrugged.

"If you'll step outside," the woman said to him, while her eyes slid over us imperiously.

Jenna sat up, even more alert than she'd been before. Neither of us had missed the dismissive curl of the redhead's lips as she looked us over. Whoever she was, she knew who we were.

Without as much as a please, the woman turned and headed back out into the front office. Through the gap in the door, I saw another man waiting near the receptionist's desk, in the same kind of business casual as the redhead. Jeffries gaped for a moment, then all of a sudden he lurched forward, like an automaton brought to life.

Jenna was muttering under her breath when the principal grabbed the door handle on his way out. The door swung closed, but didn't catch all the way. I crossed the room, nudged it open just a crack, and waited.

The three of us were absolutely still, our ears straining for what was going on out there.

"...taking them immediately."

Principal Jeffries cleared his throat. "I'm sorry, I don't understand what you're telling me."

"As long as they remain here, your students as well as your faculty are in danger," the woman said, obviously annoyed at having to repeat herself.

"I'm aware of that," the principal said in a huff. "Those students started a riot. Or didn't you notice when you stormed in?"

"Your naivety is nearly precious," the woman murmured.

"And who are you exactly?" the principal continued. "You're not one of their guardians."

"My name is Miss Virago," she said, sounding like some sort of cross breed between stuffy boarding school matron and prissy coed. "And giving you any details about what is coming here, now, is a waste of my time. You won't remember—or believe—me anyway. The only thing that will help is to get them out of your quaint little farming community as soon as possible."

"What the hell's going on?" I whispered. Next to me, Jenna looked pensive.

"Now you're going to leave with this gentleman," Virago continued, her voice suddenly cheerful and disarming. "And when he's done talking with you, the troubles these children caused will be little more than a dream."

"What?"

There were sounds of movement hidden by the door. "I'll handle the children's transport," Virago said, all business once again. "Clean up the girl's mess, and make sure the principal..." Her voice dropped, and I missed the rest.

A man's voice. "What about the rest of the school? The riot?"

The woman exhaled slowly. "I don't care," she snapped. "These people aren't our concern. Let them sort out their own problems."

They were going to make us disappear. Take every trace of us and make it vanish: yearbook photos, our houses and things, everything. This wasn't the first time. This was just a little more thorough, and that made me wonder. How bad was it really?

"Someone's coming after us?" Cole whispered, looking even smaller than normal. "Again?"

"We don't know what's going on," I said, patting him on the back. "Maybe that's just what they're telling people. Like a cover story."

The three of us jumped when the door swung open again. The redhead, Miss Virago, came in alone. As usual, Jenna beat me to the punch. "What's going on? And who the hell are you?"

Virago ignored the question. She pointed at us with the first two fingers of her hand, then pointed to the door. "Take your things. There's a van waiting on the south side of the building. Don't stop to talk to anyone, don't leave anything behind."

Jenna stood up. Even though the woman was in heels, Jenna's Amazonian height gave her the advantage. She looked down on the adult. "We're not going anywhere until you tell us what's going on."

"Get your things, Moonset," the woman spat, making the word into a curse. "And go to the van. You're being evacuated."

About the Author

Scott Tracey aspired to be an author from a young age. His debut novel, *Witch Eyes*, was named to the 2012 Popular Paperbacks for Young Readers list in the forbidden romance category and ranked among the top ten gay and lesbian Kindle books of 2011 at Amazon.com. Tracey lives near Cleveland, Ohio, and can be found on Twitter @Scott_Tracey or at his website, www.Scott-Tracey.com.